LEGACY OF GHOSTS

BOOK TWO OF THE CORAIDIC SAGAS

ALICIA WANSTALL-BURKE

Cover Art by Pen Astridge

ISBN: 978-0-6484478-3-2
Imprint: Independently published

For Mum and Dad
Without you, I wouldn't be me
(Which is actually rather terrifying when you think about it!)

There is beauty in damage,
strength in letting go,
freedom in falling
and learning to fly.

Dorfa

Redona City

Lake Lith

The Woader

Burd

Shartridor

Fort Dawa

Bata

Iscrd

Grey Cliff

Arin

Ravens

River Arris

Port Hadeen

Wolban

Syod Archipelago

Na

Marsaw

Daylin

The High Tund

pire

Marlow

Harben

Orthia

Doduvin

Usmein

anor

Visorcrest

Lativa

The Ruhen

Kederen

The Altipa

The Malapa

Fracture Pass

Jungut Mountain

Tolak

The South Lands

The Black Teeth

PROLOGUE

A brother. A promise. A choice.

All balanced on the thin, shining edge of a knife.

Her father's long-awaited son had arrived, squalling in his swaddles and mouthing for the breast, and she had a choice. In that small breathless moment, Lidan knew it for what it was. Inevitable and precarious, unavoidable and terrifying. All because she had made a promise—a frantic gesture to stay her mother's hand—a promise she had yet to fulfil.

She had sworn her father would choose her as his true heir, no matter the sons his wives produced. She had sworn her half-mother, Farah, and the unborn child would not need to die, because her father would choose Lidan instead. She had sworn to do this on her own terms and had secured her mother's word no harm would come to Farah or Ehran.

But Sellan's small mercy came at a price. Lidan's opportunity to convince the daari of her worthiness was not infinite, and her eighteenth birthday, the beginning of her matching year, would be the end of her mother's patience. Lidan had until that day to change Erlon Tolak's mind or the dana would take the matter in hand.

For four years she had studied her choice, its simple edges and plain, unremarkable lines, and knew it had not changed. She was as familiar with it as she was with the creases on her palm. It was nothing more than a wisp of thought, yet she knew the action it required and the reaction it would cause. The choice held a ripple of pain and an explosion of fury tightly bound within its walls.

Pathways to the choice presented themselves, each as alluring and seductive as the call of a mimic-bird, some pledging a faster way, a less arduous road, or a gentler path. In the years since her brother's birth her mind had followed every single one to their natural conclusion. They seemed clear and fair at their beginning, the way unmarred by trial or worry, but they all wound in tighter circles eventually, leading her into a fog of confusion and fear. All came to the same point in the end, no matter the convoluted track they took. The choice always terminated at a final precipice where nothing remained but to turn one way or the other.

Would Ehran live?

Or die.

If Ehran were dead, Lidan regained the significant inheritance lost at his birth. If he were dead, she once more had a place at her father's side. If her brother died, still too young to leave a discernible mark on the world, it would be as if he never existed at all. If he died, everything would return to the way it had been.

The end of the boy's life needn't be anything more than an unfortunate accident—her mother made this much clear. Sellan had ideas aplenty and whispered them in her daughter's ear when the clouds of jealousy were at their darkest. Whatever happened, the blame could not settle on anyone in the Tolak clan—it must look like the work of an outsider.

Her mother muttered of how simple it could be, how easy and clean. Perhaps the ngaru would attack, and there would be nothing anyone could do. Grown men hardly stood a chance against those beasts—what hope did a small child have? What if he wandered off? All children know things lurk in the shadows of the bush. What a terrible, blameless tragedy it would be if the ngaru took him.

Lidan understood the need to press her advantage, but in the pit of her gut lay the cold weight of doubt. It turned her blood to ice, and she shuddered at the thought. She knew doubt would become guilt and burrow deep until it settled in her soul, where it would eat away at her until nothing remained but a spectre of who she'd once been.

Lidan would know what she had done. Her father would know. Farah would know. They would see the lie in her eyes and in the shadow of the moment she let Ehran perish. She'd already witnessed one child's death at the whim of a ngaru and it haunted her still.

She'd watched the light fade from Abbi's eyes, a victim of the ngaru's hard blades, knowing there was not a thing she could do to reverse the damage wrought on her small body. She had held her little sister close and watched warmth and life slip away, blood mingling with rain.

She fought hard the night Abbi died—harder than she ever had to save herself—harder than she knew she had the strength to. Harder than Loge ever taught her and with abandon and anger and some sort of poisonous, furious grief he would surely frown upon. Even before she saw her sister's twisted body, she knew killing the ngaru would make no difference; Abbi was dead, and finishing the creature was but a formality—something she *had* to do, despite the futility.

It was a fight that changed her irrevocably. In the rain-soaked bush, fat drops of water smacking against the undergrowth and the night sliced by white lightning, Lidan broke.

The thin shell of her childhood innocence shattered. She cast off what remained of the child she was, a thirteen-year-old who loved her horse and her home, and let it tumble to the mud. That girl died with her sister, without ceremony or fuss. That girl had been a mask, false and as broken as Abbi's small body. For what good is a mask when it is in pieces? What is broken can never be remade, not as it was before—the Crone taught her that. Those pieces had been hastily replaced each time her mother beat her, or her father doubted her. She'd lost count of how often the mask had been mended, and she'd walked away, not once looking back at those shards of her former self now scattered amongst the leaves and twigs.

Lidan was not the girl she had once been. Not after watching her sister die. Yet, had she suffered so grievously from Ehran's birth that she would allow the ngaru to take him? To surrender him without a fight? Could she stand by while they stole her brother away, and live the rest of her days haunted by the moment he realised there was no escape?

Did she owe it to Abbi to save their brother from the horror of the same death? Did she truly want that fate for Ehran? Her mother certainly did. Given the opportunity, could she, *would* she, abandon or protect the child who had usurped her place in the clan?

A choice remained, a promise to be kept, and neither the girl she had been nor woman she had become could escape it.

Would Ehran live?

Or die.

3

CHAPTER ONE

The Hidden Keep, Ravinka, Southern Orthia

A bolt of bright blue magic arced over Ranoth's head like lightning, and he hit the ground as the power discharged with a boom that shook the building to its foundations. The air was driven from his lungs and a high-pitched ringing filled his ears, blocking out Degan's hurried apologies and requests for forgiveness.

The boy staggered to a stop, his mouth forming words Ran couldn't hear, while he looked from his hands to his teacher and back again in wide-eyed terror. Ran gave Degan a wave and the child stopped talking long enough to take a breath. At least this time, Degan hadn't actually hit Ran with the magic, so that was something.

'It's all right, Deeg.' Ran waved again, unsure if the words came out correctly. He couldn't hear them to judge. 'Go and change.'

The boy hesitated, then took off for the door. Ran levered himself onto one elbow and worked his jaw to dislodge the ringing in his ears. The back of his skull ached and the residue of Degan's magic sizzled across his skin, but the discomfort was worth it to see what Quaid had described as a "once in a generation anomaly".

Quaid had been right. In the four years Ran had been at the Keep, he hadn't seen anything quite like the things Degan could do with his magic, and so far his teachers were at a loss as to how or why. Yidda, the records master, had been digging around her library for weeks and the vast collection had yet to yield any answers. Unless she found something soon, the staff of the Hidden Keep would have to muddle through Degan's condition with a combination of trial and a shit-ton of errors.

At the door Degan stopped, bowed to someone, then hurried out to the bathhouse.

Ran's vision adjusted and his ears popped. Sasha appeared in the doorway and rolled her eyes, her red curls pulled back and looped into a knot to keep them from interfering with her work. She must have heard the thunderclap of Degan's magic from the infirmary next door.

'I'm fine,' Ran said. His words were muffled and dull, as though he was shouting under water.

Sasha pursed her lips and helped him to his feet with a none-too-subtle heave. There had been a steady stream of people attending the infirmary with ear complaints since Degan's power had come on, and while the deafness was temporary, Sasha knew Ran couldn't hear anything but the rasp of his own breath. She'd warned him about Degan, warned him to keep clear, and he'd nodded and smiled and completely ignored her. By the way her hands bit into the muscles of his upper arm, he was in for an absolute grilling when his hearing returned.

Unfortunately for Degan, the boy's troubles did not seem to be abating like the deafness he caused. If anything, they were getting worse. As Sasha led Ran from the sparring hall and across to the infirmary, he turned the problem over in his mind.

The boy was about eight years old, brought to the Hidden Keep in the summer following Ran and Sasha's arrival. He'd been a toddler then, old enough to walk and talk and old enough for his parents to realise something was very wrong with their flaxen-haired child. He singed most things he touched, couldn't be in the same room as a fire, and refused to wear warm clothes, even in the depths of winter. In a childish fit of rage, he'd burned the family cottage to the ground and had been promptly delivered to the couriers who knew the location of the Hidden Keep. Now, his simmering powers had reached a rolling boil, and despite years of training, Degan was again struggling to contain the energy.

Quaid had been the first to notice the change in his sparring class. He'd warned Ran and Keep Master Collan that the boy would need to be trained alone from now on. The risk of maiming or killing another student had become too great, but Ran had hoped Quaid was wrong, had hoped to find a way to change the sparring master's mind, or to help Degan get his power under control.

Ran had given Quaid the same nod and smile he'd imparted on Sasha and all he had to show for his efforts was screaming in his ears and terror in Degan's eyes. Ran's heart sank as he watched the boy disappear into the bathhouse across the courtyard, knowing Quaid had been entirely correct, and there was very little, if anything, Ran could do to help.

Sasha led Ran up the stairs to the ward on the second floor of the infirmary and left him on a chair by her desk. The students in her tutelage greeted the healing mistress with bows then returned to replenishing stocks of bottles and jars in nearby cabinets. Sasha reached over their heads for a tiny stoppered bottle of thick oil and Ran let her tilt his head to one side and administer the drops, closing his eyes for a moment and allowing himself to feel the pads of her fingers on his skin. Memory flashed to life behind his eyelids and a jolt rippled through his bones.

Four years...

Four years? Had it really been that long since Sasha Hale had saved him from the bottom of a Graupen mine shaft, tended his wounds and helped him escape his father's scouts?

He opened his eyes and a wisp of light vanished behind a heavy drape.

His heart skipped then thumped hard back into time.

The fuck was that?

He blinked and looked away from the curtains. He was seeing things. A side-effect of Degan's magic, nothing else.

Yet for a moment he wondered, then clenched his hands and jammed the thought away, shoving it into a shadowy crevice in his mind. No, he'd banished that creature, screamed at her, cursed her until eventually she'd faded from sight. He'd fought for that peace and maintained it ever since.

Sasha sat back on her chair and Ran dragged his thoughts to the present. He worked his jaw, popped his ears, and waited for the drops to do their work, all the while willing his heartbeat to slow. The small sounds of the infirmary crept into his head and the pain at the base of his skull eased, the tight bands of fear around his chest loosening and slipping away. He cleared his throat and fixed his eyes on Sasha. He could keep the ghost at bay if he just kept his mind in this moment, right here, with Sasha.

She moved her chair closer. 'Is it as bad as Quaid says?'

'Fuck yes.'

'Ran!' She scowled and shot a glance at the children working at the cabinets.

'Shit—I mean, sorry.' He flinched as she slapped him on the shoulder and grinned when she rolled her eyes again.

She handed him a cloth to wipe away a dribble of oil leaking from his ear. 'I told you not to engage with him.'

Ran averted his gaze, focusing on a very interesting stack of bedsheets at the end of the ward. 'He's doing something with his shots that causes the air to shift. Makes an incredible noise. I've never heard anything like it. And there's a concussion wave that just hits you like kick to the face. He's doing it all the time now, and doesn't seem to know why, or how to stop it.'

'Did he say anything about how he feels? What he's thinking?' She scratched notes on a sheet of parchment then slipped it into a thick folder. There was a collection of them on her desk about a foot high and she added this one to the top.

'I don't think he's happy about it,' Ran replied, looking at his hands and squeezing them to suppress a tremble. Degan hadn't said a word, but the way he'd hunched his shoulders and scanned the hall from beneath furrowed brows spoke volumes about the turmoil in his heart. Ran should have asked, but he hadn't. He already knew.

Sasha stopped writing another note and gave Ran a pointed look. 'Reminds me of when your powers came on.'

'That was different—'

'No, it was exactly the same.' She levelled the quill at him and looked down its length, pinning him with her stare. 'You were terrified, and Degan is probably just as scared. The changes are one thing, but now he's been told he can't train with his class. You, of all people, know what that's like.'

Ran shifted in his seat and searched the ward for something to look at other than the knowing expression on Sasha's face. He *did* know. And the weight of that loneliness still sat heavy in his chest. He hadn't wanted anyone's pity. He'd wanted to conquer his changes on his own, and the battle had dragged him into a darkness that almost killed him. Just because it had taken him an age to accept help, didn't mean Degan felt the same. The boy deserved better.

'I hadn't thought of it like that,' he muttered.

'Obviously.' She turned back to her papers and added another folder to the pile. It teetered but held. 'I'll speak with Amitty and get her to check

7

on him. Perhaps some extra meditation will help. We don't want him to turn in on himself.'

Ran's throat tightened as the memory tugged at his mind. 'Like I did...'

'Like you did,' she agreed and waved for a young woman to take the folders. The student staggered under their unstable weight and left Sasha and Ran alone.

Sasha rested her hand on his knee, waiting until he lifted his face and met her gaze. Those eyes saw right through him. They belonged to his oldest friend, one of the few people in the Keep who truly knew who he was. Ranoth Olseta: son of the duke and fugitive from his Justice.

'Don't let your past become Degan's future. You have a chance to stop that. Don't let him down.'

She was right. She always was.

Ran left the infirmary to find Quaid. He had to write a report on Degan's changes, but first he wanted to find the sparring master and confirm what they suspected. Training away from other children his age, especially his friends, would be hard on Degan. It might even be harder than Ran's experience on his arrival at the Keep. At least Ran hadn't had any friends to abandon.

Sasha had been the notable exception, though her lack of magic left her in a unique position. She was among a small number who had no magic at all, and of them, she was the only one not born to the Keep. She could have left years ago, returning to a world of freedom that Ran and the other magic-weavers were forever forbidden, but she never spoke of leaving, and he had never asked. Perhaps, like him, the memory of that bitter winter when they fell into each other's path, and the creatures that pursued them, filled her with a heady fear of the world beyond.

She'd found her brothers at the Keep, years after their parents had exiled them. They had barely remembered her, but she'd never forgotten them, and Ran suspected they were the true anchor that held her heart in this place. Zarad was an excellent manipulator of elemental magic, and he and Nicot had their sister's affinity for healing. They had been teenagers when he and Sasha arrived, but the years had swiftly turned them both into young men who towered over their older sister.

It feels like a lifetime ago… he mused.

Four years… a distorted voice muttered.

Ran spun around, hands up, blue magic sparking across his fingers, but no one was there. He almost thought he heard her laugh.

Four years you've languished—

Ran slammed a door on the voice and sprinted up the stairs of the North Tower to the teaching offices and classrooms. He willed the sounds of the Tower to fill his ears and drown the ghost's voice, burying her whispers from the past in the muffled noise of the present.

He rarely occupied his office in the Tower, preferring to remain in the sparring hall, near the pathway to the Walled Forest where he trained his students most days. They spent little time with their heads in books or focusing on theory, and that was how he preferred it. Quaid, on the other hand, loved to set his students hours of extra reading on strategy and technique. Ran wondered sometimes if the man wouldn't have preferred a role in the library with Yidda, rather than the sweaty work of teaching the students to control their power in a fight.

The sparring master was at his desk and looked up from a mess of papers when Ran rapped a knuckle on the door frame.

'How was it?' Quaid Greyling asked without preamble, setting his work aside.

Ran slumped into a soft chair by the fire and worked his jaw up and down. 'He blew my ears to bits. I can almost hear you, but you sound like you're talking under water.' Ran rubbed at a spot behind his ear that felt like it had been hit with a hammer.

'Can he control it at all?' Quaid leaned forward and chewed the inside of his lip. He was a big man, tall and broad in the shoulders, with muscles hardened from sparring. He had the light brown skin of a man from the Arinnian coast, or perhaps the Syod Archipelago, but even Quaid couldn't recall from where his family came. He'd arrived here as a child without so much as a note or an explanation of his origins, let alone a memory.

'It seems not. I think he's upset though, and it's making it worse.'

Quaid raised a brow at that, and Sasha's warning echoed in the back of Ran's mind.

'He's panicking because he doesn't want to be singled out. He just wants to be like the others, and this anomaly is setting him apart.' Ran wished

Degan's circumstance didn't reflect his own so closely, but it was becoming hard to ignore. 'The harder he tries to suppress the noise, the louder it gets. Then he panics, and it worsens again. He's not going to be able to control it until he finds peace with what's happening, and that's not going to happen until the changes stop. He's going to have to ride it out for a bit, I'm afraid.'

'Like someone else we know?'

Ran shot Quaid a look and the man held up his hands. He'd lost the ends off a few of his fingers and his arms were scared from years of training youngsters and taking the brunt of their mistakes. A few of them had been Ran's doing, suffered when Quaid turned his hand to dragging Ran back from a black chasm of self-loathing after staggering from the forest into the Keep.

Quaid had put him to work behind a sword and drilled him until his joints burned and his muscles were hard as stone. He'd forced Ran out of bed every morning, regardless of the weather, and made him run the playing fields like a reluctant horse, until finally Ran found the strength to accept what was happening in his body. Only then had he been able to channel the magic into something useful. Only then had the real training begun.

With a sigh, Ran conceded the point. 'I'm not saying he's exactly like me, but he could go that way if we aren't careful. Mistress Hale is going to speak with Mistress Slade and get him some help.'

Quaid nodded. 'And you? Do you want to work with him?'

'I can't teach him anything about controlling the noise—that will be up to you and Collan to muddle through with him. I can get him into the practise field swinging a few staves, then we can try training blades.' Ran shrugged. 'It might help him burn off that anger welling up in his chest.'

'Sounds fair,' Quaid said. 'Take it slow at first and plug your ears. If he lets off a blast you don't want to be back in the infirmary with bleeding ears.'

'True.' Ran grimaced and rubbed the base of his skull. 'I think Sash is getting sick of treating ear damage.'

A bell tolled nearby, and Quaid glanced at the window with surprise. 'Six bells already? The days are getting lighter. You hungry?'

Ran nodded and tried to not to wince at the shooting pain streaking down his neck as they walked to the West Tower for the evening meal. Midwinter had come and gone four moons ago, and as spring edged toward summer, the sun lingered longer in the sky before dipping behind the mountains and plunging Ravinka's valley into darkness.

For that, Ran was thankful.

The snow had melted away from the Keep, from the river and the lower reaches of the mountains, and for a time at least, he could go about his tasks in the warming light of the day, without every snowy shadow conspiring to remind him of the things that had hunted him here.

CHAPTER TWO

The Hidden Keep, Ravinka, Southern Orthia

Dinner was never a quiet affair at the Hidden Keep. The entire population filed into the dining hall—adults, children, and the elderly—a hundred or so people, all gathering in the massive central space on the West Tower's ground floor. Tables stretched out in uniform lines, laden with platters of roast meats and vegetables. Jugs of ale and carafes of wine stood amongst them, and any remaining space was filled with cut loaves of bread and bowls of seasonal fruit from the orchards or hothouses. The place teemed with life for most of the day, growing still only in the dead of night when the wall guards cycled through on their rest breaks. There was always a pot of stew or soup bubbling on a hearth fire should anyone find themselves hungry in the night, but at mealtimes the place filled to bursting.

Ran followed Quaid, weaving through the crowd and down the long tables. Despite the high ceiling and mezzanine floor above where windows stood open to the fresh mountain air, the hall was hot with the press of bodies and radiant heat from the nearby kitchens. It was a stifling embrace that sucked the breath from Ran's chest as he reached the table occupied by the Keep's teachers.

A squeal burst to life in his ears, growing until it drowned out the dull chatter of the gathering. He worked his jaw and rubbed at the bone behind his ear, this time to no effect. A pulse of pain rolled down his forehead and engulfed his sight. His eyes were suddenly lead balls in his skull, cumbersome, unresponsive, and aching as though Quaid had punched him in the face.

He gasped, a wave of dread crashing through him. He knew this feeling.

Once before this pain had come and banished his strength, heralding a change that began when he arrived at the Keep and refused to ease until it had irrevocably altered his sight. Agonising headaches had confined him to bed for weeks, and afterwards, his eyes had never been the same. Changes like Degan was suffering; the same, yet entirely different.

It had taken months to learn to control the new power, training to veil his eyes from thaumalux—the light emitted by magic-weavers, once invisible to him but now as blinding as daylight. It was only then they knew he would be a tracker, and only then that Ran found his purpose among the folk of the Keep.

Why is this happening? I don't... Shit, not now...

He cursed the insistent ringing in his ears and pressed his hand to his forehead. He hadn't even made it to his seat and his head told him he wasn't going to.

Something flickered and disappeared at the edge of his vision and he tried to follow it with sluggish eyes. Across the table, Sasha frowned then lifted her brows as if to ask if he was all right. He gave her a quick nod and a wave, knowing she would see straight through his lie. She was too far away to challenge him without drawing unwanted attention, and he slipped quickly into a dark corner of the hall.

Bent double behind a pillar, he squeezed his eyes shut, pushing his magic against the noise screaming in his ears and the pain throbbing through his head. It abated just enough to hear footsteps approach and stop beside him.

'Ran? How are you, my boy?' Collan's deep, throaty voice rumbled through the squeal and he squinted up at the keep master. Dressed in his usual black robes, his hands hidden so far up the excessively deep sleeves that he had to flick them back with a theatrical flourish to reveal his fingers. He was of equal height with Ran and had lost most of his dark blond hair in the years since Ran's arrival.

'Master Greyling.' Ran nodded and sucked a breath through his teeth. The headache cut across his brow and his stomach lurched. 'I'm well, sir.'

Fuck! Not again...

'I rather think you're not,' Collan said, eyeing Ran down the length of his nose and frowning. He heard someone call for Sasha and knew immediately he would be spending the night in the infirmary.

'Why did you tell me you were fine when you obviously weren't?' Quaid stood at the end of Ran's bed with his thickly muscled arms folded over his chest, his sleeves rolled up in the warmth of the infirmary. The ridges of his shoulders were damp, evidence of the spring rain washing across the forecourt of the Keep and whispering against the windows.

Ran shrugged and Sasha answered for him from the cabinets at the end of the ward.

'Because he's a sneaky little liar,' her voice echoed against the whitewashed walls and Quaid cocked his eyebrow. Ran shrugged again and pulled a cold compress down over his eyes. He didn't want to see Sasha's anger when she brought it to his bedside. There was quite enough in her voice.

'We need to understand Degan's changes,' Quaid continued despite Ran's disappearance behind the wet cloth. 'If his magic has started to affect *you*, we need to understand how before we can discover why.'

'I just wanted some dinner and a sleep, that's all. The pain will be gone in the morning.'

'You hope,' said Sasha from beside his elbow. Ran started and she touched his arm. 'It took weeks last time. Keep still and drink this.'

She pressed a cup to his lips. The liquid tasted foul, but Sasha gave him no quarter, forcing the cup's entire contents into his mouth until he had no choice but to swallow.

'It should start to work soon,' she said, giving his shoulder a squeeze before he heard her shuffle back into a chair.

Quaid cleared his throat. 'I'm going to speak with Collan, then Degan. I'd prefer you were with me, Ran, but this can't wait until you're well again. I'll be back in the morning to see how you are. Good luck with him, Mistress Hale.'

Ran heard the smile in Quaid's voice, then the man's footsteps echoed down the ward until a door opened, then closed.

Silence pressed in around Sasha and Ran, waiting to be filled. She still owed him a proper scolding for exposing himself to Degan's raw power and he was unlikely to escape it now.

'Is it like last time?' She surprised him with a question instead of a withering barrage of reprimands.

Still, the night was young.

Ran sighed and dared to lift the corner of the compress. Her eyes were on him, steady and clear, like a hawk watching a mouse in the undergrowth. One false move and she would have him. A lie wouldn't get him out of this.

'It feels like it, yes.'

Her lips pressed together into a thin, frustrated line. 'I warned you. I told you to stay away from raw magic. I kept my peace this afternoon, hoping my fears were misplaced, but I was right to worry. I knew this would happen and so did you!'

And there it was.

Her tone left no room for compromise, no room to argue. She *had* told him to avoid raw power, and he had suspected it would come to this, but he had a job to do. He needed to be around students when they used their magic. How else was he going to train them to track the stuff?

'I'm as useless as tits on a bull if I have to avoid raw magic. I need to help these students, especially those like Degan.'

'Degan has a whole Keep of teachers and minders to watch and train him,' Sasha countered. 'Teaching the average student is fine, but special cases like Degan? It's just too dangerous. Why they insist on involving you, I will never know.'

Ran scowled, his anger rising. 'Perhaps they value my opinion?'

'I'm sure they do, but they have no appreciation for what it does to you, or what it will continue to do if you keep exposing yourself.' She folded her arms as if that was the end of the conversation.

He wasn't ready to end it there, though. 'Why do you care, Sasha? It's not you who has to suffer through the consequences or the pain.'

She laughed; a cold, bitter sound that echoed like a crow's call. 'I care because it's my job. I'm the one who has to clean up the mess left behind.'

'Your job?' he repeated. He let the words sink through his skin and his eyes pulsed again with the piercing ache of a building migraine. Her treatment was slowly working its way into his head, but it could do nothing to dilute his anger. She cared only because it was her job. Not because of their friendship or their shared history. Because it was her job.

He lowered the compress and hid her face from sight. 'Don't let me keep you, then. I'm sure you've other tasks to attend to.'

'Ran, please...'

He knew in his heart he was being entirely unreasonable, but pain and anger whirled in him, mixing with a deep sense of helplessness he couldn't shake. She had warned him, and he hadn't listened but right now he couldn't bear to hear that truth.

It took a few moments, but eventually she stood and left for her apartment beyond the doors at the end of the ward.

He lifted the compress again and watched Sasha leave, her hand lingering on the door as though she might turn back, before she slipped from sight. Ran's face was numb now, entirely distant, along with the pain in his head and eyes. By morning he would know what sort of change Degan had wrought on his powers.

She didn't speak, but he knew she was there, her presence triggering a deep thrumming in his magic, as though a harp string had been plucked inside his chest. The disturbance dragged him from his drug-addled sleep until he peeled the compress from his face and forced his eyes open.

The ghost girl's form pulsed with light. It shifted gently in time with the rhythm of sleeping breath, never so brightly that it hurt to behold her, and never so subtle that she vanished from sight. It was beautiful and mesmerising and almost enough to muffle the shock that jolted through his limbs at the sight of her.

Ran blinked. 'Fuck.'

His lips slurred the curse and he tried to call his body into action, but his limbs ignored him as he watched the ghost girl glide toward him, her feet bare on the cold polished timber.

'Does your mother know you swear like that?'

'Fuck off.'

How dare she pour salt into that wound. 'Did you do this to me? Is this your work?' he hissed as she reached the end of the bed.

'I did not.'

'Then what the fuck are you doing here?'

'I could ask you the same question.'

Ran's lip curled in a sneer. 'What kind of a stupid question is that?'

'Four years, Ranoth Olseta, son of Ronart, Duke of Orthia. Ranoth, son of Merideth of Isord. Four years you've languished here.' Her face was an

16

impassive porcelain mask, unchanged since the first time he saw her in that abandoned horror house in Lackmah. Her silver-blonde hair hung in a curtain down to her waist, her body covered in a torn white shift; a gaping, ragged mess of a wound at her throat. Of course she would never change, no matter how long she chose to haunt him.

She was dead. The dead don't change. Ghosts don't change. And evidently, they don't go away either.

'Not unless we get what we want, Ranoth.'

She'd plucked the thought from his mind, and the words thrust him back into the now as he tried to lift himself off the bed. 'What do you want, then? What do I have to do to get rid of you?'

'Haven't you missed me?' She gave him a rare, sly smile and he shuddered.

'I might have, once, but that was before I found out what you were—'

'And what was that?' She titled her head, the wound at her neck warping into a hideous smirk. 'An innocent girl murdered on the cusp of womanhood? Or a soulless corpse wandering the wilds of the world, searching and suffering with a hunger it could not sate?' Her features darkened as if a thundercloud had rolled in over their heads and she edged closer, drifting toward him along the length of the bed. 'I didn't ask for any of those things, Ranoth Olseta.'

He glanced away, unable to argue but unwilling to concede her point. He had come to accept that the creatures they called dradur, the things that had hunted him through the woods to the Keep, had been created by foul magic in the farmhouse near Lackmah, but he had never reconciled that the remains of his ghost had become one of them. It was the dradur made of her corpse that had come within a breath of killing Sasha.

'Just tell me what you want,' he growled, imprisoning emotions and furious words behind clenched teeth.

She leaned over his face, glowering, anger vibrating the air between them. 'I want justice, Ranoth. I want revenge. I want payment in kind for what was done to me.'

'What? *Now?* After all this time?' Through the confusion, fear wrapped a cold hand around his heart. 'What does this have to do with me?'

'Now you're in a position to give it to me.'

Ran gaped at her. 'How the ever-loving-*fuck* do you expect me to deliver that?!'

'The way will reveal itself, if you have the heart to follow it.'

'How?' His strength was fading, but she was not. Her form remained strong, throbbing in the air beside him as his muscles gave in and he sank back heavily onto the bed. 'I can't...'

'You will, if you choose.'

The drugs reclaimed him, or perhaps the ghost let him go, dropping him back into the painless abyss that held him before she dragged him free of it. He closed his eyes and her presence pulsed against his awareness. Though he could not see her face, she wasn't leaving this time. Not until she got exactly what she wanted.

Morning yanked Ran from sleep, slicing through the blissful, painless fog where the ghost had left him. His head screamed in protest, his eyes burning as though they were on fire.

'FUCK!' he roared, arching his back away from the bed and ramming his head into the pillow with all the strength left in his aching neck. A wordless scream escaped him, followed by a sob.

Sasha burst through the infirmary door in a whirl of nightclothes. Quaid came at her heels and somewhere, a thought sprang to life amidst Ran's pain. How late was it? Surely not much past dawn. What was Quaid doing on this side of the Keep so early?

Checking on me. The thought vanished as the pain doubled down, driving knives into his eyes and dragging flaming brands across his skin. He squeezed his eyes shut and pushed back with his magic. It had been foolish to assume he would heal overnight. His power was too focused on protecting itself from the after-effects of Degan's energy to worry about healing.

Sasha pressed a cup to his lips and he drank greedily, without care for the taste or texture. His eyes fluttered open again and he immediately regretted it.

'Sweet merry fuck, Quaid, shut that curtain! The light's killing me,' Ran pleaded, and through his blinking, weeping eyes saw Quaid look about himself in confusion.

'What curtain?'

'The one behind you!'

Quaid spun again, and Sasha frowned.

'What's he talking about?' Quaid asked Sasha as if Ran couldn't hear him.

Instead of answering, Sasha moved into Ran's field of vision and put a cool hand on his cheek. 'Ran, there's no light.' She sat on the bed and pressed against him, using the weight of her arms on his chest to anchor his thoughts. 'What can you see?'

Ran furrowed his aching brow and pointed. 'Sunlight.'

Her eyes widened, and her lips parted a little. She studied him carefully. 'Is it your eyes?'

Ran's stomach flipped and he suppressed a retch. '*Please*... shut the curtain, Quaid.'

'Ran, he can't,' said Sasha, her voice steady when all else was chaos.

'*What?*' He was screaming at her now. 'Why? Fuck, it hurts!'

She took him by the shoulders. 'It's midnight! The sun won't be up for hours.'

Ran stopped cold.

'What?' He peeled his eyes open as far as he dared and tried to focus on the window across the infirmary. He couldn't get a fix on it for all the stunning light in his eyes, blocking out everything except the strange oscillating silhouettes of Sasha and Quaid.

His vision shifted and he realised only Sasha was a silhouette, not Quaid. The light not only surrounded the sparring master but oozed from him. It moved across his skin like ripples of sunlight on a lake, driving rainbows and flares into Ran's eyes. Quaid was a beacon in the darkness, blindingly bright, illuminating the infirmary as though he had swallowed the sun.

By contrast, Sasha's face fell under a shadow, her back to Quaid's light as he stood at the end of the bed. Ran shuddered as realisation dawned through the fog of the pain-relieving draught.

'Thaumalux...'

'What? Ran, I don't understand you?' Sasha shook her head and the halo of light behind her shifted.

'His thaumalux—it's blinding me. I saw it through the wall, it woke me.'

'Shit.' Sasha graced them with one of her rare curses and spun into action. 'Quaid, out now!'

Ran heard his protests as Sasha herded the big man to the door and Ran's muscles relaxed as the light receded. He heard Sasha repeat the word he'd said, heard Quaid's confused questions and her assurance she would explain—but tomorrow, in his office. He wasn't to return until Sasha gave him the word. The pull of the drug began to drag Ran under the surface of his pain.

Sasha returned, and he began to weep. She climbed onto the bed and cradled his head, humming a song she knew would cut through the anguish and the agony. The infirmary was dark once more; Quaid and his thaumalux banished to the West Tower. Sasha emitted no such light, her soul perfectly plain and unmarked by the horror of magic's curse. She was a tiny movement in the depths of the night as she held him and let her voice carry away the hurt.

Why was Quaid here? The thought slipped back into his mind unbidden. *You know why,* the ghost whispered, and Ran gave himself to oblivion.

CHAPTER THREE

The Tablelands, Tolak Range, the South Lands

Lidan crouched low. The muscles in her thighs burned as she picked carefully through the undergrowth. She licked dry lips and swallowed a hard knot of anticipation. Somewhere in the bush to the north, Loge mirrored her, creeping unseen through the trees toward their target.

Her grip tightened around the shaft of her bow and she brushed the pad of her thumb along the rough edge of the arrow's fletching. She could smell their fire; acidic smoke wafting through the trees to whisper its secrets to her. Their wood was green and smoky, unseasoned and scavenged from the bush nearby. The place reeked of tenna bark, which they had foolishly used to kindle the flames. No one familiar with the trees here would ever use tenna in a fire—the stink just never washed out.

The smoke had revealed their camp to the Tolak ranging party in the waning light of the previous day. Siman had ordered a watch, and Jessah and Nathen had scaled the face of a nearby bluff to keep an eye on the little point of light glimmering in the darkness. When the smoke billowed again in the morning, they knew the raiders had not moved on.

Shafts of morning light cut through the haze and Lidan wove through them like a spirit.

The edge of the camp appeared between the trees.

It wasn't much more than a haphazard collection of bedrolls in a small clearing with temporary hide shelters strung between the trunks of red-core trees. A fire pit sat at the centre, surrounded by a group of dark, hunched figures.

Lidan stopped as close to the edge of the clearing as she dared and sank into a low squat. The soaring trees provided only so much cover. She could not risk being seen. Not until she was ready.

The raiders gave no sign they had detected her presence, and she took a deep breath through her nose to steady her thudding heart. It had been months since a raiding party had made it this far into Tolak territory, and Lidan shuddered to think what might have been had they reached an occupied village. For a few short months after the Corron, she had thought there could be nothing worse than the ngaru in the shadows of the bush, but she was wrong.

Yorrell Namjin's wrath spawned a new evil into her world, and very quickly the ngaru became the least of the Tolak's problems. The Namjin daari's burning rage, fuelled by the insult inflicted on him by Lidan and her father, had sparked a war far worse than any border skirmish or land grab the clans had seen before. For every settlement harried by wandering ngaru, three more were attacked by the Namjin. Lidan's people found themselves fighting a battle on two fronts, never knowing where the next blow would land.

Messengers had arrived at Hummel, beaten and bloody and exhausted. Time and again they had hurried into her father's private rooms to report on the devastation. At first it was the odd running raid, scorching the earth and pillaging before racing back over the border to the safety of their own range. Then the Namjin grew bold, and their numbers increased until they were marauding across the Tolak borderlands and hill country as if they owned it.

Lidan's father ordered every ranger he had to the border, leaving reserves to manage the population of ngaru festering in the tablelands. After four years of intense fighting, the land was reclaimed and the raiders sent packing, but the Namjin were undeterred, and the incursions continued.

Erlon Tolak used every excuse he could to keep his daughter from the border—at first assigning her to the healing rooms to work and study with Grent, then to a reserve party of rangers scouting for ngaru in the table-lands. Her father thought to spare her the worst of the war, to keep her clear of the greatest danger, but she'd seen enough to know the truth of what was going on in the western reaches of the range.

She saw the wounds of the riders and the fleeing villagers who made it to Hummel. She saw their tents, pitched around the outer wall, then watched them transform into huts, then houses. The population of Hummel swelled, and the walls shifted to accommodate. She saw the remains of the western villages when her ranging took her along abandoned trackways and hunting trails. She'd seen the blackened ruins of homes, blood-soaked soil and the stinking carcasses left behind. She'd seen the price that had been paid to keep the interior villages safe—

A bird's shrill call pierced the air and Lidan's heart skipped.

She waited…

The raiders around the fire remained unmoved, muttering to each other, one hugging a steaming cup while another scratched at his crotch. Lidan curled her tongue and let out a short burst of sound that echoed through the trees—an answer to the bird call.

She raised her bow and drew the arrow back to the corner of her mouth, training the stone arrowhead on a man directly across the camp. Before she could loose the shaft, his face exploded toward the fire. Blood and brains erupted from the hole in his head and he shuddered. His body flopped into the flames and the others came screaming to their feet.

'Fuck,' Lidan hissed and shifted her aim. Her arrow sliced into the neck of a raider spinning to confront the unseen threat. He collapsed and one of his companions whipped around, keen eyes on the trees. She had just enough time to skewer an arrow through his shoulder before she stowed her bow, turned and bolted.

All pretence at stealth vanished and she crashed through the bush. Charging back between the trees, she vaguely heard someone screaming curses and orders and a decent number of other somebodies rushing to comply. To her left someone else came hurtling through the trees and burst onto the track.

'Run faster!' Loge shouted, and they cleared a log at a sprint.

The trail was faint, but the raiders seemed to be doing all right at following their ears. Loge let off a series of sharp whistles as the ground dropped away. Lidan slid down the bank toward the creek, her boot heels carving ruts in the soft dirt as she tried to steer away from the biggest obstacles.

She hit the base of the slope and rolled to her feet. Loge caught her arm and yanked her sideways as an arrow slammed into a nearby tree. Their boots thumped along another faint track, shouts and bellowed orders echoing up the valley behind them.

Arrows whistled overhead and thwacked into the trees, shredding leaves and showering Lidan and Loge in splinters. The creek curved to the right and the track followed, the valley narrowing to nothing more than a tight ravine walled on either side with massive boulders shrouded by creeping vines and undergrowth. Lidan raced toward the breach in the rock where the water flowed, a gap no wider than two horses nose to tail. The track hugged the edge of the creek through the gap, enough room only for a single ranger to pass at a time.

She shot through the space and darted around the back side of the stone wall, Loge at her heels. Arrows cracked against the stone on the other side and hurtled through the gap to splash into the rushing water.

Lidan slipped and scrambled to correct her footing as she twisted around the base of a boulder and into a crevice. Loge gave one long whistle that echoed up the sides of the canyon and into the blue sky above.

The screaming started not a full heartbeat after.

Lidan slammed back against a boulder and gulped breath after breath. Her skin prickled and the muscles beneath throbbed, the thump of her pulse nearly drowning out the shouts from the rangers hidden in the rocks above and the wails of the raiders dying by the creek. Loge leaned against the rock beside her, one hand on the wall of stone, his eyes closed as he fought to catch his breath.

'You used to be faster,' Lidan gasped. She leant forward and rested her hands on her thighs, her sweat-soaked shirt plastered to her back.

'I fucking caught you,' Loge replied.

'I beat you to the creek,' said Lidan, looking over as he shook his head. 'You—'

A raider barrelled through the gap in the rocks and turned his snarling face toward the sound of Loge's voice.

'DOWN!' Lidan cried as the raider launched himself at them.

Loge dropped. Lidan's knife flashed. Steel met flesh. The raider's throat offered no resistance to the blade's edge and blood gushed from the wound, pumping red through the man's fingers as he clutched at his neck. He slipped in the slick at his feet and went down hard, the side of his head smacking into the rock before he slumped heavily to the ground.

Between the gaping tear in his throat and the crack in his skull, Lidan was fairly sure he wasn't getting up again. She spat on the corpse for good measure.

'Fucker,' she snarled. She sniffed and pushed a stray lock hair from her face. A flash of red caught her eye and she glanced at her hand. There was blood, but it wasn't hers.

Loge straightened and rested his hands on his hips as Lidan wiped her knife clean and slipped it into its sheath.

Breathing hard, he eyed the body and the expanding pool of blood, then turned to Lidan and shrugged. 'Reckon he's dead enough, or you want put some more holes in him to be sure?'

Lidan leaned back against the boulder and pointed at Loge. 'That's going on your tally,' she said, still fighting to catch her breath.

'You're keeping a *tally?*'

'And those two ngaru up on the eastern ridge last moon.' Lidan spat a foul taste from her mouth. She needed some water.

Loge rolled his eyes and stepped over the raider and into the sunlight by the creek. 'You might as well just let the next one have me, because I'll be dead before I ever pay you back.'

Lidan grinned and adjusted the bow slung across her back. 'You're not getting out of it that easy, Loge Baker. At this rate, you'll be pouring my drinks for the next two years.'

The other rangers in their party climbed down from their hiding places above the creek and joined Lidan and Loge to finish off any lingering raiders. Loge ended two who lay gasping on the ground, while Jessah and Nathen left on horseback to make sure none had made it out of the valley alive and to search the abandoned camp. Lidan found most of the raiders had succumbed to the arrows sticking out of vital body parts and had expired before she got anywhere near them. All that was left to do was retrieve any serviceable arrows.

She collected an armful and turned to find Owin crouched beside a nearby corpse. Strands of long dark hair dangled around his face like a wild curtain as he patted the body down, fingering the pockets in the man's trousers.

Lidan frowned. 'The fuck are you doing?'

Owin glanced up. 'What's it look like?'

Lidan stared as he shuffled down to the raider's feet and began pulling at his boots. Evidently, they were the only thing of value the dead man had to offer.

Lidan's lip curled. 'Taking from the dead brings down gaden spirits. No wonder you have such bad luck.'

'Waste not, want not,' Owin grunted as he yanked the first boot free. He spared her a cold look of disdain. 'Not all of us are first born.'

'You're disgusting,' Lidan sneered.

Stealing from the dead might bring bad fortune and be generally foul, but it wasn't against the Law, so she left Owin to scavenge the bodies and made her way back to the track. Siman Jarrah, their party's leader and her father's advisor arrived with his apprentice Iema and the five remaining horses that had been tethered in the bush behind the boulder wall.

The horses twitched their ears and snorted at the smell of so much blood. Theus flicked his head, and Loge's mount, Striker, stamped his hoof on the soft soil. Lidan suspected they heartily disapproved of standing anywhere near the cooling bodies of the raiders.

Theus brought a smile to her lips. She loved that her mother hated him, loved that he took her far from Hummel without a hint of disagreement. Wild-born in the high country, he'd never been entirely content in the village stables. Striker was the older and more settled of the two, and Lidan gave them both a scratch on the nose before she accepted their reins from Iema.

Iema nodded approvingly at the carnage scattered through the bush. 'Not a bad plan after all.'

Siman cleared his throat and raised a brow at both young women. He was only just old enough to be their father, but his hair had begun to grey, giving him the odd look of a wizened elder still carrying the muscle of a much younger man. Granted, he was charged with training his niece and keeping the First Daughter of his daari alive in the most dangerous part of the South Lands, which was enough to send any man grey before his time. 'You're damn lucky it worked, Tolak.'

'But it *did* work. And no one died!' she said cheerfully. 'Except them. Which was the whole point.'

He looked around and Lidan saw him fight a smile. 'It did,' he conceded, then fixed her with a pointed look as he dismounted. 'Not a word of this to your father. I won't answer for you insisting on being running bait for this trap.'

He shot the same look at Iema, then marched away to inspect the bodies with Loge.

Iema, a couple of years younger and with the characteristic warm brown skin of the southern clans, glanced at Lidan. 'It was a good plan. And it *did* work,' she murmured with a smile.

Lidan tried not to laugh. 'Yeah, it did.'

CHAPTER FOUR

The Tablelands, Tolak Range, the South Lands

Siman led the rangers along thin game trails to another chattering stream that flowed southward from the Malapa. The water rushing past them would eventually find its way out to the creek in the grasslands beside the Caine, then past their home to where green and gold grasses met the blue of the sky in a hazy line. Somewhere beyond that horizon lay the Rinay Coast and its people with skin the colour of jet and their mischievous sea gods. Somewhere down there, across the dry, barren mountains of the Black Teeth, an ocean lapped at the land and men turned their skills not to riding horses, but navigating things called ships.

Or so the traders said. The Tolak range didn't extend past where the Jagga River cut across the plain, so neither Lidan nor the other rangers had ever seen the fruitless mountains beyond.

The ride back to their camp took most of the day, set as it was in the mouth of one of the tableland's many soaring canyons. The cliffs rose either side, bluffs of orange and white cresting the tops like great stone waves held frozen in time, bright among the dark green and brown of the bush. When the morning sun hit them, they shone with a glare that made Lidan's eyes water, and in the evening twilight, the rock threw deep hues of purple and red, as if bleeding out the warmth they had absorbed from the day.

The rangers travelled mostly in silence, listening and watching, waiting for a sign there was something out amongst the trees and cliffs that should not be. It was these long moments of silence after a fight that Lidan dreaded; when her heartbeat calmed and her muscles relaxed and her mind betrayed her. It began with a memory of lightning and rain, of booming thunder and the stench of ngaru ichor sprayed across the brush. The sound of her tiny sister's rasping breath echoed in her ears, shallow and desperate and tight, blood pumping into Abbi's little lungs as she drowned in her lifeblood.

That gurgling gasp was always loudest in the quiet moments, when her mind emptied and thoughts faded, when idle hands and little purpose gifted her too much time and space to think. Only when she stared down the shaft of an arrow, the sounds of her sister's death fled, and for a moment as brief as a few heartbeats, nothing else existed.

When she fought with her knives, the shouts and screams of her feuding parents and the crushing weight of their expectations vanished. No room for second guesses with blades in her hands, no time to overthink or worry about the consequences. With her knives, her confidence soared, and the emptiness left by her loss of purpose and place as her father's heir was filled with something far greater... survival. If it weren't for her knives and the deadly trade she plied, the pain of her inadequacy would surely boil over to scald her and anyone foolish enough to draw near.

Loge cleared his throat beside her and jolted Lidan from her thoughts. 'I'd ask where you are, but...'

She glanced down and realised she was strangling the reins, her knuckles pale with tension. Lidan relaxed her fingers and took a long, deep breath. 'Just thinking,' she said, her voice hoarse from lack of use.

He watched her for a moment, his hazel eyes bright in the sunlight. The day was well on its way to stifling, and he had rolled back his shirt sleeves to reveal the needle-etched tattana on his forearms. 'Want to talk about it?'

She shook her head. 'Same shit, different day.'

He looked up the track to the others. Lidan followed his gaze and realised with a start just how far behind she'd fallen. Theus had taken it upon himself to slacken off the pace, and in the fog of her reverie she hadn't noticed until Loge had ridden up behind her.

'It's been four years, Liddy.' He flicked a persistent fly away from his face with a wave of his hand.

'I know,' she murmured, even though the others were out of earshot. 'Still feels like yesterday, though.'

'Wasn't your fault.'

'So you keep saying.'

'And I'll keep saying it 'til you believe it.'

29

She glanced across and met his gaze. Seventeen years to his twenty-one, she was his apprentice only in name. She could just about best him in a fight, shoot as far and ride as hard. He had fewer lessons to teach her as the years passed and her skill levelled with his, but as much as he had abandoned his role as her teacher for that of her friend and confidant, he never hesitated to tell her when he thought she was being an idiot. Her lingering guilt over Abbi's death being a particular point of contention.

For years she'd played it down, dismissing Loge's concern as misplaced. It sat between them like a story untold, a song unsung, until the nightmares and the crippling anxiety, the weight of carrying around so much self-hatred and anger finally broke her and she let the whole lot spill out.

She thanked the ancestors they'd been out on a patrol when it happened, hidden from the curious eyes of the rest of their party. He'd sworn to never mention it in the company of others, and in all the time since had remained true to his word. The oath had been conditional on her promise of honesty, though. She had to talk to him, to share the burden. After all, how could he keep her safe out here if she was killing herself inside?

Much to her surprise, his strategy seemed to be working, and the pressure had eased as the seasons passed. The pain never really faded completely, and perhaps she didn't want it to. It was fuel for her fire, a reason to keep fighting.

'Siman reckons we're heading home tomorrow,' Loge said, shifting in his saddle. He glanced up at the sky visible above the canyon walls. 'It'll take half a moon to get back to Hummel from here.'

'Really? I thought we had a few more weeks out here?' Her throat tightened around her words. As dangerous as the range was, the thought of returning home always made her mouth run dry; the village walls rising high and the gates whispering shut, the stifling heat of her father's hall, and the tiny confines of the sleeping space she shared with her full-sister, Marrit.

There was no room to move and nothing to do.

Opportunities to fight or ride or hunt were few and far between, and her only escape from her parent's incessant pestering was in the healing rooms or the ranger's barracks. Hummel overflowed with the sounds of the life she wished she could escape. They grated on her nerves from the moment she returned until the moment she left again. Her parent's bickering was almost loud enough to drown out the joy of her sisters' voices, but worst of all was the deafening silence of the little girl missing from their number. Only eight sisters remained… plus the child who had taken her place.

The brother.

She never thought she'd have a brother; never thought she would have anything other than sisters. Lidan never thought the day she lost one, she would gain the other in some sort of sick trade. Ehran was four and seemed blithely unaware of the tremor his birth had sent through the Tolak clan. Did he know he shared his birthday with the death of a half-sister he would never meet? Did he have any inclination of the cold, hateful war swirling between his father and his father's first wife? Lidan pushed the questions away.

'We've been away for almost a month,' Loge reasoned, their horses wandering the track at their own pace. 'And if we don't head back now, we'll be late for the matching.'

'What matching?' Lidan frowned.

His laugh echoed into the trees. 'You forgot?'

'Forgot what?'

'Bridie?'

Her heart thumped uncomfortably; hot embarrassment prickling across her skin. Bridie had turned fifteen at the end of the last wet season, and her betrothal to Harran Daylin had been confirmed only days after. They were due to be matched this season, and Lidan had forgotten the event entirely.

Loge leaned forward, the smile fading from his lips as he realised she wasn't joking. 'Shit, you're serious. How could you forget—'

'I've had other things on my mind,' she hissed, hoping none of the others were close enough to hear. 'Staying alive, for one thing!'

She'd been so focused on the present, on tracking ngaru and watching for signs of raiders, she'd left no room for the recollection of Bridie's betrothal. Lidan tilted her head back and closed her eyes. 'Fuck. Tell me we don't have to go home.'

'Sorry. Not much chance of getting out of this one,' Loge replied. 'Some-one's bound to notice if the First Daughter is missing.'

He was right. It was strange enough that Lidan was allowed out with a ranging party and not confined to the village where her parents could keep a firm eye on her. If she didn't play the part of dutiful daughter for the benefit of her father's allies, there would be an uproar.

Lidan groaned. 'I *hate* that place, with all its whispers and stares. Do you have any idea what it's like to be watched like that? Every move noted and analysed?'

Loge fixed his gaze on Lidan. He was a head taller, so she had to look up to meet his eyes. 'Yes, I know exactly what that's like. My apprentice is the daari's daughter. Do you think they aren't watching every move *I* make? Doesn't stop me going home, though. I know you don't like it, but we can't stay out here forever.'

'At least your parents aren't constantly in your ear about what you should or shouldn't be doing with your life. Or fighting with each other about it.'

He snorted a laugh. 'Don't be so sure about that. My mother gives me a good deal of unwanted advice whenever I'm home. Why do you think I live in the barracks?'

'Is she pissy at your father for conceiving a son and robbing her daughter of her title?

'Ah, no. That's certainly not her main concern.'

Lidan sighed. 'Well, it's the bane of my mother's existence, and as long as there's breath in her body she won't let any of us forget it.'

'For what it's worth, being the first born has its advantages,' he offered carefully.

'Like what exactly?'

'First daughters and sons can't match until they're eighteen. If you were a minor daughter like Bridie, you'd have been matched off years ago.'

'That is *not* comfort—' she snapped and shot him a glare. He snorted a laugh and hid a smirk badly. He was teasing and she'd taken the bait whole. Groaning and rolling her eyes, she turned back to the trail.

One more year. I have one more year to change his mind… Lidan shoved the thought away. Despite all the years that had passed, the thought of that woman and what she was capable of made her skin crawl with fear. She didn't want to think about the promise she'd made to her mother, or that the time left to fulfil it was slipping through her fingers with each passing day.

They walked their horses into a clearing by the creek and pulled their mounts to a stop. She had expected to see the rangers unsaddling and stoking the fire, but instead they stood still as stone beside their horses.

Lidan looked at Jessah and frowned.

'Ngaru,' the ranger whispered and pointed to where Siman was inspecting a set of tracks in the sand. A year older than Lidan, Jessah had only recently graduated from her apprenticeship with Nathen and chosen to stay in their ranging party.

Siman jogged quietly back to the group. 'Get your gear. We're moving.'

Without a word the rangers hurried to comply. A pot of water was upended into the remains of last night's fire and bedrolls were secured behind saddles. Lidan ignored Theus's displeased snort and tightened the saddle's girth strap.

A bluster of wind swirled up the gorge and Lidan turned from checking Theus's saddle. She watched the imprint of the gust on the shrubs and trees, listening for its whispered warning. Her nostrils flared and the scent of the land preparing for rain assaulted her senses, a heady perfume that spoke of promise and threat in one hushed breath.

'Rain's coming,' Lidan said to no one and everyone.

Siman and Loge stopped, and the others turned to scan the sky above the gorge. A storm you couldn't see was a storm that could kill you and the walls of the canyon obscured the view to the east and west. Across the tablelands, this was the time of the turning between the dry and the wet, when the humidity of the day fed soaring storms that roared down the gorges, pouring rain into the cracks and fissures. It washed through the gullies and valleys, rushing through creeks and streams, black torrents surging out to the grasslands and past the Caine.

A distant rumble echoed across the sky.

'Mount up,' Siman ordered. 'There's a cave in the western face, across the creek.'

CHAPTER FIVE

The Tablelands, Tolak Range, the South Lands

The sky darkened as the storm crawled over the rim of the canyon and sucked the remaining light of sunset into its climbing clouds. Night fell early under the shadow of the storm and Lidan coaxed Theus into a trot, following the others as they hastened along the trail.

She strained to separate the sounds of the bush from the overwhelming noise of the storm, searching the boom of thunder echoing against canyon walls and the angry crackle of the wind whipping through the leaves. A flock of birds swooped in to roost, a flurry of wings as the circling wind in the apron of the storm whistled over the thump of horse's hooves.

Lidan searched every impact of a raindrop, every creak of a tree against the bole of another, waiting for the sound she knew lurked in the approaching darkness.

The cave stood at the foot of the canyon wall, carved by rain, wind and flood into a softer layer of stone, and she reached it moments before the first ngaru scream tore up the canyon and sent a shiver of gooseflesh across her skin. Her boots hit the ground and she turned to scan the trees.

Here the bush stood so thick there was little chance of seeing the creatures until they barrelled out of the undergrowth. Another call ripped through the trees, smothered at its climax by thunder.

'Today just keeps getting better and better,' Loge growled, releasing his axe from the straps on his saddle and tossing his reins to Iema, who led Striker quickly to the cave. 'It had to start raining right fucking now, didn't it?'

A steady hiss filled the space between the trees and the forward edge of the rain curtain washed across the clearing before the cave mouth. Lidan hurried Theus into the cave then turned to face the bush.

The roar of thunder amongst the trees muffled the hammer of her heart and the sound of her breath grating in her ears. Rain soaked through her hair, dragging black tendrils down her face. Water ran over her brow and nose in rivulets, the tears of a broken sky on her skin.

She squeezed the handles of the knives in the sheaths at her hips, the bone curved to the shape of her hands. Beyond the snug leather of her jerkin, her pale shirt clung to her shoulders and arms. She hadn't time to get her coat, so she'd have to manage this fight soaked to the skin.

The trees across the clearing lit up in a blaze of white, banishing shadows from the bush. Trees and bushes whipped against each other in the swirling wind as the rangers waited.

Loge stood beside her, his axe weighed in his right hand, his eyes wide as they scanned the tree line. Iema and Jessah trained arrows on the trees, an arsenal of shafts at their sides. The array of brandished weapons—some steel scavenged from ngaru kills, others bronze, all sharpened to a razor edge—gleamed in the flickering light. A ranger had to earn their steel by killing a ngaru themselves, and Owin was the sole exception among the group. He hung back near the mouth of the cave and gripped a stone axe, never having earned any ngaru steel in his own right.

'Ready to die?' Loge murmured in a moment when the storm seemed to take a breath.

'No.' Lidan grinned and drew her blades. 'You?'

His eyes flashed in the light of the storm. 'Not today.'

They stepped forward and slipped between the trunks of the soaring ghost-barks. The others followed without a word, vanishing into the gloom.

Her senses searched the trees and ferns for the smallest sign of a creature that did not belong. Eyes wide, she watched for a hunched shape that did not belong, her nostrils flaring, drawing in the scent of the rain, waiting to catch the sharp, putrid reek of a ngaru on the wind. She placed her feet carefully, crouched low, arms held ready for a fight, her ears pricked for the clumsy gait of creatures not trained to hide their presence as the rangers were. Her skin tingled despite the slick of water pouring across it, electrified and trembling with energy. Loge's footsteps moved at her back, watching where her eyes could not, searching for the very same threat lurking amongst the undergrowth.

Something moved to her right.

A shiver of motion illuminated by sheet lightning. A shadow behind a tree that might have been a scrubby bush had it not been moving against the wind. Lidan reached back to tap Loge on the leg with the flat of her blade.

'I've got one, too,' he whispered. 'Ten paces to your left.'

'Mine's opposite.' She leaned further into her crouch, the knives reflecting the lightning as if forged by the same arcane magic.

The ngaru must have known it was watched. It shifted, then stiffened under Lidan's scrutiny. It darted from the tree in the next blinding snap of lightning and raced away on all fours. Lidan followed, a shout echoing behind her as Loge engaged his quarry.

She pursued it through the trees, catching glimpse of long rusted blades sticking out from where the creature's hands should have been, jammed up inside the forearms until the tangs protruded from the elbows, welded in place by bulbous skin growth. The ngaru scuttled like a spider to a void in the trees only a few feet across. It meant to lure her to a battleground of its choosing, and she let it think she followed carelessly.

Lidan stayed low, knives held tight. The ngaru hissed, a low guttural sound of gargled saliva and pus. In the intermittent half-light, she saw nothing but its blades. It was not a creature from the fireside tales of her childhood, but something else; vaguely human but terribly mutated by an unknown curse. As powerful and mysterious as they were, they were as mortal as any beast as long as the spine was severed. Strong and cunning, their weapons were of a kind her people had not encountered before the first of them crawled from the bush almost five years ago. Steel had been the ngaru's greatest advantage and Lidan's people had turned it against them in a bloody fashion.

A fork of lightning struck to the south and lit the bush as bright as midday. The ngaru howled and charged and Lidan hit the dirt in a forward roll. It hurtled toward her and she came to her feet, slamming her shoulder into its chest. Inside its reach, she slashed at the neck but caught the side of its face, ripping the jaw halfway off before she spun and sliced at the ribs.

The creature shrieked and flailed its bladed arms.

Built for a fight with a wider arc, it writhed helplessly against the whipping barrage of Lidan's body blows. It leapt back and wheeled its blades, catching Lidan in the ribs with the flat of the steel.

She staggered sideways and slipped on the wet, leafy ground. The ngaru charged again, bounding forward and lifting a blade high above her head. Lidan dove away as the blade scythed down and thumped into the dirt where she had been a moment ago.

Screams and howls from a nearby struggle echoed over the thunder and for a second her gaze shifted, searching the trees for Loge. The ngaru spared her no quarter and stabbed a blade at her face. She rolled away again, and the creature bellowed with impotent rage. She might not be doing much damage, but she was sure as shit pissing it off.

Again it charged and again she let it come, ducking under the swing of the blades and dragging her knives through the flesh of its abdomen.

She came to her feet behind it and leapt, aiming for the spine and the cord connecting the thing to its power, but her knife hit a wall of thick, leathery skin and dense muscle. The blade skidded over the creature's back until it found purchase in a patch of softer flesh, the ngaru arching and wailing as the steel carved deep. A blade-arm swung around to fend her off and glanced across her forehead before she could pull her weapon free.

Lidan cried out and tumbled from the beast's back, clutching at her head with her empty hand. One of her knives remained wedged under a hard callous of skin, ripped from her grasp but causing the ngaru a great deal of satisfying discomfort.

Her vision swam as she tried to ready for the next attack, but her legs failed. She stumbled and slipped, her chest heaving as her palm pressed hard against a wound at her hairline. Searing pain lanced through her face, and she glanced up as the ngaru rushed her.

Her knife came up and she shoved it forward with all her strength. It buried itself in the flesh of the ngaru's throat, oily blue pus gushing out of the wound. Her muscles burned and she fought to fill her lungs, the creature bearing down with its weight. She screamed, battling to turn the blade so the cutting edge might find the cord of the spine.

An ear-splitting crack echoed through the clearing and the ngaru spun away, ripping the knife handle from her hands. It raised itself to its full height, challenging the new threat, and let go a keening scream.

Loge's axe sailed through the lightning and rain and connected with the ngaru's scything blade-arm. It barrelled after him as the ranger turned his smaller belt hatchet to meet each cut and thrust thrown his way. Lidan staggered upright and ran at the ngaru's back. Weaponless and dizzy, the only thing forcing her forward was the burning rage in her chest and an unrelenting need to end what she had begun.

She leapt onto the creature and straddled it, yanking her knife free of its back. The ngaru arced in a flailing protest and Lidan drove her weapon into the monster's neck, right where its malformed skull ended and the ridges of its spine began.

Shock jolted through the ngaru's body and it bucked, flinging Lidan across the clearing and into a fallen tree. She hit it with a crunch and gasped as the wind rushed from her chest. The ngaru spun and levelled a withering glare at her, sensing victory within its grasp. The head of a hatchet swung high, its edge glistening, and fell hard onto the back of the creature's neck, carving through most of the rotting flesh until the head hung by mere strips from the trunk. Loge jerked his hatchet free of the grisly mass and stumbled back as the body flopped to the ground in a twitching heap.

He spat and wiped a spray of ngaru ichor from his face, turning to search the fractured light of the storm. Lidan groaned and lifted a hand, lightning illuminating the clearing enough for him to catch sight of her beside the log. He stowed his hatchet in a belt loop and ran at a limping jog to her side. His hands closed first around her shoulders, then ran back through her rain-slicked hair.

'You all right?' he asked, scanning her face.

Lidan's vision blurred and a wave of nausea threatened to evacuate her stomach. Still, she gave his arm a reassuring squeeze. 'Course. Had it under control 'til you rolled in.'

'Horse shit.' Loge dropped to his knees and slid an arm around her, levering her up to lean on the fallen tree.

'No, you're right. I was fucked.' Her eyes rolled away from him to the corpse of the ngaru. 'It just wouldn't fucking die.'

'It was bigger than the other one. Did you see the muscles on it?'

She coughed and tried not to vomit. 'Did I *see* them? My knives are stuck in them!'

He snickered and pushed her hair back from the wound on her head. For a moment he said nothing, his gaze tracing the line of the cut before falling to meet her eyes. 'Who's going to stitch this up, then?'

'Jessah has a steady hand.' Lidan tried to smile but pain speared through her skull. Her hands trembled and she now felt every thread of her saturated clothes clinging to her shivering body. Loge's hand lingered for a moment longer, then he staggered to his feet and limped over to the ngaru's motionless body. He pushed his dripping hair from his face, worked Lidan's knives free of the creature's flesh, and wiped them clean on his sodden trousers. He found his larger axe nearby and hefted it before returning to her side and sheathing her knives.

'Best be getting back,' he murmured, pulling her up and slinging her arm over his shoulder. He heaved her from the ground and they limped together through the hammering rain, fighting mud and undergrowth to forge a path back to the cave.

Lidan's head spun and Loge held her as she retched, spitting blood and vomit into the darkness. Her legs failed when the glow of the cave filtered through the trees, and before he could drag her in from the storm, darkness claimed her.

Chapter Six

The Tablelands, Tolak Range, the South Lands

Murmuring voices drew Lidan back from the void. Gentle hands held her while others tended her wound, pressing and probing, investigating the damage to find a way to put her right again. Beyond the cave, the storm rolled on, thunder rumbling across the sky and vibrating through the ground at her back. Her eyes fluttered open, and the cave around her whirled, tilting at a sickening angle until she was forced to squeeze them shut once more.

'Nathen,' Jessah's words washed over her. 'Grab her stitch kit from the saddle bag, will you? The one on the left.'

'Can you fix it?' Loge asked.

'She taught me everything I know, and she's a good teacher.'

Lidan heard the smile in Jessah's voice, full of reassurance and confidence while the ranger's fingers trembled against her forehead.

'Open it up for me and un-stopper that flask,' Jessah instructed, and the stopper squeaked free of the bottle.

'What's that?' Another question from Loge.

What's he so damn worried about?

'The stuff she uses to clean wounds. Stinks but it works.'

Lidan flinched as Jessah poured the fluid into the gash. The burning began, washing away any filth left by the ngaru's blade.

'Not so tough now,' a deep voice sneered from a distance.

'Fuck off, Owin,' Jessah snapped.

'You're all right, Liddy. Jessah's got it sorted.' Loge's thumb traced across her cheek and Lidan turned toward his voice.

'Hold her still, please. Don't want her to jerk around.'

The needle stung as it pierced her skin and Lidan bit back a cry, a pained whimper escaping through her clenched teeth. Thread tugged the opposing sides of her wound together and hot nausea rolled through her body, her skin beading with cold sweat. Loge's grip did not ease. His thumb continued to trace a circle on her skin and Lidan retreated from the pain, blocking out the sting and tug of Jessah's work, surrendering once more to the abyss.

Morning broke sunny and clear beyond the cave and Lidan eased herself up to sit with her back against the wall of the cave. Siman glanced across the fire and smiled, stoking the coals and adding wood to the flames.

'How's the head?'

'Sore,' she croaked, but her smile turned to a grimace, the muscles under her wound bunching and sending a stab of pain down her face. 'Could have been worse, though.'

'True,' Siman conceded as he positioned a pot of water on the fire.

'What happened out there?' Lidan asked, glancing around the cave. Her knives lay against her saddle, clean and polished, barely a foot from where she sat, and Loge was nowhere to be seen.

The cave was empty save for her and Siman. The others were likely out counting the bodies of the ngaru, salvaging steel and checking for signs of others who might have escaped notice in the chaos.

'I thought we cleared this valley?'

'So did I,' Siman replied, his mouth set in a grim line. The thud of hooves outside cut through his response, and he stood, wiping his hands on his trousers and squaring his shoulders. 'Now's the time to find out.'

He went to the cave mouth and whistled. 'All of you, in here! Time to report!'

Loge appeared first, wiping his hands on a bloody rag. He'd been outside skinning a bouncer, by the look. He crouched by Lidan and pointed to the fresh stitches along her crown.

'Looks good,' he winked. 'Your mother's going to love it.'

Lidan groaned, an ache blooming deep in the muscles of her face. Her mother's reaction was the last thing she wanted to think about. 'Shut up and sit down. Siman has words for us.'

The others arrived and filed through the entry, Lidan noting each face until all of them were present. She let out a small sigh of relief. The entire party had made it through the night, even Owin, though she was yet to decide if that was good or bad. Siman didn't wait for anyone to settle. 'Right, what did you find?

'Three carcasses and no sign of any others.' Nathen nodded at Loge and Lidan. 'The two closest to the cave were where Loge said they'd be, and the other was the one I brought down. We searched them and left them for the craws.'

Iema crouched and dumped an armload of scavenged steel blades on the floor of the cave. Loge tossed her a rag to wipe blue-black ooze from her hands, and she glanced at Lidan. 'Your steel is in there if you want it. They're pretty badly worn though. Not sure if Rick will be able to make much of them.'

'Thanks, Im. If it's any good, you can take it. I've got more steel than I know what to do with.'

Forge Master Rick could do a lot with salvaged steel, but many of the scavenged weapons were in such bad condition it was hardly worth his time. Rangers brought back all sorts of blades from ngaru hunts, each kill earning them steel of their own to fashion into whatever they chose, or to throw into the armoury at Hummel. Iema smiled and nodded her thanks, and Lidan leaned her head back against the cave wall. It was difficult to earn steel when you had to stay and defend a cave while others went out to do the killing. At least Iema had that excuse for her lack of a new weapon. Why Owin had yet to manage it, she had no idea.

'And you saw none here at the cave?' Siman turned to the young women, who shook their heads. 'Good. Let's assume we got them all.' He rounded on Owin and Nathen. '*You two* said you checked the valley!'

'We bloody did, sir!' Owin glanced around with wide brown eyes and pushed his long hair from his face. He was a similar build to Siman but lacked the leader's height. 'They're like vermin. Fucking rats. They hide too well.'

'Where did they come from then? Jump up out of the ground, did they?' Siman stood with his hands on his hips, but Owin didn't answer. Instead his gaze flicked toward Jessah. Siman stepped between them. 'Don't look at her for answers! What fucking happened?'

Lidan watched the exchange and tried to ignore the throbbing in her face. Her ribs ached with every breath, promising to make the ride back to Hummel a waking nightmare. Beside her, Loge shifted his weight and stood, massaging the side of his knee. His other hand came to rest absently on the head of his hatchet and her heart gave a heavy thud. She could have cut the tension with a knife.

'I don't know, sir.' Owin's reply broke the silence. 'We didn't find any.'

'You set the traps? The lures?'

'Of course!'

Siman crossed his arms and Lidan eyed Owin, chewing at the back of her lip, wondering what he was up to. Surely, he didn't think Siman would actually swallow these lies? He'd been with their ranging party for about a year and still hadn't settled in. Hardly a journey went by where he didn't get under someone's skin or cop a spray for some mistake or failure.

Lidan suspected Siman would've happily left Owin behind in Hummel, but these days the clan couldn't afford to be picky about who patrolled the range. Anyone willing to face the danger was welcome. Such was their desperation that the wives of tradesmen had taken up weapons and reins, leaving their husbands to tend the home and children, when four years ago none of them would have even considered it a possibility, let alone a necessity. Owin was a pain in Siman's arse, but he was a thorn the chief ranger had to bear.

'Explain to me then, in simple words, how you missed these three?' Siman asked carefully, his fury betrayed only by a slight tremor in his voice. By the angle of his shoulders and his wide stance, his patience was quickly wearing thin.

After a few attempts at forming a sentence, Owin waved an exasperated hand at the canyon outside the cave. 'They must've been in the caves farther north.'

'How far north did you go?' Siman's eyes narrowed as he picked up the trailing thread of Owin's deception. He began to pull, unravelling the story like a poorly woven rug.

Owin glanced again at Nathen and Jessah. Nathen refused to meet the other ranger's gaze, and Jessah shook her head. It seemed Owin had orchestrated this ruse against the advice of the others. 'We... we went as far as Bengara Falls.'

'You *what*?' Siman's voice cracked against the cave walls and Lidan rolled her eyes. The Falls were at least a day south of Fracture Pass, the most northern point of the Tolak range. 'Why the fuck did you do that?'

'He didn't like the idea of stumbling on a dragon's nest,' Jessah said, glaring at Owin with unveiled contempt. 'Thought it best we stay out of the foothills in case one of them caught our scent and decided it was hungry enough to venture south. Told us he'd heard from another party the serpents were moving, getting bolder.'

Lidan shivered. She'd never seen an ice serpent, but she'd heard the trader's stories. For a moment, she wondered if she would have gone farther north after hearing such a tale.

'And you believed him?' Siman countered.

Nathen nodded. 'Against our better judgement.'

'Ice serpents don't leave the highest reaches of the Pass in the summer, because if they did, their ice scales would melt. Everyone knows that. They aren't even as far down as the mouth of the Pass at this time of year.' Siman stabbed a finger at Owin. 'You realise those ngaru followed you here? They must've been tracking you for days! What if they'd gone around us?'

Silence hung between them, and Owin left the questions unanswered.

'*You* didn't think this worth mentioning?' Siman turned on Nathen and his voice dropped dangerously low. When he no longer felt the need to shout, he was truly furious, all his energy channelled into controlling the action of his hands. 'What if they made it south into the grasslands? Did you even think of that, or just your own fucking needs? *This* is why we check the caves at the Pass every time. Without fail. Every. Time.'

Jessah and Iema glanced at Lidan with silent questions in their eyes—what would happen now?

As angry as Siman was, Daari Erlon was the man Owin had to fear. He'd brushed aside complaints against Owin in the past, putting Owin with Siman in the hope a strong leader might inspire the younger man to pick up his game, but this simply wouldn't pass muster.

Erlon's orders were very specific. Under no circumstances were the ngaru to cross the tablelands or come within sight of Hummel. What Owin had done was in direct violation of all the measures put in place to prevent a repeat of the attacks that had killed Abbi and hundreds of clan folk since. Erlon would tear Owin apart for this.

Owin's shoulders dropped and he sighed. 'I meant to say something, but I thought—'

'You thought yourself better than you proved to be, boy.' Siman stepped into Owin's space and the ranger leaned back awkwardly. 'You will not think so again. Understood?'

'Yes,' muttered Owin.

'You're demoted to apprentice tasks from now until we get back to Hummel, then you're confined to quarters until the daari has time to hear your case. We start back to Hummel at dawn tomorrow.' Siman ignored Owin's twisted scowl of disbelief and missed the glare he turned toward Lidan.

'Not all of us have steel at our sides!' The words snapped from Owin like a snake's strike.

Lidan snatched her knife and lurched to her feet, her instincts running roughshod over her pain. Siman's arm caught her across the chest, arresting her advance before her blade could connect with the soft skin of Owin's neck.

'You want steel?' she demanded; the point of the weapon poised just shy of his throat. Owin swallowed sharply. 'Take it.'

Owin didn't answer.

She flipped the knife and he staggered back.

Lidan couldn't help smiling as the blade landed flat in her palm, the handle angled toward the demoted ranger. Siman's arm fell away and he stepped back, giving Lidan space to challenge Owin.

She waved the handle of the knife and widened her eyes, feigning innocence. 'Go on—take it. See how it feels.'

Owin glanced at Nathen then snatched the handle. Immediately he weighed the blade, squeezing his fingers around the hilt and nodding to himself. He sneered and slashed at the air, oblivious to the roll of Iema's eyes and Jessah's lifted eyebrow—clearly unimpressed by his bravado.

Lidan inched forward, grinding her teeth against the pain in her ribs. She pointed to the knife, drawing Owin's attention to the shining steel. 'You see, it's folded over and over in the flames and hammered, not poured into a cast like a bronze blade.'

'Really?' Owin gave a nod of appreciation.

He didn't see Lidan's elbow until it connected with his nose and sent a crunch echoing up the length of the cave, his nose erupting in a bloody fountain. He howled and she gripped his shoulders, ramming her knee into his stomach, then drove her elbow down between his shoulders. The wind left his lungs, blood spurting across the sand as he struggled to breathe.

With the last of her failing energy she delivered a punch to his back, just above his hips, and sent him gasping to the ground. He'd probably piss blood for a few days but Lidan would be surprised if he could see it through his blackened, swollen eyes. Owin didn't know it, of course, but Lidan was more like her mother than she cared to admit. There was no way she would let a challenge pass unanswered, injured or not, and least of all a challenge from a dishonest, whining idiot like him.

He writhed on the sand at her feet, glancing up in the vain hope of a friendly face or a helping hand. Lidan feigned a kick in his direction and he squealed. Pitiful as he was, the display failed to bring even a mocking smile to her lips. She spat at him. Jessah scooped the discarded knife from the sand and handed it to Lidan in silence. Iema would learn a valuable lesson today, albeit at Owin's expense.

Lidan turned the blade to Owin and glowered at him. 'You think you need steel to defeat the ngaru? I killed my first with a fucking stick, and you think you need *steel*? This knife is a tool—nothing more. They don't get by me because I'm fast and I listen, and I do my fucking job. You've searched ngaru dens for how many seasons now? And with how many ranging parties?' Her lip curled in disgust. 'You're a liability, a waste of rations and a burden no one should have to carry.'

She gripped her throbbing side and turned back to her gear, sheathing the knife before Owin found his tongue again.

'That's it? You beat me like a dog then say your piece and I'm done?'

Lidan laughed sourly. 'No. What happens to you isn't up to me, or even Siman. You failed to follow orders and misled your party. You put us in danger, and worse, you put Hummel in danger. Our job is to keep the ngaru away from Hummel, away from our families, and you failed to do that.' She tried not to take too much pleasure in the pained realisation on Owin's face. 'You'll face a Hearing when we get home, and I hear the daari hasn't been in a forgiving mood of late.'

CHAPTER SEVEN

The Hidden Keep, Ravinka, Southern Orthia

A week passed and the changes to Ran's magic eased; the pain in his eyes, head and neck slowly fading until he could get through the day without Sasha's strong draughts. Impatience began to eat into his mind, a restlessness in his bones, urging him to get out of the infirmary and begin retraining his Sight.

Sasha was more reluctant; dismissing Ran's suggestion he was ready to leave her care. It took several days of nagging before she finally relented and agreed to let him test his Sight. They waited until after sunset, when the Keep folk were retiring to their beds and the infirmary stood empty. At this time of night, there was little chance of interruption.

'Are you ready?' Sasha asked, easing herself onto the edge on the bed and resting her hand on Ran's arm.

He nodded and wondered how many of his semi-conscious ramblings she'd heard over the past week. Had she heard him speaking to the ghost in his sleep, or the accusations he screamed at the shade when the pain-relieving draught wore off? If she had, she'd kept it to herself. Ran hadn't asked about Quaid's late-night visits either. The weight of unspoken thoughts hung heavy between them as Sasha unwound the strips of bandage from his head and put them aside. Thick dressing pads fell away, and she rubbed a crust of dried gunk from his eyes with a damp cloth.

'Try opening them now...'

Ran forced his sticky eyelids apart. A dim oil lamp burned to his right on a small chest of drawers, and Sasha sat at the edge of its illumination in her day dress and pocketed apron. His heart sank at the exhaustion etched in her wan skin, her eyes bordered by shadows, and he wondered for a moment if he looked the same after a week of broken sleep and no sunlight. Sasha's jaw dropped and he suddenly didn't want to know.

She lunged forward and grabbed the lamp, bringing it to his face and moving it in front of his nose. 'Ran, your eyes?'

'What? What's wrong?'

'They've changed.'

'How?' He watched her move the lamp back and forth, studying him intently; shielding the light with her hand, then revealing it again.

'The colour is… different. It's like the darkest colour has been stripped away. They're the colour of cornflowers…'

Ran's brows shot up. 'They are not!'

She stifled a laugh and took off down the empty infirmary, returning with a highly-polished looking glass about the size of her hand. 'Look.'

He took it and she lifted the lamp until the light fell over his features. 'Oh, what the fu…'

The dark blue eyes he had been born with were gone. They were pale now, and glistened with a faint iridescence. He'd seen this colour before. In the eyes of the ghost girl; the very same bright crystal blue.

'They look very… strange…' He fumbled the looking glass in his fingers and shoved it toward Sasha, running a trembling hand over his stubbled chin as his stomach twisted uncomfortably.

'When I move the light,' Sasha whispered, entranced by the oddity, 'the darkest part, the pupil, doesn't move. It should open when I take the light away, then shrink when I bring it back, but it remains the same. It's very strange.'

'Should we get Collan?' Ran shifted and cleared his throat. 'Maybe he can explain it. Perhaps it's happened before?'

Anxiety tightened a web around his heart. How would the Keep folk react to this? Would it even register as strange? Or, would it be just another weird event in a lifetime of weirdness they were all accustomed to?

He swallowed his questions and Sasha left to collect the keep master. In her absence, he focused his full attention on a shelf across the ward, ignoring the ghost with the mangled throat sitting on the neighbouring bed with her hands folded demurely in her lap.

'You know,' she murmured, 'in all the time we've known each other, you've never asked my name.'

He gaped at her then, but she vanished when the keep master pushed through the door. Collan was quelling his thaumalux, but a faint glow still flickered across his skin, leaving a discernible mark in the air. Pain lanced through Ran's face and he pressed his magic down over his eyes to filter out the light. His stomach clenched and his fingers dug into the bed sheets, throttling them until his knuckles turned white.

'Ranoth, my boy.' Collan greeted him with a cautious smile from the end of the bed. Together, Sasha and Collan were the only people in the Keep who knew his true name. To everyone else, he was Ran Harroe, a soldier's son. 'Is this all right? I'm not hurting you?'

'Yes—I mean, no—you aren't hurting me. I can still see it, the thaumalux, but I can manage the pain.'

'Good, good.' The keep master sat where the ghost had been, rearranging his robes before drawing a deep breath. 'I'm not entirely sure I could manage a stronger wall around my power if I tried.'

'I'm sorry…' Ran didn't like to ask this of the keep master, but he needed to test his condition before he could return to life in the Keep. He was determined to get out of this damn bed and back to his work. He was bored and his sanity was beginning to slip dangerously, staring at the same white-washed walls for days on end.

Collan waved away his apology. 'Think nothing of it, dear boy. Now, let's see how much you can stand.'

He dropped his shoulders a little and the light intensified like the rising sun.

Ran stared at Collan for as long as he could, then glanced away, blinking hard and tightening his magic around his Sight like a cloak. 'That's it—I can't—'

Collan backed his magic off and Ran squeezed his eyes shut until the white orbs fizzing in his vision dissolved, his hands shaking as he fought back hot tears.

Collan stood and put a gentle hand on Ran's shoulder. 'If you don't mind, Ranoth, I would like to add another element to this experiment before we draw any conclusions.'

Sasha folded her arms and knotted her lips, locking away the dissent that was written all over her face. Ran tried not to look at her and gave Collan a stiff nod.

'Mistress Hale, please fetch Nicot.'

Sasha let out a frustrated sigh and left to collect her youngest brother. Nicot was a tall, lithe young man of seventeen with hair as red and unruly as his sister's. He followed her through the ward doors, and to Ran's relief, his thaumalux shone only as brightly as a branch of tallow candles.

'What do you see, my boy?' Collan asked quietly.

'He's shining, but not as brightly as you or Quaid. I can look at him without feeling like there's scalding water running through my eye sockets.'

'Interesting. Very interesting,' the keep master murmured, then turned to Nicot. 'Thank you, Nicot. You may return to your quarters. Speak of this to no one unless I advise otherwise.'

The younger man left with a nod, and Collan cleared his throat. 'When you first arrived here, Ranoth, your magic was strong but unfocused, still unfurling after remaining hidden for so many years. Has your Sight changed at all since you first became sensitive to thaumalux?'

'No,' Ran shook his head. 'I was more able to control it, though. I could decide when I wanted to see it, like lifting a veil. That veil is gone now.'

Disappointment washed through him and he swallowed a lump from his throat. The thought of what it had taken to get his Sight under control the first time made his gut coil with dread. Would it take him half a year to rebuild those defences?

No. He set his jaw and quashed his fear of failure. He would master it again, because this time he knew how.

Collan and Sasha shared a glance before the keep master continued. 'I fear young Degan has exposed you to power much greater than you are used to. A magical form of sunburn, if you will. You will recover, I am sure, but you may be greatly changed.'

Collan paused, as if to let the knowledge sink in, then sighed. 'Nicot has very little magic, really. His skill as a healer comes from his steady hand and calm demeanour, his desire to help people and to learn, rather than anything he derives from his magic. None of our trackers can see Nicot's thaumalux. Even you struggled to see him before now.'

Ran drew a deep breath and kept his gaze fixed on Collan, avoiding Sasha's glowering eyes. 'So, Degan's new power has changed my Sight?'

'Your exposure to Degan's shot, as close and raw as it was, seems to have stripped away what was left of the filter on your Sight. You can now perceive pure thaumalux, even in relatively weak magic-users.' The man licked his lips and looked from Sasha to Ran. 'You will need to retrain to shield yourself, or it will drive you mad to be among your own people. I would also like to see if your perception of thaumalux trails has changed.'

'I can see Nicot's trail. And yours, Master Greyling. And about four others from earlier today. If I press harder, I can see more, but then it just turns into a mess of light. There are too many of us moving through the infirmary for me to tell the trails apart.' Ran squinted as Collan stared in undisguised shock. 'If I focus... I can see Quaid's trail from the day I was exposed. He's rather distinct.'

Neither Sasha nor Collan responded.

Neither of them moved.

They stared at Ran and he wished he could sink into the floor and pretend none of this was happening. But it was. It already had, and there was no reversing what had been done. He didn't want to admit it in front of Sasha, but what he had to tell Collan was important.

'Even through the bandages, I could see. At night, and during the day. They were muted, but I could see them. Even when Quaid stayed out in the hallway...'

Sasha's eyes widened and bright spots of colour rose in her cheeks. He glanced away. Perhaps she thought Quaid's comings and goings in the dead of night had gone unnoticed by her friend, but he'd seen it through the bandages and the walls. What she did in her own time was her own business, yet it hurt that she hadn't told him. He'd thought they were closer than that.

Eian came five days later, once Collan was satisfied Ran could sufficiently veil his Sight. With most of his pain under control, the infirmary was becoming more of a prison than a place of rest and healing. In his own rooms he could retrain and recover, in private and out from under Sasha's feet. Controlling his Sight while crossing the forecourt was likely to sting like the wrath of a kicked beehive, but it would be worth it to escape the pressing boredom of the infirmary and Sasha's icy demeanour.

'You look like shit,' Eian pointed out as he shouldered a pack of items Sasha had given him to take to Ran's rooms. She didn't fancy carrying them with her every time she came to check on him.

'Fuck off, Eian,' Ran smirked, then grimaced and adjusted his eyes. The magic came down over his Sight like a shield, dampening Eian's thaumalux and that of the two students working across the infirmary.

'You know you love me,' Eian said with a grin, reaching down to help Ran to his feet and Ran resisted the urge to elbow his friend in the ribs. Of an age, Eian Pollen was built like the Keep's towers—just as tall and about as wide at the shoulders—with fair hair cropped close to his head, and they had been firm friends ever since Ran's Sight first emerged.

'And seeing as I'm the one carrying your sorry arse across the forecourt, you'd better be nice or I'll drop you like a lumpy bag of spuds.' He lay Ran's arm across his shoulders, and they made their way slowly to the door. 'Old Col says your Sight has improved.'

Eian never beat around the bush. He went straight in with his bare hands, which often got him bitten by whatever topic he was attacking. They paused at the foot of the stairs and Ran caught his breath.

'Improved is one word for it,' he muttered.

'What can you see?' Eian asked with genuine curiosity. He was a capable thaumalux tracker, if the trail was strong and recently made, but he had always been better at sparring and brawling than slipping through the forest and following a magic-weaver's light.

Ran drew a deep breath and eased back on his defences as they passed the gardens and orchids and entered the forecourt. 'It's like a web. Trails of thaumalux run across the court, up and down the stairs. I can see where Collan and Quaid have been, I can see Degan and some others who are just as strong, but I don't know who they are. I'm not sure who each trail belongs to.'

'What about me?' Eian stood back and posed as if Ran were an artist about to paint his portrait.

'I see an ass.'

'A special ass?' Eian lifted his brows. 'Do I sparkle like the almighty Quaid?'

Ran frowned and feigned deep consideration. 'No, you sparkle like an ass.'

'Damn it,' Eian spat and collected Ran's elbow to support him as they moved across the court.

Ran tried not to smile too broadly. He drew down the veil and the lines of light vanished, the court appearing normal once more. 'You aren't *as* bright as Quaid or Zarad, but you're still pretty bright. Not in a clever sense though, just in a magical sense.'

'Yeah, well, I might not be as clever as you, but I'm a damn sight prettier.'

'Says who?' Ran countered.

'Everyone.' Eian pointed at his face. 'Have you seen this chin?'

'Shut up.' Ran rolled his eyes. They entered the West Tower after a swarm of small girls rushed out, then made their way slowly to the second floor. Eian swung open the door to Ran's quarters and waited for his friend to walk gingerly inside.

The apartment consisted of a comfortable sitting room with a fire and a table to take meals, and a bedroom off to the right with a wide, curtained bed, a desk and another fireplace. Both hearths were alight and roaring in an effort to expel the cold after standing empty for close to two weeks.

'Hot enough to roast a pig in here,' Eian muttered and dumped the bag on the sofa. He left Ran to ease himself into a chair and went to open a window. Every muscle from Ran's neck to his ankles protested as he sank back against the cushions.

'Did you know about Sasha and Quaid?' Ran asked when Eian flopped down on the sofa beside the bag.

Eian's features flattened and Ran had his answer. He'd learnt that little trick from watching his friend. While beating around the bush was considered more polite, diving in caught people off guard, leaving them no time to erect their shields or fold their faces into a mask. But as quick-witted as Eian was, he wasn't fast enough to avoid the trap.

'What about them?' Eian glanced at the fire.

'I don't care. Honestly, I don't. I'm just surprised.'

Eian cocked an eyebrow at Ran. 'Surprised by what?'

'That she didn't tell me, I suppose...' Ran suddenly felt a fool. Was he such a child that he could be wounded by his friend keeping her lover a secret? He flexed his fingers at the fire, and the heat came toward him. The flames in the hearth gutted for a moment, then he let them go and returned them to their purpose.

Eian went to a decanter of spirits on the table. 'It's hardly something the whole Keep knows about. Quaid let it slip to me after you were confined to the ward and your Sight came on. Couldn't quite explain what he'd been doing up there in the middle of the night.' He grinned at Ran and handed him a glass of amber liquor. 'I don't think either of them planned on telling anyone.'

'It wasn't what I was expecting to find in the infirmary, that's for sure.' Ran sipped his drink, warmth washing through his chest and into his limbs.

'Could be over in five minutes, like you and Livia,' Eian offered.

'Or it could be as permanent as you and Zarad.'

Eian shrugged. 'Zarad has his money on five minutes, and he knows his sister.' He drained his glass, refilled it and returned to his seat. 'In any case, it's Sasha's business what she does in her chambers. Would you really want to know? *Really?*'

No, he didn't. He glanced away and stared into the fire, knowing deep within that it wasn't simply the secret that had cut him. Ran would never admit it as long as the sun rose in the east and set in the west, but he'd carried a flame for Sasha Hale since the day she rescued him from death at the bottom of that mine shaft. Now, with his Sight ripped open, he saw that regard for what it was—a juvenile love—a fleeting idea of romance that could never stand exposure to the adult world. For four years he'd tended that little flame, and he wondered if now the time had come to let it burn out.

Chapter Eight

Within days Ran was jogging up and down the length of the playing fields, regaining his strength and returning condition to his muscles, even managing to kick a ball around with some of his students. Quaid put a sword in his hand and pushed him even when he hadn't the breath for it, and sometimes the sparring master even let him win.

It took immense effort to suppress his Sight around Quaid. It was like staring at the sun, no matter how hard he tried to filter the thaumalux. Yet despite the exhaustion and the strain, the more time he spent with Quaid, the easier it became to ignore the man's blinding light.

As Quaid's thaumalux receded, the trails of the other magic-weavers revealed themselves in a tangle of glowing threads woven through the grounds of the Keep. They led Ran's mind into swirling eddies of questions and tantalising possibilities until he ran aground on an idea. Quaid, of course, was the most obvious subject for Ran to use, and he approached the other man at breakfast. The sparring master levelled a dubious look at Ran's request to take a run through the Walled Forest for the sake of an experiment but reluctantly agreed. As they left the dining hall, Sasha surveyed them both with narrowed eyes, and Ran wondered if she would follow.

'Why am *I* running through the forest, and not you?' Quaid asked and stripped off his shirt. They stood in a clearing at the entrance to the Walled Forest, a massive wooded garden contained within the Keep walls. It was both a useful training ground for the children and a pleasant place to take a walk and forget the Keep was a gilded cage for birds too dangerous to fly.

'You're running so I can test how long your thaumalux trail holds in the air. I'll come back over the next few weeks and see if I can pick it up.' Ran pointed into the trees. 'Once you're in far enough that you can't see me, let your magic spool out. Just let all your walls down, then run, or walk, whatever suits you.'

Quaid nodded and took a quick sip from his water skin. 'What's the oldest trail you've ever tracked?'

'Before the change?' Ran chewed his lip in thought. 'Two or three days old, and it was Collan's, so it was strong. He disrupts the air like lightning. I know I can see weak trails for that long already. They're all over the Keep, but they get smudged by others walking through them, so they aren't reliable. This will test how long a strong trail will last without disruption.'

'Sounds complicated.' Quaid cracked his neck and jogged away into the trees.

'Take your time!' Ran shouted after him, watching the sparring master's light disappear behind the trunks and branches.

It took a few moments, but she came, her presence vibrating against his magic, singing through his bones. Ran didn't turn. Instead he found a soft place at the base of a tree and settled there to soak up the morning sun.

'Interesting,' the ghost muttered. Ran let his eyes drift to where she stood. Her fingers played across Quaid's thaumalux trail, passing through the light like dust motes in a sunbeam. 'I could never see them before now. Before your eyes changed, they were hidden from me. Now they're...'

'Everywhere?'

She nodded and her gaze followed the trail to where it wove between the trees and disappeared. 'These are important. I'm not sure why yet, but they're important.'

Ran sat forward, drawn by her words. 'What do you know of them?'

'Nothing,' she shrugged. 'I told you, I couldn't see them before the boy's magic washed your Sight clean. But I know they're important. I feel something when I see them. An... urgency. As though they're the answer to a question I haven't asked.'

Their identical blue eyes locked across the clearing.

He swallowed his pounding heart back into his chest where it thumped against his ribs. 'I'm sorry, for the things I said in the infirmary. I was... I had a lot going on.'

She looked away and shook her head. 'I know you don't want me here. I know this isn't what you thought your life would be.'

Ran opened his mouth to protest, but she held up a hand and silenced him.

'This isn't how I imagined my life either, or my after-life, for that matter. We've both had so much stolen from us. My life, my future. Your inheritance—everything and everyone, snatched away.' She crossed the space between them and crouched beside him. 'But I don't understand why you aren't fighting?'

'This again?' he snapped.

For months after arriving at the Keep she'd urged him, then berated him, then finally demanded he leave. She wouldn't listen to reason or excuse. In the end, he'd turned his magic on her and driven her away. Had she really come back after all this time to torment him again?

'I did fight!' he countered. 'I fought for my life. You were there!'

'I'm not talking about *then*. I'm talking about *now*. Why aren't you fighting to regain what was taken from you? Why aren't you at war with those who robbed you of your place in the world?'

The words hit with the force of a forge hammer. He shook his head. 'It's complicated. I can't just leave—'

She sneered. 'You're a prince of Orthia and Isord. You're a powerful magic-weaver. And you're a liar. You're lying to me, and you're lying to yourself.' She stood abruptly and spun away, stalking toward the shadows on the far side of the clearing.

'Wait!' Ran scrambled to his feet. 'Please...'

Her bare feet paused; the blades of pale green grass undisturbed by her presence.

'You were right. I've known you too long not to know your name. After everything we've been through, it was wrong of me not to ask. I would like to know, if you would tell me. Your true name, the one you were given in life, before they...'

'Before they killed me?' She glanced over her shoulder and waited for him to nod. 'Iridia. Before they killed me, I was Iridia.'

Ran asked Collan to declare Walled Forest off-limits to the Keep's folk and left Quaid's trail for seven days, despite his students grumbling at the restriction, bored and frustrated at spending their lessons in the sparring hall instead of outside. But there was nothing to be done for it. If he wanted to test his power, he had to do it properly.

He dismissed his class—half born in the Keep, half who were arrivals like him—and sent them on their way to Mistress Slade for meditation. He spotted Degan watching them across the forecourt and felt a pang of sorrow for the boy before Collan led him into the South Tower for his lessons with the records master. Ran still had scheduled lessons with Yidda, the wizened woman who held dominion over the Keep's library. She kept Ran busy with mountains of assigned reading in a strict schedule he blamed entirely for his avoidance of theory with his own students.

The children of the Keep had not only their studies, but jobs to see to daily; helping their parents or teachers with tasks like harvesting, carpentry, laundry or tending livestock. They had to learn the workings of the Keep for themselves, for one day, they would replace Collan and Yidda and the grounds master, Vespan, and train the next generation of arrivals from across Orthia. They were not many in number, with perhaps one arriving every few years, but they would continue to come, and the Keep had to stand ready.

Thankfully, Yidda had been a font of knowledge on thaumalux tracking, with her thousands of books and years of experience. But when her Sight had failed a year ago and she lost the ability to track or train youngsters, she handed the task to Ran and kept to the library. She reminded him of Perce. His old tutor and Yidda had much in common, and it saddened Ran that the two would never meet. He sometimes wondered at Perce's fate, but reckoned it was best he never knew. It was easier to pretend his tutor was alive than to imagine what befell him at Usmein's South Gate.

He made a mental note to invite Degan out the next time he went to kick a ball at the playing fields, then left the court and turned south, passing the bathhouse and continuing to the Walled Forest. He lifted the veil on his Sight and squinted as the world lit up around him. By the time he reached the clearing where he had waited for Quaid, Ran knew his experiment had worked, but not entirely as he expected.

Iridia stood nearby and offered him a small, rare smile; her eyes glistening in the glow of the thaumalux trails. Did she know something he did not, or had she merely sensed the excitement in his pounding heartbeat and quickening breath?

Quaid's distinct thaumalux wove away into the trees, and Ran followed it to the point where Quaid had dropped his defences. It flared here, became wider and brighter, then continued on. The trail reminded him of the lights sometimes seen in the night sky across Orthia's border with Marlow. It was a ribbon of colour, with the same scintillating vibrancy as the aura that surrounded Quaid, snaking off into the woods, hanging at about waist height.

The trail fractured under his fingers then reformed without fading. Seven full days and it still shone as brightly as the light Quaid left behind him this morning. Ran marvelled at it. He crouched and looked underneath it, he waved his hands around it, walked through it and beside it. No matter what he did, it remained—strong and luminescent.

He followed it into the woods, past a thicket of brambles and stopped on the other side. Iridia slipped through the trees, her eyes on Ran. Faintly glowing beside Quaid's seven-day-old trail, was another identical thaumalux. It peeled off in the opposite direction ten feet away, but it was unmistakably Quaid's.

How long ago had Quaid been in the Walled Forest before their test? Surely it had been weeks, or perhaps even a month ago? Ran glanced at Iridia then pushed through the undergrowth to the south where a well-used pathway led through the forest to the ponds, a waterfall and a small stream that emptied into the river beyond the walls.

He hadn't brought any of his tracking students here since his encounter with Degan's magic, and Collan had ordered the forest off-limits for the past week. If everything they knew about thaumalux was true and it really did fade quickly from the air, there shouldn't be any thaumalux trails visible on the pathway.

Yet, as he ducked under branches and twisted around bushes, he saw a pulsing glow growing between the trees. Ran shoved a fern aside, caught his boot on a tree root and stumbled out into a causeway of light.

The path was invisible under a river of thaumalux trails, glowing and pulsing, some with a quick rhythm, others calmer, gentler. Some hung close to the ground and whipped back and forth as if left by children running wildly along the path. Others held up at his waist height, taking a more sedate and controlled line along the track.

Ran stared at the threads of light, thoughts racing, a thousand questions all screaming to be heard above the others.

'How *old* are these?' he whispered, as if his voice might frighten the light away. How far back in time did they go? How powerful were the magic-weavers who left them?

'Generations of magic-weavers...' Iridia murmured and ran her transparent fingers through the light. 'Do you know what this means?'

Possibility unfolded in his mind like a map, each corner he revealed leading to another, then another. Could he delve back through time to pick out a thaumalux at will? How many people in the world outside left such trails and had no idea? Where might those trails lead?

What if every magic-user left a permanent, trackable trail and all that was required to follow it to its source was the ability to sift it from the air?

His heart began to thump hard.

He looked at Iridia, the river of light pulsing between them. She didn't smile now. She watched and waited. He hardly dared imagine what this might mean.

What if he could turn the curse of his magic to his advantage, and prove to his father, to his people, that this power was useful? It could change the face of the war. It could turn the tide! They could track Woaden mages in the Disputed Territory...

Iridia had said the trails were important—was this what she meant?

He opened his mouth to ask and a horn blast cut through the air. His frenetic thoughts snapped in two.

It was the gatehouse horn and shiver ran through him as if his blood had turned to ice. That horn blew only to announce an arrival.

Ran set off at a jog, dragging his magic back over his eyes and dismissing the twinge of pain in his head. The last arrival had been more than a year ago, so they were well due for some news from the outside world. The Keep would erupt with activity and people would clamour for news and pepper the riders with questions. The children would want to know if the riders had brought toys, or new books, for theirs were becoming tired and overused. The riders would smile and nod and say all in good time, and for a few days the mood of the place would lift.

He left the forest behind and passed the laundry and forge, already empty of people, and followed a small crowd of folk past the gardens into the forecourt. Shouts echoed from the top of the gatehouse and the thick timber panels began to groan open on their rarely used hinges. Collan appeared to Ran's left, on the steps of the South Tower with Yidda and Degan behind him. Degan craned his neck around Collan to see who had arrived as Ran jostled with the gathered folk to catch a glimpse of the arrivals.

A single rider moved forward, out of the shadow of the gatehouse lintel and into the sunlight.

From across the court, a pair of eyes fixed on him amongst the curious onlookers. They found him as if they had expected to see him there, staring back with widening eyes and a tightening throat.

Brit Doon had found him.

Chapter Nine

The Hidden Keep, Ravinka, Southern Orthia

A guard from the gatehouse appeared beside Brit, and from atop his horse he put a scroll tube in her outstretched hand. The crowd parted for her as she approached Collan, and Ran shot a look at the keep master. Collan's sharp eyes flicked between Brit and the guard but did not search for Ran in the crowd. The older man knew Brit did not belong to the usual group who served as couriers for the Keep, but he did not seem to recognise, or perhaps could not see, the faded crest on the breast of Brit's tunic, obscured as it was by his coat and a film of dust.

Ran knew it intimately—knew its curves and edges, its obvious and hidden meanings. It was his mother's crest—the arms of the Duchess of Orthia, Merideth Olseta, daughter of Harroe Kortson of Isord, and wife of Duke Ronart.

The guard handed Collan the scroll tube. 'He says he has news from the duchess. He offers these papers to validate his claim.'

She spoke softly but Ran caught her words as the wind blew them across the silent court. What Collan had surmised in a matter of seconds began to ripple through the crowd and more than a few people stepped away from Brit and his horse. Small children were herded behind skirts and trousered legs, and Ran noticed Eian whisper to Zarad, who slipped back through the crowd and hurried toward the infirmary.

Quaid sauntered over from the orchard, working a knife through a piece of fruit, and people shuffled aside to let him pass. Without a fuss, he positioned himself between Collan and Brit, squinting nonchalantly up at the rider. If the man on the horse made a move, Quaid would be on him in an instant. Brit had been fast when Ran knew him, but had the past four years slowed the watcher?

Thoughts tumbled through his mind, bleeding into one another. *What is he doing here? How did he find this place? Has he come for me?*

Ran's brow creased. None of it made sense.

Why was Brit wearing the crest of the duchess? He was a watcher in the Duke's Guard, not in the service of Merideth. Ran couldn't recall if his mother even *had* a personal guard. Then his stomach clenched and a wave of anxious nausea rolled over him. Had his curse and violent escape from the city caused such damage to his mother's standing that she now needed protection in her own home? He shuddered at the thought.

'What's your name, messenger?' Collan called across the forecourt.

'Brit Doon, sir.' He gestured at the scroll tube in Collan's hand. 'My credentials are in there.'

'That remains to be seen.' The keep master nodded at a man in the crowd. 'Amos, stable the man's horse please, and await instructions from my office.'

A man of middle years took the reins of Brit's horse and held it steady as the watcher dismounted and made his way gingerly to the steps of the South Tower. Brit walked like someone who had lived in a saddle for months on end, and his hips suffered for it. Collan opened his arm and waved Brit through the door, but not once did the deepening frown of concern leave his face. Quaid followed the watcher slowly, still slicing wedges off the fruit with his knife. He would use that blade if he thought for a second Brit posed a threat to the Keep. He would use it to open Brit's throat or belly and the body would be burned, the charred bones buried in the deepest part of the Walled Forest.

No one would speak of it and no one would care. It had happened before, and Ran wondered if today it would happen again.

Once Brit disappeared inside, Collan gave a quick whisk of his hand and the forecourt emptied. The gathered crowd dispersed in silence but Ran stood rooted to the spot by fear and uncertainty. Should he follow or wait? Would Collan try to convince Brit that Ran wasn't here, or would he turn him over in the hope of saving the Keep?

Collan's eyes found him and, with a nod, instructed him to follow.

Ran waited for the court to clear completely before he jogged up the stairs into the entrance hall of the South Tower. Led by Collan, Brit and

Quaid turned down a corridor and out of sight. There they would climb a flight of stairs to the second floor. Ran slowly traced their footsteps, not overly eager to stumble into their backs if they paused for any reason.

As he reached the landing, the men entered Collan's office—a huge space with windows overlooking the forecourt—and Ran hung back. He eyed the doorway as Quaid began to close the tall timber panels, leaving them slightly ajar.

There was no doubt the move was intentional, but would Brit notice? He was extremely perceptive, which made him an excellent watcher and apparently, a skilled hunter. But how had he found the Keep? Any physical tracks Ran and Sasha made on their journey had been banished by years of snowfall and rain. Had Brit discovered the Keep simply by chance?

Ran positioned himself in a niche within earshot of the door. When closed, the office was soundproof, but thanks to Quaid's sleight of hand, the doorway provided a conduit for the murmuring voices and Ran caught every word.

The hollow scrape of a metal scroll tube opening and the gentle rustle of unrolling parchment filled the silence.

'Watcher Brit Doon, is it?' Collan asked.

'Aye, sir,' Brit confirmed.

'Your papers appear in order,' Collan conceded. 'A message from the duchess is most unexpected.'

'A message of sorts, sir,' Brit replied in his familiar northern drawl, and it stunned Ran how much he'd missed that voice.

Together they'd escaped a Woaden attack on the Orthian command camp, then defended Usmein against the subsequent onslaught of Woaden soldiers. Brit had been with him at the house in Lackmah when Ran discovered the hoard of bones and Iridia's ghost. The watcher had been there the day his magic began to stir and started this whole spiralling mess. Brit had been there through it all, until Ran had disappeared from the palace dungeons, never to be seen or heard from again. Or so he thought.

'I urge you to speak plainly,' said Collan in a cool, level voice. 'I have a Keep full of very nervous folk who want to know why you have come and how you found us. I would rather not allow rumour and speculation to spread like wildfire.'

Brit's pause made Collan wait a little longer than Ran would have dared.

'Four years ago, a tragedy befell the duchess and her family,' Brit began finally. 'Her son was revealed to be a magic-weaver and was committed to stand trial by the Duke's Justice.'

Another pause, which Collan ended, his chair creaking as if he relaxed back into it. 'How very unfortunate. I did hear this tale from the riders who bring youngsters to us. News of the outside world is rare, but we do catch glimpses of the events beyond our walls. It is a shame the boy was tried. If his power had been discovered sooner, he might have been brought to us. He would have thrived here.'

'That's just it,' the watcher continued. 'The boy never stood trial.'

Brit might have expected some shock or indignation from Collan, but he received none.

It was Quaid who interjected. 'What's your meaning, messenger? The boy escaped the Duke's Justice?'

'He did just that,' Brit replied. 'He vanished. Last seen at Usmein's South Gate, four years ago this winter. We had reports from all over, sightings as far north as Harbern, some even in Wodurin, though I doubt he made it that far. An inn keeper in some far-flung mining town swore 'til he was blue in the face that the Black Prince tore his inn apart and killed his brother. No one found the boy, though. Wasn't long before the trail went cold and all sign of the prince disappeared.'

Collan wasn't about to take Brit's bait. 'Yet here you are, among us, presumably seeking him out?'

Ran wondered how quickly he could escape the corridor when Collan ordered Brit to leave.

'It is more than likely the boy died of exposure in a ditch somewhere or was taken by wolves. How long could a princeling possibly last in the frozen wilds?'

Brit chortled. 'That's true. Though, the duchess is not a woman easily vanquished. She's of the mountain people, bred on beds of stone and ice. They're hard-headed and not swayed. She never believed her son died, nor would she 'til she saw his body. She set me the task she wagered the duke's scouts wouldn't complete.'

'The duke's soldiers could not find the boy?'

'Right you are, sir.'

Collan sighed. 'I am very sorry, Watcher Doon. I fear your time has been wasted here. While I have a Keep—'

'You mistake me, sir,' Brit interrupted.

'Pardon?' Collan's question cut the air like a blade and Ran winced. The keep master was not a man who tolerated impertinence.

'What I mean is, the duke's *scouts* didn't find him.'

'Yes, and as *I* said, your time here has been for nought.' The edge on Collan's voice sharpened further.

'No, sir, it hasn't.' There was a smile in Brit's words. '*They* didn't find him, but I did. The Black Prince is here.'

A pregnant silence filled Ran's ears. Brit *had* seen him in the forecourt and recognised him for all the years that had passed.

He had to leave. He had to get back to his apartment and collect his things. He had to escape, even if it was only into the Walled Forest for a few nights. He had to make sure Brit didn't see him again, but he couldn't move.

What would Collan say? Would he continue the ruse?

Ran was acutely aware of Quaid absorbing the conversation. As far as the man knew, there was no such person as the Black Prince at the Keep.

But the sparring master was a smart man. Raised by Collan for most of his thirty years, even taking his family name for he had none of his own, Quaid was quick and clever and had been taught to read men as if they were books. He would make the connection.

'I'm sorry, Watcher,' Collan doubled down. 'You are mistaken.'

Brit laughed aloud. 'I know you're out there, Ranoth!'

Ran's breath caught in his throat and every fibre in his body flared to life. His feet found themselves and he bolted.

Behind him, the door swung on its hinges and slammed into the wall, boots pounding the timber floor faster than his legs could carry him forward. He spun and fired a shot of magic at the sound, hoping to hit something other than Collan or Quaid. He needed them if he was going to get out of this alive. The lightning strike of magic cracked over Brit's head, but the man ducked under it. He launched himself at Ran and tackled him to the floor.

They tumbled together, past the landing of the stairs and separated further down the corridor. A woman and two men peered out from doorways, but quickly retreated as soon as they saw Collan and Quaid racing after two brawling figures on the floor. Brit found his feet before Ran could catch his breath. He was weaker than he knew, his magic perilously fatigued from the constant effort of keeping a veil over his thaumalux Sight. His reserves gave him nothing as he staggered and tried to spin away from Brit's grasp.

The watcher, his old friend turned hunter, caught the back of his shirt and whipped him around, slamming him back against the wall. His forearm came up, knife in hand and held Ran in place, the shining blade an inch from his throat and poised to strike.

Quaid appeared and levelled his own blade at Brit's throat. The only thing stopping his deft hand from finishing the watcher was the firm grip of the keep master on his shoulder.

'Cease!' Collan bellowed, pushing the force of his magic against the three of them and shaking the walls of the tower to their foundations. Quaid froze and Brit staggered under the pressure shift in the air. Ran dared to swallow his terror and glared at Brit over the forearm pinning him to the wall.

Brit scowled back, gasping air into his lungs. 'You used to be faster than that, Ran.'

'And you used to be my friend,' he snapped back.

'You know this man?' Quaid demanded of Ran.

Brit carried on as if Quaid and his knife didn't exist. 'Have you got any idea how long I've been looking for you? How long I've been out in the middle of fucking *nowhere* on your mother's orders, trying to find your skinny arse? And here you are, tucked up and cosy in the Hidden Keep. Had to use a year's wages to get the location out of that rider. Then I had to fucking kill him to get my money back! Do you know what that shit does to a man?'

Ran knew; blood stained his hands right up to his elbows. It was under his nails where it couldn't be seen and would never wash out. So thick on his skin, it was like a cloak of guilt that never slipped from his shoulders. It was the price he'd paid to get to the Keep alive, and he'd be damned if he was about to throw it all away.

Quaid pressed his knife into the soft flesh of Brit's throat and leaned forward to hiss in his ear. 'Drop the knife or I'll open a steaming hole in your neck.'

At that, Brit glanced at the looming sparring master and as if only just registering the presence of the man, slowly let go of his blade. It clattered to the floor and Brit stepped back.

'Fine,' he conceded, lifting his hands and pointing a finger at Ran. 'But I'll be fucked if I'm leaving without you.'

Quaid grabbed the watcher by the lapels of his coat and aimed the knife at his throat again. '*You're* not going anywhere.'

'Let's take this back to my office.' Collan's deep and steady voice interrupted the simmering rage in the corridor and Ran glanced around. The curious faces of the tower's occupants had appeared again, and Ran wished he was anywhere but here. This story would be all over the Keep before dinner time.

Quaid shifted his grip on Brit's collar and steered the watcher back to Collan's office with Ran and the keep master following behind. Collan touched Ran on the arm as the sparring master escorted the watcher through the door.

'Let me handle this, my boy. We don't know why he's really here, but I'm not going to let him take you. Trust me—I have kept the folk of this Keep safe my entire adult life and I will not end that tradition by allowing some watcher from the capital to saunter in here and carry you off.' Collan squeezed Ran's shoulder. 'Do you trust me?'

'I do, sir.' Ran nodded and they entered to confront Brit together.

CHAPTER TEN

Tolak Range, the South Lands

Lidan's ribs ached at every jolt that came through the saddle on the winding journey back to Hummel. Siman led them home at a slower pace than she was accustomed, and she wondered if he did so for her benefit. She was grateful in any case, gulping down as much pain-relieving tea as she dared each morning when they broke camp. It was enough to keep the pain at bay and her eyes on the track ahead.

The stitches along her hairline itched like mad, and every time she reached to scratch them, she copped a scolding from Jessah or Loge. Her chest pain eventually eased, and despite a general and persistent stiffness, she was relieved to find she had escaped the ngaru attack with her ribs intact. Loge's limp lingered; his movements punctuated by hastily muffled grunts of discomfort. He switched to mounting his horse on the opposite side, and Lidan saw him riding more than once with his right leg hanging down beside the stirrup. Despite all this, he seemed intent on denying both her and Jessah an examination of his injury, probably thanks to some sort of ridiculous pride.

The others bustled around them, striking camp before their final day in the saddle, while Jessah cut away at Lidan's stitches. She winced as a thread was snipped and tugged free, harbouring vain hope she could hide her newest battle scar from her hawk-eyed mother under the curtain of her hair. She could almost hear Sellan now; the incredulous gasp, the sudden barrage of threats, the screaming fury that would erupt because her eldest child had disfigured her face and, oh by the gods of the north, who would want to match with her now!

'I need to look at that,' Lidan told Loge the fifth time in as many days.

'No, you don't.' Loge dismissed her concern and continued to pack his bedroll. 'You need to worry about your own injuries.'

'I'm fine!'

Jessah yanked on another stitch and Lidan's stomach lurched. She groaned and a flush of nauseating heat rolled in her belly.

Loge looked up from stuffing a soiled shirt into his saddle bag and cocked an eyebrow. 'Oh yes, perfectly fine.'

'At least I'm dealing with my problems. If you don't let me check that knee, you'll stuff it completely. Then we'll have to listen to your endless moaning when the dry season comes and it seizes up. You'll be an insufferable old man with insufferable old bones.' Lidan winked at Jessah and the girl snorted a laugh.

Loge swung his saddle onto Striker and tightened the girth strap. 'Next time I'll just let the ngaru chew your face off, shall I?'

Lidan gave him a sarcastic smile. 'If it spares me the sight of you hobbling around camp for two weeks, go right ahead.'

The mood among the rangers had lifted as they left the tablelands and turned for home, except for Owin of course, who rode silent and sullen within arm's reach of Siman. They'd be within sight of Hummel by midday and feasting in her father's hall by sunset. But she was caught like a straw-stuffed doll within her parents loveless matching. Her mother wanted her back in Hummel, visibly pursuing the succession and hunting the title of heir like a hungry dog. While her father seemed content to let her wander the wilds, as if her mere presence reminded him of something he would rather forget. If her mother weren't so incessantly vocal about Lidan's lack of a defined role in the clan, would her father remember she existed at all?

The inconsistency was unbearable and made leaving home far easier than staying. Yet, in the growing warmth of the morning and the laughing banter of her companions, she found herself smiling. Perhaps it was time to leave the range, and rest, if only for a moment.

The last of her stitches came free and she let go a long, steady breath before climbing carefully to her feet. Loge had moved on to fitting Theus's saddle and she watched him carefully as she approached, assessing the way he leaned his weight into his good leg and rested the other with his toe on the ground, rather than the sole of the boot flat against the soil.

'Since when do you help me with packing?' She stroked the horse's nose as he investigated her hand for any hidden treats.

Loge gave Theus a gentle pat and pointed east through the trees. 'The sooner we get out of here, the sooner I can drown myself in an urn of beer.'

Lidan lifted her hands and stepped back, smiling as her bedroll was tied behind her saddle. 'Well then, don't let me stop you. Let it never be said that I stood between a ranger and their ale!'

Across a valley of long waving grass, the Caine jutted into the sky like a wild dog's tooth, its orange stone reflecting the light of sunset. The village had grown in the years since her brother's birth, the walls shifting out into the valley and along a slight ridge to the west to accommodate the influx of refugees from border villages.

The tiny shack where the Crone had once lived on the Caine's western face, was gone. Her father had extended his stables, so the musty old hut had been torn down. Lidan had been glad to see it perish. Some of her worst memories had been born inside that building's dank shadows. Sadly, the Crone had not been inside her hovel when it was destroyed. She now resided with Lidan's mother in a hall built by the daari in the hope of appeasing his first wife and ending one of the many feuds that boiled between them.

In exchange for the new accommodations and the acceptance of her aged companion into Hummel's community, Sellan had publicly relinquished her legal dominance over Erlon's three other wives.

Privately however, Lidan's mother still controlled Hummel despite her father believing it to be under his dominion. Sellan might have allowed Erlon to decide when he slept with his wives, but she still wielded the power of first wife and dana over their children and all other domestic matters. Her father's wives still deferred to Sellan. Even Farah, the mother of his son, did not refuse the dana when she chose to press her will. Erlon may have bought himself some peace in his bedchamber, but by no means had he shackled his first wife.

Clouds climbed along the face of the eastern tablelands, soaring into the humidity of the evening. Already, dark grey curtains of rain fell from the distant rolling thunderheads. The strong east wind swirling up the valley would blow them right over Hummel, refilling water troughs and delivering a drenching to the fertile black soil.

A few hundred feet out from the village's new walls, a parallel line of pikes stood watch, severed heads glaring out at the trackway in various states of decomposition. The array of tattana marks on their foreheads marked them as Namjin raiders. The stench of the nearest rotting heads stung her nostrils and caught in her throat, but she didn't avert her eyes as she passed. One by one the rangers spat at the heads, Lidan taking her turn, cursing the spirit of the invader to never find rest while his bones were exposed to the southern sun. Punishment for crossing the Tolak border did not end with death.

A sudden horn blast startled Lidan, and the gates ahead began to ease open. Theus, to her surprise, lengthened his stride and hurried to follow the other horses. Even her wild-born horse was eager to rest in the confines of the village walls. She let him have his head and they passed under the lintel into the common.

Daari Erlon strode toward them as they dismounted, a small boy with ebony hair and light brown eyes trotting at his heels. Ehran watched with wide-eyed fascination as his father embraced Siman and shook Loge's hand. Lidan swung down beside the boy and he turned to stare at her. She thought for a moment he might never look away, and the intensity of the boy's gaze began to crawl across her skin until Erlon moved between them and Ehran disappeared behind his father's legs.

Erlon gave his daughter a small, but not unkind nod—the same nod he gave all the other rangers and apprentices—and she quickly extinguished a spark of anger that threatened to engulf any sense of joyful homecoming that had dared take root. She returned his greeting with the acceptance of a ranger—a hand to her heart, which she opened toward him with a small bow.

'Father,' she said, unable to warm the icy edge in her voice.

'First Daughter,' Erlon responded with the empty title she still carried like a yoke around her neck. It meant nothing now Ehran was among them.

She ground her teeth and turned away, leading Theus to the enormous stable complex on the western side of the village. Would anyone notice if she spent the night there with the horses?

'Lidan?' Loge hurried to catch up, Striker trotting along behind.

Loge would notice. He always noticed.

'Theus needs a rub down and some food,' she began, as if it were the sole reason she left her father and his pleasantries in the common. Loge touched her elbow and she stopped at the stable entry.

'Maybe you should ease into it,' he suggested, nodding at the huge timber and clay structure at the very centre of the village. 'We've been away a while. Let yourself get used to being back. Don't go to the hall tonight. Come to the barracks with us. Iema reckons they'll broach some of the good kegs now Siman is back.'

Lidan eyed Loge for a moment, then glanced over his shoulder at her father. Erlon didn't appear to have noticed her absence, so was unlikely to miss her at dinner.

'Do you really want to spend the night watching your father get drunk and tell battle stories, or your sisters fighting over the cake platter, or Dana Sellan glaring at Mother Farah?'

He raised a brow and she realised that was exactly what would happen in the hall tonight. The food and drink would be just as satisfying in the barracks, and the company a damn sight better, but if she stayed there, it would be her first time sleeping in the women's quarters instead of the room she shared with Marrit. Her mother despised the barracks and everyone in them, and had tried to forbid Lidan go anywhere near them. When outright prohibition had failed, the dana had resorted to nagging. As resistant as Lidan had become to her mother's methods, even she couldn't withstand an onslaught *that* relentless.

'I'll see,' she nodded, with perhaps a little too much hesitation. 'It's been a long day...'

'It'll do you good.' Loge slapped her back and went off to find Striker's stall.

As tempting as the barrack's mess sounded, Lidan wasn't sure she had the energy, or the will, to paint a convincing smile on her face; not for her father, her mother, or anyone else. All she really wanted was food, bed and some blessed, uninterrupted time to herself.

Night fell while she brushed and fed Theus. She left him in his stall and went to the far end of the stables where the doors opened to the training yards and the barracks. Thunder rolled across the sky to the east and the storms drew near, bringing rain and lightning and wind. The heady scent of the earth preparing for the downpour filled the air. She was exhausted by all of it—her parents and their fighting, the ngaru and the distant war with the Namjin. From here, she could slip across the yard to the women's quarters and find an empty bunk.

Loge, true to form, didn't give her the chance to vanish into the night. He waited by the door with a horn tankard in his hand and another beside him on a bench. He grinned and Lidan tried to suppress a smile. He'd known she would try and disappear. He'd known she would run and hide and had set a very simple trap to catch her.

She glanced into the cup as he handed it to her. 'That better be berry wine and not that horse piss ale you drink.'

He raised his brows in mock indignation. 'I'll have you know it's the best horse piss this side of the Malapa!'

'That may well be, but you won't catch me drinking it, even if my life depended on it.' Lidan shuddered and they crossed the training yard to an empty bench outside the barrack's mess hall. She unbuckled the harness for her knife-sheaths and laid them on the table. It took three gulps to drain her cup, and Loge leaned back, waving at a tine-woman to bring more.

'Happy birthday, by the way...' He lifted a nearby urn and refilled his cup. 'Seventeen winters—not bad.'

'My birthday was three moons ago, you fool,' Lidan corrected and slumped beside him. 'You carved me that little bird thing.'

'Ah, yes, I remember. What'll we celebrate then?'

'Must we celebrate anything? Can't we just drink?'

Loge shook his head and took a draw on his cup. 'No, drinking is for celebrating. You have to celebrate *something*, or the shadows in your mind will creep up and drag you down to their lair. Celebrating keeps the namorras away.'

She thought for a moment, then swung her leg over the bench, straddling it and facing him. 'We can celebrate surviving another hunt. Well, most of you survived. Your knee's probably fucked. Grent will have to cut your leg off at the hip soon.'

'Another hunt,' Loge agreed, slapping his tankard into the side of hers. 'Roose!' He shouted the salute loud enough for the rangers around them to hear.

'ROOSE!' They bellowed in unison, and Lidan laughed, racing him to drain her cup. Slowly, the pain and anger and anxiety began to slip away.

Some time and several cups later, Iema and Jessah appeared with wooden platters piled with food, and Lidan realised she was starving. The girls settled on the bench opposite and fell into conversation with Loge while Lidan levered herself up and entered the mess, her eyes roving across the tables to find the food on a board by the wall. Nathen watched her carefully from a nearby table and she grinned at him.

She probably looked like she'd been dragged backwards through a bush; her clothes and hair filthy with dust and sunburnt across her nose, but she didn't care. She was a little bit drunk and about to have a feed, and when she was little bit drunk, she could pretend she was someone else, somewhere else. She could pretend her parents didn't hate each other, and that being a ranger was all she needed from her life. That she hadn't made any promises to her mother, and that time wasn't running out to change her father's mind. She could shove it all away and just be right where she was for a single moment in time.

At the sideboard, she helped herself to the good, simple fair of the rangers. The roast meat and stewed beans weren't as highly spiced as the stuff served in her father's hall, but it was hearty, and the smell alone filled her with comfort.

'Well!' A voice echoed behind her and the lively chatter of the mess faded. Lidan rolled her eyes and continued to serve herself. She'd wondered how long it would take for Owin to drink his courage and show himself. 'Never thought I'd see the day when the *first daughter* would stoop so low as to eat with the likes of us!'

A few rangers laughed, likely thinking this was a joke between friends, and Lidan put her platter down. She turned, feeling the gaze of the gathered rangers fall on her. Her hand went to her hip, but her fingers found empty air where her knife should have been.

Shit!

'Looking for these?' Owin lifted the belt and her knives swung in their sheaths. He drew one and tossed the rest of the tangled leather on a table, well out of her reach. She looked back at Owin, the dribbling drunk that he was. She was a few cups down the wine urn, but he looked as though he'd been drowning in ale since they entered the common. He'd probably dumped his horse in the stables and come straight here without taking the time to care for the poor creature. Lidan's hands curled into tight balls of trembling disgust and Owin snarled, bearing two rows of crooked teeth.

'Reckon I couldn't use these, eh? You'll pay for that insult, ancestors as my witness.'

A murmur rolled through the crowded mess. This was not friendly banter.

'I never said that,' she spat back.

'Well, I reckon I might just learn.' He nodded appreciatively at the knife and weighed it in his hand. 'Earn myself a bit of steel on the way.'

'They aren't yours to take, you steaming sack of shit.' Rage boiled in Lidan and she fought for control. Rage wasn't going to help her win this. Brains and pace would. Owin was bigger, carrying far more muscle than she could ever hope to build, but he was drunker than ten men on a feast day, and that was an advantage she could use if she was fast enough.

'They will be,' he growled, murderous intent gleaming in his eyes.

He flung himself forward, crashing past tables and chairs, rangers diving out of his way. Lidan spun and snatched a meat fork from the table. It was a sharp thing, about a foot long, carved of bone and timber, and it sat uncomfortably where her knife should have been.

She swung back as Owin collided with her, a steel blade slicing past her nose, through the skin of her cheek, and skipping off the surface of the tabletop. Pain flared in her face and her knee rammed into his stomach. She drove the meat fork into the exposed plain of his back, aiming for his spine as if he were a ngaru. Owin shoved her with his bulk and picked her up, slamming her into the sideboard and roaring as the fork punctured his clothing and skin. She kicked and stabbed, punching at his head and clawing his face. Her finger caught the outside edge of his eye and she pushed, turning his screaming mouth away and forcing him to release her.

She heard Loge roaring over the shouts and jeers of the others, but he wouldn't make it through the throng of rangers baying for blood. Owin had challenged her, as far as anyone here knew, and they wouldn't intervene to stop the fight until someone called to yield, or died.

She kicked out, using the table as a launch point and shoved Owin across the empty space in front of a stack of ale kegs. He staggered away, corrected himself and came at her snarling, stabbing the knife like a spear. Lidan swerved and drove her fist into his face. His nose cracked and she landed a kick to his knee. He fell screaming to the floor, gasping through the blood pouring from his barely healed nose.

Despite his injuries, Owin rolled back to his feet and charged her again, arms high, the knife poised to descend on her head. They slammed into each other and Lidan shoved the meat fork up into his jaw. It speared up through his tongue, through the roof of his mouth and into the underside of his brain. A gout of blood flooded out of the wound as his life poured down her chest and onto the floor.

The room fell silent, a collective breath held, a moment turned to stone as the rangers around her realised what had happened.

Lidan let go of the fork and Owin's body slumped at her feet. She stumbled away from his twitching corpse, breathing hard and staring at the handle of the fork where it stuck out from under his chin. He was gurgling, blood rushing into his mouth, drowning him as he fought for breath. She wiped sweat and spit from her mouth with a shaking hand, smearing blood across her lips. She couldn't tell how much of it was hers or Owin's.

'Lidan!' a familiar voice broke the silence. She turned, scanning the crowd, and found her father with Siman and Loge at his back. Her heart skipped, knocking the breath from her lungs. Erlon's chest rose and fell as if he'd run from his hall and fought his way through the press of bodies in the mess. Feet shuffled, uncertain. Around him rangers stared, waiting.

Blood dripping from her a shaking finger, she pointed at Owin's corpse. 'He stole my fucking knife.' Lidan's legs began to tremble as she realised the gravity of what she'd done. 'He... he came at me with it.'

Erlon nodded, then gestured toward the door, and she stepped over Owin's twitching body, following her father into the night.

CHAPTER ELEVEN

Hummel, Tolak Range, the South Lands

Lidan followed her father across the training yard, her limbs growing heavier with every step and her stomach churning. She'd killed more ngaru than she could count, shot and killed her share of raiders too, but this…

This was different.

There were people everywhere, muttering and pointing, some shouting. The new cut to her face burned, but she ignored it, as she did the onlookers watching her progress to the hall. It was all she could do to keep pace with her father as they passed through the massive timber doors. They creaked closed behind her.

She'd hated Owin—he was a pest and a liability, disturbing in ways she could barely articulate—but she hadn't wanted him dead.

The hall stood empty and thunder boomed outside as Erlon led his daughter past the tables and benches to his private chambers at the rear.

'Where is everyone?' she murmured, glancing around.

'Outside,' her father replied without turning.

The remains of the evening meal had been cleared away and a few tine-women scrubbed at the tables. The daari's dogs licked scraps from the floor, lifting their heads to note her passing with only vague curiosity. Erlon held the door open for Lidan then followed her into his receiving room. It was a comfortable, intimate space, crowded with chairs and a few small tables. The floor was strewn with rugs and furs, and a bed chamber stood off to the left, concealed from view by a thick curtain hanging between two packed-earth walls. The gentle hiss of falling rain began on the thatched roof overhead.

Erlon went to the largest of the chairs and Lidan stood dumbly in the middle of the room, unsure of what to do or where to look. A hand rested on her shoulder and she started. It was Siman. He gave her a grim smile and she realised he was manoeuvring her toward a nearby bench. Loge materialised from somewhere and moved quietly through the shadows to her right. By the way he casually folded his arms and planted his feet wide, he looked for all the world to be the very embodiment of cool composure. Lidan might have even been fooled if it weren't for the paling skin around his knuckles betraying the tension in his hands.

Someone knocked on the open door and her father waved for them to enter. Grent put his attendee box on the floor and set about inspecting the gash on her face. He touched the hot bruise growing on her cheek and she hissed, then his finger traced the fresh scar on her forehead. His eyes searched her face.

'Ngaru?' he whispered.

Lidan nodded, unable to form the words to explain what had happened. Grent nodded and plastered her cheek wound with gummy ointment before laying a clean, linen strip over it. The daari waited, his deep blue eyes taking in every detail. He was a huge man, tall and broad, and even though Lidan had grown considerably, he still towered over her whenever she stood at his shoulder. He kept his unruly black hair tied back and had allowed a short beard to grow across his dark face in a style Lidan was not yet used to.

When Grent finished, he handed her a pouch of fresh dressings and a stoppered urn of ointment. 'Keep it clean and covered and it will heal without scarring too badly. It doesn't need to be sewn—it's not very deep. If you get dizzy or notice any redness—'

'I'll come see you straight away,' Lidan said with a weak smile. She knew what he was going to say, and it was only delaying the inevitable tirade her father was preparing to deliver from across the room.

The bone-setter stood and put his hands on his hips. 'You're lucky, but I'd wager you won't be this lucky again. Before long you'll come up against someone bigger and better and you'll end up with something sharp in something vital—' He levelled a glare at Loge. '—no matter how good your training is. Owin was a terrible fighter, and even worse when he was rotten drunk. Don't take it as a compliment that you killed him.'

Lidan glanced away, the bitter truth too much to bear. Lightning flashed outside, illuminating the shadows of the room for a fraction of time.

'Thank you, Grent,' Erlon interceded. 'We'll send for you if the need arises.'

Grent bowed and left, a pall of expectation settling in his wake.

'We need to have a Hearing. It's important the proper procedures are followed, and I want this over with before your mother comes in here in hysterics.'

'Yes, Da,' Lidan agreed, an image of her mother's maudlin wails and exaggerated horror playing before her eyes.

Erlon cleared his throat. 'Tell me what happened.'

Lidan sighed. 'He stole my knife, then he attacked me.'

Erlon's raised brow told her that he wasn't entirely convinced.

'If I may, sir,' Loge cut in. 'There's a bit more to it than that. Owin challenged Lidan in the tablelands before we turned for home, and she handled him pretty convincingly. He probably took insult and decided to deal with it personally, instead of bringing it before a Hearing.'

The daari looked to his advisor and Siman nodded.

'I didn't think that incident warranted a mention. He was already facing a Hearing for failing to inspect the caves near the Pass,' the chief ranger said, sparing Lidan a short, knowing glare. 'Evidently I was wrong. Owin was fixated on her steel, implying the knives gave her an advantage over him.'

'He had no steel of his own?' Erlon asked.

'No. He hadn't earned any as yet.'

'Do they speak true?' Her father's gaze slipped back to her.

She nodded and kept her mouth shut, gnawing the back of her lip as it threatened to tremble.

'And he attacked you, unprovoked, in the mess?'

'Yes.' She nodded again. 'I took the nearest weapon to defend myself.'

That was the line her father needed to hear. Erlon took a swig from his ale cup.

If she had intended to kill Owin then the Law required her father to punish her in kind. If she killed him in self-defence, as she rightly had, then she became the injured party. She could defend her actions, somewhat, from that point.

'Putting aside my personal feelings for Owin, I must say I'm deeply disturbed by this violence among my rangers.' Erlon fixed his daughter with stern eyes. 'I'm even more concerned by *your* involvement in this.' He held up his hand to forestall the protest Lidan opened her mouth to deliver. 'As Grent said, you've been lucky.'

His words echoed in her head and she realised this Hearing was not a cursory procedure her father was performing for the sake of appearances. He meant to punish her, publicly and firmly. Lidan couldn't look at Loge or Siman. She closed her eyes and a sigh escaped her lips as another clap of thunder cracked the air outside. 'Yes, Da.'

'I expect I'll be paying Owin's brother restitution for the loss of his life. And you must be sentenced. There must be payment made for what you've done.' He took a breath and Lidan braced herself for what he was about to say. 'Your apprenticeship as a ranger will end, in recognition of the life you have taken.'

The muscles of her face contracted, her jaw clenched and the gash on her cheek burned.

That was it. It was done.

The freedom she'd fought for and cherished for so long, was gone, leaving a gaping, bloody hole in her heart. She deserved this, she knew she did, but humiliation and grief flared white hot in her chest all the same.

Her father continued, disappointment shaking his voice, and Lidan's stomach lurched. 'You will be confined to the village until further notice. You will be permitted to ride to your sister's matching only because I can't spare the space for you in a wagon. You will assist your mothers and tend to your siblings, and—'

Lidan shot to her feet and beat her fist against her chest. 'He attacked *me!*'

'And!' Erlon raised his voice and went on as if he hadn't heard her, 'you will do all of this without complaint.'

There was resignation in the grim set of his lips. There was a sadness there too, as if making this decision cut him somewhere deep inside. Lidan smothered her anger and tried not to fall into the churning pit of rage swirling in her stomach. There were worse sentences he could pass on her for killing a man and there was nothing to be done. The daari's word was Law. She could object all she liked and it wouldn't change a thing.

'Sir, I—' Loge began, but Siman coughed and the protest ended.

'Rangers,' Erlon turned away from his daughter. 'Do you witness this sentence in accordance with the Law?'

'We do,' they responded, Loge's affirmation lagging behind Siman's. If called on by Owin's family, they would vouch for the daari's ruling.

'You may go,' Erlon said and gestured to the door.

Siman and Loge put their hands on their chests and gave Erlon a bow. Lidan didn't move. Her jaw was locked, and her feet refused to obey the commands she screamed inside her mind. She didn't look at Loge as he left. She couldn't. She didn't trust herself not to burst into tears. She thought for a moment that he hesitated at the edge of her vision, but then he vanished. She let him go and stared into the middle ground between where she stood and her father sat.

Tears pooled in her eyes, blurring the light from the candles.

'I had hoped you would come to eat with us tonight,' Erlon said into the silence. 'Bridie and the other girls all ask after you, but Lucija hardly knows you and you terrify Ehran. I thought you might come and sit with them. If you had, none of this would have happened.'

'I'm sorry…' she said. She wanted to tell him that she hadn't meant to kill Owin, that it was a terrible, unfathomable mistake, but it would be a waste of breath.

Erlon shook his head and stood to refill his cup, probably for something to do with his hands more than a need to fill it. He'd hardly drunk more than a mouthful of the contents.

'I thought you were better than this, Liddy. I thought you were better than the rest of them.' He shrugged. 'It's more than likely my fault. I've indulged you—given you inch after inch until you had enough rope to near about fucking hang yourself. Grent's right. You've been lucky. You *are* lucky. You're lucky it was Owin who attacked *you*. If it had been someone else, there's a good chance you'd be the one twitching and bleeding on the floor of the mess. And all you have to say to me is sorry?'

He paused and waited for her to speak, but she had nothing. She was empty, a ghost of who she'd been just a few hours before. He'd torn everything away, and he was right to. Sorry wouldn't undo the damage; it wouldn't bring Owin back or wash the blood from her hands. Lidan shook her head and he looked way in disgust.

'We teach children to say sorry, don't we? We say, apologise when you hurt someone. We teach them that sorry is how things are made better.'

He glanced away and drained his cup. 'Thing is, that's not how the world works. You can't fix things with a word and a smile. You can't take back an insult or repair a broken heart. Not really. Those cuts remain—they scar you and the people you inflict them on. We tell children to say sorry, and when they grow up, they believe that's how wrongs are undone, that things can be set right again. But it's not, is it?

'If saying sorry meant a damned thing, do you think we'd be in this war? Do you think if sorry fixed anything, I wouldn't be the first to walk across that border and tell Yorrell Namjin I'm sorry that my daughter didn't want to match with his son, and that my wife accuses him of perversions I can hardly stomach to think about? I can't bring back the rangers we've lost by saying sorry to their families. I can't undo *any* of that with a word. Because that's all it is—a word. It's meaningless.' He looked at her, his features rigid. 'Sorry doesn't fix what's broken. It's an empty nothing used by little children who don't know any better, and it's about fucking time you realised you aren't a child anymore.'

Chapter Twelve

Erlon's words haunted Lidan's steps as she made her way through the next morning. A night of fitful sleep had done nothing to dispel the echo of his disappointment. She hugged her arms across her chest and walked the perimeter of Hummel until, despite herself, she stood inside the door of her mother's house. To the east of the great hall, it was, at its essence, a larger version of the many other houses that stood in the shadow of the Caine. It had no adornments or extravagances, and no ornate decoration that Lidan could see. Other than its size, it was as common as the remainder of Hummel's buildings.

The interior was a different matter entirely.

Her mother's quarters were through a curtained doorway to Lidan's right, and the Crone's stood on the opposite side of the hall behind an identical curtain. Lidan had yet to enter the Crone's musty domain, thanks to a lack of desire or invitation, and she had only once seen inside her mother's clean and well-ordered sitting room. There were a number of small rooms and alcoves at the back of the structure, and it appeared the Crone's clutter had migrated straight into one of them from the old hut on the hill. No attempt had been made to disguise the mess, which looked ready to burst out into the proper of the house and overwhelm the occupants. Lidan was surprised her mother allowed it to exist in such a state, but Sellan was a hard woman to predict.

A tine-woman hurried away to alert the dana to her daughter's arrival, and in the lull, Lidan walked past the fire pit and peered into the back room, careful not to disturb anything. Surely there hadn't been *this* much stuff the last time she'd been here? Either the Crone had expanded her collection, or things had begun to spontaneously multiply of their own accord.

In the farthest corner, partially obscured by a thick curtain, was a workbench heaped with a tangle of half empty vessels, platters, tools and trinkets. On the wall above, bottles and urns of various sizes crowded a series of timber shelves, all labelled in a language Lidan couldn't read. Surrounding them were scrolls and bound parchment volumes Lidan hadn't seen before the Crone relocated to her new accommodations. They had been hidden in the depths of the old hut, shrouded and unseen for years, only now exposed to the flickering light of a few sparse candles.

Lidan's fingers itched to touch the books on the wall, her mind already craving some sort of input to overwhelm the repeating voice of her father. But as well as she knew the written symbols of the South Lands, those of the places beyond the Malapa remained a mystery. She knew the common trading tongue well enough, her mother often speaking it to her and Marrit, but neither of the girls could decipher the meaning scrawled on the parchments. She wondered if her mother had neglected to impart that education by design. That they could not read the secrets hidden here meant the world inhabited by their mother and the Crone remained unknown to Lidan and her sister.

'Don't touch the bird, girlie.' The Crone's voice echoed from the shadows. Lidan slapped her hand over her mouth to stifle a scream.

'What bloody bird?' she demanded, gripping the door frame to steady herself.

The old woman nodded at the bench. 'That one.'

Lidan glanced over and instantly recoiled. A motionless craw lay on a thick slab of stone, its legs stiff and one jet black wing slightly askew. Old, dry blood surrounded the creature, its body cut open and left uncovered, and the whole thing crawled with flies. Its eyes stared at the ceiling, unblinking and unbothered by Lidan or her revulsion. 'Why the fuck have you got a dead craw in here?'

'Language, young lady.' Sellan emerged from her rooms, chiding her daughter as if she were ten. The tine-woman appeared with a tea tray and set it down quietly before vanishing into the back of the house.

'Mother! Have you seen this?' Lidan stabbed a finger at the dead bird.

Sellan glanced vaguely at the entrance to the anteroom. 'I don't pay any attention to what goes on in there, and neither should you.' She motioned for her daughter to approach and took a seat in a chair adorned with soft woven cloth. 'Sit and have tea, Liddy.'

Lidan shot a wary glare at the Crone and slipped across the room to the seat opposite her mother, her eyes never drifting too far from the shrouded old woman. Neither of them had mentioned the plastered gash on her face, and she wondered how long that would last.

'Tea, Thanie?' Sellan asked without looking at the shadow where the Crone sat.

The old woman coughed her phlegmy cough and emerged. Her foul furs were gone, and she looked a little younger for it. No longer hidden beneath layers of lice-riddled pelts, the woman her mother called Thanie appeared to be a slender, albeit hunched woman of middle to late years. If not for the deformity of her back, she would have stood as tall as Lidan, perhaps a little more so. Her black hair, heavily streaked with grey, was piled on her head in a knot, her shoulders cloaked in a knitted wool shawl, and she clutched a worn old walking stick in her gnarled right hand. She limped to the seat between Lidan and Sellan and eased down, hunching into some rugs and pulling them around her as if the air chilled her to her bones. Lidan thought the room too warm for this time of year, but she hadn't accounted for the woman's frailty and rolled her sleeves up to cool herself.

Her mother poured three cups of tea, then leaned back into the chair, the crisp fabric of her skirt rustling gently. Her gaze settled on Lidan and the woman's expression darkened.

'What happened to your face?!' she demanded, almost upsetting her teacup as she flung it back on the table and stood.

Lidan's hands flew up to stop her mother's advance. 'Nothing! It's just a scratch. Grent has seen to it. It's fine. Please don't fuss.' The flood of reassurance only barely stopped her mother dragging Lidan to her feet. 'Really, it's nothing.'

Sellan scowled and reluctantly returned to her seat. 'If it scars, I'll kill—'

'Don't worry, Mam,' Lidan insisted. She'd worn her hair down today and hoped it covered her earlier injury, for it would certainly send her mother into a rage, but it couldn't disguise the wound Owin had given her. 'You can't kill the man who did it.'

'Why not?' Sellan demanded with an incredulous frown.

'He's already dead,' the Crone cut in. She reached for a cake as Sellan cocked a brow at her daughter. Lidan nodded. The news seemed to placate her mother, who took up her cup and sipped the steaming contents.

'So he's the one who got you into all that trouble?' asked Sellan, nonchalantly swirling the tea in her cup.

'You heard about that.'

'I did,' her mother replied with an edge of caution, and Lidan glanced up. As quickly as it appeared, the faint impression of concern vanished, waved away with a dismissive hand. 'You know what this place is like—the rumour mill runs so fast it could grind grain to flour in moments. Can't say I'm as disappointed as your father seems to be. He's been stalking around the common under a black cloud all morning.'

Lidan's brow furrowed. Of all the things she had expected her mother to say, that had not been one of them.

'You stood your ground.' Sellan shrugged. 'That's something to be applauded, even if it did put you in an unreasonable amount of danger. And now we can put all this ridiculous ranging business behind us. It's about time you focused on the task at hand.'

There it is, she thought as the Crone set to work slowly chewing on a small fruit cake. Lidan wasn't sure how many operable teeth the woman had in her mouth, but she seemed determined to bend the cake to her will.

Lidan wondered how her mother had received the news of her daughter's sentence. Had she been positively giddy at the idea? Relieved that finally Lidan had no choice but to remain in Hummel and within reach of her influence?

'What do you think I've been doing for the past four years? Riding leisurely across the range, taking in the scenery?' Lidan demanded and her mother rolled her eyes. 'How am I supposed to demonstrate my worthiness to the title of heir if I'm stuck here sewing and weaving?'

'Running around the countryside trying to get yourself killed is hardly a suitable way to win back the title, Lidan. We need to work on your appearance and deportment.'

Lidan groaned. 'Father isn't going to choose me as his heir because I look nice in a dress or because I sit with a straight back. He's going to choose me because I handle myself against our enemies as he would. That apprenticeship was the only—'

'It was never the *only* way, and you know it,' Sellan cut in, her voice thick with poison. 'It was *your* way; the way *you* chose because you refused to listen to me. *You* were the one who swore it would work, that you could change his mind, and it's all been for naught. The boy is four, you are almost eighteen and *nothing* has changed.'

Lidan had forged that path between what her mother wanted and what her father would allow. And now it had been ripped away, leaving her to wonder if all the fighting, all the conflict she had caused, had been a waste. Perhaps she should have let her mother have her way all those years ago, then none of this would have ever happened.

She sighed and looked into the fire pit. The dana would have preferred a ruthless daughter; unwilling to take no for an answer and committed to doing whatever was needed to secure her place. But the truth of what that meant sat in Lidan's chest like a stone, pressing on her heart until she was breathless with guilt and sickened by her weakness. She didn't have it in her to do her mother's bidding, or to simply turn aside while the woman did as she pleased. Neither was she prepared to shrink into a role of subservient domesticity as her father likely would have preferred. The Crone had told her once that she had but one chance to forge her own path, or risk falling into the thrall of her parent's desires. She'd never forgotten that moment, or its lesson, but she had lost sight of the path now. She was in a trackless wasteland with no idea which way to turn.

'The Dead Sisters know if I don't do something to help the situation, no one else will.' Sellan dropped the comment in Lidan's lap like a shovel load of hot coals and casually sipped her tea.

She glared at her mother. 'What's that supposed to mean?'

'It means, dearest, that for all your effort to change that man's mind, he still baulks at it.' Sellan's green eyes pinned her to her seat and she could do nothing but stare.

Since she'd been a child, those emerald depths of her mother's gaze had always scrambled Lidan's thoughts and turned her words to nonsense. 'I still have a year left—'

'Less than a year!' Sellan snapped. 'Three moons have come and gone since your birthday and your matching year is approaching faster than you realise. And when that year is gone and the boy remains his father's heir, what then?'

'Mother...'

'I want to hear you say it, Lidan! I want to hear you *say it* and I want to know that you understand what is at stake here. When you are matched and gone, too far away to be any help to anyone, who will ensure your sister and I are properly cared for? Ehran? Farah? Ha!' Sellan's laugh echoed among the rafters like a cracking whip. 'Erlon has indulged you for too long, and now he has shown you what he truly thinks of you. You're nothing more to him than another daughter; useful for making alliances and babies. That's all he has ever thought of you. We are quickly running out of time to set things back on course. So, I want you to say it. I want you to speak the words so you understand what will happen if you fail. I want to hear it from your lips, so you know there is no way out.'

'If I fail...' Lidan began, then stared into her cooling cup of tea.

'If you fail...?' her mother prompted.

'If I fail, we do things as you see fit. We do them your way. If he hasn't declared me heir by my eighteenth birthday, you may take matters into your own hands.' A ball of rage ignited in Lidan's chest as the words left her, a sickly sour taste remaining in their wake. She bit the back of her lip until it bled and could not lift her eyes away from her cup. She knew what those words meant. She knew what would happen if she failed to change her father's heart and mind. Four years had done nothing to ease the guilt of the deal she had struck.

'Good,' her mother announced. She placed her cup on the table and stood in a whisper of fabric and a whirl of perfume. Her auburn hair gleamed in the candlelight, without a hint of grey at the temples, as though the years had not touched her at all. Instead, Lidan felt them pressing on her shoulders, weighing her down and ageing her before her time. 'I must return to my tasks, child. There is much to arrange before the caravan departs for Daylin. No doubt you have tasks to see to?'

'Of course,' Lidan muttered and clattered her cup onto the tray. The Crone was still working away at her cake, staring vacantly at the middle ground, and Lidan wondered if the old woman had heard a single word that had passed across the table in the preceding few minutes. The dana swept from the room and left Lidan with the Crone, silent save for the sound of the woman chewing. 'I should go...'

Lidan stood to leave, almost unseating the table and its burden as she hurried to escape the stifling confines of the room. Near the doorway, so close to the freedom it offered she could almost touch it, the distinct crackle of magic cut through the air. Lidan had not heard that sound since the old woman had forced her to crawl, bloodied and exhausted, from the punishment of the pit beside the old shack on the Caine. She whipped around and glared at the Crone.

The woman looked at her calmly, then sucked some cake from her remaining teeth. The smell of broken air lingered, like smoke after a fire. A pair of ebony wings fluttered on the work bench behind the Crone and Lidan froze.

She stared, but it did not move again. It remained as still as stone, decaying where it lay, with no outward sign it had moved at all. Gooseflesh raced up her limbs and across her scalp, and her eyes darted to where the Crone sat calmly by the fire pit with her cake.

The Crone gave nothing away. She gazed at Lidan with her cloud-grey eyes then raised her brows. 'Something the matter?'

Had Lidan imagined the flap of black wings in the back room? Had she fabricated the sound of the magic and the tang it left in the air? She clenched her jaw to stop her chin quivering as heat coiled in her muscles, preparing for a fight, then she shook her head.

'Nothing,' Lidan whispered.

She spun away and fell out into the day. Hot morning air washed over her skin, sunlight bathing the common as she hurried across it, focused on containing the storm of emotion writhing inside. She would not show her fear, not her doubt nor her anger. She would not reveal to the world that she was shredded on the inside, coming apart faster than she could stitch herself back together, and suffocating under the weight of questions, unable to demand answers past the strangling hand of terror on her throat.

Chapter Thirteen

The Hidden Keep, Ravinka, Southern Orthia

The keep master pulled on a rope by the door and somewhere a bell rang and sent a messenger running. Ran glared at Brit across the office and wondered if the watcher had gone mad while searching the wilds for him. Or was he simply lying?

'I'm not sure I understand,' said Ran.

Brit opened his hands toward him. 'I have very particular instructions from your mother. When I find you, I'm to take you to the coast, or further if we can manage it.'

'Why would she order you to do that?' Ran frowned. It sounded absurd, but almost absurd enough to be true. Everything about his life was absurd, so why would his mother's plan to save him from his father's Justice be any different. It didn't matter in any case—he couldn't leave the Keep. No one with magic ever left the Keep.

'She wants you safe and alive, even if it means never seeing you again. What do you reckon Ronart would do if he found you here? Or if you showed up in Isord?' Brit's gaze bored into Ran and he shifted uncomfortably under its pressure.

He knew exactly what his father would do. 'He'd march an army down here, if he could spare the troops from the Disputed Territory.'

'And he might yet do it.' Brit looked pointedly at Collan and Quaid. 'I suspect the duke has no idea this place exists. If he did, it would've been the first place his scouts looked.'

'You found it well enough,' Quaid countered, his arms crossed tightly over his chest.

'Aye, well, it took me the better part of three years to track down one of those couriers and even then, this place was a trial to find. But if the duke does come, and he's bound to one day, no stone will be left unturned or a timber left untouched by flame. He'll torch the place himself if it means getting to Ranoth.'

'You're definitely never leaving then.' Quaid's finality didn't seem to register with Brit and the watcher jabbed a finger at him.

'If he finds out *you've* been harbouring his son all these years, this place'll be obliterated. If I take him, if I get him out of here, you might have a chance at arguing for mercy.'

There was a knock at the door and Collan moved to answer it, waving Quaid away. He murmured to the messenger outside, then closed the door, sealing their argument in the room. 'I have sent for meals to be brought up. I fear we have much more ground to cover before we retire for the night.'

'That won't be necessary, Master Greyling,' Ran announced. Ideas and plans were already brewing in his mind, and he needed time and space to sort through them. He couldn't do that listening to Quaid and Brit hit the same points back and forth for hours. 'I'll return to my apartments, if it's all the same to you. The law of the Keep is clear. There's nothing Watcher Doon has to say that will change that. Magic-weavers can't leave, not for any reason, ever. Even if I wanted to go to the coast, it's impossible.'

Collan studied Brit's frustrated sigh down the length of his nose. 'Ranoth is correct, I'm afraid. My remaining dilemma is what to do with you, now you are here.' He turned to Ran and nodded. 'Quaid will walk you to your quarters. I have guards here in the Tower who will assist me should Watcher Doon decide to take his frustrations out on an old man.'

Ran refused to meet Brit's eyes as he left. He couldn't shake the sickening sense of disappointment that the last four years of deception had been stripped away in one sunny afternoon, nor the creeping terror of his father's wrath. Even after all these years, the man's hatred for magic-users appeared undiminished.

'Does Sasha know?' Quaid asked suddenly. Night had fallen outside the Tower, and a breeze swirled in the forecourt.

Ran started at the question. 'Does she know what?'

'Who you are? What you are?' The accusation in Quaid's voice was echoed in the narrowing of his deep brown eyes. He wouldn't look at Ran, and the muscles of his jaw twitched under his skin as he ground his teeth. 'That you're a prince?'

'She does…' Ran admitted. It might have been the only secret Sasha hadn't shared with Quaid in the shadows of her bed chamber, but it was never hers to tell. The sparring master had no right to lay the blame for the lie at her door—that belonged solely to Ran. She had done it to protect him, as had Collan. Ran wondered whose betrayal Quaid felt most keenly of the three. His friend, his lover, or his adoptive father? 'She never met Brit though. He was lost to me long before I met Sasha.'

They scaled the steps to the West Tower and Ran shivered despite the fledgling warmth of spring. Soon enough the summer sun would bake down on Ravinka's valley, but tonight a bitterness remained in the wind, the sharp grip of winter holding tight and slicing into any hope left in Ran's heart.

'Anyone else know?' Quaid waited for Ran to unlock his door, then followed him into the apartment's sitting room.

Ran shook his head. 'No. To everyone else I'm just Ran Harroe, a soldier's son.'

'That was a terrible choice, by the way.'

Ran whipped around, an oscillating orb of magic crackling in his hand. He aimed it at the shadow sitting in an armchair by the fire but paused as the shadow lifted a glass to its unseen lips.

'Harroe? As in King Harroe of Isord? He's your grandfather for goodness sake! As soon as that watcher said the word "duchess", it all made sense.' Eian waved his whiskey at Quaid. 'And I thought *those two* had secrets!'

'How did you get in here?' Ran glanced around as his heartbeat wound down from utterly terrified to mildly unsettled and he extinguished the building energy in his hand. He stripped off his tunic and shirt and tossed them in a laundry hamper inside the bedroom door. He hadn't had a chance to change after training the students that afternoon, or to visit the bathhouse as he'd intended. He stank and he hoped a good waft of his odour might expel Eian, Quaid, and their pointed questions from his room.

Eian waggled a finger at Ran and took a sip of his drink. 'A gentleman does not kiss and tell, mister whatever-your-name-is.'

Ran ignored the jibe and dropped into a chair by the table.

'What are we to call you now?' Quaid asked, finding a place for himself among the cushions of the sofa. Iridia slipped from the shadows by the window and levelled her gaze at Ran, almost as if the others didn't exist.

Ran shrugged, pulled off his boots and dumped them on the floor. 'You can call me Ran. It was my name at home. I've got about fifteen middle names and titles you don't need to know.'

He poured himself and Quaid a drink, handed the glass to the sparring master, then sank back into his seat. All this time, all this effort, and it was all undone. Everything unravelling like a torn flag in a storm. Would it keep coming apart at the seams until he was naught but a thread in the wind, abandoned and exposed?

'The watcher said they called you the Black Prince,' Quaid said, then swallowed the contents of his glass in two swift gulps. He held the empty vessel out for more and Ran obliged.

'That was a long time ago. And it's stupid. Forget it.'

'It's poetic,' Eian mused, staring at the fire. How long had he been in here, drinking Ran's whiskey and wallowing in his own misery? Ran angled the decanter toward the light and saw it was half empty. Eian had a good head start on them. 'But you're right—it is stupid.'

Ran rolled his eyes and Quaid stifled a laugh. From the corner of Ran's eye, he saw Iridia smile.

'Look, Eian, I'm sorry,' Ran began, then stopped himself. 'No, actually, I'm not sorry. This whole thing—coming to the Keep and hiding who I am—I had to do it to protect myself, the Keep, and everyone in it. What if one of the riders from beyond the walls discovered me? There was a reward for my capture, last I heard. What if word got out somehow and my father brought his army down on us? Can you imagine what would have happened?'

'You stayed though, even when you knew it was dangerous.' The pain and betrayal in Eian's eyes shocked Ran, and he realised Eian felt exactly as he had when he discovered Sasha's heart belonged elsewhere. Eian was one of his closest friends, and the entirety of that friendship was based on a lie.

'I did,' Ran conceded. 'I couldn't leave. I had nowhere else to go.'

'Unless you wanted to end up dead,' Quaid put in.

'Well, yes,' Ran agreed, unable to fault that assessment, brutal as it was. But was that true now? 'Look, the point is, I did the best I could with a shitty situation and if I had any other option, I would've dropped Sasha here and kept going. But she was nearly dead, I was exhausted, we had those things chasing us, and nowhere else to go.'

He looked across the room at his friends; a man he relied on for support and good humour when he felt the world sucking him down into an abyss, and a man who had more than once saved him from himself through hard work and unwavering commitment. 'I *am* sorry for deceiving you both, but it was the only choice I had.'

Eian eyed him, but Quaid nodded.

'I fear I understand, more than you might surmise, Ran. None of us belong here, but it's the only place we have.' He reached out a hand and Ran took it. 'I will not hold the past against you, if you would do the same for me?'

He knew what Quaid was asking, what he wanted him to do. If Ran would forgive Quaid's deception, then Quaid would forgive his. But it meant more than simple forgiveness—it meant letting Sasha go. Ran suppressed a smile at that. Sasha was her own woman with her own mind and would go where and with whom she pleased. She had proven that when she abandoned her parents to lead him through the wilderness. She was no more his to give than she was Quaid's to take. All Ran had to let go of was an idea; a silly, foolish, childish idea. He gave Quaid a nod and squeezed the other man's hand.

Across the room Eian frowned at the ceiling. 'What did Collan call those things that hunted you? Dravors?'

'Dradur,' Ran corrected and shuddered. 'It's an Altipan word—means "dead walkers".'

A silence fell between them then, but Ran couldn't let the subject rest. 'Am I forgiven, Eian? Or are you going to spend the next two moons sulking and drinking yourself stupid?'

Eian eyed him again, then held out his cup. 'Get me a refill and I'll think about it.'

That was the closest he would get to acceptance from Eian. He knew that and wondered how Zarad would react when Eian delivered the news.

He took the cup from his friend and poured the required refill. It was not a perfect peace, but it was an understanding. For now, that would do. Tomorrow he had to deal with the reality of Brit Doon and the lengths Collan Greyling would go to protect the Keep and the folk it sheltered.

Quaid eventually levered Eian out of the chair by the fire and helped him through the door, leaving Ran alone with his thoughts and his ghost. He went to his bedroom, intent on readying for sleep, but found he made it no further than the end of the bed. For a while he sat there, leaning on a polished timber post, staring at the dwindling flames in the hearth as silence settled in the room. He hardly knew where to start.

'Quite a day,' he said finally, and Iridia nodded.

He closed his eyes and rubbed the bridge of his nose. The warmth of the fire and the liquor held him in an embrace he wished he could remain in forever, but a draught of cool air shifted across his exposed skin and he looked up.

Iridia stood between him and the fire, more opaque than he had ever seen her.

'What is it? How... how are you doing that?'

Magic rolled off her like heat from a forge, and her chest rose and fell as if she drew breath for the first time in almost two decades.

She pinned him with her gaze. 'What we saw out there today—do you know what it means?'

Unable to move, he swallowed a choking tightness in his throat. The fire behind her began to disappear, her shift and the body beneath it becoming solid. 'No, I don't, not yet. What are you doing? How are you doing this?'

'I need you to understand. I need you to see.'

'See what? I *don't* understand!' He lurched to his feet and grabbed at her shoulders. His hands found something not quite solid, but not entirely of the vapour she had been for the past four years. She winced, dragging in a ragged breath.

'I need you to see... I need you to see *me*. What I was. I need you to understand.' She sucked a breath through her teeth as if the effort of forcing herself to solidify was agonising.

'I do, I see you!' Ran pressed his hands against her, as if to emphasise his point, and suddenly her hands were on his face. Ice cold, solid as stone yet yielding as flesh.

'Those trails. Every magic-weaver ever living has made one. Every magic-weaver, including those who *murdered* me.' Her hard, frigid hands held him like an eagle clutches its prey, and he finally understood. 'They did this to you, to me, to us! They made us what we are, took everything we had and burned it to ash. I want justice, Ranoth. I want revenge, in kind, and now the way has revealed itself. Follow the light, Ranoth.'

Her hands shook and the space between their bodies diminished until there was nothing between them but the thin cloth of her shift. Bodies moulded together, fire in her eyes and ice in her hands, she held Ran and made him see, forced her will upon him, pressed down on his mind and against his body until nothing else mattered, nothing else existed.

Revenge.
Justice.
Follow the light.

Chapter Fourteen

The Hidden Keep, Ravinka, Southern Orthia

Ran kept to himself the following morning while rumours swept through the Keep—whispers of the brawl in the corridor, speculation of Ran's connection to the newcomer, and conjecture about what Collan would do about the mysterious man on the horse. Ran made a show of going about his day as he normally would, but there was only so much hushed conversation and poorly disguised pointing he could ignore.

The Keep was in such a spin that when he slipped into the dining hall for the midday meal, he almost choked on his own tongue to see Brit sitting beside Collan at the highest table.

He frowned and reached for a bowl, ladled soup out of a pot on a side table, then took a seat in a quiet corner. He watched Brit and Collan, remembering his days watching tap-rooms in far-flung inns as he fled for his life. It had been a long time since he'd felt the need to guard his back with the solid presence of a stone wall.

He'd never feared the people of the Keep before today, but their lingering eyes and whispered conversations put him in mind of a pack of alley dogs—placid enough when safe and secure in their territory, but vicious and deadly when cornered or threatened. What might the folk of the Keep do to him, and to Brit, if they thought for a moment their presence put them at risk?

Ran suspected Collan's open display of trust with Brit was a strategic move toward avoiding any such violence; a signal that Brit had been accepted and was to be honoured as a guest. It might go some way to quelling the anxious speculation swirling through the Keep. Locking Brit up somewhere in a tower would only fan the flames of fear. If Collan allowed Brit to move freely, that meant he was to be trusted.

Ran watched the two of them and the gathered Keep folk as he scooped out the last of his soup, wondering as he did when he might have an opportunity to speak with Brit alone without the watchful gaze of so many suspicious eyes.

Iridia's words from the previous night chewed a hole in the back of his mind. He *had* remained in one place too long, despite all his reasons and excuses. He'd never intended to simply accept the fate forced on him by the arrival of his magic, and he'd never truly given up on the idea of one day returning home to regain what he'd lost. Remaining at the Keep had been a necessary evil, something he'd fallen into through circumstance and a lack of a better option. But Iridia's return had ripped the bandage off a wound in his heart that had never fully healed.

The Walled Forest was still off limits to the Keep folk, and would afford him some privacy with Brit, even if only for a short time. As he dropped his empty bowl in a dish bucket, he wondered if he and Brit could get out there under the guise of a tour of the grounds.

Collan stood and motioned for Brit to follow, moving to leave the dining hall as Ran approached.

'Keep Master,' Ran called over the hubbub of conversation echoing against the stone and timber of the hall, feigning nervousness as if he'd never met Brit before in his life. 'I wondered, as I have no classes to supervise this afternoon, if I might offer my services to your guest?'

Collan let his momentary confusion slip into an easy smile. 'Of course, Master Harroe! What did you have in mind?'

Ran had to give credit where it was due—Collan wasn't about to let Ran and Brit wander off together without knowing their plans.

'I thought a tour of the grounds, perhaps through the forest? The lake is quite nice in the afternoon, and there are still some blossoms in the orchard.'

'I've no objection,' Brit put in, doing his best to suppress a smile at the mention of picturesque lakes and blossoming orchards. 'Could do with a walk to get these knots out of my back.'

'Very well,' Collan agreed, and his smile fell away. They probably wouldn't be alone for long, but Collan would allow them this. It might be their only chance to talk privately, and Ran planned to use every second.

He held his hand out to the newcomer, playing ignorant. 'Ran Harroe, Tracking Master, at your service.'

'Brit Doon.' Brit smiled broadly, gave Ran's hand a good shake, then slapped him on the back. He clearly hadn't lost his love of that particular gesture.

Ran led his old friend from the dining hall and into the afternoon sunlight, turning south past the gardens and the stable, making sure to point out every building and sub-structure in sight. He'd never played the part of a tour guide before, but he would make damn sure it was a convincing show for anyone watching.

'Tracking Master?' Brit glanced around as they passed the infirmary. 'What are you masterfully tracking in this prison?'

'Oh, you'd be surprised.' Ran lifted a hand and gave a casual wave to Sasha, who was waiting for the last of her students to arrive at top of the infirmary steps. He lengthened his stride; Sasha had too many questions in her eyes and Collan would expect them back before long.

'How long do we keep pretending not to know each other?' asked Brit as they left the common areas of the Keep and strolled down the path to the Walled Forest. Ran relaxed his magic and let his Sight open up. The thaumalux trails were exactly as he'd left them—strong and pulsing like blood through a vein.

'You can't admit you know me. Folk will lose their minds,' Ran replied. 'Admitting you know me implies you tracked me here, and the only thing keeping these people sane is the idea that they're safe and hidden from the outside world. If they thought for a minute they could be found, or that the couriers of the arrivals had been compromised, their world would collapse.'

'I see.' Brit left the topic and hurried to keep up. He had aged, as had Ran, but the years showed in the stark, hard lines of Brit's features. His face was creased at the edges of his mouth and eyes, and his skin weathered from years spent on the road. Time had been much kinder to Ran. Perhaps he *had* been tucked up and cosy in the Keep while the world went on without him.

They followed the path past the first clearing and along a slight ridge. They would come to the ponds eventually, and then the falls. Ran hoped the distance and the sound of the water would be enough to obscure their words from anyone following.

Iridia was there, just out of sight, matching them through the trees with no effort whatsoever, her form immaterial and transparent once more. He could still feel her hands on his face and the press of her body against his. The memory left him gasping, like a punch to the gut, and he rolled his shoulders to shake it off.

It took an hour of hiking to reach the place where the stream spread into a series of pools, then plunged into a steep gully before meandering away again to the south.

'I'm going out on a limb here,' Brit grunted as Ran led him down a series of stone steps to the base of the falls. 'But I suspect you didn't bring me out here to see the sights?'

'You'd be correct in that assumption.' Ran let his magic spool out completely, checking the forest for trails nearby, but sensed nothing he thought was recent. The trail from his experiment with Quaid had turned back to the Keep some time ago. Ran felt comfortable no one, at least not anyone with magic, had been to this part of the forest for quite a while.

'Well?' Brit slumped onto a boulder by the edge of the water, just beyond the reach of the waterfall's misting cloud.

Ran turned from scanning the trees. 'Can you get me out of here?'

'What?' Brit almost choked on the word.

'Can *you*, get *me*, out of *here*?' Ran said it slowly, pointing at Brit, then at himself, then into the forest.

The watcher frowned. 'I'd planned to, but after last night's little performance I thought you might prefer to stay.'

Ran sighed and put his hands on his hips. 'It's not about preferring to stay or not. No one can just choose to leave. If you have magic, you're stuck here. Those guards on the gate? They aren't keeping things out so much as they are keeping us in. I can't just up and leave. As far as they're concerned, I'm here until I'm dead.'

Brit crossed his arms and chewed on the back of his lip, eyeing Ran. 'What's wrong with your eyes?'

'My eyes?'

'They didn't used to look like that.'

'It's a thing,' Ran said with a wave of his hand, and tried to find words Brit would understand. 'It's a magic thing. I have Sight. I can see magic in the air, like a game trail, except it's invisible to most people. That's the tracking I do. Tracking magic that even most magic-weavers can't see. It's getting stronger though, and now I can see trails that are old—*years* old— when we thought they faded within a day or so. I think magic-users leave a permanent trail, but only someone with very strong Sight can pick up the thread.'

'If I get you out of here, you aren't planning on going to go to the coast, are you?' Brit's questions were like punches in a boxing match. Just as Ran thought he'd recovered from one, another came from the side and slammed him in the jaw.

'What makes you think that?'

The watcher might not have a speck of magic in him, but Brit Doon knew how to read people. 'I've seen that face before. You've got an idea in your head and it's got nothing to do with making a break for the coast and a relaxing sea-side life in the Archipelago. *I'd* go for the sea-side life, but you? No, you've got something brewing in there, something to do with this Sight thing.'

Ran sighed. 'Are you going to help me, or not?'

'I can't tell you that 'til I know your plan.'

Fair enough, Iridia muttered and Ran bit down on a smile. He glanced at where she crouched by the water and eased away from the desperate sense of urgency she pressed against his will.

He settled on a log that had fallen near Brit's boulder and spent the remainder of the afternoon explaining his plan, as basic and infantile as it was, watching the changing expressions on Brit's face. At first, when Ran told him he had found a way to prove that his magic, that all magic, was useful, Brit frowned. Ran understood that—Brit came from a place where magic was an evil thing, and Ran didn't expect him to take to the idea easily.

He found himself explaining the dradur, and how he and Sasha were hunted by them. He explained what they were, and where they had come from, how they had been made, and by whom. He did not mention Iridia, keeping to himself that the vision they had seen in the house at Lackmah had travelled with him ever since.

When he began to reveal the mechanics of how he might use all of this to change his father's mind about magic, Brit's eyebrows rose so high Ran thought they might disappear under his unruly hair forever.

'You can't be serious.' At the end of it, that was all Brit could come up with.

'I am. Deadly serious.'

'You want to follow some magic dust left behind by witches who murdered a whole village, to fuck-knows-where, in the hope you'll find them at the end of it?' Brit shook his head and for a moment Ran thought the watcher might actually vomit. Brit stood and began pacing, scratching absently at the stubble on his chin as if it might help him think.

When he says it like that... Iridia was sitting at Ran's feet, unseen and unheard by Brit.

'It's not magic *dust*—it's a thaumalux trail,' Ran corrected. 'And if I can pick up the trail of the people who committed those murders and created the dradur, then I can bring them back to Usmein and the Justice they deserve.'

There it was. The entirety of his thoughts and Iridia's demands, laid bare in the fading afternoon light. If he looked at them from any other angle, they were complete madness, but straight on, there was a slim chance he could make it work.

'And you'll do all this, hoping to catch your father in a good mood when you return? Hoping he doesn't execute you with the witches you risked your life to bring back?'

Ran glanced at Iridia, who was staring up at him. Could she see the doubt in his eyes? His fear erasing the need she had shared with him? He wanted this as badly as she, but was the risk worth the reward?

'Ranoth,' Brit pleaded. 'Have you forgotten the man your father was? He hasn't changed; not one bit. If anything, he's angrier and more bitter than he ever was.'

'I'm sure if I can just get him to listen—'

'He's burning them, Ran.'

Ran looked up, perplexed. 'Burning who?'

'Magic-users! Once upon a time they just cut the heads off the few derramentis mages who popped up across the countryside, but now he's hunting them, slaughtering them, burning them in village squares, decapitating

103

the corpses! Whole families are interrogated if one among them is found to possess even the slightest power.' Brit's hands grasped at the air as if searching for a way to make Ran see the futility of his plan.

Ran's stomach lurched and he stared at the watcher in disbelief. Surely Brit was wrong. Surely, the man was exaggerating.

'How long has it been since a child arrived here?' Brit asked, catching Ran off guard.

His mouth ran dry as he opened it to answer. 'A year, maybe longer?'

'You know why that is?' Brit pressed, wild anger in his eyes. When Ran shook his head, Brit leaned close enough to whisper. 'He's killing them too. Men, women, wee ones—the lot. People in my village, members of *my* family have been taken…'

A shiver rushed across Ran's skin. 'Baylah?'

Brit shifted his feet, scraping the toe of his boot through the dirt. 'No, not Baylah.'

'She's well, then? She's safe?'

'As far as I know,' Brit murmured, looking away into the trees. 'I've not seen her since she was small. I trust she *is* safe, but I have no idea. Last I heard, she was with my parents in Revel. They're more parents to her than I ever was. I hardly went back after her mother…' The words caught, hard and thick. 'The duchess said she'd see they were cared for, and I trust her word.'

'Who then?' Ran asked softly, almost afraid to know; as if knowing made it real, made his father's actions indisputable.

'My sister's family. Her boys…'

Ran's stomach twisted, a mirror of the anguish on Brit's face. 'How did you… find out?'

'They post lists. In each village square. A roll call of the cursed…' Brit cleared his throat and met Ran's gaze. 'Your father was always a single-minded man. That much was clear from the body count in the Territory, but what happened to you broke something in him. You would do well to remember *that* man, not the father you think he might be underneath all that noise and cruelty. Why do you think your mother wants you as far away from him as possible? Mark my words, Ran; he'll not play this game you're imagining.'

'I have to do something, Brit.' Ran set his jaw and met the watcher's gaze, dousing the hot wave of horror rolling through him. If Brit had thought to use that harrowing tale to frighten Ran into running, he'd wasted his breath. 'I can't stay here. Have you seen this place? I can't even walk out of my room without a veil of magic over my Sight. It's excruciating!'

He stood abruptly and stabbed a finger in the direction of the Keep. 'And my people, people like me, should not have to live like this—huddled in the mountains, caged like animals. If there is even the *slightest* chance I can change his mind, to make things better for people like me, then I have to try. Even more so if what you say is true. At least help me get out. Then go off to the coast, or back to Usmein or Revel. Go back to your daughter, or wherever you want but get me out of here before you do.'

A shriek echoed faintly through the gully and Ran froze. It came from the north, from the apex of the valley where the Keep stood at the foot of a mountain as the sun set in the west.

'What was that?' asked Brit, stepping back and scanning the forest.

Ran knew that scream.

Iridia vanished.

'We have to go,' Ran managed to squeeze out of his tightening throat.

'Go where?'

Ran was already running, climbing the stone steps beside the falls and hurrying back to the pools at the top of the ridge. He knew that scream. It had been four years—four boring, painful, empty years—but the memory of *that* scream had never faded.

'What is it, Ran!?' Brit sprinted behind him, bellowing questions, but suddenly Ran's tongue was too big for his mouth and the words wouldn't come.

Would he make it back in time? Would there be anything he could do, or would it be too late?

A hand caught his shoulder and wrenched him to a stop.

'What *is* it?' Brit demanded.

'Dradur.' Ran swallowed the choking terror. 'At the Keep. It's the dradur. They've come back.'

He saw the glow of flames through the trees before they reached the edge of the Walled Forest; thick, acrid smoke billowing into the twilight. They hurried into the Keep's open common area and Ran knew immediately that he was too late.

From the chaos and dancing flames, a figure charged. A grisly maw spread wide and full of broken teeth. A blade scythed toward Ran's head. He ducked as the edge whistled past his ear, and his magic flared in his hands.

A shot of blue light arced forward and he fell to one knee, slamming his fist into the abdomen of the roaring dradur. He drove the power through the centre of the creature like a white-hot knife then jerked his fist sideways, slicing the dradur in half at the waist.

The halves of the corpse fell away and Ran staggered to his feet, blinking as the world around him tilted and spun. Brit grabbed him from behind and hurried him forward, over the smoking ruin of the dradur and into the forecourt.

'There!' someone cried, and magic cracked the air like lightning. Ran turned to follow the sound and saw a black figure scuttle across the face of the North Tower.

Magic boomed again and his ears screamed as a concussion wave slammed into his chest. Pitched backward, he crashed to the ground, vaguely aware of Brit flailing behind him. Everything was wreathed in flame and smoke, screams echoing up the walls of the towers and into the approaching night.

Ran crawled back to his feet, gasping for air and squinting through the smoke. Across the court, Eian and Zarad raced away from the North Tower stairs mere seconds before the building exploded into a soaring ball of flame. The force of it shoved them in the back and sent them sprawling across the cobbles. Ran and Brit staggered forward and dragged them clear of the greedy flames engulfing the tower.

Somewhere nearby Quaid howled orders and Ran saw a cluster of people hauling lake water toward the flames with their magic, while others pressed their power against the flames in an attempt to suffocate them. From the corner of his eye Ran saw a flicker of disjointed movement and someone started screaming. He whipped around to see a dradur slither out of the gatehouse and into the courtyard.

He found his feet and ran toward it at a limping jog, pooling his remaining magic into his hand and drawing his only weapon, a small belt knife, from its sheath.

'Hey!' he shouted over the pandemonium in the courtyard. The dradur turned and eyed him, crunching something bloody in its mouth.

It was a seriously malformed creature, with a mace for an arm and a protruding lower jaw that reminded Ran of a fighting dog. Its teeth had been replaced by rows of jagged little blades that glistened with a dark slick of blood in the dancing light of the flames. It swallowed whatever it was chewing and took a single hulking step forward. Ran pushed down on his fear, ignoring the shiver of fatigued muscles in his legs and the way his knife shook in his fist.

'Come on,' he whispered.

He reached for his magic and found it fading, weakened and depleted by the effort of shielding his eyes and carving up the first dradur. He reckoned he had one shot left, a single chance to take the thing out before it turned the considerable weight of the mace to pulverising him. He willed his magic to spool out into a thread, rather than an orb, and it snaked down like a rope from his hand.

Now or never... 'Come on!' he roared.

The dradur bellowed and charged across the space between them, hefting the mace. Ran took a few quick steps and backhanded the energy rope across the creature's face. It connected with the foul, rotting flesh and tore off the jutting lower jaw.

The skin and outer muscle of the neck peeled away, leaving the inner workings exposed to the smoky air. Ran buried his knife in the creature's neck, driving it in hard until the blade punched through a space between the bones of its spine.

It gave an almighty jolt, then shuddered. Its weight shifted, and Ran ripped the knife out through the side of its neck, severing the pulsing vein of magic hidden between the bones.

Chapter Fifteen

The Hidden Keep, Ravinka, Southern Orthia

Ran slipped in the slick of dark blue slime leaking from the crumpled body of the dradur, then stumbled and turned, his knife falling from his fingers to clatter on the stones. The forecourt was complete mayhem; people racing back and forth, animals bellowing over the screams and cries of terrified children.

Sasha stood in the middle of it all, shouting orders at the able-bodied to move the injured away from the burning buildings. Ran heard Brit cursing and his throat tightened as he limped toward the cluster of injured. Many lay directly on the cobbles without so much as a blanket to shield them from the cold, nursing burns to their faces and arms, covered in soot and ash. A good number were marked by savage bites and bloody gaping wounds that the small infirmary staff and a handful of older students desperately tried to sew back together in the light of the flames.

The North Tower groaned ominously and the water bearers backed away, no longer able to confront the inferno. On the third and fourth floors of the West Tower, folk hurried to dismantle the timber bridges joining the teaching block to the accommodation tower, lest the fire crawl across the spans and take hold on the other side. As Ran watched, the lowest of the bridges collapsed in an explosion of splinters.

He found Quaid staring at the destruction, and the older man flinched when Ran touched his arm. 'What happened?' he asked, breathless and shivering.

'Monsters. Those creatures—the dradur.'

Ran rubbed his stinging eyes and blinked through the smoke. 'But how? How'd they get in?'

'No idea.' Quaid shook his head as a group hurried past leading horses and livestock away from the stables. 'There was magic going off everywhere. So much energy. Then the fires started...'

'How? Dradur can't control fire.'

'Degan,' a faint voice croaked from behind him.

Ran turned and searched the injured, cold shock tightening his chest when his gaze fell on Collan, lying on a ground with a bloody mess of a wound from his shoulder to his hip. Sasha knelt beside Collan now, her hands pressed against the blood pumping from the monstrous gash. Her brother Nicot sat nearby, his hands and forearms coated with blood, staring at Collan, his features pale and drawn. He'd been trying to stop the keep master from bleeding to death before Sasha had taken over.

Something in the grim line of her lips and the strain in her shoulders told Ran she was losing that battle, Collan's magic unable to keep pace with the loss. There weren't many ways to kill a magic-user aside from severing their spine, but old age and draining the body of blood would do it every time. One of Collan's hands was wrapped completely in bandages, and the air around the keep master stank of charred flesh.

Ran dropped to his knees and Collan reached out, his long fingers trembling as they closed around Ran's hand. 'The fire began with Degan.'

'I don't understand,' Ran shook his head. 'Why would Degan start a fire?'

'No... the children were afraid. Degan was afraid. The dradur... I saw them this time. Saw their eyes. They are searching...' Collan coughed and a wad of bright blood splattered on his lips.

Ran tried to make sense of Collan's words amidst the screaming and crying. 'The creatures frightened the children, and they started the fires in their fear?'

The keep master nodded, and behind Ran, Quaid swore.

A moment later, the huge timber support beams in the North Tower gave in. The structure collapsed with a deafening boom and a wave of heat and ash swept across the forecourt. The Keep folk huddled beside the wounded and watched the tower consume itself; bright, hungry flame soaring into the night.

'Sash?' Ran whispered into the firestorm. He suddenly realised why Eian and Zarad had been inside the tower—he could only see the faces of half the Keep's children gathered in the court. 'How many...'

'I… we don't know yet…' Her voice was small and brittle against the roar of the flames. 'The young ones had evening meditation.'

Grief flared across her features. In the light of the fire, her red hair seemed to glow with fury.

'Where is…?' His question died as he glanced around. Amitty, Vespan and a slew of others were nowhere to be seen. Those remaining stared at the burning tower, tears streaking through soot and char from blood-shot eyes. 'Degan did all of this, because he was *frightened?*'

'Not just Degan,' Collan croaked and blood spilled from his mouth. 'He started it, but… there were many young ones in our midst.' The keep master's uninjured hand gripped the front of Ran's shirt and pulled him in close. 'Don't—'

The word ended in an exhaled breath, and Collan's hand fell away.

The flames were all Ran heard as Sasha placed shaking fingertips on Collan's throat. Her lips trembled as she let go and pressed the back of her bloody hand against her forehead.

Ran stood and stumbled, leaving Collan on the cobbles of the forecourt. *Collan… Collan's dead…*

A fissure cracked open in Ran as he turned away from the keep master's body. He searched the forecourt for something, anything… Anything to distract him from the chasm ripping his heart apart, but all he found was devastation.

He glanced at Quaid, and immediately wished he hadn't. Despair creased the man's brow and his face tightened, a flood of emotion threatening to break him. Sasha stood and rested her head on the tall man's shoulder, her blood-soaked hand slipping into his.

A wave of sorrowful whispers rose like a tide as the news of Collan's death spread through the diminished crowd and Quaid's gaze levelled at Brit.

'You. Those things followed you! *You* brought them here!'

Quaid lunged at Brit and Ran threw himself in front of the watcher. He had no idea what he would have done if Sasha hadn't spread her hands across Quaid's chest and stopped him with a word. Fury flared in Quaid's eyes and he glared at Brit until the fuel of his anger burned out. His face crumpled, then his legs gave way. He went to the ground in Sasha's arms and sobbed.

Ran turned away, his heart pounding, and raked his hands through his hair. 'Fuck,' he whispered, and tried to set his thoughts straight amidst the noise and the grief.

'Can you see them?' Brit asked quietly at Ran's shoulder. 'The trails of the things that came here?'

Ran glanced at him, waiting for the meaning of the words to come. 'The thaumalux trails of the dradur?'

'Can you see them?' he repeated. 'They were made by magic, so shouldn't they leave one of those trails you can see? What if there's more? What if they come back? These folk are in no condition to take another beating. We need to find where they got in and make sure none of them got away.'

Years of suppressed military training lurched to life in his mind and Ran scanned the battered Keep folk and the blackened walls. Brit was right—they couldn't weather another attack, and he had no idea if more of the creatures were lurking outside the walls or within. Ran took off.

Brit followed behind, and among the wounded and the dead, they found Zarad and Eian sitting together as one of the infirmary staff bandaged Zarad's hand. Of the three Hale siblings, Zarad was the tallest, with the same rambunctious red hair and green-hazel eyes as his sister. Eian watched his lover with wide, worried eyes until Zarad gave him a small smile and murmured something Ran could not decipher.

Ran squeezed Zarad's shoulder as he crouched beside Eian. 'Any chance you're up for tracking?'

He'd never seen Eian so visibly shaken, and the sight of his ashen face and shaking hand on Zarad's leg turned Ran's stomach. He swallowed his shock, crushing down doubt and horror at the unseen wounds his friend must now be carrying, and waited. Eian glanced at Zarad, then nodded, and Ran helped him to his feet.

'What's on your mind?' asked Eian, his voice diminished and lacking all its usual swagger.

'Years ago, Collan told me those creatures were created by magic, so it stands to reason they might leave a thaumalux trail. If we can sift out their trails, we can hunt down any that escaped. We can split the grounds between us and see what we find.'

Eian nodded, pointing to the space between the two largest towers,

III

one consumed by unrelenting flame, the other standing silent in the night.

'They came over the wall near the kitchen garden.' He cleared his throat, hacking a deep, chesty cough after inhaling so much smoke. 'We were in the sparring hall when we first heard the shouting. At least one of the things went into the North Tower, but the others scattered across the Keep like birds caught indoors. The place went mad.'

'Any idea how many?' Ran pressed.

Eian shook his head. 'No.'

'Right,' Ran said, trying to take a breath though the air was thick with choking smoke and ash. 'See what you can find here in the forecourt. I'll head over to the kitchen.'

Eian nodded and Ran hurried to the gardens. He dropped his walls and let his Sight open. He was dangerously weak, his power barely holding as he searched the hundreds of thaumalux trails pulsing across the forecourt. For a moment it was all white light, an unreadable mess that made no sense. Then a smudge appeared across the trails of the Keep folk, a ribbon of blue-black rippling with the colour of the night sky. Five such trails swirled across the forecourt, one veering off and disappearing amongst the flames where the North Tower had been.

He looked over his shoulder at Eian. 'Can you see that black trail, the colour of midnight?'

'Barely. It's faint to my eyes,' he called back.

Ran turned slowly toward the gate. There he saw a trail disappear inside the gatehouse and emerge to terminate beside the corpse of the mace-wielding dradur he'd taken out with the rope of energy. The remaining three trails wavered and darted around the forecourt, bouncing like wild cats from one side of the Keep to the other as if running from something and unable to find an exit. Ran chose one and followed it, moving toward the orchards.

'Eian?' Ran called.

'There are only these three,' he confirmed. 'They fade, then reappear. It's like trying to catch sand.'

Ran nodded and continued past the wounded, Eian falling in beside him as they came to the corpse of the dradur Ran had ripped in half. The final two trails fled into the gardens. 'Three are dead, and two have gone.'

'Who the fuck did *that*?' Eian stared at the remains.

'Me,' said Ran. He stepped between the top and bottom halves and into the rows of apple and plum trees, ignoring Eian as he stood gaping for a moment before hurrying to follow. They mirrored the thaumalux to the edge of the lake, then along the shore, until finally, the trails scaled the wall of the Keep and vanished over the top.

Ran touched the cold stone. 'South…'

South… Iridia's voice echoed from between the orchard's trees.

'Pardon?' Eian asked.

'Collan told me once that the dradur are always heading south. Tonight he said they were searching for something…' He had thought it the disorientated babble of a dying man until he saw the trails. The way they darted around, unfocused and wild. Collan's words from years before echoed in his ears. 'Always moving south…'

Eian played his fingers through the thaumalux where it arched up and leapt over the wall several feet above his head. 'What about the dradur who attacked you and Sasha, the year you arrived? Where were they going?'

'South,' replied Ran. 'Every dradur I've ever encountered was moving south.'

Eian looked back at the glow of the fires against the churning smoke. 'Well they're not moving like that for no reason. No creature ever does. There's always a reason, even if they don't know it.'

Ran met Iridia's eyes through the trees. 'They seek their makers.'

The days following the attack dawned bright with spring sunlight, as if the world hadn't noticed the smoking ruin of the North Tower or the folk digging graves while wrapped bodies bobbed in the cool shallows of the lake. Ran watched the work crews from Yidda's window with a very full glass of her favourite brandy in his hand. His fingers were blistered and etched with cuts, testament to the hours he'd spent clearing land in the cemetery. He'd tried to use magic for the heaviest of the lifting, but he had nothing left. He was exhausted, as were all the magic-weavers in the Keep.

The remaining masters and mistresses sat behind him, arranged around Yidda's sitting room, cradling their own glasses in various states of sobriety. Thankfully Eian wasn't among them, or there'd be no brandy left for anyone else to dampen their sorrows. Sasha stared into her drink as though it might begin answering the questions she seemed to be pouring into it, while Quaid eyed the bottle on the little table beside Yidda's chair.

In the silence, Amos leaned over and asked Katia, the kitchens mistress, if there was something in the cold room that might line their stomachs before the brandy went to their heads, and they and a handful of others left to see what was to be had.

Ran had expected opposition to his plan. He had expected vehement opposition actually, but he hadn't received it. Yidda, newly appointed as keep mistress, had nodded as he told her what he wanted to do, and presented her with a reasonable motive that didn't include "a ghost told me it was a good idea". As far as Yidda was concerned, Ran intended to pursue the dradur and eliminate them, ostensibly to ensure they didn't double back and attack the Keep again.

'Eian and Zarad have volunteered to help me track the dradur.' Ran turned from the window and continued his proposal. 'The watcher, Brit Doon, will also travel with us. He's got no reason to remain here and we need him for hunting and navigating. That's four, including me.'

Yidda gave a resigned sigh. 'I think this is terribly foolish, but I can't deny a certain understanding of what you're feeling. I may not see thaumalux anymore, but I remember. I remember how the light calls you. I still remember the first time I saw it as a child, and I knew I couldn't remain among ordinary folk. I've not seen these dradur trails, my Sight is too weak, but I *know*, Ran. I know what is in your heart. There's also the none-too-small matter of revenge for what was taken from us. That's a score I would very much like to see settled.'

Sasha's head jerked up and she glowered at Yidda. 'You aren't actually going to let him do this, are you?'

The keep mistress regarded the younger woman and gave her a sad smile. 'Sasha, please know that I say this with all the love I have for you, but you cannot possibly understand how magic can drive a person. Unless you've felt it, you cannot hope to comprehend it.'

'Perhaps you're right. What I can *comprehend* is that you're sending three magic-weavers, one of whom is my brother, into a world that despises them. What benefit can this Keep possibly derive from such recklessness?'

'I'm not sending anyone anywhere. Ran's companions, including Zarad, have volunteered.' Yidda opened her hand toward the window. 'I'm sure they're aware of the dangers that lurk beyond these walls, but if recent days have proven anything, it's that we're not immune to such threats. Do not presume that I am unaware of what I am agreeing to. I simply hope they are able to succeed and return here when their task is complete.'

Sasha slammed her glass onto the table and surged to her feet. 'This makes no se—'

'Keep Mistress,' Ran cut across Sasha's rage and bore the glare his friend levelled at him like a punch to the face. 'May I speak with Mistress Hale alone?'

Yidda nodded wearily. 'Of course. I'll take Master Greyling to the kitchens. Perhaps the others have found something for us to eat.' She took Quaid by the arm and gently led him from the room.

'I don't see why you have to take the boys with you,' Sasha snarled into the silence left behind.

'Zarad isn't a boy and Nicot is staying here, where he's safe,' Ran replied in a low voice, unwilling to match her anger. 'And if Zarad wants to stay, or if Eian wants to stay, they can. I'm not forcing anyone to come with me.'

'As if either of them would choose to stay! They're loyal to a fault and gods-know why. It'll just get them both killed.'

'Four of us against two dradur? I think we're in with a good chance of winning that battle,' Ran countered, trying to keep the bitterness out of his voice and failing.

'And what if you get *caught?*' Sasha hissed, bright spots of colour in her cheeks and anger flaring in her eyes. 'What happens if Ronart's soldiers find you and figure out who you are, *what* you are? You'll be dragged back to Usmein and have your heads sliced off in the market square! And for what? Revenge? Glory?'

'For revenge, yes. For the lives the dradur have taken, here and out in the world. For Amitty and Vespan and Collan.' Ran swallowed and lifted his chin. 'For the Parry family. For you and me, and what we suffered. For all those people who were made into those *things!* This has to *end*, Sasha.'

'How does this end anything?' Fury shook her voice and her white-knuckled fists. 'Killing two dradur won't stop others coming for us.'

'Killing their makers might.' The truth spilled from him before he realised what he'd said, but he squared his shoulders against Sasha's response.

She glared at him for a moment, her jaw clenched, then turned her eyes on the window. 'I knew there was more to this than hunting dradur. You're a fucking liar, Ranoth Olseta. You know it won't end there. You won't come back, despite your promises. I know you. I know what you're like and I know this will not end with the deaths of the witches! You'll go north—'

'We deserve respect, Sasha!' he growled, not daring to raise his voice lest anyone hear. 'And the only way we earn that respect is by proving what we can do. Our people shouldn't have to live like this!'

'My arse this is about *respect!*' Her anger was a physical thing, simmering between them, threatening to boil over and scald them both. 'This is about reclaiming what your father stole from you and proving him wrong. You don't want respect—you want your life back. And that will *never* happen, because your father is a monster and monsters do not *ever* change. You're chasing a ghost, Ran. The ghost of a life you thought you would have, and it's time you accepted that it's dead and buried.'

He stabbed a finger at the hazy morning beyond the window, smoke coiling into the blue spring sky. 'And what kind of existence is this? What's left for me here, for Eian and Zarad?'

'Life!' Sasha opened her trembling hands. 'You have a life here, among people who understand you, and who love you...' She faltered, her brow creasing as tears pooled in her eyes. He knew it went against all her instincts to let him go, after so long watching over him, healing his wounds and keeping his mind all in one piece, but he would not be dissuaded. It was not her job to save him from himself.

Ran took her hand, absorbing her anger and sorrow and holding it tight. 'I know you imagine we can live out our days in safety here, but this place is no safer than Graupen or Usmein. Brit found it, then the dradur. How much longer before someone sympathetic to the duke discovers us? The life you want for us is no life at all. I can't stay, Sasha, and I'm sorry. I have to go, and I have to try.'

She winced as if slapped, and he collected her into his arms. She buried her face in his shoulder and wrapped her arms around him. Ran held her, the beat of her racing heart hammering against his. His throat tightened around his words as he murmured them into her hair. 'If I stay, I'm only delaying the inevitable. This is my chance to play the only card I have left in my hand.'

Iridia might have pushed him toward it, but he realised now how badly he wanted this for himself. He needed to find the witches and make them pay in kind for the suffering they had caused, and he needed to prove his father wrong or die in the attempt. There was a great power lurking within Orthia's people, and it was wasted if not used against their enemies. It was the one thing that could break the deadlock in the Disputed Territory, their only hope of ending an endless war.

'I can't stop you if Yidda lets you leave.'

Sasha didn't look up as she spoke, and Ran was glad of it. He didn't want her to see the pain etched in the lines of his face, or the tears. He just wanted to stay like this for as long as he could, imprinting this moment on his mind. He didn't know when he would see her again, or if he ever would, but he would hold this memory along with everything he had ever felt for her and bury it so deep it could never be lost.

She took a shuddering breath. 'I will say this, Ranoth—I didn't keep you alive all these years to let you go out there and die. You come back here when you're done. You bring my brother and my friend back to me. And don't you dare die.'

Chapter Sixteen

Hummel, Tolak Range, the South Lands

Owin's funeral took place two days after his death. Erlon, Siman and a handful of rangers escorted the wrapped corpse to the southern face of the Caine, where generations of the clan's dead rested in tumals beneath the earth. Lidan's family had their own tumal, as did other family groups, all clustered together where the tunnels and alcoves could burrow deep under the Caine.

Lidan was neither invited nor barred from attending the ceremony; Owin's brother indicating to her father that he was content with the daari's sentence. Lidan had expected a flood of grief from Guner, or perhaps a burst of rage, but as she watched the great hall through the woven reed screen at its perimeter, she saw the man's shoulders drop as he let out a long sigh and gave a resigned nod.

'My brother seemed to attract trouble. I'd wager, all counted, he had more adversaries than friends.' Guner shook his head. 'I wish he'd done better with the time he had.'

Erlon nodded from his audience chair. 'I had hoped time was all he needed. And I am aggrieved it was my daughter who ended him. Are you certain the ruling she faces is enough? You're well within you rights to demand restitution.'

Lidan went rigid behind the screen, clamping her jaw shut lest the tiniest sound escape.

'I... Yes, sir,' Guner said after a moment. 'It's common word about Hummel that the First Daughter lost her apprenticeship over this. It's also common word it was my brother who challenged her. There's a mess hall full of rangers who attest to it, so I've no reason to question them. I've no desire to punish her for defending herself against a drunk idiot.'

'Very well,' Erlon gestured to his tine-man, Kaito, who sat at a nearby table with a quill and a sheaf of parchment. 'My household will provide what is needed for the ceremony and burial. No, I won't hear it, Guner. My house will pay for what's been done. Tell Kaito here all you need, and it will be seen to.'

And so the arrangements were made and the ceremony fixed, and Lidan retreated to her family's private rooms at the back of the hall.

'I thought I might find you here,' Bridie said as she slipped through the heavy curtain.

Lidan shoved her sad attempt at mending a shirt to one side and embraced her sister. 'It feels like an age since I saw you last!'

'Oh, that's because it has been!' Bridie hugged her tight, then stepped back to scan Lidan's face. 'I bet your mother loves that new scar.'

'She was surprisingly relaxed about it. Probably because she hasn't seen the other one.' Lidan lifted her hair and Bridie cringed.

'Best keep that hidden or she'll have kittens.' Her sister picked up the shirt Lidan had abandoned, clicked her tongue, and immediately set about unpicking the stitches. 'I see they haven't improved their needlework lessons over at the barracks.' Bridie glanced up, her deep blue eyes and dark features mirroring their father almost perfectly. 'Oh no, I'm so sorry. I didn't mean—'

Lidan forced a smile. 'It's fine. Even the best tales have endings, though some come a little sooner than you think.'

Her sister's hand found hers and they shared a moment of silent under-standing. Lidan marvelled at how much Bridie had grown, how much older she seemed even in the past few months.

'Are you excited?' Lidan asked, changing the subject.

'About the matching?' Bridie returned to rescuing Lidan's mending. 'I'm not sure if I'm nervous or excited, to be honest. One moment I'm afraid to leave, afraid to be among people I don't know. The next I'm desperate to be anywhere but here as fast as a horse can carry me. I suppose that's how you felt too, after Abbi...'

'I think I felt that even before Abbi.'

A whirl of excited voices and hurrying bodies burst through the doorway. Farah, her father's fourth and youngest wife, bustled in, herding a throng of children before her and leading a troop of tine-women into the large common room. A beaming smile broke across her face as she spotted Lidan. 'Liddy! You're here, you're finally here!'

Lidan was engulfed in a crushing embrace and found herself laughing as Farah rocked her back and forth and attempted to squeeze the air from her chest.

'Your father said you were back. You've been busy, I hear?' The woman planted a kiss on Lidan's cheek, her chestnut curls bouncing, the very embodiment of her joy.

Lidan nodded. 'I've been a little occupied.'

'Well, you're here now. We have to sort these gowns before we pack them in the wagons. Your mother will have yours and Marrit's along in a moment.' Farah spun to glare at a pair of children screeching beside a chest near the opposite wall. 'Lucija, just give him the horse, please. There are a hundred others in that box, you don't need every single one.'

'But the black one is my *favourite!*' Lidan's youngest sister relinquished the dark, timber horse figurine to her brother's hands and sat back, returning her mother's glare.

'Your black horse is probably buried in your room under that pile of dolls I keep telling you to put away.' Farah turned to where a tine-woman had begun unpacking gowns from a nearby chest. They shared a few murmured words, shaking their heads and glancing back at the children. The tine-woman clicked her fingers at a younger girl, who hurried away, most likely to go and look for Lucija's lost toy.

'But *this one* looks like Theus!' Lucija countered. 'Mine looks like Titon. He's a boy's horse and Theus is a *girl's* horse!'

Lidan left Farah to sorting gowns and Bridie to mending and slowly approached the rug where Lucija sat sulking. Beside her, Ehran played with a herd of small horse figures, most of them light brown, and only one jet black. Lucija glanced up as Lidan settled on her knees, the small girl's shimmering brown eyes widening in surprise.

'I'm not sure if Theus thinks of himself as a girl's horse,' she said softly. Lidan pointed to a roan figure Ehran had abandoned beside the chest. 'That one was my first ever horse. Da gave it to me.'

Lucija eyed the figurine, then collected it carefully, watching her brother in case he took a sudden interest in it. 'He doesn't look like Theus.'

'No, he doesn't. I never had a horse like Theus until he came from the high country. I think the only reason he let them catch him was so he could show off to Titon.'

'Da said I can't have a horse 'til I break it in.'

Lidan smiled at the memory of breaking in her wild-born horse and nodded. 'He's right—that's the Law. But until then, why don't you look after Sunspear for me?'

Lucija looked up with a frown. 'Who's Sunspear?'

'This little roan. He was my companion for many years, and if you look after him, Da will see that you can be trusted to look after a big horse.'

The little girl's smile broke like sunrise after a night of roaring summer storms. 'What do I do? What does he need?'

'Well, first he needs some feed, Ranger Lucija. You better get some from the—'

A small snap and a cry of frustration cut through Lidan and Lucija's play. Ehran had broken the leg from one of his galloping horses and was staring at the two pieces as though they might go back together through the sheer will of his mind. To her left, Lidan saw Farah pause, her eyes darting over the three of them. Lidan lifted her fingers and Farah grew still.

'Ehran? What happened?' Lidan asked in a whisper.

'Icewind's leg broke.' The boy's voice was thick with emotion. 'Da said he would fix him.'

'Does he break all the time?' Lidan shuffled a little closer, leaving Lucija whispering to Sunspear and trotting him along the rug. Ehran nodded and Lidan opened her hand. 'Did you name him Icewind? It suits him. He's the colour of the high-country snow.'

Ehran turned the broken figure over to Lidan and looked up at her. This time, Lidan didn't meet his eyes. She let him look, his gaze roving all over her face, searching for a clue that would tell him she was lying. The horse was made from light, fragile timber that had been painted with a thin layer of white. It was nothing like Sunspear, who had been made from a heavy, solid wood that had survived almost two decades of intense love.

'You've seen snow?' Ehran asked. His small face crumpled into a dubious frown.

'I have,' Lidan replied. 'At least once a year, up near Fracture Pass. It's the brightest thing you'll ever see aside from the sun.'

'I want to see it,' the boy said in an awed whisper.

She gave him a smile and a wink. 'You will one day, when you're big and have a horse of your own. Da will take you.' She expected to see Ehran's face light up as Lucija's had, but instead he looked down at his hands and fingered the hem of his trousers.

'Da's too busy.'

'He's got too much work,' Lucija chimed in, burying her horse's nose in the rug, pretending he was eating grass.

The children's loneliness hung heavy on their small shoulders, like a wet blanket smothering the joy that childhood should hold, and Lidan's heart sank at the sight of Ehran absently fidgeting with a nearby toy and Lucija's nonchalant acceptance of their father's absence. Lidan looked down at the broken horse and wondered if her father had ever actually fixed Icewind's leg as promised, or if instead he'd had someone quickly carve a replacement from poor quality timber just to appease an overeager child. A headache began to grind at the bones around Lidan's eyes and she blinked to dispel it, making a mental note to fetch some peppermint oil from her room.

Her own childhood memories of Erlon flooded back—doting and attentive one moment, distant and uninterested the next. She'd thought it was because she was a girl, an unwanted and inconvenient heir, but as she sat with her youngest siblings and heard them for the first time, it seemed their father was indiscriminate in his treatment of them. She had expected Ehran to be spoilt, fussed over and favoured above Erlon's other children, but he was as ignored and confused as she had been.

'Ehran,' she began, aware that somewhere behind her, Farah was watching the exchange. 'Would you like me to fix Icewind? I have a friend who's quite good at carving. He could make Icewind better. Would you like that?'

Ehran nodded. 'Can he make him so he doesn't break again?'

'Oh, I think he could. He made me a little bird for my birthday. It's very lovely.' Lidan pocketed the pieces of the toy. 'He's very good at riding too. Maybe he'll let the both of you sit up in the saddle and hold the reins for a while when we're riding to Daylin.'

'Only if I can hold Theus's reins!' Lucija practically launched herself at Lidan in her excitement.

'Well, I'll have to speak with your mother, and Theus, but I think he'll let you, for a small fee.' Lidan leaned very close as the children craned upward. 'He has a weakness for carrots.'

Lucija shot off, charging toward her mother, shouting questions and begging to be allowed to ride Theus, even for the shortest while. Ehran was right behind her, proudly proclaiming that Lidan had a friend who was going to make Icewind even better *and* let him hold the reins of a big horse. Lidan smiled at the astonished expression on Farah's face as she sought to calm her children, but her smile faded as Sellan swept through the doorway.

Lidan clambered to her feet and followed the convoy of tine-women carrying chests and bundles into the common room. They began to set out gowns and outfits beside those Farah had brought, and the two women acknowledged each other with small, polite nods.

That was unexpected... Lidan turned her attention to the chests as they were unburdened of their cargo. Had her mothers finally found a shared interest they could bond over instead of sniping at each other in a never-ending power play?

'Liddy!' Sellan's voice cut across the room. She stood back and motioned for Lidan to attend her. Marrit was already at her side, quiet and unassuming. There were two packages wrapped in linen cloth on a table to Sellan's right, and she motioned for a tine-woman to unfold them. A gown of emerald green and one of deep mauve appeared, the green longer in the skirt, while the smaller mauve had a higher neckline. 'These will be your matching day gowns. You will not wear them on any other occasion unless expressly instructed, do you understand?'

'There's at least four mares' worth of cloth in the green one,' Farah put in, not looking up from her deliberations over two small blue gowns.

'Four mares!' Lidan pulled her hand back from where her fingers had almost touched the fabric.

Farah nodded seriously as the woman beside her took Deliah and Iscah to try on the dresses. 'Your father paid a ridiculous amount for all this. You should see the cloth going with Bridie in her dower chest.'

It was a stunning value, but a worthy expense. The Daylin were a clan the Tolak needed as an ally, and a strong alliance was purchased with expensive demonstrations of status. Lidan wondered how much steel and bronze would be in the dower chest, then glanced at Bridie. The young woman now had bronze cuffs on both wrists and her mother, Raeh, was clipping her daughter's hair with brightly polished rings as Bridie continued to fuss over Lidan's shirt. The adornments screamed wealth and power, designed to leave a lasting impression on Horice Daylin. He would know the kind of family he had as an ally. Lidan wondered if her father would gift any metal weapons to Daylin, though a set of eating knives would likely outshine anything the Daylin had in their armoury.

'You will both be wearing these for the matching ceremonies,' Sellan continued, handing her daughters decorative timber boxes. Lidan lifted the lid to find a set of bronze cuffs similar to Bridie's, although less ornate, a set of earrings and a huge bronze comb that would sit in her hair. They shone with polished stones and bone embellishments, worked with dot patterns and horse motifs. They made her fighting knives look like primitive clubs. Did she dare wear this much wealth on her body? What if she lost it?

'Who made these?' she whispered, tracing her finger down the fine edge of the comb.

'Behn,' Farah replied. 'He's Behn Hammersmith now he's a master. Rick is still the man to see for knives and axes, but Behn is the one with the eye for detail.'

Sellan held out her hands and Lidan and Marrit returned the boxes to their mother. 'You will not mention these items to anyone outside this family. The Daylin cannot know we carry such treasures until the last moment.'

'Yes, Mam,' the girls replied.

'These are your other garments for the duration of the matching festival and the Corron.'

Lidan stiffened. 'What Corron?'

Sellan waved a dismissive hand. 'There's been a message, calling for a Corron after your sister's matching. Something about the war. Promises to be fabulously tedious, but your father is in a lather about it for some reason.' She gestured to two larger chests. 'I will have them stowed for the journey to Tingalla. If there is anything else you wish to bring, make sure it is packed and stowed by tomorrow night.'

Marrit nodded and bowed. 'Grent requires me in the healing rooms, if we're done here?'

'If you must.' The dana shuddered. 'Filthy place…'

Lidan hardly heard them. The news of the Corron echoed in her ears, pulsing with the beat of her heart and drowning the noise of the room to a dull roar. Her fingers shook and she smoothed them down the front of her dress. This was… This wasn't good…

'I see you finally found something decent to wear,' Sellan noted, breaking into Lidan's thoughts.

Lidan glanced down at the red linen dress she'd found in her room. She swallowed and found her voice. 'Strangely enough, this gown and five more like it were all I had in my room. You wouldn't happen to know where my trousers are, or my leather jerkins?'

'Me? No, I haven't the slightest idea.' Her mother folded her arms as Farah tried to get Ehran to stand still for his fitting. 'Perhaps the tines have them somewhere. I'm certain you said you'd outgrown everything in there.'

'Actually, I'm still growing into some of them.'

Her mother turned and raised an eyebrow.

'The jerkins? They look like a vest with laces in the bodice?' Lidan probed. Surely her mother knew what she was talking about.

Sellan's eyes narrowed. 'What about them?'

'I need them.' How obvious did she need to be?

'Whatever for?' Her mother gave Kelill a small smile as she hurried Cerise, Elva and Hanne through the door and over to a collection of unopened trunks and bundles.

Lidan cleared her throat. 'For riding. I've been told I'll be doing quite a bit of it on the journey to Tingalla, and unless you think my nipples would look better nearer my knees than my face, I'll need my jerkins.'

For a long moment Sellan simply stared at Lidan, and she wondered if her mother had heard her at all.

'I shall see that they are found, my sweet.'

'Thank you. And the boots that vanished from my room. It would be a shame to ruin these pretty indoor slippers.'

Sellan fixed Lidan with a glare. 'Will you be insisting on wearing those horrendous knives?'

Lidan returned the glare without hesitation. 'They speak of our clan's status as much as any of these *trinkets*. And if you recall, the last time we rolled up to one of these "gatherings", those horrendous knives saved my life.'

A charged silence stretched between mother and daughter until Sellan finally inclined her head and turned back to the trunks. 'There is a belt in your trunk that will allow you to wear *one* knife on your waist when you are required to dress formally. It was your father's idea.'

The words washed over Lidan and she rode the surprise of her mother's admission to its end. Her father was not a man to bother himself with the outfitting of his children. Had he harboured fears about the matching even before the Corron was announced?

She forced a little lump of fear down into her belly and let the thought go. Her focus had to be on the journey ahead. She was about to embark on several weeks of travelling, living in close quarters with people she hardly felt she knew anymore. She didn't want to dwell on what the next few weeks might bring, or what might happen on the journey west, or when they reached Tingalla, not while the memories of the last Corron were so fresh in her mind that she could still feel the blood on her skin.

CHAPTER SEVENTEEN

Hummel, Tolak Range, the South Lands

Her hands worked with deft purpose, carving away the handle of the knife until hardly any of it remained. She reached for the hand, gently, as a lover might, and carefully turned it over. She pressed the cool flesh of the palm against the hilt.

It would fit.

She let the hand fall back to the bench, the arm thudding down, and laid the knife beside it. Taking up the needle and thread, she frowned. What was this black muck under her nails? It was dry, flaking away from the fine creases of her skin as she flexed her fingers.

Her hands did not stop moving.

Once again, she reached for the hand that was not her own. The needle pierced the flesh of the smallest finger, then penetrated the skin of the next. The thick thread pulled through the holes with a whispered hiss, again and again, drawing the fingers together until they touched. There was no blood.

Her head tilted as the needle worked along the length of the pallid, supple fingers, sewing each to its neighbour in turn.

Why was there no blood?

She positioned the knife handle in the palm of the hand and curled the sewn fingers around it. The needle worked until the thumb locked over, creating a fist, then bound the ends of each finger to the ball of the palm until the knife was secure. She lifted the hand by the wrist and angled her work to the light.

It would hold.

She glanced up the arm to the body. It was pale; the anaemic hue of raw fish flesh, and utterly bloodless. There was a wound at the throat, but it had not been stitched. The jaw hung slack and the eyes stared into the void between life and death. The colour was almost gone from the iris, fading to the colour of high cloud even as she watched. She put her filthy hand on the body's shoulder. It was as cold as the stone of the workbench.

The skin shivered and she pushed against it; firm but gentle. It began to shake, and she pushed harder, her fingers pressing against the dead flesh.

The body shuddered and the jaw snapped shut, cracking teeth down to the bone. Blue-black ichor oozed from between the thin line of the lips.

She was shaking but her hand held tight to the corpse. Her mind screamed at her to let go but her hand refused to obey. It was not her hand, and this was not her body.

She had never been to this cold, dank room; never sat on this hard, unforgiving chair or sewn a body with no blood to the hilt of a knife.

She had never been to this place, but she knew the face of the corpse.

She knew those knives.

The dead eyes found her, and she screamed.

Lidan jolted awake and gasped. Her heart pounded, knocking the breath from her throat before it could reach her chest, and her hand trembled, strangling the linen sheet clinging to her sweat-slicked legs like a winding vine.

Her eyes searched the room. There were no candles or strange glowing shapes with bulbous metal bases. There was no stone bench.

The body was gone.

The room with the bench was gone.

She was home, in her quarters, with moonlight streaming through a gap in the curtains.

She tried to catch her breath.

A dream. Just a dream. Her skin prickled and she turned to the bed across the room. It was empty, a sheet hanging over the side, abandoned in the hot night air. Marrit was gone.

Lidan untangled her legs and stood to peel the curtain away from the window. Silver moonlight drenched Hummel, throwing shadows at odd angles across the ground. Bands of thin cloud streaked the sky and the moon slipped behind one as if it were suddenly ashamed to show its face. She turned away and wriggled her feet into a pair of boots.

Slipping from her room into the darkness of the corridor, she rubbed her hands up her arms as if to wash the ravenous gaze of the corpse from her skin. The icy chill of the body's sallow skin lingered on her fingertips, burning as if she held them to a flame, and she curled them into a clammy fist, taking a deep, shaky breath.

Dreams like this weren't new. They crept in like thieves, stealing away her peace and leaving her with a gnawing disgust that persisted long after sunlight had burned away the night. She never spoke of them; not to Loge, not to Jessah or her sisters. It was better to keep the horrors trapped, trussed up in the shadows of her mind, lest giving them voice might also give them life.

The dreams were all the same; hands sewing weapons into corpses before the dead jerked to life on the cold stone of the bench. They differed only in the kinds of weapons used and the body to which they were bound. Each nightmare was a birth, a new creature built and unleashed on the world, a new curse sent out to destroy and murder and—

Lidan gripped the doorframe and vomited into the shadow beside the kitchen steps. Gulping air, she wiped the back of her hand across her lips.

Had anyone seen her? Torches flickered beside the gateway to the barracks and along the top of the walls in the distance, marking the edge of safety with a dancing orange glow. She leaned against the doorframe, shivering despite the warmth of the night. There was no denying what those things were, even if the passage of time had ruined their features and rusted their blades. No one else ever entered that dark little room, and the face belonging to those industrious hands remained hidden.

She hugged her chest and cut through the kitchen's garden and across the common. The eastern sky held the palest hint of the approaching day, but night still held dominion, and paths and trackways between the village's buildings stood empty. Lidan crossed an intersection and her stomach growled, responding to the scent wafting from the Baker's house down the street. Loge's father would be up, sliding all sorts of breads and cakes in and out of the glowing mouths of his ovens.

The healing rooms appeared at the end of a trackway in the shadow of the looming walls. These were not the healing rooms she had known as a child, but a newer, larger complex of connected stone buildings around a rectangular courtyard. Grent kept his home in one corner, sharing the rest of the building with a dormitory of beds, a room for procedures that required the use of knives, some curtained spaces for examinations, an abundance of storage rooms and a smaller chamber where the clan's written healing knowledge had been collected.

This was Marrit's favourite room—a musty place stuffed full of books and parchments and charcoal for her drawings. When she wasn't hovering at Grent's elbow helping him treat his patients or rushing after Moyra when a baby needed pulling into the world, she spent hours poring over the tomes, adding to the collection in recent years with her own observations.

Lidan eased open the door to the records room and Marrit looked up from the bound volume open on the table. A collection of thick candles burned beside a sheaf of parchment and a sharpened length of charcoal.

Marrit nodded and turned back to the book. 'Couldn't sleep, either?'

Lidan coughed to dispel the lingering acidic burn from her throat. 'Something like that. How long have you been up?'

'A couple of hours.' Marrit stood and pushed a kettle over the flames in the hearth. 'Thought I might as well do something instead of staring at the ceiling until dawn.'

She eased herself back into her chair and Lidan settled opposite, wishing she'd brought a shawl. The bare stone walls and floor refused to hold any heat from the day, no matter how high the humidity rose outside. On a stinking summer day the healing rooms were a relief, but tonight the chill sunk its teeth into her bones.

Lidan reached over and lifted the cover of the tome from the table. 'You've already read that one.'

Marrit shrugged. 'Never hurts to refresh your memory.'

Lidan cocked a brow at her sister. 'And how many times have you refreshed your memory on the Structure of Bones and Muscles in the Bodies of Adult Men?'

Marrit pressed her lips together in thought. 'A few times…'

Lidan closed the book and slid it off the table.

'Hey, I need that!' Marrit protested, untangling herself from the chair and stalking after Lidan as she carried the book to a trunk by the door. She dropped it in, closed the lid and turned to take her incensed sister by the shoulders.

'No, you don't.' She spun the girl around and walked her back to the table. 'You've read every book in here at least three times. You could rewrite most of them from memory. You do not need to read them all again.'

'But what if something happens—'

'Four years of training should help, Marri.' Lidan angled her into her seat and went to attend the kettle. Marrit sighed as Lidan sprinkled leaves into a pot and waited for the water to boil.

Of the two, Marrit most closely resembled their mother. She had paler skin than Lidan and Sellan's gleaming green eyes, but thankfully the fourteen-year-old had inherited none of the woman's personality. Grent and Moyra's guidance had produced a healer as competent as Lidan had ever seen, and a girl on the verge of womanhood who on one hand had very little tolerance for horse shit, and on the other, crippling doubt about her abilities when left alone with her own thoughts for too long. In that, Marrit was Lidan's mirror image, and it pained her to see her sister so conflicted.

'Why are you even packing all those manuals? It's all in your head.'

A collection of trunks stood along the wall by the door, each packed tightly with provisions; bottles and urns wrapped in wool and soft fern husks, dressings, bandages, splints, needles, thread, and utensils along with an assortment of other items they might need on the journey to Tingalla. Marrit often ran the healing rooms on her own, especially when Grent was called away, and he had decided she would be the appointed healer on the journey to the matching. This announcement had evidently sent the girl into an anxious spiral, and she'd spent the past three nights rereading every book she could get her hands on while the rest of Hummel slept. She had also insisted on packing a trunk of books and reams of drawings, only to chew the nails off her fingers when she realised she couldn't take *all* of them.

'What if I forget something?' Marrit whispered, leaning over the table as Lidan poured the tea. 'What if something bad happens?'

'You won't, and it will,' Lidan said with a shrug. 'Things go wrong here all the time. The first year I was training with Grent, we lost more people than I could count. People got sick... people had accidents. Wounds festered, or they bled out from some injury or other. Some of them died while we were still stitching them together.' An image of the sewn hand flashed before her open eyes and she gulped a mouthful of scalding tea, instantly regretting it. 'My point is, bad things happen. People die. How many times have you saved a life one day only to lose another the next?'

Marrit chewed her lip and didn't answer.

'Grent wouldn't let you do this if he didn't think you capable. Da wouldn't either. In any case, you won't be the only healer, and you won't have to do any of it alone. You just get to be in charge of all this… stuff. All you have to do is your best. That's all you can ever do.'

Marrit sighed heavily and laced her fingers together around her teacup. 'I think Da's only letting me do it because he couldn't be bothered arguing with Grent. He's got enough to worry about with the war and the matching and the Corron.'

Heat prickled across Lidan's skin and she looked into the fire. 'I'm sure he and Ehran will be just fine at the Corron.'

'Ehran?' Marrit said with a derisive laugh. 'He can't take Ehran to the Corron.'

Their eyes met and Lidan's brow furrowed. 'He has to take Ehran. He's the heir.'

Marrit looked at her like she was an idiot. 'He's four, Liddy. He's far too young. Haven't you ever read the Law?'

Lidan shrugged a shoulder. 'A while ago…' And if she was perfectly honest, it had bored her to tears. She'd abandoned it after the first volume, reasoning she could pick it up later, but "later" never arrived.

'Heirs have to be ten years old, at a minimum, to attend a Corron. You got to go because you were the only heir, and you were what? Twelve?'

'Thirteen,' Lidan corrected, and Marrit waved her hand.

'Older than ten—that's what mattered. Old enough to remember what was said.'

And what was done.

'That's the point of taking the heir to the Corron in the first place. They have to remember what was said; they have to witness it so when they take their father's title, the memory survives.' Marrit gestured in the direction of the hall. 'Ehran can hardly remember where he left his boots. How is he going to remember what's said at a Corron?' Marrit leaned forward again, as if the walls had ears. 'But that's not what's got Da in a twist. I overheard him talking to Siman.'

Lidan's eyes narrowed. 'What did you hear?'

'Apparently, Merk Marsaw has agreed to treat with us,' Marrit told her. 'That's why they called a Corron for after Bridie's matching. Da has been trying to win him over from the Namjin side since the war started, and now they've finally got him to talk. But Da has to appoint a witness to stand with him at the Corron, or he's barred.'

'Marsaw wants to treat with us?' Lidan couldn't believe it. Was this the message her mother had mentioned? If true, this was huge. No wonder her father was on edge. 'Siman could—'

Marrit shook her head. 'Has to be someone in Da's immediate family.'

'And you know that, how?' Lidan eyed her sister.

'It's in the Law books—'

'Of course it is,' Lidan groaned, rubbing the bridge of her nose.

Marrit ignored her. 'Witness of the Blood, they called it. There was a Corron to decide the borders of the clan territories, just after our people settled into villages, and one of the daaris had only one child, still in swaddles as it happens. He had no heir to witness the Corron's rulings, so he had to appoint a witness.'

Marrit swirled the tea in her cup and Lidan dragged up every memory she had of her father's stories. He'd taught her their history with stories by the fireside when the darkness and biting chill of the dry season drove them all indoors. The story of the borders sounded familiar, but she couldn't recall anything about a special title.

'This other daari chose his brother, but Da doesn't have any brothers. They all died before we were born.' Marrit's green eyes gleamed in the firelight and a bird warbled outside, announcing the approach of dawn. 'It has to be one of us girls.'

'Why hasn't he appointed anyone yet?' Lidan asked in a breathless whisper.

Marrit shrugged. 'I don't know. I haven't asked.'

'Why the fuck not? We leave for Tingalla in *three days*. He has to appoint someone before then—it's a war Corron, for fuck sake! This is important, Marri!'

'I know that! That's why I'm telling you!'

Lidan's brows shot up in surprise. 'You want *me* to ask him? You have got to be joking.' She pressed her hand against her forehead. 'He's not going to like this.'

Marrit blinked and opened her hands toward Lidan. 'You're the obvious choice.'

'You cannot be serious?' Lidan hissed across the table. 'I skewered a ranger with a meat fork four days ago! There's no way he's going to appoint me as witness. I'll be lucky if he ever lets me leave the village!'

Marrit's features flattened and she suddenly looked very much like their mother. A shiver rolled across Lidan's skin and she wished she hadn't come down here. She should have gone to the barracks, or the stables, or stayed in the kitchens.

'Liddy, all of that is very true and completely irrelevant. The facts are the facts. He doesn't have a choice. You have to tell him.'

'Fine,' she growled through her teeth and jabbed a finger at Marrit's face. 'But you're coming with me.'

Chapter Eighteen

Hummel, Tolak Range, the South Lands

Lidan and Marrit waited outside their father's rooms until Farah appeared hugging a shawl around her shoulders. Their half-mother yawned, gave them both a kiss on the head and wandered off to her quarters, leaving the girls alone in the silent hall. Lidan's heart thumped uncomfortably. The last time she'd been in her father's rooms things had not gone well, and she'd left with the distinct impression she'd only just escaped with her head attached. Barely four days had passed and here she was, standing outside, certain she'd gone completely mad.

Marrit cleared her throat and Lidan started. She'd been staring at the doorway for several moments without moving a muscle. Marrit sighed and rapped her knuckles on the doorframe.

'Enter,' Erlon called from inside, and the younger girl snagged Lidan by the wrist and dragged her through. The air inside the sitting room was still and musty. Early morning light streamed through the windows on the far wall, dust motes sailing through the beams like leaves in a creek.

'Da?' Marrit called.

'Marri? You're up early—' Erlon's head appeared from behind the curtain to the bedroom. His eyes found Lidan and his brow furrowed. 'Give me a minute.'

He vanished, leaving the girls to stand awkwardly in the centre of the room while he shuffled around in the back. Lidan wound her fingers into the fabric of her night dress, scratching at the stitching while she waited. Erlon eventually emerged with the hem of his shirt between his teeth as he laced up his trousers, and he gestured to a collection of empty chairs around a table.

'Can't say I was expecting to find you two in here at this time of day,' he said as the girls sat. 'What's wrong? If your mother has something to say to me, she can come and—'

Marrit held up her hand and gave him a quick smile. 'No, Da. It's Lidan. She has something to tell you.'

'I what?' Lidan snapped, and her father stared at her. 'No, *you* found it. You tell him.'

'I really think you should—'

Erlon cleared his throat and eyed them. 'It's a bit early for this, isn't it?'

Marrit glared at Lidan for a moment, then turned to her father. 'I was… I heard…' Marrit shifted in her seat and Lidan rolled her eyes.

'Marrit was reading the Law recently and stumbled on a part about Corrons. Apparently the daari's witness has to be older than ten or the daari is barred from the meeting. Since a Corron has been called, she was worried that Ehran is too little to be your witness and—'

'I'm aware of that,' Erlon interrupted.

Lidan glanced at Marrit but the girl offered no help. Her voice began to shake despite herself. 'It said something about a witness of the blood, and given that you don't have any brothers, you… you have to choose one of us.'

She pushed the words out through her tightening throat, cursing herself for a fool. This was madness! Why had she agreed to this?

'I'm aware of that also,' said Erlon.

Lidan's heart skipped. Beside her, Marrit was a picture of confusion. She gaped at their father, her eyes searching his face. Lidan licked her lips and looked away as Erlon turned to Marrit. 'Did your Law book tell you what a witness does?'

'I…' Words failed the girl, and she shook her head.

'And based on what you read, you thought Lidan was the obvious choice?'

Lidan's shoulders dropped and Marrit nodded.

Why isn't she saying anything?

'Marri, look at me,' said Erlon. The girl glanced up from her hands. 'You're one of the cleverest people I know. There's more knowledge in that head of yours than all the masters put together, but sometimes knowing something doesn't mean you understand it.' He reached over and squeezed Marrit's hand. 'Go get something to eat.'

Marrit left without another word. Lidan would have followed her sister if she could, but her body refused to move. She sat glued to the spot, staring at her father across the table. Her eyes stung, dry and burning with fatigue. She should never have gone down to the healing rooms. She should have just stayed in bed—

'Is that all she told you?' Erlon asked, resting his elbow on the arm of the chair and his chin in his hand.

'She said you have to appoint a witness of the blood for the Corron.' The room shrank around her; the walls pressing in. Her voice shrank with it, as if afraid to be heard. 'Ehran is too young and you don't have any siblings, so it has to be one of us girls. That's all she said.'

He rubbed his fingers across his lips and glanced out the window. 'She's right on all those counts.' He stood to pour two cups of water from a nearby ewer. 'There are seven of you who are old enough, and you *are* the obvious choice.'

'But?' she put into the pause.

He watched her over the rim of the cup.

'There's a "but",' Lidan said. 'There's always a "but".'

'But, I'm not sure you're...'

'Good enough?' A sneer threatened but she pressed her mouth into a hard line. 'Or do I embarrass you so much that you can't abide me being there?'

'No—'

'You think I'll stab someone in the neck for no apparent reason?'

'No!' he shouted and Lidan jolted in her seat. 'I'm not sure you're *ready*.'

'That didn't seem to worry you last time,' she countered. 'I was barely thirteen.'

'That's not what I mean.'

'Then what is it?' Lidan stabbed her finger into the tabletop. 'If you don't have a witness, Merk Marsaw can treat all he wants but you won't be there to hear it.'

Erlon's eyes narrowed. 'How did you know about Marsaw?'

Lidan attempted a casual shrug. 'Just rumours. It doesn't matter how I heard—what matters is this Corron. You're not going to get another chance like this. Look, if you don't think I'm good enough, then choose one of the others. I don't care. Just choose *someone*. Take Marrit! She's got a mind like a trap. Once something's in that head of hers it's never getting out.'

'Marrit's a good girl but being appointed witness isn't just about remembering what was said.' Erlon put a cup of water in front of Lidan and stepped back. 'Or keeping a cool head when arguments run hot. Marrit knows what the mantle of witness is, but she doesn't know what it means. She has no idea what it will require of you if I place it on your shoulders.'

Lidan slumped into her chair, all the fight going out of her. 'I... I don't understand.'

'A witness is appointed if an heir isn't old enough to attend a Corron, but they can be appointed at other times too; usually if a daari is gravely ill or they die unexpectedly.' Erlon paused, then sighed. 'A witness is a care-taker, Lidan; a direct blood relation to the daari and the heir, who publicly renounces any claim they have to leading the clan and swears to defend the heir with their life.'

Lidan stared at Erlon, certain she hadn't heard him correctly. When she'd woken in the small hours of the morning, this was not where she thought the day would go. She might have escaped a nightmare, but she'd walked straight into something that was shaping up to be far worse. Her stomach clenched and her fingers twitched as she ached to escape, but there was nothing to be done but see this through.

'When I said you weren't ready, I didn't mean you weren't old enough, or strong enough. If I appoint you, you would be bound to Ehran's fate, called to put your life before his if need be. And you could never claim the daari's chair in your own right... I'm not sure you're ready for that.' Erlon watched her with his intense blue eyes, his frame towering over the chairs and table.

What did he see? An unruly child, or a restless young woman? Did he see someone he could trust with the care of his son, or someone who would eliminate the boy at the first opportunity? For certain Lidan was the only one of his children who could defend Ehran if it came to it; the only one who could cut a man down if the need arose. She'd proven that.

Her father shook his head slowly. 'We're in the middle of a war, Liddy, and this Corron could change everything. This isn't a meeting of casual foes in the face of a common enemy, like last time. This is our chance to put an end to the blood and the death. Ever since shit went sideways with the Namjin, we've been hunting for an advantage, and now, we might have something. It's taken four years to get Merk Marsaw to the table, and if we can win *him* over, we might just turn the tide.'

'But the only way you get a seat at that table is if you appoint a witness… and it has to be one of us; someone willing to swear to protect Ehran.' She looked up at him and her mouth ran dry. 'And willing to renounce their inheritance?'

Erlon nodded and put his hands on his hips.

She gave a nervous little laugh. 'It couldn't be any more dangerous than hunting ngaru across a range infested by raiders!'

The look in his eyes burned that assumption to the ground. 'At any other time, it wouldn't be. It would be a damn sight safer, actually. But right now, with the way this war is going, with the Namjin crawling into our lands and ngaru haunting our steps, it would be the most dangerous thing I've ever asked you to do.'

He swivelled Marrit's chair around and sat facing Lidan with his elbows on his knees. 'I've put you in more danger in the last four years than I had any right to. First the Corron with Yorrell, then letting you go ranging. *That* was a decision I've wrestled with every day. I've lost count of the time I spent watching that gate, wondering if you were coming back. The ancestors know your mother has never let me hear the end of it. I underestimated Yorrell once and it almost got you killed. If it weren't for Marsaw offering to talk, there wouldn't be a Corron and we wouldn't be having this conversation.'

'But?' she pressed quietly.

'You're the only logical choice.'

The room seemed to tilt on its axis, but all Lidan could do was stare.

'You don't have a choice,' she whispered over the deafening thud of her heart. 'There isn't anyone else.'

Their eyes met, disbelief etched in the lines of his frown. 'Do you understand what this means? What you would have to give up; what you might have to do? This has to be something you want, Liddy, because you can't ever take it back. You can't change your mind once it's done.'

'It doesn't matter what I want. It doesn't matter what you want, either.' Her vision blurred and she blinked away tears that threatened to spill. Her mother was going to hate her for this. 'This is the path that's been put before us, and denying it is as foolish as denying the sky is blue. This whole mess started with me, when I refused that Namjin match and killed Yorrell's second.' Her father moved to deny it, but she held up her hand. 'It started with us, Da, and this Corron could end it. We have to be there; *I* have to be there. It isn't the logical choice—it's the *only* choice.'

Sellan took Erlon's announcement with all the grace and composure of a cat dunked in rain barrel. At least Erlon had the good sense to deliver the news in private, away from curious eyes, but Lidan was fairly sure the fallout had been heard for a mile.

'You've done what?' Sellan hissed at her husband. 'You made her do *what?*'

'I didn't make her do anything,' Erlon said, folding his arms across his chest. 'Lidan volunteered.'

'What?' her mother snapped, turning a withering glare on Lidan that almost took the air from her lungs. 'You cannot be serious. Tell me he's lying.'

Lidan lifted her chin. 'It's the truth. I chose this.'

'You *chose* to completely excise yourself from the succession? Are you insane?!'

Lidan took a deep breath and tried to appear outwardly calm, when inside, her heart was slamming itself against her ribs and her mind was screaming at her to run. She hadn't seen her mother this furious since she'd dragged her into the Crone's hut almost five years ago, and the memory of that punishment was carved in her skin to this very day. 'We're at war, Mother. Our people are on the brink, fighting for survival on two fronts. We need to attend this Corron—'

'Oh, for the love of—I don't give a shit about the Corron! What I give a shit about, is my eldest daughter—' she jabbed a finger at Erlon '—your *First Daughter*, putting herself in mortal danger for the sake of a *child*!'

'Mother,' Lidan kept her voice as even as she could manage. 'This is about more than my place in the succession. We need to be at this Corron. We have to be there when the decisions about Yorrell Namjin are made. That is not something we can be apart from. And if Father doesn't have a witness of the blood, then we're barred from the whole thing. We can't rely solely on our alliance with the Daylin. We have to bring them and the

Marsaw over to our side, or we're adrift, fighting the ngaru and the Namjin on our own.'

Her mother seethed where she stood, glaring at Lidan with unveiled disgust, while her father tried to hide the smile creeping across his lips. Emboldened, Lidan pressed on.

'And if you think I'm putting myself in danger by taking this title, then perhaps we should just sit here and wait until the Namjin are pounding on our gates, throwing our people's severed heads over the parapet. This is how we stop this war, Mother. *This* is how we keep ourselves safe.'

Sellan's hands balled into fists, and Lidan wondered if she was imagining wringing her daughter's neck for this defiance. If Erlon hadn't been standing a few paces away, she probably would have tried.

'If you insist on taking this path, Lidan, I cannot stop you. It is not the way I would have chosen for you, but you have your own mind. I suppose years running around in the wilderness will do that to a girl.' The dana put her back to her husband and pointed an accusing finger at Lidan. 'I will not be held responsible for the consequences of this decision. Do you understand me? When it all goes wrong—and it *will*—I will not hear of it.'

She had more to say. Lidan could see it locked behind the furious twist of her lips. But she left and Lidan watched her go, wondering as she did if she had made a terrible, irreversible mistake.

Chapter Nineteen

It took two days to organise the appointment ceremony, alongside the final preparations for the journey west, and Lidan hardly had time to scratch herself, let alone sleep. She packed and repacked, chased after her sisters and tried to keep Marrit calm as the day of their departure loomed.

She had expected nerves from Bridie, but the girl seemed inexplicably calm, as though leaving the only home she'd ever know for a new life was a matter of course.

In an effort to escape the chaos, Lidan found herself wandering down to the healing rooms to check on Marrit, then fabricating rather flimsy excuses to do so. She searched the common for a familiar face whenever she went to the stables, then fussed over Theus, whispering to him about who had said what to whom and when. If the horse understood a word of her ramblings, he never gave it away. Instead, he shoved his head into his feed bin, probably wondering why she was brushing him for the third time in a day. Despite all this, she never saw the pair of eyes she was searching for. At least, not until the final night before they left Hummel.

Lidan saw him across the gathered clan, under a blood orange sky. Pink and violet played at the edges of distant thunderheads, and a warm southerly wind flowed across the common. She should have been thinking of her ancestors travelling on the breeze to witness her appointment, but when she saw Loge standing with his parents and younger siblings, her carefully ordered thoughts scattered. She had so much to tell him. They hadn't spoken since her Hearing, or trained, or gone riding. Neither of them had had the time.

She turned from the crowd and faced the steps of the hall, taking a deep, shaky breath. Behind her, families clustered together with furs draped over shoulders, feathers and polished bone woven into braids. Their faces bore an array of markings, lines of pale paint highlighting their features in the waning light. The men had discarded their shirts and the women wore only trouser-skirts and simple chest wraps of dyed linen, leaving their shoulders and arms bare, exposing their black tattana etchings to the air. The ancestors would know them and their achievements by the tattana on their skin, and they would surround the people of the clan and banish any darkness that might seek to mar the proceedings.

Lidan kept herself very still. She could feel their eyes on her back, the weight of their expectations pressing down on her shoulders. She held her forearms turned outward, revealing the thick band of Abbi's mourning tattana and the winding branches of her ranger markings to the evening. Where Siman's ink tree stretched from his wrist, up his arm, and had begun to reach across his shoulder toward the centre of his back, hers was small—a tiny sapling intended to grow through her years of apprenticeship and mastery. From tonight, no more branches would be added to that tree, and she clenched her hand to stop her fingers shaking at the thought of what she'd lost.

Lidan heard a small squeak and Ehran shifted on the step beside her. 'Wriggle your toes,' she whispered, and the boy grew still.

Behind them, Raeh and Kelill moved among the gathered clan. They carried bowls of blood, fresh from a sacrificed goat, and dabbed a little on each forehead, marking them as protected by the presence of the ancestors. Raeh finally appeared in front of Lidan and dipped two fingers in the blood. She drew them down Lidan's face, from her forehead across her eye and down to her jaw.

'May the ancestors see you and keep you,' Raeh murmured. 'May their sight never waver or wane. May they guide you and protect you. May they witness your victories and cast aside your failures. May their will be yours, and yours be theirs.'

Kelill came next and repeated the ritual, drawing her bloodied fingers down over Lidan's other eye. Her half-mothers painted Ehran with the same bloody lines, spoke the same ancient words, then climbed the steps to where Farah and Sellan stood either side of the hall's door. Both mothers were marked with a pair of lines across their foreheads, then the remaining

143

blood was poured down the steps, crimson waterfalls connecting Lidan and Ehran to them.

Nearby a drum boomed twice and a hush fell over the crowd. From the open doors of the hall, Daari Erlon appeared. At his back stood Siman and Forge Master Rick Anvail.

Erlon's voice echoed across the common. 'Ancestors—hear us. Today we seek your blessing. We call you to witness this ceremony and to hear our decree.'

Her father's hand opened to her and Ehran, then reached back to touch his bare chest. His own tattana had grown over the years, telling the tales of his victories over the Namjin and the loss of his small daughter.

'First Daughter and First Son, approach.'

Lidan stepped off her mark immediately but Ehran hesitated. She bit down her fear and scooped up his hand, squeezing it and drawing him with her. At the top of the stairs, Dana Sellan stiffened and Lidan heard a murmur at her back. She kept Ehran at arms-length so his bare feet travelled up the cascade of blood before him, while she walked through her own, her toes squelching through the wet, sticky trail.

They could not do this alone. They had to do it together. The ancestors were watching, weighing her intentions against her actions, watching to see if she was true to the role her father was about to bestow. If she left Ehran at the bottom of the stairs, frightened and alone, what did that say about her? If she was so willing to abandon him here, surely she would do so again.

They stopped halfway up the stairs and waited.

Erlon approached his eldest and youngest and touched their shoulders. There was a smile in his eyes as he glanced to where Lidan gripped Ehran's little hand.

'You are the light of my life. You are the sun and the moon, and my regard for you is ever present and unchanging.' He shifted to face Lidan. 'First Daughter—you are called to become a Witness of the Blood. You are called in this time of need to protect your clan and our heir. You are called to witness, to advise and to guide. You will deny any claim to rule these people and pledge yourself to the heir alone. You are called to protect his life with your life. You are called by the ancestors and by your daari. Do you accept this burden?'

Her heart thumped hard, a knot of anxiety throbbing in her throat. Somehow, she squeezed out the words she'd practised in the silence of her room until her head hurt.

'I accept this burden. I will bear witness. I will advise and I will guide. I will protect this clan and its heir with my mind, my body and my soul. I… I renounce all claim to my birthright as a daughter of the blood. I swear this to the ancestors, to my daari, and all those present.'

Her voice shook, and her vision blurred, but her father didn't seem to notice. The daari turned to his small son. The boy craned his head back to squint up at his father's face, his tiny hand clenching in Lidan's grasp. She gave it a gentle squeeze of reassurance and hoped it was enough.

'First Son—you were brought forth to this place to lead these people. Your spirit was chosen by our ancestors to come among us, to take my place when I join them, and to take this clan into the future only the ancestor's sightless eyes can see.' He crouched and he took the boy's other hand. His voice was not that of a booming announcement, but that of a father seeking to explain something very complex to a small child. 'You have many years left to grow, years your sister has already moved through. She has seen things in her life that I wish you to never behold. She is brave, and she is strong. She is wise,' he turned and winked at Lidan, 'mostly, and she is kind.'

Lidan's throat tightened. She didn't dare look down. She didn't dare look at her mother. Instead she fixed her gaze on Siman's boots and crammed her emotions deep into her chest. There would be a time to feel the things her father was saying, to recognise what he was doing, but it was not now.

'Lidan is to be your protector, when I can't be. Lidan is to be your teacher, when I can't be. She is to be your eyes and your ears and your heart if she must, until you are old enough to know yourself and this clan. Do you understand?'

Ehran gave a stiff nod. 'Yes, Da.'

Their father leaned close to the boy's ear. 'When I ask you this next question, I need you to say "I accept" as loud as you can, all right?'

Ehran nodded again, and Erlon stood to scan the assembled crowd. 'Ehran, First Son of the Tolak—do you accept Lidan, First Daughter of the Tolak, as Witness of the Blood?'

'I ACCEPT!' Ehran shouted and Lidan started. A murmur of laughter rippled through the clan's folk.

'Very good.' Erlon smiled and turned to wave at Rick. The forge master held out his hands to an unseen assistant in the shadows of the hall. Two sheathed blades appeared, and Rick carried them down to Erlon without fuss or flourish. Lidan's skin rushed with goosebumps.

They were longer than her knives, each encased in an ornately wrought scabbard. One was slightly shorter than the length of her arm, shoulder to wrist, and the other considerably shorter again, but they were otherwise identical, with a horse motif at the pommel and a minimal cross-guard where the blade disappeared into the hard casing of the scabbard. Lidan met her father's gaze and tried not to let her shock show in the lines of her face.

'These were made in the image of the first sword our forge ever wrought. They join that blade as the only swords to ever rise from those flames. They are not of scavenged steel, but ore mined in the farthest reaches of the South Lands. They are symbols of our people and of our future, and they are yours.' Erlon handed the swords to his children and Lidan was forced to relinquish her grip on Ehran.

Ehran took the weapon and stared at it as if it might leap up and bite him, while Lidan closed her fingers around the hilt of hers and wondered if her father had gone mad. She might be competent with a pair of knives, but neither she nor her brother knew how to handle a sword. What was he doing giving a four-year-old boy a weapon like this? Perhaps he meant them to be worn for ceremonies, symbols of the clan's power and wealth?

Her father looked at her and she knew she was wrong.

'You can't be serious?' she whispered, careful not to let her voice carry beyond the space between them.

'I am,' he replied and bowed his head toward her, shielding their conversation. 'Ehran's blade is as blunt as a tree branch, but yours has an edge sharp enough to scythe through a man's arm. You will wear it on your body at all times. You will use it, if necessary, to defend yourself and your brother. Do you understand?'

'But, I—'

'Rick will train you on the way to Tingalla. We'll discuss it further once we're underway.'

Lidan quelled her questions and met her mother's furious eyes over Erlon's shoulder. She had not forgiven either of them. Nor would she. Sellan hadn't spoken a word to Lidan outside of what was absolutely necessary. She had only agreed to stand at the top of the stairs because Farah had accepted without hesitation. If there was one thing about the dana that never changed, it was her absolute refusal to let another of her husband's wives upstage her.

And while her mother didn't believe in the ancestors shifting through the air around them, Lidan did. There was a heaviness, like steam, hanging about her, clinging to her skin, seeping through her clothes. It was the weight of them watching her every move, reading her every thought. She knew her forefathers and foremothers were here, their dead eyes reaching across the generations to see what their bloodline had become. She couldn't fail or falter. She had sworn an oath.

Her father retreated up the steps and his voice boomed across the common. 'Witness,' he declared.

'Witness!' the crowd bellowed in answer, their hands thumping into their chests in collective confirmation.

She glanced at Ehran, met his wide, wondering eyes, and gave him a quick smile. A sword was just a big knife. How hard could it be to wield? Together they turned to face the gathered clan, swords held in their outstretched hands. She found Loge among the gathered folk, his golden hazel eyes glimmering in the twilight.

Could he see her hands shaking where she gripped the scabbard? Could he sense the anxiety roiling in her belly? He didn't look away while the rest of the clan shouted and cheered and clapped. He didn't smile, or nod. He just stared. She had meant to tell him what all this meant before now, but there just hadn't been time.

But he knew now. She could see it in the tight line of his lips and the muscle that jumped along the line of his jaw.

Lidan's life belonged to Ehran. They were one; welded together by the clan and the ancestors and the swords in their hands. It was her fate to defend him, to save him if he was ever threatened, to put her body before his and take the brunt of whatever came his way. There was no going back, no reversing what had been done.

If Ehran died, so did she.

CHAPTER TWENTY

The Altipa

The trails of the dradur led south from the mountains and foothills of Ravinka and the Hidden Keep, breaking out across the high Altipan plain. It was a sparse expanse governed by tent-dwelling nomads who followed the seasons and game herds. Howling winds scoured the land unhindered, whipping across the plain, biting and clawing at anything that dared stand in their way.

Five days out from the Keep, Eian whistled from the head of the group and waved at the others to hurry.

Ran's heart thumped up into his throat and he nudged his horse forward. 'What is it?'

'Either my Sight has gone loopy or these trails are converging with more of their kind.' Eian pointed at the air a few yards ahead of his horse.

They had been sharing the task of tracking, resting their magic as often as they could to avoid exhausting themselves. Eian had power enough to see the newest thaumalux trails, which allowed Ran to focus on teasing out anything left behind more than a few months ago. Ran's Sight peeled back time to reveal a throbbing causeway of shimmering black dradur thaumalux.

Brit reined his horse in beside Ran. 'Which way?'

'They're going south,' Ran said, but Brit shook his head, following the direction of Eian's hand then squinting at the sun.

'Southwest, by the looks.'

Ran licked his dry, cracked lips and scanned the miles of nothing. The alpine tundra, carpeted with short grass and dotted with stunted, shivering shrubs seemed desolate. The hundreds of dradur trails criss-crossed the landscape—some as old as he was, others left no more than a few years ago—told a different tale. The two newest trails wound around the others in a familiar embrace, as if they had found kindred spirits out here in the wilds. The sheer number turned Ran's blood to ice, and he shuddered. *So many...*

For each body in that house there was a monster made... Iridia's voice crackled like a fallen leaf on the dry wind. Ran looked for her but found no trace. She kept herself hidden, and he wondered for a moment how much of his bone deep foreboding belonged to her. So often he felt like nothing more than a vessel for her vengeance, but she was not the only reason he pushed south into this barren, wind-scoured wasteland.

'Southwest, then?' Brit's words broke the silence.

'Southwest... What's out there?' Ran turned his head to see Brit suck at his teeth.

'More of this.' He nodded at the barren plain. 'And the biggest fucking mountains you'll ever set your eyes on.'

Another five days brought them within sight of the looming jagged heights of the Ice Towers. Elsewhere in the world, spring had turned to summer, but up here they didn't dare take off their coats and gloves. They pulled woollen hats down over their ears and wrapped scarves around their faces to ward off the frigid wind, wicked as knives against exposed skin. Some nights it fell away just enough for them to rest and eat, free of the relentless buffeting gale, but its bite never eased entirely.

They set camp, pitching their small tents as best they could in the wind, pegging them down in the icy soil. Zarad turned his elemental magic to sparking a fire, digging a hollow into the ground to protect the tiny flames, while Brit found something for them to eat in the packs. Eian had slumped onto a bedroll by the fire almost as soon as they'd dismounted, exhausted from another day of tracking while Ran rested, and Ran wondered how much more his friend could take.

Even with the rest days, Eian was struggling, the strain evident in the dark circles under his eyes and the drawn look on his face each morning. There would come a time when his power would simply stop responding, and Ran would be faced with tracking the dradur on his own. He finished hobbling the horses and stuffed his hands into his pockets, trying not to think too hard on how long his own magic would hold up when that day came.

The lingering sun finally retreated from the sky, and Ran stood with his back to the fire. As daylight faded to twilight and night drew its cloak around them, he unveiled his Sight and stared at the thaumalux trails. Despite sharing the load, exhaustion crept toward him, each day proving a little harder to pull his magic up from where it gathered. If he lost sight of the trails could Brit track the creatures by the prints left in the soil? He kicked at the ground with the toe of his boot. The earth was hard and unforgiving here; frozen, unyielding and unlikely to hold tracks for long, if at all.

Ran chewed the inside of his lip. He'd hoped to have found something by now—either the dradur or their makers, or some material sign of their passing, but all they had were the shimmering midnight trails he was certain he would lose if his magic failed him.

Something flickered amongst the trails in front of him and he narrowed his eyes. Was it a trick of the firelight, dancing across the ground under the thaumalux? He stepped closer and pressed his Sight against the trails, the magic unwinding the past until deep within, a faded rope of light appeared that pulsed with a slow, steady beat. It was faint, even to Ran's eyes, smothered by the bruise-blue light of the dradur. Their thaumalux wound around the lighter one, strangling it until it could hardly be seen at all.

Zarad appeared at Ran's shoulder and passed him a share of supper. Ran shied from the sudden appearance of Zarad's thaumalux, and he shuddered as he reeled his magic back in.

'You all right?' Zarad asked with a frown, before flicking away of his unruly red ringlets from in front of his eyes.

'Just...' Ran coughed and shook his head. 'Trying to see something hidden under the trails.'

'What is it?' Zarad glanced around. Sasha's brother was a powerful magic-weaver, skilled at manipulating the natural elements and detecting the vibrating frequencies of worked magic that were too faint for even Ran to perceive, but his eyes had never opened to Sight. To Zarad, the air in front of them was as empty as it was dark.

Ran shrugged and accepted the bowl of broth. 'Maybe nothing, but there's a lighter thaumalux underneath all those dradur trails. It's buried deep, but it's there. Are you getting any frequency disturbances?'

Zarad's frown deepened and Ran felt the man's magic roll away from them like swirling cloud flowing down a mountainside. He shivered and pulled his magic tighter around his Sight.

Zarad shook his head. 'No. Whoever left that trail didn't lay down any spells as they passed. The only magic at work here is ours.'

Ran looked back to where he'd seen the trails but kept his veil down. How old was that thaumalux hidden beneath the winding darkness of the dradur? Old enough to be the witches who made the creatures?

Witch, he corrected. Only one trail glowed beneath that throbbing thaumalux, not two. He tilted his head to one side as his mind slowly pulled the puzzle pieces together. *That* didn't make sense. Collan and Iridia had repeatedly told him there were two witches at Lackmah. But here there was only evidence of one...

Collan could have been mistaken, but Iridia had been there. She'd seen two witches, hadn't she? He glanced around. The ghost was nowhere to be seen, so Ran tucked his questions away and tried to focus on what he knew. 'I guess we just keep following the trails and see where they lead...'

Zarad gave him a sympathetic pat on the shoulder. 'We'll find them. It might take longer, and the road may be harder than we imagined, but we'll find them. They probably have no idea they've left a trail as bright as sunlight in their wake, and I'd wager they think themselves safe and sound wherever they've holed up all these years. They won't be expecting to be found, not after all this time.' They looked at each other and Zarad gave him a small smile. 'We're not going home empty handed.'

Ran hugged the bowl in his frozen fingers as Zarad returned to sit by the fire. The broth was a faintly meaty concoction with a few mysterious floaters on the surface. Still, it was better than nothing out here in the frigid expanse of the plain, and they had to make their supplies last. No one knew when they'd have a chance to replenish their stocks. He bit the inside of his lip again. They'd probably starve before they found what they were looking for, but at least he'd squirrelled away a couple of bottles of liquor in his pack. Not for the first time he wondered if he was leading his friends on a long, drawn out march toward death.

The warmth of the bowl in his hands did little to distract him from the whipping wind and the thaumalux that drew his attention again and again. It called to him, a persistent whisper he couldn't shut out. He didn't want to see it again, didn't want to waste his magic standing out here staring at the night, but the thaumalux called and his Sight answered. It eased back the veil and the trails materialised; the single bright vein glowing in the suffocating embrace of the dark light. There was a familiar pulse to them, as if they were all parts of a greater whole.

The bright trail, for all its years, was powerful. It radiated strength, like the heat from a fire trapped behind a door. It was barely contained; a shimmering raw energy that hurt to look at after too long, and he glanced away.

He wanted to speak to Iridia. Questions piled up in his head that needed to be given a voice, but she was gone. She'd so far lingered at the edge of his perception, breaking cover only when she thought he was alone. She had developed a wonderful habit of gate-crashing his dreams though, and he suspected she might do so again soon, especially since he'd found this trail. Answers meant waiting. He didn't fancy wandering off into the night to try and coax her out of thin air. That was a sure-fire way to break an ankle, or convince his friends he'd finally gone off the deep end when they found him talking to himself in the dark.

He looked up at the stars; a dusty band of twinkling light arced across the sky, bright despite the glow of the moon peeking above the horizon. How far would they have to go? As far as the coast, or across the sea? Did all of this lead to a cave in the mountains, or a nondescript hut in the hills somewhere south of the Altipa? Certainty slipped from him and his Sight stuttered as he forced the veil back down. The movement of the dradur, collected as it was over time, winding south to only the gods knew where, was his only lead. But would they find naught but graves at its end?

They had not yet caught up with the dradur who attacked the Keep. Unhindered by the needs that slowed him and his friends, they raced ahead without horses that required rest, or a hunger for food that required catching and cooking. They could go on through the night, free from the fear of snapping a horse's ankle in the deepest shadows. But Ran could not afford to take such risks. He chafed at any delay and found comfort only in knowing the dradur were unwittingly leading him across the wilds of the world to the doorstep of those who made them.

He hoped.

He bit down on his doubt, crushed it and swallowed all the sharp, bitter pieces. He didn't have time for this shit. But the doubt, the questions, Sasha's disappointed eyes—they all pressed in on him as he was forced to concede that ten days of searching had turned up nothing but more trails to follow into the unknown.

Ran clenched his jaw and turned back to the fire. He wiped out his empty bowl and stuffed it into a supply bag, then crawled through the doorway of his little tent. Iridia wasn't there, so he wriggled under the canvas of his bedroll and curled himself into a shivering ball.

He couldn't see his ghost, but her anger and doubt mirrored his own—one feeding the other, back and forth until a hot ball of emotion burned deep in his chest. He might never find the dradur who attacked the Keep. He had to accept that. He might never make them pay for the lives they had stolen, but he *would* hunt out their creators, and in that act, seek restitution for the blood spilled for those dark ends. He had to. Iridia had not given him a choice.

This revenge, this hatred that had been entirely Iridia's, belonged to him now. She had poured it into him, an all-consuming molten flow, and now he nurtured it, protecting it from the relentless doubt that battered against him. The white-hot hate urged him on when the logical voice in his mind cried foul, despairing at the utter folly of his goal. He squeezed his eyes shut and a wave of exhaustion washed over him. He sighed, giving in to the fatigue. The plan was as ambitious as it was foolish, but it was the only one he had.

It was the only path that led home.

Chapter Twenty-one

The Altipa

Tiny flowers dotted the grassland of the Altipa. Snow had been banished where sunlight touched the ground and hopeful buds of colour slipped free of the freezing soil, turning their faces to the sun, eager to see what the new season had to offer.

Ran and his companions devoured the distance, racing toward the soaring mountains on the southern horizon. On Brit's map, high peaks and ranges enclosed the Altipa on all sides, but none were as formidable as those directly to the south. On the map they had two names; the Ice Towers, as they were known by the people of the north, and the Malapa, the name given to them by those to the south. They dominated the space on the vellum sheet, as if the spine of the world had broken the surface of Coraidin and arched its bare bones toward the sky.

'Reckon we'll have to cross those?' Ran asked, his lips stinging as he spoke, burnt and bleeding from the insistent wind. Zarad passed him a tiny pot of lanolin ointment, which he hurriedly smeared on his dry skin before passing it on to Eian.

'If that's where your light-path leads, then I wager we will. We'll have to go through here,' Brit said, pointing at a tiny space on the vellum. 'Fracture Pass. It's only clear in the height of summer, and if we miss the window, we won't get through for another year.'

'How do you know that?' Ran eyed the watcher from under a doubtful frown.

'Trader's chatter in the taverns in Usmein. Every few years caravans from Arinnia and Isord go through to trade with the southerners, then they head home before the weather closes it again. They should be crossing about now, if I've got my timing right. They did tell some stories, those traders.'

Ran looked over at the others and the pair of them shrugged. Neither Zarad nor Eian had been beyond the walls of the Keep since they were children. All they knew of the outside world came from the books in Yidda's library and the couriers who visited the Keep.

'These traders—did they say the Pass was safe? Can it be crossed?'

'We've probably got a better chance in a small group than if we were taking a great big caravan of wagons through. We'll go faster too.' Brit's tone did little to allay Ran's anxiety. He hadn't anticipated impassable mountains. Perhaps a hard trek through some tough terrain, but not a pass that could only be crossed in a short window of time. Brit shrugged. 'Don't worry, I'm sure we'll be fine. As long as there's no avalanches or land slips or blizzards or anything. Should be fine.'

'Fuck's sake.' Ran spat dust from his mouth and took a swig from his water bladder. What if the thaumalux trail led straight through the Pass but it couldn't be traversed? Would they have to find another way around? *Was* there another way? He couldn't afford to lose the trails while searching for another path across the mountains. 'Where are we?'

'Here.' Brit pointed to where the thin lines of two rivers snaked northward out of the Ice Towers. 'Unless the trail cuts west along the foothills, I reckon we're going over that pass.'

Ran snorted and shook his head. 'Yeah, fuck it. Why not? It's not like I haven't seen enough fucking snow to last me a lifetime. What's a bit more between friends?'

'What's that?' Eian asked, his voice raw from lack of use.

Ran whirled to where Eian pointed at the foot of the mountains. In the distance, barely perceptible against the grey stone of the peaks, a finger of smoke rose into the sky.

'We might have some company tonight,' Brit murmured. Eian and Zarad looked at each other, silent questions in their eyes.

Ran glanced at the watcher. 'A settlement?'

'A camp, most likely.' Brit rolled the map and stuffed it into a saddle bag. 'Let's hope they take Orthian coin. Could murder an ale.'

Ran's heart beat harder with each step toward the rising smoke. He hadn't anticipated stumbling onto an Altipan camp, or traders. He hadn't thought they would come across anyone out here who might want to know who they were or what they were doing. And he hadn't put any thought into the horse-shit story he would need to deflect their questions.

His mind flipped back into the self-preservation that kept him alive when he escaped Usmein and Graupen, and he realised how foolish he had been to dismiss Sasha's concerns. *She* had anticipated this. She had warned him, and he'd brushed it off like it was a trifling thing he could deal with if the need arose. But now the need had arisen, he had nothing, his mind suddenly abandoning him to his fate. He worried at it as they rode, his eyes on the dradur trails beside his horse, fighting to come up with a story that was reasonably believable, something that wouldn't land him and his friends in a dungeon somewhere.

'Fellas?' Eian shouted and Ran's gaze snapped up. 'Not sure that smoke's coming from a cooking fire.'

He looked out over Eian's broad shoulder and his blood ran cold. The pale wisp of smoke rising from a pinpoint on the horizon had become a thick black column and his fear of capture found itself edged out by a newer, more visceral terror.

He squeezed his heels against his horse and gave it its head. The animal loped toward the haze, dark smoke stinging Ran's eyes as the remains of a camp materialised on the far side of a chattering mountain stream. He urged his horse on, and they splashed through the clear eddies and vaulted up the opposite bank. He eased the exhausted horse to a stop then dropped down from the saddle.

Strewn across the tundra, criss-crossed with the black trails of the dradur, were scores of collapsed tents. Most were smoking ruins, barely recognisable piles of charred poles and rags. A line of wagons stood to the west, smouldering carcasses of timber and steel, their wheels shattered to splinters and the draught horses dead in their harnesses. A few lay further west, as if someone had tried to drive them away from the chaos. Or perhaps the horses had bolted. It was impossible to tell.

Dozens upon dozens of corpses lay among the carnage—bits and pieces of humans strewn through a congealing mess of horse and goat—all twisted and broken and oozing as they festered in patches of dark, bloodied soil. A black form shifted on the ground and Ran's heart skipped, thudding hard back into time. It took but a second for him to realise it was flies. Hundreds of thousands of flies, buzzing clouds lifting from the bodies as he approached, giving each corpse a moment of shuddering life that dispersed, then reformed as the insects settled back to continue their feast. Black birds circled above, swooping through the smoke to land on the remains of their choice, sharp beaks slick with blood, macabre quills poised ready to record the final chapter of these lives.

The stench hit him like a punch in the face and Ran covered his mouth and nose with the sleeve of his jacket. The smoke and the smell coated his tongue; foul, sickly sweet death swilling around in his mouth. Someone behind him coughed and retched. He didn't turn to see who it was. He couldn't take his eyes off the camp.

A figure launched from the smoke and slammed into Ran, shoving him off his feet. He hit the dirt hard, legs and arms flailing. Without command, magic discharged from his hands and hammered into the body wrestling him on the ground. The energy boomed amongst the shouts of his friends and the attacker sailed backward into the swirling smoke.

He scrambled to his feet and sprinted in the direction of the figure's flight, searching the corpses for movement that was not a carrion bird or a swarm of flies. A shadow staggered upright a few feet away and stumbled, the grey light of day glinting on a brandished blade. Ran drew his sword and let his magic pool in his opposite hand, the blue light of his power glowing in the choking haze.

Eian appeared, weapon drawn and magic pooling. This was what Quaid and Collan had trained them for—the moment they had to turn their power to defend themselves. Behind the figure, Brit and Zarad emerged from the smoke, creeping forward but remaining out of sight. Brit edged closer on silent feet. He nodded at Ran.

The figure staggered and waved its blade at the two men in front of it. Ran's brow furrowed. This thing was not a dradur.

'Name yourself?' he called into the haze.

'You first!' a woman snapped back, and he froze. A familiar accent. One he knew from his mother. This woman was Isordian.

'We mean you no harm,' Ran told her, and withdrew his magic into the skin of his hand, extinguishing the power in a gesture of good faith.

'Your sword says otherwise.' The blade in her hand swung around again. Her coat billowed as the wind blustered through the camp, but her hood remained in place, obscuring her face.

Ranoth glanced at Brit and the watcher took a silent step toward the woman. 'I'll put it down if you come closer, so I can see your face.'

She laughed. 'Like fuck I will! Put it down. And your friends—they put theirs down too.'

'Not going to happen.'

She staggered again and sucked a breath through clenched teeth.

'What happened here?' Ran changed the subject, hoping to distract her.

'Monsters. Or maybe your friends. I don't know. I don't—' she wheezed again and wavered where she stood. She lunged at Ran with her knife swinging, before her strength failed and Brit darted forward to scoop the woman up as she fell. Her knife toppled to the dirt, abandoned by limp fingers, and Ran arrived at the watcher's side.

Her head lolled against Brit's arm; her body cradled across his chest. Blood caked her right hand, and an ugly dark stain spread across the clothing under her coat. She was pale; paler than she naturally should have been. There was no colour in her cheeks and dark circles under her eyes made her face seem sunken and gaunt. She looked like Ran's cousins from Isord, but half dead and slipping closer to an endless sleep with each passing moment.

Zarad shoved past Ran and put his hand on the woman's forehead, then neck. 'She's alive, but barely. Carry her back to the horses. I have a healing kit in my bags.' Brit nodded and they hurried away, leaving Ran and Eian in the swirling smoke.

'They took the camp, didn't they?' Eian asked. His voice was distant, as if trying to reach Ran through a thunderstorm.

A memory from long ago tore its way out of the cage he had locked it in. The farm. Bodies hunched under the snow. Drifts stained black with frozen blood. Butchered. He'd almost convinced himself it was nothing but a terrible nightmare. Almost.

But the mess of bodies around him, their silent screaming faces and their empty glaring eyes... The memory of the Parry farm howled back to life and dug its claws deep into his mind. He lurched, his legs crumpling beneath him.

The dradur did this. *Their* dradur; the pair who had survived the Keep and led them south. Ran hadn't thought he needed to catch them. He hadn't considered the price that might be paid for allowing them to run unchecked across the Altipa. He hadn't thought…

He cursed his stupidity and clambered slowly to his feet, looking over his shoulder at Brit's retreating back. That woman might yet die, like everyone else in this stained and smoking ruin, because he hadn't been fast enough. He'd let the dradur streak away, intent on letting them lead him to the source of all their chaos, not once thinking of the cost. He should have found these creatures and destroyed them before they could wreak havoc on these people. He could have, and he should have hunted them harder, and with more urgency.

But he hadn't.

This slaughter was the price paid for his failure.

Brit sat by his bedroll, within reach of the camp's sole survivor while Zarad crouched at her side, tending to her wounds. Ran recognised something of Sasha in Zarad's calm, steady ministrations. A pang of guilt and self-pity snapped in his chest and he turned from it, forcing himself to look at the smouldering camp, hoping it might burn the sensation away. He didn't have time for what might have been, for should have or could have. It was done. The dradur had murdered again and no amount of self-flagellation would bring these people back.

He itched to do something other than stand around waiting for the woman to wake, so he left and patrolled the remains of the camp with Eian, kicking soil over smouldering ash and searching the bodies for anyone who still clung to life. He sought solace in the perimeter, searching the extremities and remaining distant from the others. The tears in his eyes were as much the product of the smoke as the sheer horror surrounding him.

At nightfall he returned to their small cluster of tents and hobbled horses by the bank of the stream. He found Zarad staring vacantly into the fire, his face drawn and streaked with sweat, ash and tears. Ran's heart fell into his boots.

'Is she…?' he ventured, unwilling and unable to utter the words.

Zarad blinked once and shook his head. 'She lives, but she's got a wound in her side. It's ugly but not too deep. I've cleaned and stitched it. If she survives the fever, she should pull through.'

A sense of relief surprised Ran. Amongst the wanton butchery of the ruined camp, he had not expected such news. He'd expected to add her body to the pyre and to watch her burn with the rest of her people. The notion that she might survive, after all this destruction, lifted his heart.

He turned to where Brit sat by the bedroll. He'd hardly moved in the hours Ran had spent patrolling and searching, and sat a little closer to the woman with one arm hugging his chest. Ran moved and the firelight fell on one half of Brit's face.

'Brit?'

The older man didn't look up right away. Slowly, his head turned, and one eye settled on Ran. Exhaustion and anger radiated from him, sharp against Ran's raw senses. The ferocity of it caught Ran off guard and stole the breath from his chest.

'What is it?' whispered Ran as he fell to his knees and faced his old friend across the bedroll.

'They killed all of them, didn't they?' Brit's words were hoarse and broken.

It occurred to him then that Brit's experience with the dradur was limited to the attack on the Keep. He'd not seen what Ran had seen; the aftermath of the weapons and the teeth. Ran balled his trembling fingers into a fist.

'They did…'

Just like the Parrys… The thought shivered through him. Brit's gaze dropped to the woman and Ran looked at her. Brit clutched something tightly in his lap, so tightly that his knuckles paled, as if it he held the most precious thing in the world. Hidden by shadow, Ran hadn't seen it at first. The woman's hand, cradled in his lap, sheltered from the horror and the death. Her fingers clung to Brit, her broken nails biting his skin hard enough to draw blood.

The watcher shook his head. 'She won't let go. She screamed when Zarad stitched her side, clawed at the ground until her fingers bled, so I held her hand. She hasn't let go.' Their eyes met, but Ran couldn't find the words to comfort his friend. What could he possibly say? 'She's lost everyone…'

Ran reached over the bedroll and squeezed Brit's shoulder. 'She survived, and that's no small feat. We have to help her now, help her get well again. If she can survive this long, then she's strong.'

'And the creatures? The dradur?' Brit's voice shook with rage, and fresh tears welled along the red lines under his eyes.

'We follow them, and we destroy them. We destroy them and the monsters who made them.' He squeezed Brit's shoulder again and the watcher nodded, the muscles in his jaw jumping as he ground his teeth and tried to lock his anger behind them.

Ran helped the others with food, but Brit ignored the share Ran set beside him. Zarad checked on the woman again and Eian took a spare blanket to Brit, who bundled it under his head and lay on the ground with only his coat to shield him from the icy soil and a rudimentary windbreak at his back. His hand remained locked in the woman's grasp, even as sleep took him into its arms.

CHAPTER TWENTY-TWO

The Ice Towers

Ran wanted to get moving as soon as the sun rose over the mist shrouding the blackened camp, but Zarad wouldn't hear it.

'She needs at least another day of rest,' he insisted in a hushed whisper.

'I know…' Ran's whole body was tense, his senses on edge, waiting for something to leap out of the haze. He released a sigh. 'But we can't stay here. We have to keep moving.'

The drive to move on was a burning urge he couldn't shake no matter how he tried. He knew he was asking the impossible of Zarad, knew the woman needed rest if they wanted her to survive the ride, but a cruel, selfish part of him didn't care.

'You're welcome to try and get her on a horse, but I'd wager you'll get a broken nose and two black eyes for your efforts.' Zarad tilted his head at where Brit sat beside the sleeping woman. 'No way he's letting her go anywhere yet.'

Ran nodded and smothered the irrational need to leave. 'Keep an eye on them, will you? And see if you can get that big idiot to eat something. I'm going to see if I can find something that tells us who these people were.'

He headed into the destruction. After several hours of rifling through the ruins, he found what he was looking for in the least mangled of the wagons, the only one to have survived the flames. It was the farthest from the centre of the campsite; the wheels naught but a collection of splinters and the flat bed tray cracked down the centre. Ran had recovered the driver's body yesterday; its face carved off and innards feasted on. The horse bound within the harness had its throat torn out. Both had been added to the pyre, leaving the wagon listing on its side in the shadow of the Ice Towers.

In the bed of the wagon were several small timber chests. By the way they jingled when he dragged them free of the wreckage, they were full of coins of some sort. He gripped the lock and forced his magic into it, willing the metal to crack under the pressure, but succeeded only in heating the steel to the point that it seared the skin of his hand.

One chest among them was unlocked and he set it atop another and eased back the lid to reveal a shroud of oiled cloth. He removed the bundle and unwrapped it, peeling layer after layer of tightly wound fabric from a collection of leather document wallets and vellum scrolls. Someone had gone to great lengths to protect the contents. Ran opened the top-most wallet and leafed through the pages inside. A map as well as a long-winded list of instructions.

Eian crouched beside him and reached over to shake one of the locked chests, tilting his head to listen to the clinking of the contents inside. 'No wonder he tried to get this wagon away. This thing was loaded.'

'Not that it did him any good,' said Ran. 'Still ended up with his insides on his outside.'

'I would have tried to save the wagon with the wine casks, but that's just me.' Eian abandoned his effort to pick the lock and sat atop the chest. 'What's in there?'

'Maps. Documents. Letters. An invoice or two.' Ran held the map up to the early afternoon light. 'Must be the Pass and the trail south. Look,' he pointed at a line marked on the northern most point on the map. 'They've come from Kotja in Isord by the look of that, via Kederen.'

Eian studied the map over Ran's shoulder. 'What's that in the Pass?'

Ran eyed the two large ink dots at either end of a gap in the mountains. 'No idea. But these people were traders, not Altipan nomads. Did you find anything in the other wagons?'

Eian shrugged and picked up a scroll. 'Some food, but the fresher stuff isn't far off spoiling. Plenty of wine casks, like I said. Lots of cloth, furs and the like. Zarad went looking for healing supplies and found two wagons chock full of weapons. Spears and lances mostly. Loads of bows, arrows and some weird looking Isordian thing that shoots bolt-shafts. Brit reckons it's a crossbow?'

Ran nodded and continued to scan the documents in his lap. 'That's a weapon you don't want to stand in front of. My uncle has a whole armoury of them in Kotja. Nasty things, but slow. Mostly used in sieges when you can fire from cover.'

'Weapons traders, eh? Fat lot of good it did them.' Eian tossed the scroll back in the chest.

Ran's heart thumped hard against his chest and his train of thought vanished. Amongst the pages and pages of instructions a single word glared up at him. He knew enough Isordian to know he hadn't mistranslated it. He leapt to his feet. 'They're not trading the weapons. They're for defence.'

He ran through the veil of lingering smoke, and Brit looked up and frowned. 'Is she awake?' Ran called through the wind.

Brit nodded and beside him the figure of the woman shifted, her head turning toward the sound of his voice. Ran lifted the pages flapping in his hand and stabbed a finger at the lines of carefully scribed Isordian text. 'What is this? What does this mean?'

'Mind your tone, Ranoth,' Brit growled into the air between them.

Ran continued to glare at the woman watching him from the bedroll, impassive and unmoved by his demands. He switched to Isordian and repeated his question, thrusting the page toward her. 'What does this mean?'

She slowly lifted herself onto her elbow and took the paper. A small smile spread across her cracked lips. 'You've never crossed the Pass, have you?'

'That wasn't my question.' The others stared, unable to understand any more than a few words of the language spoken in the highest reaches of the Ruken. 'What does that word mean? I know what it says, but what does it *mean*? Why are there more wagons of weapons than food in this convoy?'

The woman grimaced as she pushed herself up to sit and slipped into the common trading tongue. 'Have *any* of you crossed the Pass before?'

She looked at them each in turn and found only shaking heads.

'And you?' She eyed Ran with a frigid stare. He ground his teeth to confine a retort and shook his head. 'Ever heard the stories?'

He nodded this time, his anger simmering down under her scrutiny. Zarad and Eian shook their heads, but Brit stayed strangely still. What did he know of this place?

'If you heard the tales, then you know what that word means. You have enough of our tongue to read it. You aren't a native speaker but you're good. You grew up on our words, our stories, didn't you?'

164

He had, but he'd thought them bedtime tales his mother wove to scare him off wandering alone in the wild places of the world, but he had never considered they might be true. 'They're nothing but legends told to frighten children.'

'Are they?' She dragged herself to her feet and squared her shoulders, biting down on a groan and clutching her side. 'You think all those spears were to defend us against myth and legend? There are things in those mountains, hungry things, sleeping for entire seasons until they smell human flesh venture into their domain. Things warned of in stories, if the blind are wise enough to see it.'

Zarad leaned forward. 'What's she talking about, Ran?'

'Ice dragons,' Ran murmured. He suddenly felt very small in the shadow of the soaring mountains.

'Fucking *what*?' shouted Eian, and Zarad swore.

'Did you know about this?' Ran turned to Brit, but the watcher's eyes were on the woman and didn't seem willing to shift.

'There were mutters. Stories. Nothing worth mentioning.' Brit's voice cracked and he cleared his throat. 'No one said anything about fucking dragons, Ran. Not once. Not in any of the taverns or markets. Not once.'

'Why would they?' the woman cut in. 'Why warn a competitor and give them a chance to break into your market? They come south, they try to cross the Pass, they freeze to death or get eaten.'

'Well that's fucking cheery, ain't it?' Ran snarled.

'Look, I don't know why you're here, or what you thought you were going to find up there.' The woman winced and Brit stood, wrapping a steady hand around her elbow. 'But if you think the *snow* is the reason people don't cross the Pass more often, then you're in for a rude surprise.'

'A bit like when the dradur happened upon your camp, I suppose.' Ran was fairly sure she would have hit him if it hadn't been for the injury biting into her side. Her gaze, bright with fever and pain, bored into him with an intensity he could never hope to match, and he glanced away from her challenge.

Brit turned toward the woman. 'Aelish, do you know the Pass well enough to cross it? Safely, I mean?'

Aelish? Ran baulked. He hadn't even asked the woman's name before berating her about what lurked in the mountains.

What a surprise? Iridia smirked from beside a pile of charred timber that had once been a wagon.

Where the fuck have you been? he demanded, shooting a quick glare in her direction before turning back to Brit and Aelish.

Sometimes you really are a dunce. Maybe next time you meet a woman, start by asking her name. Iridia shrugged. *Maybe introduce yourself. She might be more willing to give you the time of day.*

Ran looked away and coughed awkwardly. His cheeks flushed with heat and he sighed. 'Wait. I'm sorry. I started this all wrong.' He extended his hand toward Aelish. 'I'm Ranoth, but this lot call me Ran.'

Aelish considered him for a moment, then slowly accepted his hand with a cautious squeeze. 'Aelish Yordam.'

'Have my friends been better mannered than I and introduced themselves?' he asked, nodding at Zarad and Eian. Aelish inclined her head and Ran sensed her hostility begin to soften. 'Let's get some food in our bellies. Then we can talk properly.'

Night crept up on them from the east, surrounding them in violet twilight and impending darkness. Aelish watched as they moved about the campsite, Brit stoking the fire with wood scavenged from ruined wagons, murmuring the odd word to her that Ran failed to catch on the whipping highland wind. Ran guessed her to be somewhere in her early twenties, though it was hard to tell through the grime, blood and soot plastered across her features and staining her braided blonde hair.

By the time the sun dipped behind the mountains on the western horizon their supper was ready. Eian shouldered a scavenged wine cask and carried it into the camp, sharing the contents among the group in an assortment of mismatched cups.

'Found some supplies in a wagon.' Ran nodded at the platter and bowl he handed to Aelish. 'Hope that's all right.'

She shrugged. 'Won't do the dead any good to leave it. Someone might as well have it before it spoils.'

The five of them ate quietly, Eian and Zarad sharing a few whispered words where they sat on the other side of the fire. Ran imagined it wasn't easy finding time alone out here in the wilds, so he left them to their conversation and stared into the flames.

'What are you all doing out here?' Aelish's voice cut the silence and she put her empty bowl on the ground.

'I could ask the same of you,' Ran countered.

'I asked first though.'

Ran couldn't help smiling. Even though she was clearly exhausted and fighting intense pain, she was going to make him work for every skerrick of information. Time to roll out his shitty story and see if it held water. 'We're tracking those things that attacked your camp. They killed people in our village and we're hunting them. You?'

Her finger ran idly along the rim of her cup. 'We're traders. You know that already. We were going south to trade with the people across the Ice Towers. It's warm this season, warmer than it has been for years, so the Pass should be clear.'

'Who were you among these people?' he asked, waving his cup toward the ruins. The warmth of the wine washed through him, but it hadn't blinded him just yet. He saw how Brit glanced at him, casually enough, but there was an edge to his gaze. If Aelish noticed, she didn't give anything away.

She looked up from her cup and studied him. 'My mother is the principal holder of the East Ruken Trading Company. I am—I *was*—the superintendent of this crew.'

The soft murmur of conversation across the fire faded as Zarad and Eian paused, their attention drawn away from their quiet conversation.

Ran's eyes never left her face. 'Do you remember what happened?'

She chewed her lip for a moment, as if running the memories through her head, searching for the words. 'I was scouting the mouth of the Pass when they came. We weren't expecting an attack from behind. It's the things in the mountains we watch for. The plain is a safe place... or at least we thought.

'We hadn't sent a crew out to the Pass for years, but there were rumours from other companies of crews failing to return.' She shifted where she sat, staring into the middle distance, eyes bright with fear and firelight. 'We thought it was the dragons. We thought... we thought traders were trying to cross in cold seasons, when the serpents are more active, more aggressive. They hate the heat. It makes them sick. They pull right back into the highest reaches when the melt comes, and the Pass is clear. We didn't think it anything more than bad planning on the part of the other crews.'

She rubbed the bridge of her nose and a heavy, dreadful pause filled the air, her hand shaking where it gripped the cup. 'When I got back, the camp had been overrun. Fires everywhere, people screaming, horses shrieking. So much blood. The smell was…' Aelish shuddered, a single tear slipping from her glistening, bloodshot eyes. 'Something hit me, and everything went dark. I woke up to silence and smoke.'

Ran glanced at the others, firelight flickering across their faces, entranced by Aelish's story. The flames of the Hidden Keep danced in Ran's vision, screams echoing through his mind. He saw Sasha and Quaid and closed his eyes against their pain.

'You can track those monsters who savaged my crew?' Aelish asked. Ran and Eian nodded and she gestured into the darkness beyond the firelight. 'You think they went through the Pass?'

Ran turned to the mountains and unveiled his Sight. The dradur's thaumalux flared to life, weaving through the remains of the trader's camp before streaking away and vanishing into the night. 'Yes.'

'And you want to follow them?'

He looked at the others. They sat around the camp, silent and expectant. They were with him on this journey, but it was his vengeance that drove them. If he turned for the Keep, he doubted any of them would protest. Except Brit—Ran would never hear the end of it from the watcher.

Eventually, Ran nodded. 'They're driven by a hunger they can't sate. They can't be reasoned with. They can't be deterred. Those who made them must be brought to Justice, and the only way we force them to that end is if we follow where the trail leads. If it leads over the Pass, then that's where we have to go.'

'*Through* the Pass,' Aelish corrected, accepting a refill for her cup from Brit. Ran frowned. 'That's what I said.'

'No, you said *over*. You don't go *over* Fracture Pass—you go *through* it.'

'All right…' He glanced at Brit, but the watcher just shrugged and stretched out on the ground behind Aelish.

'If you're going to kill them, then I'm coming with you. They have taken from me and mine, and I won't be turning for home until the score is settled. In any case, I doubt you're going to make it through the Pass without help.' She nodded at the collection of bedrolls, saddles and weapons behind Eian and Zarad. 'I hope you know how to use those blades. We're going to need every inch of steel we can carry.'

CHAPTER TWENTY-THREE

The Western Reaches, Tolak Range, the South Lands

Travelling with a caravan was as tedious as Lidan remembered. Used to crossing the Tolak range at speed, travelling light and unimpeded by the needs of cumbersome wagons and their occupants, a party of rangers could have made the journey to Tingalla in a fortnight, weather and adversaries permitting. With wagons full of children and inexperienced travellers, it would take twice as long to cross the country between Hummel and the border village.

Even when the travelling was good, it took them hours every morning to strike camp, pack, herd the children and adults into the wagons, harness the massive draught horses and begin their slow, lumbering progress westward. They stopped frequently over the course of the day and were forced to make camp well before the sun touched the horizon. If Lidan hadn't had the relative freedom of moving up and down the column as she wished—scouting ahead and circling back—she was sure she would have gone mad with frustration within the first three days.

When the caravan stopped for the evening, tines bustled around the centre of the camp like bees tending a hive, preparing food and setting up sleeping shelters for the daari, his family and the other clan folk travelling with them. There was Forge Master Rick, of course, and a pair of apprentices, as well as a number of other trade masters brought along to manage the maintenance of weapons, saddles, harness and wagons. The Crone travelled with them also, but for the most part she remained inside a wagon set aside for Sellan's exclusive use.

On the fourth evening out from Hummel, Lidan gave up trying to help her mothers with the children. Her presence was superfluous, and the sheer unrelenting noise and chaos of so many demanding little bodies overwhelmed her entirely. She retreated toward the edge of the camp and tethered Theus behind a small pavilion some tine-men were pitching for her.

Here, among the smaller tents and bedrolls, there was an easy sense of quiet, a dull murmur of conversation and movement punctuated only by the call of birds and the snort of horses. So far, they hadn't encountered any ngaru or Namjin raiders, and the mood among the rangers was one of peace, if not a little boredom. Her tent was all but ready, and the tine-men began moving a collection of furniture into its confines. Lidan slipped off the leather harness that supported her scabbard and handed it to a tine who took it into the depths of the tent. The sword wasn't heavy, but she hadn't yet grown accustomed to the leather straps biting into her shoulders. Rick would arrive before supper to continue their daily training ritual, but for a while at least, she had time to herself.

There were freshwater pools to the north of the campsite, and in the oppressive humidity of the day, the thought of splashing her face and cooling her feet drew her past the watch posts and sentries and along a sandy creek bed. A multitude of tracks wound along the bank, left by rangers watering their horses and tines carting tubs back to the camp for washing and cleaning. A lone pair of boot prints veered away from the rest—the left foot pushing in deeper than usual into the sand, while the right dragged, gouging a trench beside it.

Lidan's eyes narrowed and she followed the trail as it turned upstream and down into a gully. It didn't take long to spot Loge through the trees, his leather jerkin, belts and left boot discarded on the sand. He struggled with the other boot now, pushing at the heel with his left foot; his knee refusing to bend enough for him to reach with his hands. Her stomach lurched. His face awfully pale and beading with sweat, his fingers trembled as he finally got a purchase on the leather.

She moved through the bush, making as much noise as she could as she uncorked her water bladder and knelt at the creek to fill it. On her periphery, Loge snapped around, staggering to his feet.

'Lidan?' he called, and she turned, feigning surprise and dropping the bladder in the shallows.

'Oh! I didn't see you there!' She scooped the bladder from the water before the current could carry it past the reeds and worked the stopper into its mouth. Loge cleared his throat and looked about himself, searching for something Lidan couldn't see. Perhaps an excuse for being out here on his own, dishevelled and sweating as though he'd run all the way across the range to get here. Of course, he hadn't run anywhere. He'd limped, dragging his crooked right leg through the sand to somewhere he could hide his pain and the injury he refused to acknowledge.

'I was just—' he started.

Lidan raised a brow and he stopped. He sighed and slumped back on a boulder.

'Why are you doing this to yourself?' she asked.

He wouldn't look at her, staring instead at the light dancing across the surface of the water. Did he even know why? Or was it something he felt driven to, unable to stop himself? He shrugged and Lidan pushed through the thin bank of shrubs separating them.

She crouched at his feet and pulled off the offending boot and its accompanying sock. She sat back on her heels and crossed her arms, studying his face even though he refused to meet her gaze. 'Are you going to let me see it? Or, are you going to keep pretending everything's fine?'

He looked at her then, fire in his eyes, his lips set in a fierce line. For a moment he said nothing, and she waited, her face an impassive mask she hoped hid her pounding heart and thundering pulse.

'Turn around,' Loge said finally, the words forced between clenched teeth. Lidan stood and turned, scanning the trees as she heard him unfasten his trousers. He sucked in a breath and Lidan fought every instinct not to turn around. She bit her tongue and waited. 'Right. You can turn back now.'

She took a breath and turned. He was back on the boulder with his trousers across his lap, his legs bare from the mid-thigh down to his feet. At the sight of his knee an involuntary groan fell from her mouth and her shoulders sagged. 'What were you thinking?! No, wait, don't answer that. You clearly weren't thinking at all. Are you mad? Look at this thing?'

He bore her tirade through closed eyes until she ceased her onslaught. Lidan sank into a crouch and put her hands either side of the joint. Loge hissed and shifted when her fingers settled on the livid black bruises, but he didn't pull away. It was swollen, and the bruises ran halfway down his calf, a deep, angry blue-black that was yellowing at the edges. What he had done exactly, and to what degree, she couldn't tell, but the sinews holding his knee together were badly damaged. Bearing weight on it for weeks had made it worse, as had the lack of attention from a healer.

'You shouldn't be walking on this, let alone...'

It took but a second for the realisation to slap her with its harsh sting. It was written all over his face; the set of his jaw and the stoic determination in his eyes. It was like staring into the blazing furnace of the forge.

It was for her. All of it. The pain, the dogged refusal to reveal the extent of the injury. Somehow, it was all for her.

'Why?' she whispered.

Loge shook his head. 'If you'd seen it, you'd have told Siman. If Grent had seen it, he would have told Siman.'

'Siman knows, Loge. He's not an idiot,' she countered, anger cutting at the edge of her voice.

Loge continued as if he hadn't heard her. 'If Siman knew it was more than a bit of stiffness, he would have ordered me to rest. Even then, it might never have healed.' She opened her mouth to protest but he kept going. 'I'd end up guarding the wall with Jac and all the others who aren't fit to ride. They'd have left me and taken you. In four years, I haven't let you ride out that gate alone...'

He looked away, but Lidan couldn't.

'Lidan?!' her father's voice echoed through the gully.

She spun around, searching the trees for the daari. Loge found his feet and somehow vanished behind the boulder in a flurry of curses and pained grunts.

'Get out of here!' Loge demanded.

Lidan glanced over her shoulder. 'What are you—'

He was wrestling with his trousers and scowled up at her. 'Would you get out of here? If he finds you down here, with me, like *this*, we're dead. Get going!'

It took a moment for her to realise what he meant. 'Oh.'

'Liddy?!' Erlon called again and she heard something large and angry crashing through the bush.

'I'm here! Just filling my water bladder,' Lidan shouted. She left the bladder on the ground, collected Loge's boots and gear and rounded the boulder to where he was fighting with his pants. She grabbed the belt of the trousers and reefed them up over his injured leg. He bit down on a scream and a mouthful of curses and she crouched to shove his right boot back on his foot.

'You all right down there?' Her father's tone was cautious this time, less concerned, less agitated.

'Of course! I'll be up in a minute!' she called back as Loge stuffed the hem his shirt into his pants and fastened the laces. She came to her feet and glanced out past the largest of the boulders. Her father was still far enough away that the trees and undergrowth kept them hidden.

'What are you still *doing* here?' Loge demanded, panting and clutching the top of his knee.

She didn't know what to say. She was furious at him, worried, and completely confused all at once. Of all the thoughts whirling in her mind, she chose the one that made the most sense, the one she could articulate. The others were all too raw, too new, too unformed to be given voice just yet. 'That leg. It needs tending.'

'I told you—'

'No, you shut the fuck up and listen to me,' Lidan hissed and closed the space between them. 'If you don't let me treat it, this will be the last ride you *ever* go on, Loge Baker. You want to stay with me? You want to be where I am? Then let me fix you. Stop being a fool and let me do this. Fuck! The ancestors know you've kept me alive these past four years, so just let me do this.'

She was sure he would refuse, sure he would push her away again, as though allowing her to help would be admitting defeat and inviting a fate he couldn't abide.

'Please,' she whispered. She couldn't hear her father's calls anymore, or the sound of the rushing water in the stream. There was just her breath and the rapid thud of her heart.

Those bright eyes settled on her face. 'Fine.'

Then he reached forward and shoved her out from behind the rocks. She staggered to a stop beside her abandoned water bladder and turned to see her father pushing his way through the bush at the top of the gully.

Erlon spotted her and waved. 'There you are! Your mother is screaming the camp down trying to find you. Better get back, eh?'

Lidan scooped up her water bladder and jogged up the bank to her father's side. She didn't dare glance back to where Loge hid. Could he get out of the gully on his own? If he wasn't back at camp for supper she would have to sneak away and find him.

'Where's your sword?' Her father frowned and looked over her shoulder to where her scabbard had been.

'Oh, ah… in my tent. Still getting used to the straps.'

Erlon nodded and glanced away, as if averting his eyes would hide the glimmer of disappointment.

She'd only meant to be gone a few moments, and while she was getting better at using the sword, her knives were always going to be her weapons of choice. Besides, she hadn't thought he would come looking for her, or that she would need the thing on a short trip to the creek. Then again, she hadn't thought she would stumble upon Loge either, half dressed and struggling. Her skin prickled with heat and she hurried to change the subject. 'I didn't realise I'd been gone so long.'

'You haven't been gone *that* long,' said Erlon. He grinned and shrugged. 'But you know what your mother's like.'

Lidan forced a laugh, her feet sinking into the sandy bank. 'Can't even get a moment alone without her throwing a fit. Is she going to be like this the whole way to Tingalla?'

'Probably.'

'I'm not sure I can last that long,' she muttered.

Her father smirked. 'Neither am I.'

The shadows grew longer and Lidan watched the northern edge of the camp, wondering if Loge hadn't fallen down a creek bank and snapped his neck. The thought made her stomach clench, and she was about to find an excuse to slip away and look for him when Rick and Ehran arrived at her tent to begin their daily sword training.

It was an odd feeling to be trained by someone who wasn't a ranger, and stranger still to see a man she associated with swinging hammers turn his hand to cutting and thrusting with a sword. And although it was a welcome distraction from worrying about Loge, Lidan spent most of the afternoon quelling a tide of childish jealousy rising in her blood.

Ehran either had a freakish natural affinity for swinging a blade, or unbelievable beginner's luck. He copied the steps Rick taught them, picking them up as if they were moves to a dance. He managed to remember them better than Lidan and moved with a fluid grace she thought no four-year-old should have. What was worse, she couldn't seem to force her muscles to replicate any of what seemed to come so naturally to her half-brother.

She stumbled and her arm twisted, and Rick's blunt training blade touched the skin at her neck. Ehran turned and stabbed his training sword at a bug on the ground and a small cluster of rangers murmured approval at Rick's skill, having stopped their own training to watch. Breathing hard, she waited for Rick to release her.

'You're trying too hard,' he said, holding his position.

Lidan sucked air deep into her lungs. 'What?' she panted.

Rick relented and withdrew his sword. 'You're trying too hard.'

'As opposed to *not* trying?'

He lunged before she could think and her arm came up. Their blades crashed together and Lidan parried his away with a hard flick, then whipped her sword back in to attack. He shuffled away under her blows and Lidan stopped, her practise blade poised above the soft skin of his shirtless belly.

Rick laughed. 'See? When you stop thinking, you start fighting.'

She stepped back and Nathen threw her a water bladder from where he sat with Jessah. So *that* was her problem? She was too focused on getting the movements to *look* right when she should have been focusing on how they *felt*. Somewhere in the distance, thunder rolled across the sky, and the sun sank further into the west. The soft leather of her jerkin and undershirt were drenched in sweat. It dripped from her nose and other places she hadn't thought it possible to sweat from and she hoped the nearby storm would bring some cooling rain to their camp.

'Your instincts will always go back to your knives, and that's not a bad thing. This is just a big knife. But when you get your head out of the way, you find your feet. The fighter comes out.' Rick accepted the water bladder and took a long draw. 'The rest is just fancy footwork.'

'Never took you for a fighter,' said Lidan. 'Who taught you?'

'My father was a forge master for a great house. He made their weapons and taught their children, and me, 'til we were old enough to start our apprenticeships. I took up the hammer, they took up pens and books. But they still had to practise fighting, so they practised with us. I was never one for books or scrolls or pens.'

Lidan frowned. 'Why not?'

'Can't read,' he replied with a grin then gestured at Ehran. The boy jogged forward swinging his wooden practise sword and Rick absorbed the blows. He twisted away from the onslaught and tapped Ehran on the ribs. They repeated the dance a few times, Rick winning and losing at even intervals, correcting movements and stances, then laughing when Ehran's sword slapped him on the back of the arm. 'Ow! All right, that's enough for today, wee man.'

Ehran beamed and Rick tousled his hair. This was exactly what the child craved. Lidan had too when she was his age and for years after—all she had ever wanted was someone to spend time with her, to show her something new and exciting. It had taken a threat to her life before she'd found someone willing to do it, someone who knew what it was to stare down the steaming maw of a ngaru and see death wedged between its rotting teeth. As jealous as she was of Ehran's innate skill, at least he was being given that chance now, before his life depended on it.

CHAPTER TWENTY-FOUR

The Western Reaches, Tolak Range, the South Lands

The sun set and supper was dished out among the travellers in the camp. Loge emerged from the bush not long after, his jaw clenched tight as he forced his leg to bend and bear weight, and Lidan's heartbeat rose as she watched him limp through the tents. Had it really taken him *this* long to get back from the creek? His usually healthy brown skin was drawn and sickly pale, and his wavy black hair a slick, sweaty mess. His suffering wrenched her stomach, and she turned away, her appetite evaporating.

She'd been wrong to leave him out there. She should have found an excuse to get rid of her father, helped Loge back to camp, then eased his pain before training with Rick. But would he have accepted her help, or found a reason to push her away?

Ehran sat beside Lidan, chewing loudly on a roasted bird's leg and ignoring the vegetables he'd carefully pushed to the edge of his platter. He reminded her of Abbi in ways she couldn't quite reconcile. Tiny movements, little things he did without prompting. He hated crowds and noise, just as Abbi had. He was curious and determined, but adventurous in ways Abbi hadn't been. They shared their father's smile and his frown of concentration, but that was where the resemblance ended—Ehran had too much of his mother in him.

In fact, Lidan recognised more of herself in the boy than she cared to admit, as if he was becoming her reflection rather than her opposite. Each day that passed made it harder for her to dislike him, a little harder to resent him and his role in all this. He hadn't asked to be born their father's heir. Neither of them had. All either of them really wanted from life was a little freedom and a horse.

Lidan suddenly remembered Icewind and her promise to have it fixed. The toy was buried in a bag in her tent. She put her bowl aside and brushed her trousers down.

'Ehran, you stay here with Marrit and Elva, all right? No wandering off, or your mam will have my eyes for earrings.' The boy grinned at his older sisters, then shuffled under Elva's outstretched arm. Lidan turned to Marrit. 'Keep him close. Never know what might be beyond the fires. I've got something to sort out.' Her sister nodded, and Lidan hurried away before she could ask any questions.

When she arrived at her sleeping pavilion, Loge was perched on a log nearby. He had a bowl beside him, but the contents looked untouched. She folded her arms and looked him up and down. He had a pretty healthy relationship with food, and in the years she'd known him, had never missed a meal by choice. 'I thought I'd have to hunt you down?'

'Yeah, well, I did promise you could try.' Loge shrugged. 'Doubt it'll do much good, but you can try.'

'Let's see if I can't prove you wrong.' Lidan held the tent door aside and he ducked through the opening.

At this time of year there was no need to burn a brazier for heat, so the tines had arranged thick bee's wax candles around the place for light. The tent was tall enough inside that they both stood comfortably without brushing their heads on the roof, and on one side of the space was a low pallet topped with a mattress of furs wrapped in a linen sheet. To the left stood a small table and a chair, her trunk of riding clothes, and carefully positioned on the table was her sword, still hidden within its scabbard. Beside that, a bowl of fresh water and a cloth, a small hand mirror and a variety of combs and pins her mother insisted she use to keep her hair in presentable order.

'Well, I suppose—' she began.

'Pants off and on the bed?' asked Loge, his light hazel eyes gleaming in the candlelight.

Lidan burst out laughing. She tried to reply, but the smile on his face was too much. She could only nod and turn around while he stripped and made himself comfortable. Earlier that afternoon she had pilfered some supplies from the wagons and stuffed them in a small leather bag, anticipating that she would have to go searching for him. She grabbed all she needed and conveyed them to the floor beside her pallet. From the depths of the bag she retrieved a stoppered urn, a roll of linen bandage, a pot of mashed snake vine and bouncer berries, and a handful of linen dressings.

'So, how many ales did you have for dinner?' she asked, kneeling to arrange her provisions.

He might have had the forethought to cover his nakedness with one of the linen sheets, but he couldn't hide the unnatural shimmer in his eyes or the smell of ale on his breath. He shrugged. 'A few. Wasn't going to be able to walk over here without at least a few.'

'Afraid I'm going to hurt you?' Lidan soaked the cloth in the water and bathed his knee.

'Ah, no. Not afraid of you.'

'Whatever you say,' she smirked and held up the stoppered urn. 'This oil will make it warm and take out some of the pain. You don't need much. Don't drown it, or you'll run out before we get to Tingalla. Massage it in twice a day. This stuff,' she held up the little pot, 'will take down the swelling and *hopefully* give the damage a chance to repair. You need to put it on twice a day as well, maybe more. If you need help, come and find me. Marrit can help too, or Jessah, but if you're still fragile about people knowing what you've done, then come find me.'

'Did your father suspect anything?' he asked.

Lidan fumbled the oil urn and caught it before it tumbled from her fingers. Heat rose in her cheeks as she started to massage his knee, and she cursed herself. Four years they'd been out in the wilds together, often alone, often for days on end. Why did she all of a sudden feel like she'd been hit by lightning whenever he looked at her? 'Not a thing. Why?'

'Do you have any idea what he would have done if he'd seen us?' All the affected bravado and humour had vanished from his voice.

Lidan cleared her throat and jammed the stopper back into the urn. 'What was there to see? I was examining your leg—your injured, fucked up, fucking leg—that you *should* have let me see to the day after that ngaru fight. But no, you left it and hid it away thinking no one would notice.'

She sighed and met his gaze. His face was drained of colour and sweat beaded his brow. He looked exhausted, broken, but something beneath all that still burned bright.

'Why?'

'I already told you why,' he replied.

Fine. Let him try and hide his motivations, just like his twisted knee. If he wasn't going to say it outright, then she wasn't going to waste her time trying to get it out of him. 'You look awful, by the way.'

Loge rolled his eyes. 'Oh, good. I was worried I didn't look *quite* as shitty as I feel.'

She held up the urn again. 'How many times a day?'

'Twice.'

'Good.' She put it aside. The mash in the pot was potent, stinging her eyes as she unwrapped the cloth cover and levered out the wax seal. She scooped out a portion the size of her thumbnail. The thick, fibrous mixture spread well over the oiled skin.

Loge looked down at his knee, now plastered in the greenish ointment. 'Ugh, that's disgusting!'

'All the best treatments are,' said Lidan with a smile. She put the cloth pads either side of his knee and began wrapping the whole thing with the bandage. 'This will need changing in the morning. Give it a little while to work and you should be right to walk back to your tent. Take this with you.'

She started to pack the supplies into the leather bag, but Loge's hand wrapped around hers. 'Keep it here. No point in me taking it. You'd never be happy with my efforts anyway.' They shared a smile and she nodded.

'When you're feeling better, can you look at something for me?' Lidan took the bag of supplies to the table and dug around in the bottom of her saddlebag for the broken horse figure. 'This is Ehran's. I told him I knew someone who could fix it. I doubt it's actually salvageable, but he loves it, and...'

Loge took the horse and its dismembered leg and turned it carefully in the candlelight. 'Who made this?'

Lidan shrugged. 'No idea. He was playing with it in the common room.'

His eyes met hers, shadowed by a frown. 'This is balter wood. It's useless for carving anything but priggin dolls.'

'What?' Lidan's pulse quickened. 'Are you sure?'

Priggin dolls were never deployed against children. Their parents, perhaps, but no one would ever make a figure carved with curses for a child.

Loge levered himself up from the pallet and swung his legs over the side. He held the horse toward the nearest candle and Lidan sank to the floor. As he angled it toward the light, the thin white paint glistened, revealing tiny symbols carved into the horse's belly, neck, and the inside of its legs.

'It's a priggin doll, all right.' Loge rolled the horse over in his hand. 'Don't know what it says though. Ehran had this?'

The world inside Lidan's tent suddenly seemed very small and very hot. They weren't the symbols her father had painstakingly taught her when she would have preferred to be riding, but she knew them all the same. She'd never been taught their meaning, or how to write them, but she knew who did. She licked her lips and tried to find a way to explain. 'It was in a toy box, in the family common room.'

Loge shifted and straightened his injured leg. She realised then she was crouching between his knees and her skin tingled. He turned the horse so she could see the underside in the light of the candle. 'Someone carved this with bad blood in mind. Someone who knows nothing about horses but a lot about curses.'

With hesitant fingers she took the figurine from Loge and cradled it in her lap. A pain stabbed down her face from behind her right eye and she rubbed the bridge of her nose. 'Do you think it was working on him? Or the other girls?'

Loge snatched the figure back and tossed it at the doorway of the tent. The bright spots fizzing in Lidan's vision began to fade, the screech of an approaching headache eased, and she sagged forward. Loge caught her shoulders. 'Does that answer your question?'

Lidan groaned. 'Why didn't it make you ill?'

'Because it wasn't made for me, or for someone who shares my blood. Who did this, Liddy?'

Anger surged in Lidan like a white-hot flood. 'You know who.'

Loge shook his head, never taking his eyes from her face. 'Why? Why would she do that?'

She glared to where the horse figure had fallen, pushed from the ground, collecting the figure and wrapping it in the discarded washcloth by the bed.

'Because of me. It's always because of me.'

CHAPTER TWENTY-FIVE

The Western Reaches, Tolak Range, the South Lands

Her parents would be at the centre of the camp, talking and eating with the other folk travelling to Tingalla. Lidan stormed between the pavilions and Loge hurried to catch up, his trousers forced on over the bandage and dressing, his footsteps muffled by soft soil. The treatment had taken effect, and despite his limp, he kept pace, tents blurring past until they fell away.

She emerged into a clearing dotted with fires. Folk sat about chatting and drinking, at ease in the lull of an evening lacking in any apparent danger. Ngaru screams had not yet split the night, but a threat lurked here, hidden deep at the heart of her world.

Two huge fires burned at the centre of the clearing. Her father, Siman, and several other men sat around one, while her mother, the Crone, and Raeh sat with Bridie, Elva and Marrit around the other. Farah, Kelill and the rest of the children were nowhere to be seen.

Lidan staggered to a stop and sucked in a deep breath. She glared at her mother and the Crone with all the silent poison she could muster, and a ripple of uncertainty shivered across her skin. She couldn't accuse them outright. Couldn't demand they explain themselves. And while she couldn't read the symbols on the horse figure either, she knew they were northern. No one else here knew the symbols of the north, or that Sellan and the Crone had a stash of texts in their little hall. No one else went in there, not even Erlon. All her proof was circumstantial, yet here she was, staring at them with a broken toy in her hand and no idea what to do next. The conversation faded, leaving the whispering wind and the crackle of hungry flames to fill her ears.

Sellan turned toward Lidan and furrowed her brow. 'What is it, Liddy?'

She took a steadying breath. 'I found this a few days before we left home. Ehran was playing with it.'

Lidan opened her hand and let the washcloth fall away. She held the horse between her fingers and dangled it in the firelight, ignoring the pain that lanced down the side of her face. Her mother stiffened, but the Crone didn't flinch.

'At first I thought it a badly made toy, but I was sorely mistaken.'

The headache began to scratch at the back of her eyes.

Erlon turned at the sound of her voice and the mention of Ehran's name. He came to his feet. 'What is that?'

'A priggin doll,' called Lidan, projecting her voice as far as it would carry. She tilted her head to where Loge stood at her shoulder. 'Neither Loge nor I can read the curses, so we can't be sure who made it or why, but he's certain it was made in bad blood.'

Sellan stood and narrowed her eyes. 'A priggin doll? In our hall? In our *home*?'

Her indignation was so perfectly affected Lidan almost believed her mother was horrified by the idea. But there was something in the woman's stance that spoke a silent truth. Sellan was furious, and not because someone had placed a curse in her husband's hall but because Lidan had found it and figured out what it was.

'Should she be touching it?' Erlon shot a glance at Sellan, and for a moment they shared a genuine moment of parental concern. Lidan rolled her eyes; it was a bit late for that now.

'No,' Sellan growled, 'she shouldn't. Put it down, Lidan.' Her mother didn't move to take the figure. Instead she pointed at the ground in front of Lidan's boots.

'Of course.' Lidan leaned forward and tossed the wooden horse into the fire.

Her mother screamed.

The balter wood exploded. Bright blue flames erupted from the fire. The blast hit Lidan in the chest and shoved her backwards.

She slammed to the ground and winced away from the heat washing over her face and arms. Screams echoed amongst the trees, rangers shouted orders and somewhere a child began to cry.

Loge's arm lay across her chest, a solid band of protection where he'd tried to get between her and the flames. Lidan lifted herself from the ground and he rolled away with a groan. She leaned on her elbows and stared.

A blistering inferno roared to a height twice that of her father, a swirling column of blue flame reaching for the sky with a power Lidan could not name. Heat radiated from the column, pulsing to the beat of a frantic heart, but Lidan shivered despite it. People staggered back, shielding their faces and hurrying away.

A craw's harsh call echoed through the clearing and a smoky blue bird swept from the depths of the fire toward Lidan. It landed, ruffling its mangy wings and angling its head to flash an accusing eye at her face.

It hopped toward her, its long dark beak snapping as its talons scoured the dirt. Lidan stared, fixed in place as if turned to stone by the creature's bright blue eye. It snapped its sharp beak again, calling and cawing, its voice raking against her senses. She began to shake, her fingers trembling as the craw took a final hop and landed on her boot...

The world around Lidan evaporated into a white abyss.

The fire, the rangers, Loge, her parents, all vanished; replaced by a gleaming white vista that went on forever and surrounded her completely. There was one small black smudge, far off in the distance behind the shoulder of the blue craw, but it did not move. Lidan ignored it, her attention drawn to the craw perched on her boot.

It scuttled up her leg, across her abdomen, and stood triumphant on the bone between her breasts. It was unbothered by her hammering heart and heaving chest. It turned its eye on her again and blinked. Lidan's breath caught, terror strangling her, choking the air from her lungs and crushing her voice.

She knew this bird. Had seen it dead as a brick on the Crone's dusty workbench. It wasn't the whole craw though. It had no weight, no substance that she could feel. It was a thing of smoke and shadow.

What did it want? How and why the fuck had it brought her here?

It waited, watching her, fluttering its wings and ruffling its feathers. Slowly, it leaned forward and she flinched away. It kept coming, its head tilting curiously back and forth until it darted forward and nipped her nose. Lidan screamed and slapped it away. The bird squawked and flapped off in an indignant flurry of blue feathers and smoke.

The spell broke.

Lidan slammed back into the present with brutal force. Chaos reigned around her in a kind of sticky slow motion. There were screams and shouting but the sounds were muffled, the voices broken by distance and stretched by time. Her father bellowed and the Crone cackled hysterically, but it was all so far away it hardly felt as though it were real.

The craw was real, though.

It spread its wings and leapt, beating the air and thrusting up into the night, screaming accusations back at Lidan as it disappeared above the trees. It was gone in seconds, the blue glow vanishing above the canopy, leaving confusion in its wake.

Erlon whirled around and thundered orders in Lidan's direction. 'Get her out of here! You don't leave her side unless one of us relieves you!'

He turned away and shouted something about Ehran and the girls, and Siman sprinted off with a pack of rangers at his heels. Loge's arm appeared from nowhere, wound around her and dragged her to her feet. Somehow, he managed to keep her upright as he steered her away from the fires.

She stumbled and stared up at the black patch of sky where the craw had vanished. Was that it? Had it gone for good? Questions whirled in her head, screaming over the hammer of her heart and going unanswered in the clamour of shouted orders and running feet.

They arrived at her tent before she knew what was happening and found it ringed with rangers bristling with weapons. She almost laughed. As if stone and steel could do anything against what had been unleashed. Loge shoved the door flap aside and ushered her through the gap, pausing to mutter something to the rangers outside.

Inside the tent, the noise fell away. Lidan stood in the middle of the floor, shivering, her eyes darting from one shadow to another. She half expected the craw to swoop through the wall of the tent and carry her off to the white place, but nothing moved.

The tent was empty.

She gulped and balled her shaking hands into fists.

Loge's hand settled on her shoulder and she flinched hard.

'Liddy?' he whispered, searching her face.

Lidan closed her eyes and the world slowed. The craw was there. Its eye settled on her, undeterred by distance, burning a hole through her skin right down to her soul. Everything tilted and spun; the tent, the camp, the sky. The memory of the heat of the fire rushed up her arms. She bit back bile and staggered under the weight of the nausea.

Loge caught her before she fell, his hands wrapping around her arms, cutting through the churn and pulling her back. His fingers were warm, so she focused on that. Warm and firm, but trembling.

Why were they trembling?

Those hands were the only solid thing holding her back from the sucking quicksand of the white place. It called to her, beckoning at the edge of her consciousness, inviting her to explore that black smudge in the distance…

'Liddy, come back to me.' Loge's voice reached through the fog. She opened her eyes. He was there. He was real. Her skin prickled and she took a deep, ragged breath.

'I'm here,' she replied, though she felt a thousand miles away.

'You vanished, Liddy. Where did you go?'

'I… I don't know…' She shook her head. 'Did you see the craw?'

'Yes. Everyone did.' Its call echoed above them and he looked up, as if he could see the offending bird through the ceiling of the tent. 'What *was* that thing?'

'A dead bird. A spirit trapped in the priggin doll.' Lidan clamped her jaw shut to stop her teeth chattering. Her whole body shook, her fingers dancing across Loge's shirt where her hands rested against his chest.

He looked at her with a deepening frown. 'The curses need a sacrifice to give them power. The bird must have been it.'

'Have you ever seen that before? The blue fire? The ghost?'

'No… But I've never seen anyone burn a priggin doll before. I never thought any of that shit actually worked. You should sit down.' He nodded at the bed across the tent.

'I, um—'

'I wasn't asking.' He guided her to the pallet and deposited her on the mattress. He turned—

'No!' She leapt to her feet and pulled him back. 'Don't go.'

He turned, winding his hand into hers. Lidan licked her lips, her mouth suddenly as dry as chalk. Hardly a foot of space stood between them, but it might as well have been the width of the world.

'I'm... I'm not all here...' she whispered. The craw banked in the air, not far off, its eyes trained on something more interesting, and she shuddered. 'It has me. It has part of me and if you go, I'm not sure if...if...'

Loge put a hand to her cheek and touched his forehead to hers. 'I'm not going anywhere. I'm staying right here.'

Lidan closed her eyes and ignored the craw calling in the night. The whispers of the white place faded, relinquishing its hold and releasing her to the world where she belonged. She pulled her thoughts into line and focused them on the tiny points where Loge's skin touched hers.

Her heartbeat began to slow. She had her anchor. It couldn't pull her back if he was here. As long as he was here, with his hand in hers, she was safe.

CHAPTER TWENTY-SIX

Fracture Pass, The Ice Towers

Fracture Pass began innocuously enough; a track worn into a wide riverbed, winding between the soaring peaks of the Ice Towers, the sides of the valley growing steadily taller as the days passed. The snow line was high above, lost to sight most days amongst clouds and mist. Aelish's solid confidence in her company's weather predictions held true, until the third morning when they woke to a blizzard screaming through their camp.

'Is this normal?' Ran shouted over the howling wind, clutching at his horse's dangling reins and shielding his face against the onslaught of ice whipping down the valley.

Aelish hugged her chest. 'No! We need to get into the Pass before it gets worse and the mouth closes!' She pointed up the valley. 'It's a few hours walk. We can't ride in this.'

Behind them Brit and Eian dismantled the tents while Zarad did his best to wrangle and harness the remaining horses. At Aelish's insistence, they each had a bow and a quiver of arrows strapped to their backs, and whatever blades they could carry arrayed about their bodies. A pair of sleds had been retrieved from the campsite, repaired and harnessed behind the largest of the horses, then packed with food, firewood, pitch torches, and a veritable arsenal of spears, lances, and slingshots. Aelish had added a crossbow to the pile, which Ran had raised an eyebrow at, given they weren't embarking on a siege.

Brit shouted and waved from behind a pile of boulders. Ran turned into the wind and pushed through the stinging snow to reach him. 'We're done. Need to move before this gets worse.'

Ranoth looked at Aelish. 'You ready?'

She squinted up the valley, nodded, and pulled a thick scarf up over her chin, mouth and nose. Ran and the others followed suit, and then stepped out from the meagre protection of the boulders into the roaring white.

Ran hadn't really understood what Aelish meant when she talked about the Pass. After a several hours of trudging, she vanished from the storm and Ran hurried after her, dragging his horse behind. The wind died away and he found himself standing in the yawning mouth of a cave surrounded by a dizzy sense of weightlessness after so long fighting to remain upright in the roaring wind. Eian bundled in after him, leading his horse with one hand and holding Zarad's hand with the other. Aelish took all but a few seconds to realise Brit hadn't followed them into the safety of the cave, and she dove straight back into the blizzard before Ran could stop her.

'The fuck—' Zarad looked up from stomping snow off his boots as Aelish darted past.

Eian was the next to move but Ran grabbed his arm. 'She knows what she's doing. Best we wait.'

Ran's muscles twitched tighter as the seconds passed. Each moment they didn't appear was a moment closer to him leaving the cave to start searching. Aelish might know what she was doing, but if Brit had collapsed or broken something, there was no way she would get him back to the cave on her own.

Aelish and Brit burst from the swirling white, horse and sled in tow, and Ran sighed with relief, lunging to take the reins. 'What happened?'

The watcher pulled his face mask away and stomped snow from his boots and pants. 'Bloody sled got caught. Didn't you hear me shouting?'

Ran glanced at the others. They all shook their heads.

'I thought you were right beside me,' Aelish murmured, the colour draining from her face. 'It shouldn't be like this. It's the wrong time of year. This doesn't—'

'What's that?' Eian pointed down the cave.

A lone wagon stood at the edge of the light, hunched against the side of the cave, the drawbars angled down to the ground. A skeleton, or at least some of one, lay crumpled near the front wheels, and the body of the wagon had been crushed by something extremely heavy. Aelish started toward it, then pulled up short, staring down the throat of the cave.

'Aelish?' Brit asked after her, his voice echoing against the cold stone.

'It shouldn't be like this…' She turned and scanned the ground, her figure dwarfed by the height of the cave. She slipped a glove from her hand and touched the wall beside her shoulder. 'Did those creatures come through here?' she called back at them.

'Ah, let me check,' Ran replied and gave Brit's shoulder a squeeze. 'See if you can't find some of those torches and get Zarad to light them.' The watcher nodded and took the reins of Ran's horse.

He opened his Sight as he drew closer and Aelish frowned at him. Had she sensed the change when he set his magic free? He sometimes thought he could smell it; a tang in the air, like a wisp of smoke left in the wake of a flaring spark. Ahead, dradur trails darted off into the darkness, the most recent circling the broken wagon several times, then seemingly hesitating at the edge of the day-light. What had they sensed as they passed by? Was it the same thing that gave Aelish pause and sent a shiver of fear crawling across Ran's skin?

Behind them, torches flared to life and Aelish turned. There had been no clack of flint echoing up the cave, just the hiss of flame bursting from the end of the torch. 'What…'

'Zarad has some hidden talents.' Ran shrugged.

'I noticed,' she replied, and stepped closer to the wagon. 'My sister had it. Burnt one of our barns to the ground. Thankfully the boy she was cross with got away unscathed.'

Ran cleared his throat. 'Your sister had what?' Could she hear the way his voice cracked?

Aelish looked at him sideways. 'You think I don't know what you are? What trail is in here, or out in that blizzard, that normal eyes could follow?' He had to concede that truth. The cave floor was solid rock, without sand or even a layer of loose stones to record the passage of passing footsteps. 'Did they come through here or not?'

'They did,' he said. He rubbed his hands together and stomped his feet, hoping to encourage some warmth back into his toes, while Aelish crouched beside the wagon and ran her hand along the deep gouge marks that scoured the timber.

'What is this place?' asked Ran.

'Fracture Pass,' she replied, her voice thick with emotion.

'This is a cave, not a pass,' he countered.

Aelish rounded on him. 'I've been crossing this Pass since I was twelve. Do not presume to tell me what it is or is not.'

'Fracture Pass is a *tunnel*?' Ran turned back to the mouth of the cave. 'Brit—anyone tell you the Pass was a tunnel? Seems like something worth mentioning, wouldn't you think?'

The walls around them trembled. It was a gentle shudder, distant and soft, but Aelish darted forward and slapped her hand over Ran's mouth. The tremble became a roar, and beyond the cave something gave way. A bank of snow and ice thundered down and the horses screamed, tearing their reins from their rider's hands and bolting for the depths of the cave.

Aelish threw herself into Ran, pushing him away from the flashing hooves. His magic flared, surrounding them in an orb of blue light as the horses charged past. The force of it shoved them against the wagon, his ribs taking the impact as the rotten timbers collapsed beneath them. The others were shouting, Eian cursing his horse and Brit swearing about the sleds.

The clatter of frantic hooves faded, and Ran realised he'd landed on top of Aelish. 'Sorry,' he groaned, and rolled away.

She snorted a laugh, then winced. 'I don't think that was you.'

'No, I meant for—'

Brit appeared with Zarad bearing a pair of burning torches. 'You two all right?'

'Of course,' Aelish grimaced and Ran nodded, clutching his ribs and wondering how long his magic would take to heal the bruises.

'Those stitches holding?' Zarad asked Aelish and she nodded, pressing a hand against her healing wound.

Down the cave, Eian's torch bobbed back and forth as he drew closer. He threw his arm up in frustration. 'They've gone in pretty deep. One sled is busted a hundred yards or so down, and the other must still be attached to the horse.'

'We'll find them once they run out of puff.' Aelish slipped her glove back on and brushed herself down. 'They won't go far in the dark without us.'

Eian's eyebrows shot up. 'We're going *in* there?'

Aelish glanced at what had been the mouth of the cave. 'You're welcome to stay here until that melts, but I'm going out the other side.'

'What's she talking about?' Zarad eyed Ran with suspicion.

Ran hunched over to catch his breath, but already the magic was moving. Heat swirled through his chest, and he thought he felt tiny sparks of magic singing through his veins. 'This is the Pass. We have to go that way.'

'And the dradur?' Eian frowned, as dubious as his partner.

Ran waved down the throat of the cave. 'In there.'

'Oh, wonderful. I fucking love confined spaces, don't you?' Eian's voice had a slight edge of hysteria, cracking as the pitch rose and he turned to stalk off down the tunnel.

'It's going to be fine,' Zarad assured him. He handed Ran his torch and followed Eian, reasoning with him as one might a frightened child. Their voices trailed off, Eian hissing something about a pass being something that was *above* ground and not signing up for any sort of quest that involved going down a dirty great hole. Brit went after the horses, leaving Ran and Aelish by the ruined wagon.

'So, this is the Pass?' Ran asked, as if time and circumstance might have changed matters.

Aelish met his gaze in the orange glow of the torch. 'It is.'

'No other way around?'

'Not any I would recommend.'

He grinned to mask his fear and they started off after the others.

Aelish hugged an arm around her stomach and threw another glance over her shoulder. Ran couldn't tell what she was looking for and hadn't the heart to ask. It had been hours since they'd followed the light of the torches into the Pass. The sun might have been setting in the world above, but there was no way to tell down here.

'You sure you're all right?' he asked. 'We can stop if you need.'

'It's nothing,' she replied quickly and turned her eyes to the path ahead.

The others were farther down the passage, their torches illuminating the walls as they chatted amongst themselves in low tones, soothing the frayed nerves of their horses. Yet despite the bobbing circles of light, the darkness pressed in, their voices and the clatter of hooves echoing against the hard stone and disappearing into the gloomy distance.

They had collected most of the scattered supplies and repaired the harness on the damaged sled, Brit and Zarad rigging up something to secure it to the horse's saddle. Ran had no idea how long it would last. It creaked and groaned as he rode beside Aelish. Zarad had given over his horse to her and decided to share with Eian, while Brit and Ran pressed their mounts into hauling the sleds. One of their torches had already burned out, a few had been smashed to splinters by the horses, and Eian was somehow, miraculously, holding himself together as the path inched further under the mountains.

Iridia lingered at the edge of Ran's vision, slipping through the darkness where it met the light of the torch; a beautiful spectre in a dank, dripping tunnel that stretched on endlessly into nothing. She was a silent, distracting presence that drew his eyes from the task at hand, and his mind back to the night she pressed her will on him at the Keep.

He rolled his shoulders to shake the sensation away and lifted his torch toward the ceiling. They could have illuminated the tunnel with magic, but he was loath to waste the energy on something other than tracking. 'Can't say this is what I expected. I knew it would be dangerous, but this is something else.'

'I've known this place since I was a child, Ran. I could almost say I grew up down here.' She hunched the collar of her coat closer around her ears. 'The Pass *is* dangerous—it always has been. That's why it's hardly ever crossed. But that,' Aelish gestured back at the avalanche blocking the tunnel mouth, 'should never have happened this time of year.'

'It did strike me as odd…' muttered Ran, looking up at the roof. It was at least twice as high as he was tall. 'Is it natural, or did they mine it out?'

Aelish followed his gaze. 'The fissure was here long before northern eyes ever found it. My grandfather said they mined along it, widened it, installed a halfway post, that sort of thing. It took my people years to build it. It was only opened up a few decades before my mother was born.'

'You're kidding, right?' Ran raised his brows. 'It's only been accessible for, what, half a century?'

She inclined her head. 'Maybe a little longer. It's not the *only* way through the Ice Towers, but it's the safest. I thought it was solid—immutable, infallible—but something is wrong here. Something has changed. I've known it all my life, but now it feels like a stranger.'

'Well, that's saying something.'

Silence fell between them as the torches ahead disappeared around a bend. Aelish pulled up her horse and glanced over her shoulder again, her green eyes lingering on the darkness at their backs. Her fear shivered in the air between them, visceral and consuming, and Ran opened his Sight to the thaumalux trails glowing in the passage, throbbing with the beat of his heart. There were dradur trails, but also others left by magic-weavers. Decades of human life had traversed this path, but in this moment, surrounded by nothing but darkness and the sound of hooves on stone, it felt like a sucking abyss they might never escape.

He reached out and touched Aelish's elbow. 'We better catch up or Brit will be riding back here to find you.'

She smiled at that, and they started after the others. 'He reminds me of my brother, although Brit's not quite as overbearing. Loyal to a fault, and kind. Insufferably protective. Always worried about my safety, worried I'd get eaten by an ice dragon. The usual things older brothers do, I suppose. Thank the gods he found himself a wife to fuss over, or I'd never be allowed anywhere on my own.'

'Brit certainly is loyal,' Ran conceded. The man had searched the wilds for four years on the duchess's order, and if that wasn't loyalty, he didn't know what was. 'Can't say he ever struck me as the protective type, though.'

Aelish winked at him. 'It's always the ones you least suspect.'

CHAPTER TWENTY-SEVEN

Fracture Pass, The Ice Towers

Hours dragged past in silence and darkness, nondescript stone pressing in, mile after mile no different from the next until the shape of the wall ahead bowed out dramatically and their torches lit up a cavernous space branching off from the main tunnel. Aelish grinned, then swung down from the saddle and led her horse inside, Zarad holding his torch high as he followed.

Aelish staggered to a stop and gasped, setting Ran's skin to crawling. He cast around, looking for what had brought her up short, his eyes straining in the dim light.

At first, he thought it a collection of buildings—stone and timber huts that might have been storehouses and sleeping quarters for weary traders, and at some time in the not too distant past, they had been. But his mouth ran dry as he realised they were nothing more than broken ruins; collapsed roofs clinging to the edges of demolished stone walls, doors hanging from hinges, furniture abandoned in the centre of pathways. The broken skeletons of a group of wagons stood in what might have been a central square, and beyond it all, a lake glimmered, stretching away past the reach of torch light.

He should have guessed when he saw the wagon at the entrance that nothing down here would be as it should. He should have pressed Aelish to reveal her thoughts and fears, but he hadn't wanted to push her. He hadn't given voice to his own fears either, as if speaking the words might summon the monsters dwelling deep in this place. Now he wished he had. He dismounted and tied his horse to a tumble-down awning on the side of a ruined building, then picked his way through the rubble to Aelish.

She stood at the centre of it, her hands balled tight and trembling, her eyes wide as she searched the dim cavern for something Ran couldn't see. 'Aelish? What happened here?'

She didn't answer immediately, just shook her head and stared.

'Those trading caravans, from the other companies,' he continued, 'they didn't fall victim to the weather or the dradur, did they?'

She darted forward, limping around rubble and piles of broken masonry. Ran gave chase, torch in hand, light bouncing frantically off the jumble of surfaces around him until Aelish slid to a stop at the edge of the lake, her boots kicking stones out across the water. He waited for the distant *plop* as they fell beneath the surface, but instead, a series of icy clinks echoed back to him. Aelish yanked off her glove and flattened her hand against the water, and Ran stepped forward, holding his torch high, the light spreading out over the surface of the lake.

'It's frozen,' Aelish whispered.

It was solid ice for as far as he could see; opaque and glistening with a layer of frost.

'There *was* a blizzard on the surface,' he pointed out.

'This water never freezes. *Ever.*' Her fingers withdrew and coiled into a fist. She staggered as she came to her feet and Ran caught her elbow.

'I need you to tell me what's going on,' he pressed. He was about to bring his magic to bear, impatient and afraid, but Aelish shuddered as if something inside had given way. 'What happened here?'

She looked at him, green eyes turned to black pools. 'I don't know. Something has changed. It's too cold; it's never this cold. That's why the Pass was built down here—it's too warm for them.'

'For who?' Brit asked, his question echoing from beside a crumbled building. He turned a stone over with his boot and the bright white bones of a severed arm glared up at him. He flinched away, almost crashing into Eian.

Aelish wouldn't look at any of them as they approached. She just stared into the middle ground as if a litany of memories danced before her eyes. 'This lake is fed by a thermal spring. The last time I was here the water steamed. It shouldn't be covered in ice. That's why this Pass is safer than all the other ways over the Towers. It's below the snow line and it's too fucking hot for them to come down here.'

'The ice dragons?' Eian folded his arms. 'They built this to get past the ice dragons?'

Aelish nodded and glanced back at the line of destroyed wagons. Nothing had been spared. Ran wasn't even sure they would find documents among the ruins to prove who these people were.

He turned back to Aelish and pointed at the destruction. 'The *dragons* did this?'

Aelish threw her hands out, exasperated. 'I don't know! I wasn't here! But by the fucking great big bite marks on the side of the wagons and the serious lack of corpses, I'd say they were probably involved.'

'We need to get out of here,' Zarad put in. Brit spat on the ground and they both turned back to where the horses waited at the cavern entrance. Eian stood at the lake edge, broad shoulders hunched, watching the ice in silence.

'There's no point in running,' Aelish called after Zarad and Brit, and Eian whipped around, his eyes wide. 'If they're down here, they already know where we are.'

Ran's heart lurched in his chest. 'What? How?'

Brit stopped walking and the others grew still.

'A lot of fancy words my uncle tried to teach me once, but it boils down to vibrations. They squeeze a fluid out between their scales and it freezes. The ice scales vibrate, and they follow the sensation to track their prey.'

Ran rounded on her. 'You didn't think this worth mentioning *before* we got in here? Maybe at the mouth of the Pass?'

'What good would it have done?' Aelish snarled back. 'We couldn't get out that way! And how was I to know the whole Pass was compromised? That wagon at the entrance could have been attacked from *outside*. There was nothing to say they were down here. But this,' she stabbed a finger at the icy lake, 'and this,' she pointed at the ruined halfway post, 'tell an entirely different story. Something has changed their habitat and this place is no longer the safe passage it once was. The best thing we can do is eat, get some rest, and prepare to fight if they show themselves. If we run, they'll only wait until we're exhausted.'

Ran turned his eyes to the roof and ground a curse out between his teeth. This was not how he'd imagined this journey going.

Aelish looked at each of the men in turn. 'You can make for the end of the Pass if you want, but I guarantee they're listening. Terrible eyesight, but they can feel the beat of your heart in their bones. They *will* attack if you run.'

Eian looked deeply uneasy, Zarad dubious, and Brit seemed to be holding a ball of fury tightly in his chest. Did he blame himself for not taking the stories of the dragons seriously? Or was he angry at Aelish for not revealing all the cards in her hand?

The watcher looked at Ran. 'What are your orders?'

Brit must have been boiling with rage if he was asking for orders. Ran sighed heavily. 'Set up a camp and feed the horses. Give them plenty of rest. Keep everything packed in case we need to move out at short notice. Check your weapons, maybe get some of those spears ready in case something tries to sneak up on us. We should probably set up some fires—' He looked at Aelish and she nodded. 'It might go some way to deterring them. Eian, can you check the ruins with your Sight? See if there's anything we should know about? I'll do the same at the perimeter.'

Iridia followed him away from the others, slipping between the buildings, shifting through the walls until she was ahead of Ran. He dropped the veil on his Sight and the cavern lit up, Iridia glowing white hot before him.

'Ow, fuck!' Ran shielded is eyes and squinted, waiting for his vision to adjust.

'What?' She turned, hands spread as if expecting an attack.

He had no idea what could possibly do her harm, but she was as much on edge as he was.

'You! Shit, that's bright.'

Iridia looked down at her hand and turned it over. 'Oh. Would you look at that...'

She was as bright as the midday sun, surrounded on all sides by decades of throbbing thaumalux and a good number of midnight-blue dradur trails. She held her hand toward Ran and giggled when he flinched. He glanced at where the others were setting up the camp. No one looked his way, and he assumed they hadn't heard him cursing.

'Look.' Iridia pointed at the darkness behind Ran, and he turned, his gaze following a pale shimmering trail that glowed in an entirely different way to any of the others. Beside it was another he thought he knew, and he peeled back the years. 'You know who that belongs to, don't you?'

Ran nodded, unwilling to use his voice in answer.

Fine, she said in the depths of his mind. *Is this better?*

They're less likely to find me talking to myself, if that's what you mean.

I'd say they're a little too preoccupied to notice. She looked back through the jumble of buildings and Ran followed the weird shimmering trail around the outpost. It appeared to him like a frequency left by worked magic, but he couldn't be certain. Zarad would have to confirm it.

Did you know about this? Ran asked Iridia. *These dragons and the Pass?*

She drifted out over the icy lake. *The Pass, yes; but not the dragons. No one I knew ever took those Isordian stories seriously.*

But now?

Their eyes met over the ice.

I don't think your new friend is lying. What other explanation is there? Iridia shrugged. *Here there be dragons...*

Ran shivered despite himself and reached out with his magic toward the strange shimmering trail. It vibrated the air under his hand. *What's this, then?*

Iridia appeared beside his ear. *Touch it.*

Not sure I want to, if I'm honest.

Go on...

He eyed Iridia. She was in an odd mood, goading him with a wicked gleam in her eyes. She was bathing in the magic in the cavern, absorbing it into her being as though she were dying of thirst and it was the only water for miles. She practically shone with it, taking on the same iridescence as strange trail circling the cavern. *Iridia, what are you doing?*

Just touch it, Ran.

He pulled his glove off and unfurled his fingers into the shimmering glow. It was cold, so cold it burned, and he yanked his hand away. *The fuck is that?!*

Stop lying to yourself. Smell it. Feel it. Just let go and touch it! She forced herself into a more solid form, drawing magic from the air. She took his hand and plunged it back into the trail and Ran bit down on a scream. She glared at him, fire burning in her sky-blue eyes, willing him to submit, and he did.

He let go.

He dropped every wall and veil, undid every lock, threw away all the keys. He let the magic spool out and he heard someone shout. Time fell away and he plunged with Iridia into the abyss...

It was white here.

Completely white, as if a blizzard had roared through and covered every inch of the world in blinding ivory. There was one black smudge, far off in the distance, too far away to make head or tail of. He could smell smoke.

'Where are we?' he asked.

'Who cares,' Iridia replied.

Ran scowled at her and she shrugged. 'How do we get back?'

Iridia looked at him as though he were simple. 'It will spit us out when it's done with us.'

He grabbed her shoulders, ready to shake her, and a figure moved behind her. A woman, possibly of an age with him, but the cut of her clothing spoke of a different time; before he was born, when his parents were much younger. She moved through the space, walking across a floor he could no longer see, muttering as she moved, her fingers spread wide, coils of smoky blue magic trailing after her. In her wake, a blurred rendition of the cavern under the mountain appeared, as if viewed through a pane of filthy glass.

'What is she doing?' Ran whispered at Iridia.

The ghost stood motionless beneath his hands, staring with unveiled horror at the woman drifting toward them.

'You know her, don't you?' He leaned forward and scanned her face. 'Who is she, Iridia?'

The woman passed, muttering words Ran couldn't understand, and Iridia shivered. 'One of *them*...'

Ran's grip on Iridia loosened and forced his voice to work. 'One of the *witches* did this?'

'She cursed it. To cover their tracks. To bring the dragons down from the mountains and bar the way.'

'What are you doing here?' a deep male voice erupted beside them.

Iridia screamed and Ran swore. The white abyss vanished, and the cavern materialised. Ran slammed into the floor and Iridia disappeared.

'Ran?' Eian shouted his name over the echoing thud of boots running across stone. He lifted himself up and opened his eyes, the cavern was as dark as it had been before he'd opened his Sight and followed Iridia's foolish demands.

'Mate, you all right?' Eian arrived at his side and grasped his shoulder.

Ran nodded and tried to speak, but his throat was on fire. Zarad appeared behind his partner and staggered, screwing up his face as though he'd caught a whiff of something foul. 'Ugh, what *is* that?'

'Magical discharge,' Eian replied and hauled Ran to his feet. 'Quaid's sparring hall used to reek of it some days.'

Zarad coughed and suppressed a retch as Ran fought the urge to do the same. The pungent odour reminded him of the fumes from the Keep forge when the blacksmiths welded metals. It lingered like a fog, heavy and oppressive. 'I'm not sure I've ever smelt it this bad before.'

'Zarad, is there frequency here?' Ran croaked. The man glanced at him then spread his fingers wide, Ran's ears popping as the magic rolled past like a wave.

'Oh yes, that's a good one.' Zarad curled his fingers into a fist and the pressure in the air receded. 'It's old, but it's strong. A pretty decent spell, or a curse. A slow burn if I'm not wrong, set to grow stronger in time.'

Ran nodded and Iridia's voice echoed in his mind. A curse to cover their tracks... It must have been a powerful one if *he'd* seen it hanging in the air beside the thaumalux trails, given his affinity for sensing frequency magic was infantile compared to Zarad. He shuddered and swallowed, trying to dislodge the burning in his throat as the cavern started to spin.

'Here, get under his other arm and help carry him,' Eian ordered, his voice cut by a squeal that burst through Ran's ears. 'I don't think his legs are working properly.'

Ran looked down and saw his feet dragging listlessly across the stone. He tried to lift his head and focus on the camp, tried to centre his consciousness, but it slipped like sand through his fingers, and the cavern plunged into the black.

Chapter Twenty-eight

Fracture Pass, The Ice Towers

The scent of food dragged Ran from wherever his exhaustion had sent him, and he wondered where exactly that had been. A fire warmed his face, and his stomach growled. He reached down within himself and found his magic recovering; weakened, drawn and depleted by his excursion into the white place, but recovering.

'You called them dradur?'

He looked up to find Aelish's eyes fixed on his face. For a moment he wasn't sure what to say. He glanced around and found the others asleep, curled up in bedrolls not far from the fire. Ran sighed and lifted himself up carefully. 'How long have I been out?'

'Only a few hours. It was my turn to take watch.' Aelish cradled a mug in her hands, the contents steaming, and his stomach growled again.

'Is that soup?' he asked.

'You can have some if you answer my question.'

Ran frowned at her. 'You're holding the food to ransom now?'

'Just answer the question.'

'Yes. That's what we call them.'

'Dead walkers?' She translated the Altipan word into common and Ran nodded. 'How do you know what they are?'

'Well, they attacked our village and—'

'Bullshit.'

'Excuse me?'

'I call bullshit. What village? A village in Orthia that accepts magic-weavers? No such place exists.' She leaned forward, the glow of the fire casting eerie shadows across her face. 'You got the truth from me, now I want the same from you. Who are you?'

Ran scratched at the crop of stubble on his chin. 'Suppose there's no point keeping secrets out here. We're magic-weavers and we can track the dradur's magical signature in the—'

'I fucking know *what* you are. I saw that blue light you were fixing to fling at me when you rode into my camp. You've been using it to track creatures when there are no tracks to be seen, and I felt you use it to shield us from the horses. Zarad has been setting fire to things without flint for days. I know a magic-weaver when I see one.' Aelish stood and crossed the few feet between them, dropping to her knees. She never once looked away; her eyes scanning his face under the shadows of furrowed brows. She slipped into Isordian. 'I know what you are, but I want you to tell me *who* you are.'

A wave of heat prickled across Ran's skin. 'Why ask a question you already have the answer to?'

Iridia materialised from the darkness and stood at the edge of the light. *That's impossible*, she hissed.

Aelish flinched toward where Iridia stood, then looked back at Ran like a hawk watching its next meal quivering in the undergrowth. 'You have their look—that nose and that hair. You're that Orthian prince, aren't you? Word came across the mountains when you vanished. Merideth's son was gone, missing, and they were hunting him across Coraidin. They wanted to commandeer the crews to search for you but King Harroe wouldn't have it.'

Was he so easy to spot, or was this just a terrible case of being in the wrong place at the wrong time with someone who apparently knew his mother's family better than he did? He dragged his voice from where it cowered in his chest. 'How long have you known?'

She barked a laugh and it echoed against the ceiling.

'Almost straight away. You did introduce yourself as Ranoth. But I suppose you thought no one out here would think you were *that* Ranoth.' She shrugged. 'I grew up with your cousin, Villia, and she had just the same look when she tried to hide something from me.'

Villia. He hadn't seen her since they were children. Ten years ago, perhaps. The last time his mother had gone home to see her family, when Ran's uncle, the crown prince had been married a second time. 'How could you possibly know her?'

A smile broke across Aelish's face and she spread her arms wide. 'The East Ruken Trading Company is the largest in Isord, and for twelve generations the Yordam's have controlled the majority of trade in the kingdom. You think my family aren't intimately entwined with yours? That I don't know a son of Merideth Kortson when I see one, out here in the wilds, balling up magic and chatting away in our tongue?' She leaned forward. 'My brother is *married* to Villia Kortson.'

'Fuck off.' The words shot out of Ran and Aelish laughed. 'If that's true then why didn't the crews come after me? Surely their trackers would be more than capable of finding me?'

She sniffed and wiped a tear from her eye. 'Because King Harroe and Crown Prince Peytr fucking hate your father.'

Ran started at that. Duke Ronart was a difficult man to like, true enough, but outright hatred? Had the world changed so much in the four years he'd been in hiding? 'They *hate* Ronart?'

Aelish nodded. 'His very name boils their blood.'

'I don't understand. My parent's marriage was an alliance—'

'And every year your father demands more troops for his war with the Empire. Every year he wants more gold, more gems, more ore, more horses. He wants our blood to stain his soil just so he can hold it in his greedy hands for a little while longer. When the demands came to hunt down Merideth's son, that was it. Harroe was done.' Aelish turned to the pot on the fire and filled a mug with steaming broth. She handed it to Ran and settled beside him. 'Harroe had the principals of the trading companies brought to his hall and forbade them from taking a recovery contract from your father. If any of them had, you wouldn't be here.'

Ran sipped at the broth, hoping to drown the uneasy sense of complete vulnerability and exposure burning in his gut. 'Did Ronart's message happen to mention why he was hunting me?'

'Yes,' she said.

'What did the king think of that?'

Aelish shrugged. 'Probably the same as most Isordians—he didn't care. If he did, he made no mention of it. No one gives a shit about magic in Isord. It can get messy, but you're not going to lose your head over it.'

A pregnant silence filled the camp and Ran glanced at Aelish. She knew exactly what she had said.

'Another reason Harroe has no time for Ronart, I expect. Can you imagine? An Isordian handing over a prince of the blood for an Orthian execution? And they call *us* backward cave-people.' She spat into the fire.

He had to smile at that. 'So you won't be turning me over to my father when we get back?'

'*If* we get back,' she countered. Iridia laughed and Aelish flinched again. 'Did you hear that?'

Ran's body went rigid and he forced an impassive expression to keep the surprise from his face. 'No, what was it?'

'Since we came in here, earlier today, I keep hearing this… It's nothing. Probably just an echo.'

He caught sight of Iridia across the fire, glimmering at the edge of the darkness. She looked down at her hands and frowned. He had no explanation for it. Perhaps the proximity to the witch's curse was amplifying Iridia's presence. Perhaps the exposure to the sheer weight of magic here was drawing some sort of latent power of Aelish's to the surface, but Ran hadn't noticed her leaving any sort of thaumalux trail.

Aelish gave him a pat on the shoulder. 'Rest up, Ranoth Kortson. Only a few more hours and we have to get moving.'

She called you Kortson… Iridia whispered. She pressed against him, a heavy presence where once she had been no more than a wisp of thought. She was becoming more adept at forcing herself into a physical form and seemed to enjoy watching him squirm whenever she did so.

Yes, thank you, I did hear that.

She lay beside him on the stone floor of the cavern; had been there for hours—the entire time he'd been trying to sleep. *I thought you must have, and I wouldn't have remarked on it, but I could have sworn your name was—*

His eyes flew open and he glared at her.

Do you want to talk about where we went? The white place? she asked, rolling toward him and trying to pick up a stone with her transparent fingers.

No, not really, he said.

Oh. Didn't you think it was strange?

Yes. Absolutely fucking terrifying actually. But I'd really rather get some sleep so I'm not dead on my feet if these dragons decide to show up.

When, she corrected and looked back at the roof.

What?

When the dragons come, not if.

You aren't going to let me sleep, are you?

She smiled. *No. You have things to do.*

Ran groaned and rolled onto his back, blinking up at the darkness. A tiny shower of dust peppered his face and he blinked again. Something in him sparked and his magic rolled across the floor of the cavern, spreading like mist; reaching down, sensing, listening, feeling. Deep in the earth, down in the bowels of the mountains, something rumbled. He looked over at Aelish and found her wide green eyes fixed on the ceiling; gentle showers of dust raining around them.

'Did you feel that?' he asked.

'Yes,' she said in a hoarse whisper. 'Wake the others and I'll get the horses. But move slowly. We can't run.'

Ran did as Aelish ordered, shaking the others awake while she collected their belongings and packed them back on the sleds. He pressed his finger to his lips when Eian started hissing questions at him. 'We do as we're told, all right? I don't like this either, but she knows this place, and we'd do well to listen to her.'

Eian gave a reluctant nod, shouldered his bow and quiver and went to help Aelish and Brit. In the centre of the ruined outpost, Zarad stood with one hand splayed wide at his side. Ran stepped toward him and grimaced at the magic radiating from his friend like heat from an oven, his wild red hair seemingly alive with energy.

'What can you feel?' Ran whispered.

'Life...' replied Zarad. He closed his eyes and flinched. 'This was a place of death when we got here, empty except for the curse. Now...' He looked at Ran and a muscle jumped in his jaw. 'Something is very much alive down here.'

Ran chewed his lip and nodded. 'We better get moving then. I'd rather not join it for breakfast.'

They rode for hours, nothing moving in the tunnel except for them and their skittish horses. There were no strange sounds, nothing to indicate anything lurked just beyond the reach of their senses, but the animals felt something in the air. Whether it was the approaching danger or the simmering apprehension in the riders, they responded all the same. It was eerily quiet, a silence filled with expectation and threat, like the world itself held its breath. If not for his magic, Ran would have sworn he and Aelish were mistaken, wrong to worry and too quick to jump to conclusions.

But when he unfurled his power and let it swirl around him in a mist, his perception tingled like a spiderweb disturbed by unsuspecting prey. While nothing obvious shifted around them, his magic told him otherwise. Somewhere, something, was moving.

Eian shielded his eyes and looked away from Ran several times as they walked their horses through the Pass, and he realised he probably looked like a blinding orb of thaumalux to his friend. Zarad traced his bare fingers along the wall, frowning and muttering to himself, distracted by the presence he sensed deep in the mountain. From their shared horse, Brit and Aelish watched the three magic-weavers with guarded curiosity, whispering to each other as the group pushed on.

They maintained the pretence of calm, unbothered travellers wandering through the Pass without a care in the world for several more hours before Ran realised the gait of the horses had quickened, their breath clouding from their nostrils.

'Is it—'

A dragon burst from a fissure in the rock behind Ran's head and his horse screamed. The serpent moved like quicksilver to the sound of shattering glass, its ice scales rattling together as it slithered from the wall and coiled itself in the cave behind him. There was no controlling the horses. They shot away, sleds bouncing dangerously behind them, riders clutching at whatever purchase they could find.

CHAPTER TWENTY-NINE

Fracture Pass, The Ice Towers

Ran's horse raced after the others, hooves clattering across the ground as they rounded a bend. The dragon roared, a bone-shuddering sound that seemed to rise from the very rock around them to an ear-splitting pitch higher than anything Ran could hear. Somewhere ahead light shimmered. Was it from the torches? Or had they travelled far enough that daylight was within reach?

Behind him, the dragon closed the distance—much faster than his terrified horse could run—and the tunnel began to climb, incrementally inching upward. His horse began to labour, clouds of frantic breath steaming from its nostrils, its sides slick with sweat despite the freezing air.

Beyond the silhouettes of the others, the entrance to the Pass opened to the day, a gleaming oval of pale light bordered by solid black rock.

Freedom.

Safety.

'DRAGON!' Brit bellowed. A long, snaking shape wound down from the roof, coiling on the floor and filling the exit. Their horses baulked and reared, skidding to a halt. Ran wheeled his horse around as the first dragon lopped around the bend and braced itself against the walls, illuminated by the light at the end of the Pass.

Its body wound like a snake poised to strike, and a pair of muscular fore-claws gripping the wall, talons scoring the face of the rock with a crackling screech. Thick bands of muscle bunched in its powerful hind legs, and its immense tail coiled like a spring under the body. A pair of wings remained tightly pinned against the length of its back, as a series of long spines flexed in and out around the beast's crown. It was crystal white from snout to tail, and an exoskeleton of icy scales glistened in the daylight leaching from beyond the exit. The serpent tilted its head and fixed pale grey eyes on Ran, his horse shivering and stamping under the unwavering scrutiny.

Ran took his chance and rolled out of the saddle. He pulled his sword free and put his horse between him and the creature filling the tunnel. He snatched the dangling reins and started to run, his horse jogging beside him, ears back and eyes rolling. A small fissure in the rock appeared to his left, just wide enough to crouch in and he dragged the horse to a stop. The sled behind it bounced into the space and he swung the sword, slicing the leather straps securing the sled to the saddle.

The serpents keened, shrieking in some sort of reptilian conversation he couldn't understand. Ran spun, searching for the others, and found them pinned behind rock formations with their horses circling or standing shivering against the wall. Eian had an arrow trained on the dragon at the exit, while Zarad crouched behind a boulder clutching his ears and clawing at his head.

'Eian!' Ran shouted above the cacophony of dragon chatter. 'What's wrong with him!?'

'Searching for their frequency!'

A loud *thunk* echoed up the tunnel and the dragon at the exit screamed. Another *thunk*, followed by a grinding metallic clanking, then another *thunk*. It took him seconds to find the source, but much longer to comprehend what he saw.

Aelish knelt at the lip of a fissure several yards down the tunnel, the crossbow wedged against her shoulder, shafts streaking away with each echoing *thunk*. Brit hefted a spear and sent it sailing down the tunnel, the head smashing into the scales of the creature's foreleg. Aelish grabbed a metal lever on the top of the crossbow and hauled it back, bracing the stock against her shoulder. She loaded another bolt and fired.

'Ran!' Eian cried out, slicing through his stunned observation.

He whipped around and the first dragon arched its neck, sucking a breath deep into its chest. It began to swell, its neck bulging, the scales separating as the skin beneath stretched. Ran shoved his sword back into its scabbard and leapt toward Eian and Zarad.

'Take cover!' he roared.

The dragon let go.

A super-heated jet of water shot up the tunnel and hit a wall. The wave crashed and rolled, pouring back toward the bellowing dragon.

Ran's hands burned, his fingers spread wide, crackling blue magic filling the tunnel from the ceiling to the floor, blocking the scalding water and turning it back on the dragon.

The *thunk* of Aelish's crossbow had stopped, and he glanced over his shoulder. She was pressed against the wall of the tunnel, Brit's considerable bulk shielding her from the boiling jet of water that never reached them. If it had, there would be nothing left of any of them but gleaming white bones floating in steaming puddles of gore. Aelish and Brit stared at Ran, unable or perhaps unwilling to move.

He started to pool his magic. 'Aelish! Brit! Clear the exit. We need to get out of here.'

He looked over his other shoulder and saw Eian stow his bow. Zarad was on the ground, pale as a dead man, his eyes rolled back in his head, his lips moving quickly while his fingers flicked in and out. Evidently, Zarad had found the dragon's communication frequency and had set about disrupting it. They had stopped roaring, and were now growling, deep in their throats, the very same sound his sister's cat had made when the stable pups had tried to play with it many years ago.

'Eian! You ready?' Ran shouted over the guttural sound of the dragons, and his friend gave one stiff nod before stepping out from the boulders. His hands sizzled with power, blue lightning arcing between his fingers. 'NOW!'

Their magic exploded, tearing the air in the tunnel as it screamed toward the dragons at both ends. The creature facing Ran lunged, slithering forward as the bolt of magic scythed over its head and singed the tips of its wings. Steam clouded the tunnel and the dragon roared. Where the magic found purchase, the thick icy plates evaporated, exposing soft, pale scales.

Behind him Zarad's voice dropped into a throaty chant and Eian let off shot after shot of sizzling magic. The dragon charging at Ran shuddered and flexed, then suddenly drove its head into the side of the tunnel. It drew back and slammed into the wall again, roaring as Zarad pressed himself against its mind. Ran fired again and hit the dragon's shoulder, melting scales and blistering skin.

'Aelish?' Ran managed to shout between shots.

'It's gone!' she called back. 'It's clear!'

'Go!' he ordered. 'Get out and find cover!'

He barely heard the thud of boots and clattering of hooves echo over the whining keen of his dragon. He held his hands in front of his chest, filling the cavernous tunnel with a wall of thick blue magic as the others ran to the exit. Eian continued firing booming shots of power at something—laying down covering fire, Ran assumed, just in case the other dragon decided to stick its head back into the cave.

Ran retreated toward the tunnel mouth, dragging his magic wall with him, and the dragon flattened itself against the floor, following him, glaring through the energy with simmering hatred. It growled, low and harsh, shaking the tunnel, swinging its head and smashing its skull into the wall, stone and dust raining down. It hit the tunnel again and a boulder the size of a horse came away from the roof.

It's trying to bring down the tunnel. It's trying to collapse the Pass! He picked up the pace, shuffling backward out of the cave, abandoning the sleds to their fate.

'Ran, hurry!' Brit shouted from the entrance, his voice reverberating off the wall of magic. Ran flinched and the dragon pounced forward. It lunged and swiped, its great claws screeching across the surface of the magic sending a shuddering jolt down Ran's arms.

'Drop the wall!' Aelish ordered.

'Fuck no!' he yelled over his shoulder. 'Get clear!'

She fired her crossbow and a bolt smacked into the energy plane. It disintegrated into a cloud of wood smoke and a blob of iron slag slopped to the ground. 'DROP THE WALL!'

He did as ordered. The blue shield of energy vanished. He turned and sprinted, the dragon at his back bellowing with triumph. He made the exit and raced across the clearing as Aelish brought her crossbow to bear, facing the serpent thundering up the throat of the tunnel.

'Eian—fire at its face,' Aelish ordered.

Magic arced through the air toward the charging dragon and exploded in front of its snout. It scuttled to a stop at the edge of daylight, remaining in the protection of the tunnel, burning rage flaring in its eyes. It planted its claws, arching back and sucking air deep into its chest.

'Melt the scales!' Aelish shouted and Ran lifted his hands. His magic boomed against the cliff above the tunnel and caught the dragon in the neck, right where its water reservoir was beginning to bulge. The protective layer of icy scales evaporated, exposing a thin membrane of flexible skin and softer scales. Aelish fired the crossbow and the bolt sank deep into the flesh of the serpent's neck. A spear sailed over their heads and buried itself beside the bolt.

'Go! Run, now!' Aelish shouted, but Ran couldn't move. He stared at the dragon as its reservoir burst open and water gushed to the ground. The others ran, but he stayed rooted to the spot, his muscles frozen by the glare of the dragon.

It held him, fixed where he crouched outside the cave mouth. Disarmed as the beast was, it was not dead, or even mortally wounded. It let go an ear-splitting scream that shook the snow and ice at the mouth of the cave, then charged.

Zarad appeared, no longer entranced, and slapped his hand down on the back of Ran's neck. Ran thought for a moment he meant to drag him from the path of the beast, but when he glanced at Zarad, sweaty and breathless, he saw nothing but singular purpose in his eyes.

Oh, shit.

'Sorry. I need a loan.'

Ran didn't have time to ask questions. Instead he screwed his eyes shut. 'Do it!'

Zarad's fingers clenched and Ran's magic responded. He let it go and it surged up Zarad's rigid arm, roaring as the magic tore from his spine into Zarad's bones. Zarad clenched his other hand into a fist and drove it into the ground beside his boots.

He forced every ounce of magic he had into the stone, glowing blue fissures streaking away toward the tunnel mouth. The earth responded with a deep shudder. Ran sensed Zarad press his will into the ground, granting it no quarter, demanding it release the ice and snow above the mouth of the cave.

The ice above cracked. It echoed up the valley and the dragon turned, tilting its head and bleeding throat upward. It realised what was happening and lunged as the sheet came down, crashing across the mouth of the Pass in a blinding shower of ice and snow.

Ran didn't think he'd been crushed under the weight of the avalanche. He couldn't feel it on his chest, pushing the air from his lungs, or filling his mouth and nose. There was no burning cold against his hands or face, but the world around him was a white-out.

He grimaced and blinked. Had he been sucked out of his reality and dumped into the white abyss again?

No. It was raining here, freezing droplets falling across his face in an icy shower. He groaned and reached up to touch his neck. A cluster of finger marks were burned in his skin—blistered pressure points where Zarad had drawn the magic away. He rolled over, came to his knees and peered through the falling snow. The dragons had fallen silent, and there were no wailing screams of people being eaten alive, so he assumed Zarad's plan had worked.

Zarad. Someone nearby groaned, then someone else called their names.

'Over here!' he shouted in a distant, muffled voice. He worked his jaw and popped his ears, the sounds of the world sliding slowly back. 'Zarad?'

His friend coughed and spat.

'Here,' he croaked, and a body rolled out from under a thin layer of snow. 'That hurt more than I expected…'

Ran snorted. 'It worked, though.'

He squinted through the settling snow to the place where the cave mouth had been. They had been extremely lucky. If Ran hadn't conceded the power to Zarad, the transfer would have cracked his spine and killed him. If Zarad hadn't been sufficiently strong enough to hold and direct the power, it would have killed him too, burning him from the inside out.

'You all right?' he asked Zarad. 'Your sister will fucking skin me if you go back home with so much as a scratch.'

'Ah…' Zarad looked down at himself. 'I'll live, I think.'

'You two having a nice time?' Brit appeared, followed closely by Aelish and Eian, who knelt down beside Zarad. Eian embarked on a tirade of scolding, apparently objecting to Zarad making outrageously dangerous decisions, and Ran decided to leave them to it. He took an offered hand and Brit pulled him to his feet.

Aelish nodded at him, cradling her crossbow across her chest. 'Nice work, your highness.' Brit chuckled and hefted his last remaining spear onto his shoulder. Ran glowered at the pair. Aelish must have told the watcher of her revelation during the ride.

'That was Zarad's idea,' Ran told her, turning to the sealed tunnel mouth and frowning. 'How long will that hold, do you think?'

Aelish shrugged and looked at the sky. It was clear, the sun dipping behind the mountains to the west. 'If this weather holds, it will melt away in a week.'

'And the dragon?' Their eyes met and he saw fear swirling in the depths of her gaze.

'If it's dead, well, it's dead. If it's not...' She let the idea hang in the air.

'And the other one? Is it dead?' Ran pressed. Aelish shook her head and Ran's blood froze in his veins. 'Where is it then?'

'It took off pretty soon after Eian started firing. Ice serpents aren't big on anything that will melt their scales, hence the general dislike of warm sunny places or thermal hot springs,' Aelish said. Eian and Zarad stopped talking and turned, and Brit's brow furrowed. Aelish sighed, then continued. 'The females would rather starve than risk leaving a nest unguarded. She had to choose—stay here and fight, maybe score a meal, or save herself and get back to the eggs. She'll probably go there and lick her wounds, then wait and see if the male comes back.'

'A nest?' Ran hissed.

'What? You think they magically spring up out of the ground? Of course they have nests!' Aelish stabbed a finger at the snowy peaks above. 'Up there usually, in the fucking snow. But seeing as nothing around here is as it should be, I'm not going to hang around waiting to see what else might come slithering out of the shadows.'

Ran couldn't disagree. They had to leave the mountains as quickly as they could manage and not simply because of the impending dragon threat. Their sleds had been lost in the tunnel, along with whatever surplus food they had scrounged from Aelish's camp. He didn't know how good the hunting was this side of the Ice Towers, but he didn't want to take any chances. He nodded and Brit handed his spear to Aelish.

'Hang onto this for me? I'll go see if I can round up some horses.' The watcher left, and Eian helped Zarad to his feet. Ran glanced around and opened his Sight, but nothing happened. He blinked and tried again. Again, nothing changed. 'Fuck,' he muttered.

'What's wrong?' Aelish asked.

'Zarad drew off my magic to bring that ice sheet down,' he told her, rubbing at the hard bone behind his ear.

Aelish cursed and put her crossbow and the spear on the ground. She took hold of Ran's collar and turned it down, revealing the marks where Zarad's hand had been. She clicked her tongue. 'You better hope Brit finds all those horses. Zarad's healing supplies are in the saddle bags and that needs dressing.'

'That's not the worst of it,' he said. She frowned and he shrugged. 'I'm empty—my magic's gone. I can't see the dradur trails. I don't know which way they went from here.'

A smile broke across her lips and she pointed down an incline a few hundred feet to her left. 'Unless they can fly, that's the only way south from here.'

'Ah,' he replied, and his face flushed with heat. 'Right then...'

'There's more than one way to track a monster, Ranoth.' Aelish grinned. 'And from what Brit tells me, he's the best tracker around.'

CHAPTER THIRTY

The Western Reaches, Tolak Range, the South Lands

'How much longer do I have to suffer this indignity?' Loge asked.

Lidan smirked at him from Theus's back. 'Until you're sufficiently sorry for refusing treatment, and you're well enough to ride.'

'I've hardly even got a limp anymore,' he said, and blew some wood shavings from the pale lump of timber in his hand. Relegated to the back of a supply wagon and insufferably idle for the past three weeks, Loge had set about carving a new Icewind figurine for Ehran.

'Getting back on your horse too soon won't help matters,' Lidan pointed out. She glanced up the column and watched Siman weave his horse between riders and wagons, checking and re-checking, asking questions and issuing orders. 'We'll be at Tingalla in four days. You can spend as much time as you like out of the wagon when we get there.'

'I knew you'd report me.'

She glared at him until he cleared his throat and looked away uncomfortably. 'You weren't giving yourself a chance to rest. What was I supposed to do?'

'Not tell Siman!' he shot back.

'You were making it worse! And I don't have time to worry after you *and* Ehran. I told you that.'

His knife scraped loudly over the timber. 'Off you go then. I don't need a nursemaid.'

'Could have fooled me. You're behaving like a child.'

He leaned out of the wagon and gripped the tailgate. 'I'm being *treated* like a child!' He was always like this when he had pain. He let it build, refusing to drink the tea Lidan found in the store trunks until the slightest irritant caused him to boil into a rage.

Lidan loosened her grip on Theus's reins. 'If your knee is sore, put something on it. Drink some of that damn tea. Do *something*, but don't take your frustration out on me. You're a ranger. Grow a pair and take your fucking medicine.' She gave Theus his head and pressed her knees into his sides. He didn't need any further encouragement, and leapt forward, cantering along the outside of the wagon line.

Loge wasn't the only one among them chaffing at restriction. Since leaving Hummel, ranging parties had been circling the caravan, scouting for ngaru and dealing a quick death to any they found. Lidan wanted so badly to be with them. She needed to be out in the wilds, hunting, fighting, even tracking; anything to distract her from the guarded looks and barely disguised whispers of the folk around her.

Three weeks had done little to dispel the simmering fear and confusion about the night she'd burned the priggin doll. People were on edge, wondering who among them might have made a curse doll into the shape of a child's toy. Erlon's silence spoke louder than any whispered conjecture, and she was not alone in wondering what her father was thinking. If he shared Lidan's suspicions, he made no move to act on them, and she reasoned that he probably had bigger problems to deal with.

Every few days a ranging party returned with a pile of salvaged steel for Rick's wagon, leaving the ngaru corpses to rot into the undergrowth. But the last party to go out was well overdue. The remaining rangers scanned the trees with cautious eyes, their hands never far from their weapons as the days rolled past and the others failed to return.

Lidan slowed Theus as she drew close to Jessah and Iema.

'Anything?' she asked.

Iema shook her head. 'There's talk of sending riders out to track them, but Siman isn't sure the daari will spare them from guarding the wagons.'

'We should have heard something by now.' Lidan pursed her lips and looked out at the trees.

'If they got held up by that rainstorm it might take them a few days to catch us up,' said Jessah.

'Maybe...' It didn't sit right, no matter how Lidan turned it over in her head, but there was nothing she could do. It wasn't like her father would let her go off searching for the lost party. She clicked her tongue and gave

Theus his head again, weaving up through the wagons toward the front of the line.

Loge's wagon was the last in the caravan—one of the many supply carts laden with food, tents, weapons and trunks. The passenger wagons carrying her family, clusters of tines and a variety of other clan folk were at the head of the column, and she pulled Theus in toward the wagon her mother shared with the Crone, angling him to the back of the cart and lifting the hide door flap. The soft snuffling of someone snoring reached over the gentle creaking of the timbers, and her mother looked up immediately, meeting her gaze across the gloomy interior.

'Liddy,' said Sellan in a low, rumbling whisper.

'Mother,' Lidan replied.

'I hope you've got better questions for me today. They've become rather tedious.'

'So have your answers,' Lidan countered.

Sellan's eyes narrowed. 'Mind your tone—'

'Or what? You'll get your pet to hide a curse in my saddlebag?'

Her mother scowled, and Lidan let a charged silence fill the space between them. Sellan had insisted her wagon be driven by a tine-man who'd lost most of his hearing, and since the priggin doll incident, Lidan understood why. The dana could speak freely here without fear of her words being repeated elsewhere. It also meant Lidan could loosen her tongue and speak her mind, but never so much that she might provoke her mother's ire.

Sellan shifted, rearranging the pile of cushions and light summer throw rugs at her back. 'I honestly have no idea what you're talking about.'

It had been years since her mother had dared lay a finger on her, but Lidan knew better than to think the woman changed. The threat had not abated, it had merely shifted focus. Sellan was a practical woman. Lidan matched her for height and easily outstripped her physical strength, and Sellan knew she was no longer a danger to her daughter's person. The physical dominance had been lost, so that required more creative methods of keeping Lidan in check, but even the bite of the dana's words had a limit. The sharpest weapon the dana had now was the threat she posed to Lidan's siblings. It was an ominous thing, looming on the horizon like a swelling storm—the priggin doll only the beginning of a greater campaign to get Lidan to fall into line.

It had been deployed well before Lidan had renounced her inheritance, and only the ancestors knew what her mother was plotting to avenge that defiance, but Lidan braced against that fear. Her confidence had soared since the incident with the priggin doll. Something had hardened in her heart that night, a strengthening she hadn't expected. She'd found a hole in her mother's defences, one she couldn't yet see through, but with a little persistence, she might widen the crack enough to catch a glimpse of what lay on the other side.

'So you keep saying.' Lidan let her gaze wander. 'I think we both know that isn't true, though.'

She'd been on the back foot ever since she could remember, unable to predict her mother's next move, always glancing around to see from where the next blow would rain. But now she had an advantage, a sliver of truth her mother could never snatch away. It was as wicked a weapon as her knives.

Everyone had seen the priggin doll explode. Everyone had seen the craw jump on Lidan and steal her away. Everyone had seen what had burst from the fire. It was magic—pure and simple. And as rare as it was in the South Lands, her people knew it when they saw it. No one could prove who had made the priggin, but everyone had their suspicions. The Crone sat atop the list, and there was nothing the dana could do about it. Her only defence was a flimsy shield of deniability. The burden of proof was on the accuser, and she knew no one, including Lidan, could publicly bring a case without something solid to back their claim. Speculation just wasn't enough. The only physical evidence had been destroyed, but that didn't deter Lidan. She'd ask as many awkward and irritating questions of her suspects as possible.

'We both know you can't prove anything, blossom.' Sellan shrugged and examined her perfectly-shaped fingernails. 'If you could, you would have made your father call a Hearing.'

Lidan was sick of this game. Tingalla was four day's ride away, and once they arrived she wouldn't have time for this. She hadn't come to her mother's wagon to trade barbs for the fun of it—she wanted answers. She climbed from Theus's saddle into the back of the wagon and tied the reins to a hook on the tailgate. 'It doesn't matter what I can prove. What matters is that you lied to me.'

Sellan looked incredulous. 'I would—'

Lidan stood inside the wagon and held tight to one of the roof bars, jabbing a finger at where her mother reclined. 'You told me you wouldn't move against Ehran until I turned eighteen, and only then if I failed.'

Her mother sat bolt upright. 'You renounced your inheritance! You chose to fail.'

'*After* you had the old bag make the priggin doll!' Lidan seethed, glaring at the dana and balling her hand into a fist. 'You went behind my back with the intention of harming Ehran, which was exactly what you promised you wouldn't do.'

'I will not continue to go around in circles! I did no such thing, Lidan. You can choose not to believe me if you wish, but I will not be accused of something I did not do. Call a Hearing or let it go!'

'Fine. But before we get to Tingalla, I need you to know something.' Lidan squared her shoulders despite the rocking of the wagon. 'The oath I took to protect Ehran? They weren't empty words to me. I take that oath very seriously.'

Her mother's expression darkened. 'You made a promise to me as well, Lidan.'

'I did.' Lidan cleared her throat and lifted her chin. It had taken weeks to work up the courage to speak these words. Weeks of interrogations, each day laying out another round of probing questions in the hope her mother might admit what the Crone had done. She'd spent days whispering the speech to herself, trying to predict what her mother might say or do in response. 'In exchange for the one you have broken.'

Sellan's eyes narrowed and her jaw clenched. 'Mind yourself, child. Remember who you're talking to.'

Lidan's muscles bunched and she fought the urge to reach for the knife at her hip. 'I am a woman of my word, Mother. If you move on him, if you touch a single hair on that child's head, I will come for you.'

'Is that a threat?' Sellan growled.

Lidan turned away and threw the wagon cover aside to unwind Theus's reins. She urged him closer and stepped out onto the saddle. She vanished from her mother's sight and heard a hurried scuffle as Sellan rushed to the back of the wagon. Lidan settled into the saddle and slipped her boots through the stirrups as Sellan yanked the cover back and glowered at her daughter.

'I said—'

'I heard what you said,' Lidan cut her off. 'Just as clearly as you heard me. I don't make threats, only promises. Leave the child alone and we have no reason to quarrel.' Lidan pointed at the shadows inside the wagon. 'That goes for her as well. Touch him, and all bets are off.'

She clicked at Theus and drew him away, leaving her mother to glare in her wake, her hand gripping the side of the wagon so hard her knuckles turned white.

Somewhere above the trundling caravan, a craw called.

Lidan didn't glance up. She knew what she would see—an unbelievable sight invisible to everyone else. The craw showed itself only when it wanted, and then only to her and Loge, tormenting him most evenings. After three weeks she'd grown accustomed to its presence, while he'd come to despise the strange little creature. It hadn't helped its case by hopping around the tent, teasing him, threatening to jump on her then flapping away and vanishing through the roof. He'd taken to sleeping inside the doorway of her tent, convinced the craw would try and steal her away again, and equally convinced he could stop it if it tried.

Each day, once the caravan was underway, it circled above them, then dropped down to sweep through the trees, wisps of blue smoke trailing from the tips of its wings. When they stopped to eat and let the children stretch their legs, it perched on a nearby branch and watched her go about her tasks. Sometimes, it found a spot atop one of the wagons, twitching its head to the side and glaring with one of its unnerving little eyes. It might not have bothered her so much if she knew what it wanted, or why it was there, but she had absolutely no idea. Was it watching her on behalf of the Crone, or for some other spirit lurking in the shadows of the world? Or was it trapped here, bound to her since she released it from the priggin doll? As much as she'd grown accustomed to its presence, it was as distracting as it was irritating, and she wished a quick arrow to the head could rid her of it.

For the rest of that afternoon she wondered if she could get away with shooting at empty air without alarming the entire caravan and looking like a complete fool.

One arrow.

She could get away with one arrow, surely, just to see what would happen.

Lidan swung Theus around and headed back to Loge's wagon for her bow. He was asleep when she got there, leaning where she'd left him at the tailgate with his head on one of the wagon's timber support posts. Theus snorted and Loge jolted awake, blinking at the glare, and Lidan grimaced, wishing she'd stayed away. He looked utterly exhausted; the dark rings under his eyes making him appear drawn and weary beyond reason. He might resent her reporting his injury to Siman, and his restriction to the wagon, but his fatigue ran deep. He slept for hours at a time during the day, and at night she heard him groaning from his bedroll beside the door. He was restless and listless all at once; exhausted but driven to return to what he knew.

Pain did that. Unrelenting, merciless pain. It sucked the light from your soul, devoured your joy, and ravaged any strength held in reserve. Lidan tried to remember that when he snapped at her, railing against his confinement and the oppressive boredom of the wagon. She tried to remember it was the pain swiping its claws at her.

The craw screamed behind her shoulder and Lidan spun to the noise.

The world slowed as though time itself was caught in a stream of honey.

An arrow sailed past her ear, whispering through stray tendrils of hair precisely where her head had been a second before.

Loge cried out and swore, and Lidan whipped around. Theus shied beneath her as the caravan burst into panic. Arrows rained down on the riders and wagons, and Lidan dug her heels into Theus's sides.

He lurched forward and she slipped her boots free of the stirrups, using his momentum to launch herself at the wagon as the draught horses quickened their pace. She tumbled into the bed of the cart and rolled to her knees before spinning back to Loge. The arrowhead had sliced through the muscle of his upper arm and lodged in the timber frame behind him, a deep red stain spreading through the pale green of his shirt sleeve. Lidan took one look at it and tossed him a spare shirt from a nearby bag.

'Keep the pressure on it.' She turned and collected her bow and strung it in one practised motion. The arrow was steady in her hand as she nocked and trained it through the gap in the wagon's cover, her training taking over. It isn't skill that wins battles, it's who keeps their nerve long enough not to die, and Lidan was ice as she sighted along the shaft.

Loge shuffled, clearing a space for her and sucking pained breaths through his teeth as he moved. 'What is it? Who's out there?'

She spared a quick glance at the arrow sticking from the post. There were two red lines painted on the end of the shaft, just before the fletches. 'Fucking Namjin raiders.'

A flicker of movement through the trees caught her eye, and she loosed her arrow. The rangers at the rear of the caravan spread out to cover the back of the line but were pinned beneath an onslaught of arrows. The driver of their wagon pulled the horses to a reluctant stop and the timber under them jerked and rolled, arrow shafts ripping through the cover above their heads like razor sharp rain drops. Children and adults screamed, orders were bellowed and answered along the line. The thrum of firing bow strings vibrated in the air.

Loge hunted around for something among the bags and trunks, cursing as he did, but Lidan didn't dare take her eyes from the trees around the trail, her arrows flying true to their targets. The screaming from the front of the caravan intensified and the attack at the rear diminished. Her stomach clenched and she realised they were concentrating on the passenger wagons, where her sisters and Ehran were.

'I need to go,' she said. She flung her bow aside and saw Loge hefting one of his new steel hatchets. 'I told you to keep pressure on that arm!'

Another arrow sliced through the wall of the wagon and Loge pulled Lidan from its path.

'What's that smell?' He glanced around.

Lidan paused, searching the chaos beyond the wagon with every sense she had. 'Smoke. Shit—they're firing the wagons! I have to go! I have to find Ehran!'

'Liddy!'

She turned and his hand wrapped around the back of her neck. He kissed her and her body jolted, her breath knocked clear from her lungs. He pressed her closer and her lips responded, returning his kiss before she knew what was happening.

He let her go and they stared at each other—a moment of breathless silence cocooning them from the madness outside. She couldn't move. Her entire body tingled, her skin singing with an urgency she didn't recognise.

'Go find Ehran,' he managed in a thick voice.

Lidan broke free of whatever spell held her. She swung a leg over the tailgate then looked back, her mouth dry and her heart racing.

'Don't die,' she whispered. Loge nodded and she rolled out of the wagon and into the fight.

CHAPTER THIRTY-ONE

The Western Reaches, Tolak Range, the South Lands

The craw swooped alongside Lidan as she ran. Her pulse thudded in her ears, blocking out the frantic cries of passengers and desperate rangers. Her lungs burned, black smoke billowing from a pair of wagons fully ablaze in the middle of the caravan. She raced past them to her brother's wagon at the very front of the line, angled across the path and surrounded by rangers firing arrows into the trees. Jessah and Iema were nearby, as was Nathen. She heard Siman shouting something, and beyond that, her father.

Lidan reached the wagon and slid to a stop. She flung open the cover and the occupants screamed.

An arrowhead gleamed in front of her nose and she stared up the shaft at Kelill. Her half-mother nodded, moved to one side and loosed the arrow into the trees. Someone wailed from the shadows and Kelill loosed another. Behind her, Farah huddled among trunks, bedrolls and blankets with four children crouching under the protection of her arms.

'Liddy?' Farah asked, gaping as she clutched the children closer.

'Get down, flat on the floor!' Lidan stabbed a finger at the bed of the wagon then whirled to survey the battle. 'Nathen?' she shouted over the chaos.

'What?' The ranger demanded without turning from where he knelt by the wagon. He loosed an arrow into the bush.

'Take the fight to them!'

He shot to his feet and tossed his bow at Lidan. She snatched up an arrow and put it in the eye of a Namjin raider who broke from the tree line. Nathen leapt over the convulsing body, axes in hand, and led a cluster of rangers into the bush. Other rangers hurried to follow, swarming toward the Namjin crouching in the protection of the trees.

The enemy charged, flint and bone flashing as they raced down an embankment to the wagons. Kelill's withering barrage faltered and Lidan stepped into the pause. She whipped the bow across the face of an oncoming raider and drew her knives, the blades singing as they left their sheaths and sliced the throat of the next raider tearing toward her.

Her knives scythed through flesh and sinew, carving into the next raider in a blur of blood and rasping breath. Spurred by rage and building terror, her steel against stone, the knives tore into the raider's reinforced leather armour, snapping the bands and plates beneath. His body slumped to the ground and the wagon jerked forward.

Lidan whipped around and stared as the wheels began the turn, her throat tightening as the flames of her anger were doused by the rising flood of her fear. Someone in the driver's seat cracked the reins against the rumps of the horses and the pair of them lurched forward, hooves pawing the ground, eager to oblige the driver and escape the melee.

The wagon jolted again and Kelill lost her balance. She tumbled, flipping from the rear of the wagon to the ground, and Lidan started forward as the wheels turned faster. The wagon pulled away and picked up speed as Kelill rolled onto her belly and screamed.

Lidan broke into a sprint, sheathing her blades.

The horses found their stride, and she launched herself at the back of the wagon. She caught the hide cover and hauled herself up from the ground flashing past beneath the wheels, the crack of the reins echoing against the trees. Glancing back at the caravan, she watched a Namjin raider make for the driver's seat of the wagon behind them, only to be beaten back by the rangers guarding it.

They want hostages!

She spun back as her own wagon thumped over uneven ground, the frame shuddering, timbers creaking and the cover flapping wildly in the wind. Lidan swung her leg over the tail gate and crawled inside. Farah snapped up from where she huddled with the children, brandishing a knife, and Lidan pressed a finger to her lips. The knife retreated into the gloom.

The wagon bounced and crashed along the track, throwing the occupants into the air before slamming them down again. Ehran and Lucija screamed, Cerise let out a pitched wail and her older sister Hanne dropped a curse no one cared to admonish. Farah soothed the four of them as Lidan slipped past.

Outside, the driver whipped the horses again, flicking the reins hard and shouting at them to move. The idiot seemed intent on pushing them into a frenzy, and they weren't far off as Lidan steadied her breath and peered through the opening in the cover.

The driver was a lanky man, with dark hair tied high and tight on his head. His clothes were filthy and torn, bloodied and by the stench, covered in a good amount of ngaru ichor. If this ranger had survived a ngaru attack, then he was no novice.

She stepped back from the opening and tried to order her thoughts. Farah's expectant eyes didn't help matters. Drawing a knife, its edge glistening with congealing blood, she stuck the blade through the cover of the wagon and waited. The wheels hit something hard and the wagon jerked up and down. No one heard the rip of the hide cover as the steel sliced through it over the crash of the trucks and the cries of weeping children. It tore a hole big enough for her to climb through, and she sheathed the blade, edging out and along the outside of the wagon as quietly as she could manage. At the front, Lidan paused and glanced at the track ahead.

Except there was no track—just an old overgrown trail that hadn't seen use in a decade or more. It was uneven and gullied by rain, and she realised the driver had taken them off the road. They were probably swinging to the north, making for a camp or maybe just straight for the border, and if she didn't stop this madman, they'd be lost in the bush and all the harder to find with every mile they travelled.

Gripping the wagon's frame in one hand, she drew her knife again and held it tight. This was either going to work spectacularly or she was going to end up minced under the whirring wheels—there was no third option.

The next jolt came and she jumped, swinging on her hand hold and sailing around from the side of the wagon to the front. The driver glanced up a second before her boots slammed into his chest, shoving him back into the cover. He dropped the reins and Lidan rolled away, staggering and flailing for a moment at the far edge of the seat. The driver recovered first and snatched a club from his belt while the frantic horses thundered unchecked through the trees.

The raider's fist hammered into her face. His club came next, swinging at her head and she leaned away, the swoop of the bulbous end barely audible over the rumbling of hooves and the crashing of the wagon across the ground. She ducked under the raider's arm and slashed with the knife then kicked him where she'd opened a gash in his side.

He roared and came back with a fury, the backswing of the club smashing into her hand and sending her knife scything through the air, slashing the cover of the wagon and disappearing inside. She went for her spare and he landed a kick to her knee.

Lidan cried out and crumpled, and the raider took his chance.

He leapt and bore her down, his legs straddling her hips as one of his hands found her throat. Somewhere, someone screamed her name, but a high-pitched squeal blocked it out.

Her lungs began to burn; iron-hard fingers squeezing her throat. She gasped, her hand clawing for her remaining knife, and the ranger's lips contorted into a grinning snarl when he realised what she was trying to do. He lifted his club high, his teeth bared, his face painted with blood and dirt.

Something landed beside her head and she glanced up. The craw perched above her shoulder on a leather-bound handle.

The sword.

She'd been so consumed by the fight, relying on her training and focused on her knives, she'd forgotten it was there.

With a single beat of its wings the craw vanished and Lidan let go of the raider's arms, reaching up to yank the sword free. The raider's club barrelled down. Steel flashed past the club, biting into the soft flesh where the man's neck met his shoulder.

He released her and roared, staggering back and pawing at the wound. Blinking black spots from her vision, she hauled herself upright, gasping for air as the man clutched desperately at the blood gushing from his collar.

She followed him as he stumbled back to the edge of the seat. From here, the only place left for him to go was down. Lidan gave him a moment to absorb the knowledge, then skewered her sword through his gut. He doubled over the blade and she gripped his shoulder with her free hand, shoving him backwards and tearing her weapon free.

He lingered there, disbelief and anguish rippling across his face as blood pumped from his wounds, followed closely by a slithering rope of greyish-purple intestines. She kicked him when he didn't have the decency to fall on his own.

'Far—' she tried to call, but her voice squeaked and cracked. Her strength faltered—the unnatural fire that burned in her limbs guttering as fatigue washed over her. Her hands shook and her legs trembled, threatening to give out.

Lidan sheathed her sword and clung to the edge of the seat, bouncing hard against the timbers as she gaped at the horses galloping ahead of the wagon. The reins snaked along the ground between their flashing hooves. Retrieving them was out of the question.

She had to stop the horses, though. The wagon wouldn't survive much longer at this speed, and letting the horses run out their fear and energy would kill them and likely everyone else. Farah shoved the wagon cover aside as Lidan began to inch out from the driver's seat, her hand reaching for a purchase on the harnesses.

'Liddy! What are you doing?' her half-mother's voice cut through the chaos but Lidan couldn't respond.

Farah shouted at Hanne to keep the other children inside as Lidan slipped.

Her hand snagged the harness just fast enough to stop her falling beneath the thundering hooves as the collar of her leather vest jerked tight. She glanced up to see Farah, teeth bared in a fierce grimace as she pulled Lidan up from the blur of the ground below.

Clawing her way up the harness with Farah's help, Lidan threw her leg over the back of one of the frantic draught horses. She leaned against its neck, her fingers stretching, her eyes screwed shut until her hand found the leather of the bridle. With one hand wound tight in the creature's mane, she pulled gently at the bridle, easing the horse's nose back toward its chest, cooing in her most soothing voice.

It felt like an age before the horse responded, its breath easing and its hoof-falls slowing. The horse beside it began to slow, sensing its mate's panic lessen, until finally the pair of them stood panting and shivering on the track, their sides slick with sweat and foam.

Lidan held tight to the leathers, too afraid to move, shaking all over, her hands locked into fists that would not unfurl. Farah's voice reached through the ringing in her ears and the woman stretched from the wagon to pull her back to safety. She deposited Lidan on the seat and swung down, stumbling around to the front the check the harnesses and collect the reins. Somehow, between the two of them, they turned the wagon around before exhaustion drove Lidan down hard at the foot of the seat.

Lidan shook for the entire journey back to the caravan, her injured hand tucked tight against her chest as her muscles shivered and her neck burned. Each breath was a trial, as if the very air was filled with merciless thorns.

Sentries from a search party spotted them first, and riders wheeled around to take the news back to the daari. A ranger climbed up to the driver's seat but Farah refused to relinquish the reins, instead turning the ranger's attention to checking on the children. Grim determination set Farah's lips in a line, her voice commanding and strong as she issued orders but Lidan couldn't make out what she said through the ringing in her ears. The ranger heard her clear enough though, nodding and hurrying to obey.

The wagon finally rolled to a stop and Lidan glanced up. Among the reaching branches of the tangled canopy, her craw circled, watching.

'Lidan!?' A shout cut through the dull hum in her head and she looked around. Her father rushed through and took her shoulders in his bloodied hands. 'You all right?'

She nodded dumbly and gave him what she thought might have looked like a weak smile. Her lip split and blood trickled into her mouth, pain lancing from her bruised and swollen nose. Erlon helped her from the wagon, but her legs went to water beneath her. Her father scooped her up before she hit the ground and carried her from the track to a hastily erected pavilion crowded with wounded—rangers and other healers scurried between bed rolls and pallets of blankets.

The daari deposited Lidan on a bedroll and Marrit noticed them across the pavilion. She collected a box of supplies and darted over, crouching at her sister's side.

'Go on, Da,' Marrit urged when he hesitated. 'She'll be fine.'

He spared Lidan one last, uncertain glance then disappeared into the shifting crowd. Lidan looked away as Marrit examined her hand, deep black bruises rising where the raider's club had crunched into it.

'Wait here,' her sister said, as if she was likely to get up and sprint off. 'I need to get one of the others to check this.'

Beside her bedroll lay Jessah, her shoulder wrapped and wadded with bandages. The ranger noticed Lidan and shifted closer. 'What happened to you?'

Lidan fought to push the words out through her throat, and when they did break free, they were hoarse and broken. 'Raider took a wagon.'

Jessah gave a rueful smile. 'I bet he regretted that?'

Lidan nodded and tried not to laugh. Her aching ribs and searing neck wouldn't thank her for it if she did. To their right a commotion rose and they both sat forward, craning their necks to see through the crowd. Siman shouted something unintelligible at a group of rangers and clan folk and Lidan climbed to her feet, pulling Jessah up with her. They moved toward the noise and shoved their way through the tangle of people at the edge of the healing tent.

They broke through the crowd and Lidan lurched to a stop.

Able-bodied rangers carried the dead away, lifeless bodies swinging between bloodied hands. Among the twisted limbs and swarming flies, Iema lay on the dirt, motionless and pale among the ruined corpses. Jessah's scream split the air and Lidan braced her hand against her lips, her stomach responding as her mind revolted against the truth. A pair of rangers reached for Iema while a few others pushed Siman back, their faces twisted in anguish.

'Immy!' Jessah cried and darted forward, scrambling toward the rangers. Lidan forgot her pain and hurried after her as Jessah slid to a stop and clutched at her friend, her body wracked with sobs. Lidan's throat contracted and she shuddered, staring down at Iema's sightless eyes and bloodless skin. An image of the corpse from her nightmares flashed before her eyes and she faltered, tears spilling from her eyes as she looked at the ranger holding Iema's shoulders. His hollow, haunted gaze met Lidan's.

'Should we leave her?' he asked.

'No,' she replied in a harsh rasp, her voice cracking as her heart broke.

She choked on a sob and worked herself between Jessy and Immy. 'Take her. Put her with the others.'

Lidan held Jessah, and they sank to the ground together. She rocked her friend like she might a child, Jessah's repeated cries echoing among the trees, mingling with the sorrow of the survivors. The rangers came back, collecting body after body and carrying them away, working around Lidan and Jessah, a dark blood stain growing in the soil beside them.

Sickening fear rolled through Lidan then and she scanned the faces of the dead. Some were ruined beyond recognition, their faces melted and charred by flame or beaten to a pulp by the raider's heavy clubs. Others she knew.

Nathen looked like he was sleeping, his blood-splattered face peaceful; his lips relaxed, his eyes almost closed. The last she'd seen him was running into the bush, taking the fight to the raiders, following her order... The rangers picked him up and his head rolled away, revealing a gaping hole where the side of his skull had been caved in by a club. Her stomach lurched and she sucked huge breaths into her chest as Jessah's keening cries redoubled. Her friend, and her ranging master, killed in a brutal fashion by rangers that should have been their allies.

Lidan couldn't see Siman, but she heard him; his apoplectic rage echoing through the trees, cursing the Namjin and swearing revenge. Tears blurred her vision and she buried her face into Jessah's good shoulder. She let herself weep, let her loss rip through her heart and bleed.

CHAPTER THIRTY-TWO

The Western Reaches, Tolak Range, the South Lands

Sunset closed in and Siman limped from the lingering smoke to collect Jessah from the healing tent. He'd only been released from care an hour or so before, after relenting to the insistence of the daari that he have his own wounds tended. Lidan watched him leave with her friend, her eyes finally empty of tears and her heart aching. The weight of grief pressed into her chest until she was sure she would suffocate, and she looked away.

Marrit lifted her hand by her wrist and began wrapping it with a linen bandage. Her fingers stank of oils intended to hasten healing and though the blood had been washed away, she felt it still, clinging to her skin like mud.

'It's not broken, thank the ancestors, but it's badly bruised. You need to take care—'

'Where's Loge?' Lidan asked, cutting her sister off.

Marrit glanced up and frowned. 'I think he's helping build the pyres.'

Lidan let out a shaking breath, relief diluting her panic, and she flinched as her sister secured the end of the bandage at her wrist. The younger girl placed a gentle hand on her sister's leg and their eyes met. 'Go. The clearing is that way,' she tilted her head toward the sun slipping below the horizon.

Lidan crawled to her feet and left the pavilion, weaving between the tents and wagons toward the setting sun. The wagons had been pulled from the track and arranged in a circle, rangers arrayed beyond that, with the remaining survivors clustered in the middle. They'd lost a score of folk defending the wagons, yet the loss would not be fully known until they returned to Hummel.

That seemed like a lifetime away—a possible future among many. How many of them would make it back? How many more of her people would they burn by the side of the track, their bodies consigned to ash upon the dirt, destined never to rest in a tumal with their ancestors? The thought sickened her, and she shook it away, hugging her throbbing hand to her chest.

The small clearing emerged through the trees, funeral pyres jutting up from the ground; sombre timber pedestals for the dead. The remains of the two burnt-out wagons had been stacked up with scavenged timber, along with any unsalvageable supplies and she searched the milling crowd, blinking dancing lights from her eyes as the last of her energy faded.

She staggered backward into the trunk of a soaring tree and sank to the ground, dizziness spinning the world around her as grief closed its cold hand around her heart. She drew her knees up under her chin and wrapped her arms around her shins, balling her good hand into a fist and willing her fingers to stop shaking and her heartbeat to slow. It hammered against the wall of her chest as if she still fought for her life, as if she still wielded her blades, spilling blood and tearing flesh.

The craw squawked by her boot and she started. It tilted its shiny blue-black head and she gave it a small, grim smile. Without the bird, she'd have died before the fight had even begun. Without the bird, that raider would have ended her while her sword sat unused and forgotten in its scabbard. Her fingers itched to touch the creature, to find out if its sleek blue-black feathers felt as silken as they appeared, but she didn't dare. As horrible as this place was, stinking of death and smoke, she didn't want to slip away to the white place. Yet, she wanted to run. If her legs had been strong enough to carry her, she would have.

She didn't want to be here among the mourners and the pyres, but she hadn't the heart to turn away. She was stuck, unable to escape. Her only way out was to let the day fall away like a discarded snakeskin, to leave it all behind in the tangled undergrowth, among the ants and the spiders, a feast for the carrion birds when she was gone.

A ranger touched a torch to a nearby pyre and it burst into flames with a loud *whoosh*. A silhouette tracked across her vision and she glanced up. Farah led Ehran by the hand, firelight dancing across faces streaked with grime and the tracks of tears. The boy held tight to something in his other hand.

'Mama found this in the wagon.' He stepped free of his mother and lifted his burden toward Lidan as she shuffled onto her knees. It was her sword and the missing knife, cleaned of dirt and blood, wrapped in a strip of soft cloth.

'And what do you say to your sister?' Farah prompted, her voice strained and hoarse.

Ehran's brown eyes fixed intently on Lidan's face. 'Thank you, Liddy.'

Lidan looked up at Farah. 'I was only—'

'No. I won't hear it.' Farah took Ehran's hand again, the woman's fingers shaking as they closed around the small boy's fist. 'Duty or not, I can't repay you for what you did. And after everything that's happened... Thank you.'

Lidan bit the back of her quivering lip.

Farah knew.

How could she not? It was obvious what Ehran's birth had done, how it had changed everything for her husband's eldest child, how it had set Lidan adrift and left her scrambling for a handhold in a world shifting beneath her feet. And she surely knew how desperately the dana wanted to shove Ehran out of the line of succession.

Was it pity or sadness Lidan saw in Farah's eyes? No, it was guilt shimmering just beneath the surface, fuelled by the knowledge of what Lidan's protection of Ehran meant. Lidan could have stayed at the back of the caravan and left her mothers and sisters to defend themselves and the boy. She could have stayed with Loge—where she suddenly ached to be—but she'd fought and watched her fellow rangers return from the bush, beaten, bloodied and worse. She could have ignored the oath she'd given, thrown it to the wind and let the Namjin do their worst, but she hadn't. She'd done the thing she had sworn to do—the thing her mother hated her for.

Farah knew all of this, and in that small, silent moment, Lidan thought the woman understood the cost; what Lidan had given up, and the war she fought within herself every day. With a stiff nod, Farah led Ehran away, and left Lidan kneeling with her sword. She unwound the cloth from the blade and shrugged the scabbard harness from her shoulders. The muscles in her arms were like stones under her skin; heavy and lifeless, moving only because she forced them to, protesting every twitch. She slid the sword into the casing and looked up at the shifting crowd of mourners gathered by the funeral pyres.

Her father moved among them, offering words of sympathy and sharing the grief. The lines of his face were drawn, dark shadows reaching where they had not been before, painting fatigue across his features for all to see. She stood as he approached, and when his gaze fell on her, he waved for a tine-woman to bring a drink. Lidan opened her mouth to refuse, but the steel in Erlon's eyes pulled her up short.

'Don't drink it if you don't want,' he said. 'But honour them, even if you won't honour yourself.'

She accepted the cup in silence, then tipped a portion of the wine on the ground. The ancestors had their share, and she drained the rest. The tine refilled the cup without hesitation and moved on through the gathered mourners. Lidan hugged the cup to her chest, the warmth of the drink washing through her weary body as orange flames consumed the pyres. Timber popped and sap sizzled from cracks in the branches, smoke swirling up past the trees and into the sky where the light of the stars had been all but banished by the glow of the fires.

'What happened out there?' she asked her father in a coarse whisper, turning toward him so her question stayed between them. 'Where were the scouts? How…'

Her questions died on her lips, her thoughts scattering across a plain littered with bodies and screaming craws. She couldn't think straight, and she flinched as the words caught in her throat.

Her father chewed the inside of his lip, tears glimmering in the corners of his eyes. Erlon held himself together with bands of steel no one could see, glancing at where Siman stood staring at the flaming pyres with arms crossed over his chest, his features fixed. Jessah sat nearby, her legs crossed and her hands folded loosely in her lap. They were like statues, solidified by grief and loss, their faces carved into stony masks to hide their boiling anger.

'The northern scouts didn't cycle back on schedule, so we sent more out to find them. It was too late. The raiders slaughtered them all.'

Lidan's throat tightened and she squeezed the cup to stop her hand shaking. 'We lost so many…'

'And we'll lose more if we don't end this war.' Erlon put a heavy hand on her shoulder with a gentleness that belied his strength. 'Farah told me what you did. I'm proud of you, Liddy.'

'I can do more, Da. Please,' she implored him, keeping her voice low. His pride in her was all well and good, but it wasn't going to keep them alive. 'You need me out there, now more than ever.'

He hesitated, scanning her face, doubt furrowing his brow. Finally, he shook his head. 'I need you with Ehran.' He lifted a finger as she opened her mouth to protest. 'You are exactly where you should be, exactly where I need you to be. I can't...'

His voice cracked and he looked at the fires. His hand shook as it fell away from her shoulder. 'I can't lose you, Liddy. I won't lose any of you. Not again.'

She blinked away threatening tears and accepted his decision in silence, swallowing it like bitter medicine she knew she had to take. She wasn't going to fight him today. Neither of them had the strength for it, and for once, she thought her father might be right.

Loge limped from the darkness and Lidan's heart leapt into her throat. Erlon's face broke into a strained smile and he stepped forward to clasp the ranger's forearm. 'Siman said you made it through. I was glad to hear it.'

'Thank you, sir. Not without a few stitches, but...' He shrugged and Erlon nodded, giving Loge's uninjured arm a gentle squeeze.

Loge's eyes found Lidan and he stepped past the daari. Her pulse quickened as he walked slowly toward her, leaving her father to stare into the flames. From the way his mouth fell open, no one had told him about her injuries. She had wondered how livid her bruises were, and the naked horror on his face told her all she needed to know. He stopped his hand reaching for her face and cleared his throat. 'How'd that big knife go?'

'Better than expected,' Lidan replied, her voice hardly more than a whisper above the sound of the hungry fires. 'Almost forgot I had it.'

'You all right?' he murmured. A rumble of conversation surrounded them—folk drinking, some weeping, others talking—all of them mourning.

Lidan swallowed her heart and nodded. 'I think so.'

All she wanted was to feel his hands on her skin again. Despite the trauma and the bruises, her neck tingled where Loge's hand had been when he kissed her. The sensation consumed her thoughts until a fire deep in her belly flared to life.

His hand came up and rested behind her shoulder, a gentle gesture that made her heart give a single heavy thump. 'Got all your parts in the right place?'

She nodded.

His hand lingered for a moment then clutched at the wound in his shoulder. Her heart thumped again, and she clenched her jaw.

What was wrong with her? What was this madness shifting across her skin, taking over her thoughts like some sort of sickness? She'd lost count of how often they'd shared that exact exchange—a hand on a shoulder, checking to make sure they'd each made it through the turmoil in one piece. It was so normal, so utterly unremarkable, that no one around them even spared a passing glance. But something *had* changed.

Subtly, without her realising, *they* had changed. It had been there for some time, an energy growing between them that she couldn't name or explain. It had changed the way they looked at each other, the way they touched or asked after the other's wounds. It had driven her to help him, clawing at her heart whenever he winced with pain, or flashing like lightning in her chest when he smiled. Slowly, yet suddenly, Loge's regard, his hands, his eyes, his very presence, had become something else—something powerful and meaningful and intoxicating and she needed more.

'Might need you to check these stitches,' he said, scratching at the torn, blood-soaked sleeve. 'Just to make sure they're as they should be.'

She drained the contents of her wine cup. 'I think my bag is in your wagon.'

Erlon turned at that. 'Speaking of wagons, we won't be setting up tents between here and Tingalla. The rangers will maintain a perimeter, but I want everyone else in the wagons in case we have to move out quickly.' Her father nodded at her, then Loge. 'I need both of you to guard the youngest children. Take whatever weapons you need and get settled in with them.'

Loge pressed his fist into his chest, acknowledging the order, and Lidan found little reason to disagree. She didn't relish staring at the ceiling of her tent, waiting for a raider to slip from the shadows and cut his way through the wall.

They left the funeral and slipped into the dancing shadows. Loge limped a little, but not as heavily as he had in Hummel and Lidan rubbed a chill from her arms, despite the warmth of the evening. Her body shook from a place deep inside. It was uncontrollable and insufferable and nothing she did quelled it.

Loge drew level with her and slipped a hand around her elbow to bring her gently to a stop. The air between them was thick with unshed tears and barely controlled pain. Lidan didn't know how much longer her legs would hold and she locked her knees in the hope she wouldn't collapse in front of him.

'What happened?' he murmured. The mournful wail of a coylew rippled through the night, echoing off the trees, calling to its mate. The swelling around her nose was obvious, but she lifted her chin and pulled her shirt collar down. Loge sucked air through his teeth, grimacing as the light revealed the bruises around her neck.

'Everyone was pinned down. No one was attacking, they were just *being* attacked. Then a raider hijacked the wagon with the little ones in it. They were looking for hostages, I think.'

His finger traced down her neck and his features darkened. 'You fucking ended him, right?'

She gave him a wry smile and raised her brows. 'Stuck him with the big knife.'

He nodded approvingly and they kept moving along the border of the camp, skirting around to the supply wagons on the far side of the circle. It was late by the time they found the right wagon, a cold full moon riding high in the night above.

'What about you?' she asked, holding her throbbing hand in close.

'Kept as many pinned down at the rear as I could manage. Wasn't like I could run off and get my axe wet with my knee the way it is.'

'Nice to hear some sense from you, finally!'

Loge rolled his eyes and climbed up into the wagon. He dragged a pair of bedrolls and her treatment bag to the tailgate, then handed them out to Lidan. She shouldered her bedroll and he tucked his under his good arm, then they wound through the camp until Lidan found her family's wagons, the campfire beside them burning down to coals.

She sensed a presence in the shadows and looked over at the Crone sitting motionless by the dying fire. They regarded each other in silence, the Crone absently chewing on something like the old nanny goat the Knapper's kept out the back of their workshop. Loge stiffened as he caught sight of the old woman and Lidan put her hand on his arm.

'Ignore her,' she whispered. 'She delights in unnerving people.'

Lidan quietly checked each wagon in turn, aware of the Crone's steady gaze on her back. The dana and Marrit were in the one closest to the Crone, and the eldest children were in another. She carefully lifted the cover of the middle wagon and peered inside. Farah lay curled around Ehran and Lucija at the far end, and Raeh slept between Cerise and Kelill's youngest, Hanne.

The trunks and belongings had been moved into a new wagon, then arrayed around the edges in some sort of makeshift fort. Lidan climbed under the cover and tied it back, then rolled her bed out in the empty space near the tailgate. Loge stood frozen, staring at the Crone, and started when Lidan touched his shoulder. He dragged his eyes away from the old woman and handed Lidan his bed, which she unrolled beside hers.

'You've got to rest that knee,' she muttered. 'I can't keep this lot safe on my own.'

'I'd say you did just fine without me,' he whispered, pulling himself up into the wagon.

'If by "fine" you mean losing my knife, getting kicked in the leg, punched in the face, almost choked to death and forgetting I had a sword, then yes, I did really well.' Lidan unlaced her leather jerkin with her good hand and tossed it on a pile of dirty clothes in the corner of the wagon.

She sat down and yanked off her boots, then went to work on Loge's. She didn't ask—she just did it—then pushed both pairs over to the tailgate beside the clothes. Loge managed to unbuckle his wide belts but the wound in his shoulder conspired against him as he fought to pull his shirt off. Lidan took hold of the hem and eased it up over his head, careful to release his wounded arm last. She tried not to stare at the moonlight gleaming across his arms and chest. She threw the shirt on the laundry pile and sat to examine the dressing on Loge's arm. 'Who fixed it?'

'Marrit. Much to your mother's disgust.' He grimaced when she poked at the bandage. 'She gave the dana one of your looks.'

241

'One of *my* looks?' Lidan glanced up with mock indignation. She could just see her sister glaring at Sellan, small and determined with blood up to her elbows, a needle and thread in her hand. Her sister wouldn't say a word, and Sellan would turn on her heel, scowling and hissing, and Marrit would return to sewing bodies back together.

The bandage around Loge's arm was clean and sturdy, and Lidan saw no reason to remove it. 'Looks fine to me. She can check her work tomorrow.'

Loge reached up and carefully touched the bruised flesh under her eye. 'He got you good, Liddy.'

'Does it look as bad as it feels?'

'Maybe even better. Are you sure you're all right?' he asked again, just in case she hadn't been truthful last time.

Lidan leaned her head to one side and studied him. 'Since when are you so worried about me?'

He gave her a rueful smile. 'I've always worried about you. I've just gotten worse at hiding it.'

The heat burning in her belly flared and she kissed him, her fingers combing through the thick waves of his hair. His hand found her waist and her breath caught. She moved closer, drawn by her need and his hands as they slid under her shirt. Things could only go so far in the confines of the wagon and when Loge eventually pulled away, it was well before she was ready, and her body mourned the loss. Fire burned through her veins, her whole being charged and tingling. She knew why he'd retreated, and in the rational depths of her mind—the parts her heart had kicked into a small dark place in the hope they would never emerge again—she knew this was not the time or place.

Loge leaned his forehead against hers. 'Here I was thinking I'd over-stepped back there, when the fight started...'

She smiled and shook her head. The grin that broke across his face made her heart jump. Looking around in an effort to distract herself she found a collection of blankets in the middle of the wagon and handed a pair of them to Loge, then bundled another into a ball and stuffed it behind her head as she lay staring at the roof of the wagon. Loge eased himself down and rolled onto his back beside her.

'Did you hear about Nathen and Iema?' he whispered into the darkness.

A sliver of moonlight cut through the gap where Lidan had tied the cover back. In the distance, the sounds of mourning tinged with drunkenness, the pyres roaring and crackling, filled the deepening night.

'I saw them…' Lidan shut her eyes and heard Loge turn toward her.

'I'm sorry, Liddy.'

Their hands met in the tiny space between the bedrolls.

'Don't be sorry,' she whispered. She wound her fingers around his and turned toward his voice. 'There will be a reckoning for what they did to us. There will be a bloody toll to pay for what was taken. And when it comes, that dawn will break hot and red, and they will curse the day they turned their ire on our people.'

CHAPTER THIRTY-THREE

The South Lands

The air grew warmer the further south they travelled. Coats and jackets were stuffed into saddlebags along with gloves and scarves, shirt collars were loosened and Ran seriously considered riding his horse without his boots and socks. Other than the odd dradur scurrying around in the shadows of the ravines, the weather was easily the weirdest thing about the place.

It was hot—a steamy, suffocating heat that sucked every drop of moisture from his body while simultaneously drenching him in sweat. Rain poured from the sky one minute and vanished the next, the clouds rolling away to reveal blinding sunshine. The ground literally steamed around them, and the nights offered no relief. He slept on top of his bedroll, swearing off blankets and coverings, wearing a shirt and trousers to protect his skin from the biting insects humming around his ears at all hours. The air hardly shifted in the confines of the endless canyons and gorges, the trees whirred and creaked with the large sounds of tiny creatures, and the whole experience put him in mind of the steam room in the Keep's bathhouse.

Truth be told, they pushed the horses hard to get out of the place, riding by the light of the moon as it grew fuller and taking advantage of the extended hours of daylight the summer season offered. They covered an extensive amount of ground in a short time, making the edge of the canyon-riddled tablelands in a week, relying on Brit's tracking skills and Aelish's memory to guide their way. There were no dradur trails to follow, Ran and Eian's power exhausted fending off the dragon, leaving them bereft of magic to use their Sight.

By the time his Sight returned, Ran had lost the thaumalux trails of the dradur who attacked the Keep and the camp. Instead, he faced a mess of thaumalux ranging in age from a few months old, all the way back to before he was born. They whipped across the landscape, scattering into the bush-land like a flock of frightened birds, and the single trail of the witch he'd found in the Pass vanished under decades of light left by other magic-weavers travelling with the trading caravans. Try as he might, he couldn't sift that single thread from the tangle, and he eventually conceded defeat.

Late one afternoon, at the mouth of a gorge, they encountered a group of riders bristling with weapons; some wrought of shining steel and others of bronze, while a few of the men hefted wicked stone axes as deadly as anything forged in the north. Thankfully, Aelish proved to be a skilled negotiator, and after a short exchange, one of the riders slipped down from her saddle and drew a map in the sand. She pointed east, listing off direc-tions to Aelish while Ran remained with the others at a respectful distance, trying his best not to stare at the riders or their weaponry. He burned to ask them about the dradur, but Aelish warned him off. Were they so armed *because* of the dradur, or some other threat? Was this a regular patrol, or something out of the ordinary?

Soon enough Aelish had the information she needed, and permission to proceed into the territory, but by the time she returned to the group, the riders had melted back into the trees, leaving Ran with a distinct and creep-ing sense of being watched from afar. After a small meal of dried meat and weak tea, he volunteered for first watch.

He sat apart from the others, staring at the thaumalux trails as dark-ness fell. Worry rolled in his stomach, a cold shiver of fear he worked to shake off. The thaumalux of the witch was in there somewhere, taunting him, hidden under decades of magic he hadn't expected to find. He couldn't understand why the dradur weren't following it as closely as before, and he couldn't decide if it had something to do with the strange magic in the Pass.

At first light they struck camp and followed the rider's directions through thick bushland as the sun rose. The eastern sky brightened, and Ran glanced over his shoulder at the thaumalux trails winding along beside his horse, visible only to him while Eian reserved his strength.

'Those riders we saw yesterday... Did they know you?' he asked Aelish, who shared his horse today instead of Brit's.

'They know my name, and that I'm a trader from north of the mountains. They were rangers from the Tolak clan, who control this part of the South Lands. My people mostly trade with them for horses.' She tapped him on the shoulder. 'Speaking of horses, we should get an extra one when we get to the village.'

He turned in the saddle. 'What? Don't you like my horse anymore?'

She grinned. 'No, your horse is lovely. You just take up too much room on his back.'

'How far is the village?' he asked.

She glanced up at the sun, orientating herself against the face of the tablelands marching off to the east, then pointed into the trees. 'The rangers said it was a day's ride that way. Why?'

He didn't answer at first, his attention drawn back to the thaumalux trails. 'Is that where the clan live?'

She handed him a canteen of water. 'The clan leader and his family live there. It's nice, if a little basic. Hot. Gods, it gets hot there. Friendly people though, as long as you don't insult them.'

'That's where your people go to trade?'

'Yes,' Aelish replied cautiously. 'Why?'

Ran sucked water from his lips. 'There are a lot of trails left by magic-weavers, which isn't surprising if they travel in the trading crews. But you know how I told you about the witch? Well, I can't pick that trail out anymore. It's buried too deep, disguised by the rest of them.'

Aelish lowered her voice and accepted the canteen back from Ran. 'Do you think the witch is in the village?'

'Maybe…' This galled and worried him the most. 'It's been a long time since they passed this way.'

'What are you going to do?' she asked, shifting behind him.

Ran rearranged the reins in his hands. 'You're right—we need another horse. We've got enough coin to pay for it and some supplies. And maybe someone in the village will know who we're looking for.'

Aelish led them south-east and Ran relinquished the tracking to Eian at about midday. By sunset the bushland fell away completely and ahead of them, illuminated by the setting sun across an undulating grassland, a soaring stone monolith broke through the surface of the earth like a thorn on the stem of a rose. It shone with the colours of sunset, reflecting the warmth of the day, framed by crackling lighting on the horizon. He pulled his horse to a stop and Aelish put a hand on his shoulder.

'See the village at the base of the rock? That's Hummel.' She glanced back at the others as they emerged from the trees. 'Let me do the talking. I've been here before; their leader will know me and my family name. Don't mention the creatures or what you're looking for yet. Keep your weapons and your magic to yourselves. These people aren't especially fond of those who have power.'

The others nodded and Ran loosened his reins, letting his horse walk calmly down into the valley, following a track beside a gurgling stream to a ford. They crossed, splashing through the eddies and winding up a gentle incline to a gate which looked to be shut tight. They drew closer, and Aelish leaned forward, peering over his shoulder.

'Where is everyone?' she muttered.

A figure appeared at the top of the wall and trained an arrow on the riders. Ran baulked and tightened the reins. His horse shied and Aelish swung her leg over its back and jumped clear. Heart rate climbing, Ran squeezed his legs against the horse's flanks, meaning to urge the animal after her, but he paused as she raised her hands and her voice echoed off the timber battlements.

'Jac?' she called in the common tongue. 'Jac Tolman?'

The figure at the top of the gate multiplied into several more as Aelish climbed the track. In the falling darkness, Ran pushed his horse to follow slowly, and noticed a buzzing swarm of flies gathered at the top of a series of pikes to his right. The pungent stench of rot hit him, and the flies lifted away from a mangled skull. It leered at him in the twilight and he swore, the hair on the back of his neck standing on end. There were more, a whole line of them along the length of the wall, a good distance from the battlement, decorated with severed heads in various states of decay. He fought down the gorge that rose in his throat. Eian made a disparaging remark under his breath, drawing a hissing shush from Zarad and a snort of laughter from Brit. Was this what happened to those who insulted these people? Aelish, on the other hand, seemed unbothered by the heads, and directed her attention to the guards.

'Who's ask'n?' a voice called down, his common as thickly accented as Aelish's.

'Aelish Yordam, of the East Ruken Trading Company. We have crossed the Malapa to trade with your people.' She brought her hands to her chest then opened them in a wide, sweeping gesture.

'Party's a bit small, young Yordam,' the man on the wall observed with an edge of suspicion.

Aelish nodded. 'We encountered trouble before the Pass, then again as we came through. This is all that's left, Jac. We've got hardly any food and not enough horses to carry us all. I've got coins to trade, but not much else. We just need some supplies and a horse if you can spare one—we'll keep moving if you want.'

There was a murmur of conversation on the wall, then Jac nodded and gestured toward the tablelands. Ran's heart felt as though it had crawled up into his throat, hammering away and attempting to choke him.

'We can't bring you in,' Jac told her. 'The daari's away and left orders to keep the gates secure. There's a war going on.'

That explained the severed heads.

Aelish's shoulders dropped and she sighed.

'Guner's saddling a horse, and rangers will bring it out with some supplies. You wait by the creek.'

'Thank you, Jac!' Aelish shouted as the man disappeared. She turned and waved at Ran and the others. 'Get down to the creek and set a fire. This might take a while.'

They unsaddled their horses and let them graze along the creek bank, lit a fire for light more than warmth, and waited. An hour or two passed, the sun sinking behind the hills to the west, and in his boredom, Ran unveiled his Sight and stared up at the village. Thaumalux trails wound straight up the trackway and through the gate, shimmering bands of light oscillating in the evening, and he frowned, peeling back time, sifting and searching for a single thread that might be the witch he'd discovered in the Pass.

Witches, Iridia murmured.

What? He blinked and looked for her.

You keep talking about a witch, as if there was only one of them.
I can only see evidence of one—
There were two—

He shot a withering glare over his shoulder. *I don't know what to tell you.*
I can only see one. And whoever it was isn't here anymore... He turned back
to the ropes of thaumalux pulsing by the gate. In the end he hadn't needed
to search through the distant past. It had been many years since a magic-
weaver had entered that gate, but one had recently left. The light wound down
the track, past their camp and off to the west. *They left maybe a moon ago.*

'Ran?'

He started and looked back at Zarad, who stood at the edge of the fire,
squinting into the night. His fingers flicked in and out, as if plucking at
strings in the air.

'I can feel something,' Zarad said, rubbing the pads of his fingers across
his palms. 'There's a blur through the air. It's familiar, like the magic—'

The village gate rumbled open and Aelish came to her feet, waving at
Eian to do the same. Glancing down, Ran realised he looked no more
presentable than a drunk after a night in a city gutter, and furiously brushed
road dust off his sleeves and straightened his shirt.

A man led a horse down the hill, followed by a group with woven baskets
slung over their shoulders. Accompanying them was a short, stocky man
with greying hair and a face furrowed with wrinkles. His skin was a dark
shade of brown, and his smiling eyes gleamed as he approached their fire
and offered his hand to Aelish. She reached and clasped his forearm, squeezing his shoulder with her free hand.

'Good to see you, Jac,' Aelish said with a smile. 'Still manning the wall?'

'The daari don't trust anyone else, young one.' Jac winked, then turned
his attention to the four men arrayed behind Aelish. 'Not much of a crew.'

'These are all that survived.' Genuine sorrow raked her voice, and she
cleared her throat. 'The caravan was attacked north of the Pass. By creatures... Things that might once have been men but...'

Jac's eyes narrowed as Aelish's voice trailed off. 'Nasty fuckin' things?
With blades stickin' out of their bodies?'

'Yes!' Ran blurted. Aelish glared at him and he almost swallowed
his tongue.

Jac spat on the ground, as did the others behind him. 'Ngaru, we call them. They've been a plague on this land for years. Had no idea they wandered so far north.'

Aelish turned slowly back to Jac and licked her lips, seeming to carefully consider her next words. 'We think they might be *from* the north, from a place far from here. They attacked our camp at the Pass and we tracked them across the mountains. We lost their trail in the tablelands.'

Jac sucked at his teeth. 'Haven't seen one in this valley for near on four seasons.'

'They don't come here?' asked Ran, unable to help himself. He ignored another scathing look from Aelish and stepped toward the gateman.

'Only one ever got within spittin' distance of the gate.' Jac nodded at the tablelands, shrouded in darkness. Ran couldn't quite believe what he was hearing. 'Broke through the trees over there. Got killed for its trouble. Daari Erlon's rangers have been scouting the tablelands ever since. Beasts are still out there, but not as thick as a few years back.' As if that were the end of the tale, Jac waved the basket-laden villagers forward and gave the northerners an apologetic smile. 'You can camp here the night or keep going— up to you. Sorry about this. If I let you in and the daari finds out, he'll feed me to the pigs.'

Aelish grimaced. 'I've seen those pigs. Not the way I'd want to go.'

The villagers deposited the baskets on the ground, and it took all Ran's strength not to dive on a pile of flat bread peeking from the basket nearest his boot. Jac turned to the man with the horse. 'And this is for you, young Yordam. May she carry you with the strength and spirit of her ancestors.'

He passed the reins to Aelish and stepped back. The mare was beautiful— a sleek, rangy roan with a wide blaze down her nose. The leather of the saddle and tack shone in the firelight, worked with horse motifs and swirling symbols.

'Has she got a name?' Aelish asked.

'In the common, it's Ember.'

Ember snorted and nuzzled Aelish's hand, then sniffed at Ran's trouser pockets as Aelish turned to Eian. 'Could you pass me the bag of coins, please?'

Jac held up his hands and stepped back again. 'I won't trade you these, young Yordam. You come seeking aid and shelter and I could only supply you with half of what you need. These are gifts.'

'Are you sure?' Aelish eyed him, and the villagers began their trek up the incline to the gate. 'I don't want to—'

'Offend anyone? You northern folk are so worried about offending people, it's almost offensive.' The gateman reached forward with a smile and Aelish took his offered arm again. 'Take them, Aelish. And next time you pass by, I hope we can show you better care.'

Jac started back up the hill, the gate inching open just wide enough for him and the others to slip through before it rumbled closed again. Aelish turned on Ran as soon as it eased shut. 'What did I say about talking?'

'I had to ask! Did you hear what he said? They've been fighting a plague of dradur down here, but only *one* has come within sight of the village?' He gave her a dubious look.

'Jac said the daari has patrols out searching…' Even as she said it, her voice wavered, and he knew she wasn't convinced. It didn't sound right, not like the dradur he knew. Walls and arrows and flame were hardly a deterrent at all, so what was it about this place that kept them away?

'No, something else is going on here,' Ran insisted.

Eian stepped between them. 'The gateman spoke true. There hasn't been a dradur in this valley for years. If there had, we'd see the trails.'

He was right, of course, but it still made no sense.

'How is this valley, of all the places in Coraidin, immune to the dradur?' Ran lifted his arms wide, exasperated. 'I can see the witch's thaumalux now. They've been here, hidden for years behind those gates, but not a single dradur has made it over the palisade?'

'Maybe we were wrong about them following the witch?' Eian suggested with a shrug, folding his arms over his chest. 'What if they were coming south for something else?'

Ran shook his head and stalked up the hill away from the group, Aelish hurrying to catch him with the others at her heels. He lengthened his stride and climbed the path toward the gate, boots crunching on the rocky path.

'Ranoth!' Aelish hissed through her teeth. 'Get any closer and they *will* shoot you!'

He turned to her, walking backwards up the hill. 'Have you ever heard of a crissan web? Did anyone in Isord ever talk about them? Any of the magic-users you know?'

Aelish flinched to a stop and shook her head, but behind her, Zarad nodded. 'Master Collan mentioned them a few times. He said the Woaden lay them around homes or towns to ward off magic-users with bad intentions. He'd never seen one though.'

'I've only ever read about them, and I'd wager that's why there wasn't one around the Keep,' Ran ventured. 'Crissan webs are frequency magic, yes?'

Zarad nodded and Ran dropped his veil completely. Trails flared around him, illuminating the track up the hill. He blinked at Zarad, his figure shining with thaumalux, his red hair aflame.

'Is that what you can feel? The blur you were talking about?'

Zarad extended a hand toward the valley and muttered a string of curses. 'Ugh... yes. The place is smothered with it. It's a damn clean spell, too. It's vibrating so fast I almost couldn't feel it.'

'It's a crissan web, laid out to deter someone—or some*thing*—from entering.' Ran opened his magic and beyond his Sight, a web of energy broke through the darkness; looping, criss-crossing lines of shimmering power fanning out from the village like the petals of a multi-layered flower. He marvelled at it, horrified and enamoured all at once. This was powerful stuff, created by someone with extraordinary strength and talent; crisp lines cutting the air as if it had been scored by the needle-sharp tip of a blade. 'A crissan web all the way around the village... And it runs right out to the tree line, right to where Jac said the dradur appeared.'

Zarad started explaining the web to Brit, and Aelish studied Ran with a deep frown.

'I wish I could see it...' she whispered.

Ran hesitated, heat gathering in his fingers. He could show her. It wouldn't take much effort. She had an affinity with magic that gave her a sense of Iridia's presence, but he wondered if she knew what she was asking, if she knew what she would be exposed to if he showed her what he could see. But then, who was he to deny her? He held out his hand, and she took it; long, cool fingers wrapping around his searing skin, soothing the burn in a way that made him gasp. He willed her eyes to see through his own, pressing his vision over hers like a painted pane of glass.

She cringed, and Ran felt a shiver run through her body from her skin down to her marrow, then she swore and grew very still. 'Is that it? The shimmer?'

'That's it.'

'It looks as though it was painted with starlight...' Aelish wondered at the valley, then turned to look up the hill to the village. 'Can you sense the witch you're looking for?'

'Yes, but their trail leads away from here. Tomorrow, we'll follow it. You could stay here if you—'

The look of absolute disdain Aelish levelled at him ripped the offer from his lips.

'No, Ran. I'm going with you. Someone needs to answer for what happened to my crew, and I won't get that justice sitting here waiting for it to appear out of thin air.' She took one last look at the valley before slipping her hand from his, her fingers shaking as she tucked them under her arms. 'We'd better get some rest.'

She started back down the hill and he watched her go, thankful her questions had ended there. There were things here he could not yet explain, things he wasn't ready to give voice to. Zarad had felt it—the similarity between the spell worked in the Pass and the web around the village. The magic in the tunnel had changed the air, making it colder as the years passed, drawing the dragons down from the surface to deter anyone, or anything, that might come looking for them.

A cold shiver rolled over Ran's skin. The curse the witch had worked in the Pass was not meant for any living, breathing pursuer. It existed to deter something darker, something hungrier than any Orthian soldier sent to find a fleeing murderer. Yet it had failed to stop the darkness following the trails of light.

He glanced around, his eyes open to the magic in the air, and swallowed hard. All about him the crissan web shimmered, and his preconceived notions of what the witch had done fell away. What if the web around this village was not a defensive wall, but a cage—a gleaming prison of starlight woven by someone living in terror of the creatures they had created?

CHAPTER THIRTY-FOUR

Hummel, Tolak Range, the South Lands

Ran took first watch again and waited for the others to fall asleep. Brit had reclaimed his bedroll after the trade with the clan produced a new one for Aelish, and they succumbed to sleep beside one another; Aelish on her stomach with one arm twisted under her body, the fingers of her other hand an inch shy of Brit's. The experience at the trader's camp seemed to have welded the watcher and the Isordian together in a way Ran didn't really understand. Danger often did that to people. Perhaps that was how he and Iridia had ended up as they were—bound together by invisible chains that had not broken no matter how hard he'd tried to sever their hold.

She looks like you did, the first time I saw you in the farmhouse, Ran whispered to Iridia.

A small smile danced across her lips. *Except she's not dead.*

True. He glanced up and watched the ghost. Her form passed over rock and through grass as if she were nothing but cloud on the hot southern wind. *Seems like yesterday.*

And a thousand years ago, all at once.

At that, he stood and walked into the night, opening his Sight and letting his magic go, reaching out to reveal the crissan web swirling around the base of the rocky monolith.

It's the same as the magic in the cave, Iridia said in a whisper, her voice a crawling shiver up his spine.

Exactly the same, he replied. His gaze followed a line of magic until his eyes met hers. *She used frequency magic to disrupt the air in the cave. That's what we saw her doing when we were pulled into that white place.*

The place between.

The what?

It's called the place between. Iridia shrugged and wandered along one of the crissan lines. *You're not dead, but you're not alive. You're just in-between. I was there before you found me in the farmhouse; before your terror fused me to your mind and you dragged me back here.*

Is that what happened?

She glanced at him, ice blue eyes gleaming in the light of the distant campfire. *It took me ages to figure it out. I wondered for years if I was something you dreamed up to make sense of what you saw. Or if I was some broken part of your conscience that fractured when your magic woke. It was only after I saw the place between when we were under the mountain that I remembered. I remembered after I saw her...*

Ran stepped toward her. *This is exactly the same as the magic in the cave, because it was made by the same person, for much the same reason. It's a curse. Someone cursed this valley, barring the dradur. They worked the same magic through the Pass to draw the dragons into the tunnel.*

Why would they bar the dradur? They made the dradur! Iridia's voice rose, edged with confusion.

Ran wanted to take her hand, as if it might help her understand. Instead, he fixed her gaze with his own and took a deep breath. *They barred the dradur from the valley because this is where they live. And they had to lock them out because they can't control them.*

What? Tears glistened in her eyes like diamonds in the sun.

Nothing else makes sense, he continued. *Why bar the creatures if they could simply order them not to attack, or command them to cease? Why go to all this effort unless you've got no other way of keeping yourself safe?*

They aren't here though, are they? They've gone. Iridia folded her arms and hugged her chest. *Coming here was a waste of time.*

I thought so too, but there's still something to be gained from this.

She glanced up at that and drifted a little closer. He had her attention now. Would she go with him? Would she trust him?

We're so close, right on their heels. But I need to see her face again. Once more, so when I find her, I'll know her on sight. We saw her before, after we touched the magic she left behind, but she was young then. This was made recently, so maybe it will show us what she looks like now.

Her eyes widened with realisation. *I don't know if I can...*

I can't cross into that place without you. Ran extended his hand, inviting her to take it, wondering if she would.

Iridia stared at him and unwound her fingers from her arm. She closed her eyes, effort creasing her brow as she gained form. Her skin flushed, a wave of pale light coursing through her. Ran lunged, pulling her close and wrapping her in his arms as they fell into the shimmering magic...

The place between expanded as Ran opened his eyes. Bright light spread in all directions, illuminating where he stood with Iridia curled against him, her head buried in his chest. Her heart thumped and he glanced down. She was as corporeal as if she lived and breathed; her silver-blonde hair coiled around her face, her eyes squeezed shut. Her cheeks were flushed red, as were her lips, and she trembled as he held her.

He thought for a moment he'd hurt her and let go, jolting her away from him. Iridia's eyes flew open and scanned his face. 'What is it? Is she here?'

'Ah, no, I don't...' Ran looked around. There was nothing but white, stretching into infinity—no movement, no sign of the witch. 'Did we do it wrong?'

Iridia stepped away. 'I don't think so... but this feels different. Not like the cave.'

She was right.

There was a presence, a warmth that wasn't here last time. Ran turned, searching the abyss, and his eyes settled on a black smudge in the distance. It was the same as he'd seen the first time they'd fallen in here; the same shape, immobile and steady, resting at the farthest edge of his vision.

'What do you reckon that is?' he asked, pointing across space.

'Don't know,' she said, not looking at where he indicated. Instead, she glared in the opposite direction. 'But *that* shouldn't be here.'

Ran turned and followed her gaze to a dark, lumpy figure nearby, much closer than the black smudge. 'Why? What's wrong with it?'

Her eyes narrowed. 'It's alive.'

They moved toward it, and space contorted around them. In three steps they were right beside it. The sleeping figure of a young woman lay on the ground, her head rolled toward them, her eyes closed and her breathing low and steady. A blue raven perched on the girl's arm, its talons squeezing the flesh above her wrist. It turned to face them, glaring with sharp sapphire eyes. It called and snapped its beak and Ran staggered to a halt.

'The fuck is that?!'

'It's dead, like me,' Iridia told him in a breathless whisper. 'It pulled her into this place. It's what brought her here.' She glanced around as if expecting to see the witch at any moment.

The girl on the ground had jet black hair woven into a braid, and wore a loose linen shirt, and a pair of trousers. Both the shirt and trousers had seen better days. Dusty and blood splattered, they reminded Ran of the clothing he'd seen the southern rangers wearing. He glanced to where the raven perched on her arm, his heart thumping hard, and realised the stignada marks on her forearms were strikingly similar to Jac's.

'She's one of them...' he whispered. 'She's a southerner.'

A deep scowl darkened Iridia's features. 'Her face—'

Iridia stepped forward and the raven flapped its wings, beating them hard against the girl's body, wisps of smoky blue magic swirling around it. It screamed and the girl jolted awake.

A pair of bright green eyes fixed on Ran.

'Who are you?!' Iridia snarled and lunged at the girl. 'Where are the witches?'

The raven launched at Iridia and the girl vanished. Iridia stumbled back into Ran under the force of the bird's assault, then it disappeared.

Ran spun around. 'Where did she go?'

'The bird sent her back.' Iridia spat and wiped a line of blood from her mouth.

'Are you bleeding?' He took hold of her arms, turning her to face him. 'I didn't know you could bleed?'

She rolled her eyes at him. 'Usually I can't, but the usual rules don't apply here.'

Ran gestured at the place the girl had been. 'Why did you attack her? She was just lying there!' Iridia glared at him for a moment then looked away. 'What happened, Iridia?'

'I don't know!' she snapped. 'I just reacted. Something about her face, her eyes. I don't know...'

'Maybe next time let's give her a chance to speak before you try and rip out her throat,' Ran suggested.

'After that performance, I doubt there will be a next time,' a deep, reverberating voice said from behind them.

Ran and Iridia whirled around and froze. A man sat on a horse nearby, his skin smooth ebony, his eyes a vibrant shade of indigo. He crossed his hands on the pommel of his saddle and shrugged.

'Would *you* come back after that?' His midnight black horse stamped a massive silver hoof and a boom echoed through the air. Ran's ears rang, and pain lanced through the bone of his jaw.

'I remember you...' Iridia whispered behind Ran.

'And I, you.' The man pointed at Ran. 'But he is not supposed to be here.'

'Ran, we have to go.' Iridia gripped the back of his shirt and pulled, but he was rooted to the spot, unable to move, unable to look away. The man's eyes were intoxicating and terrifying, dragging him in and pulling him down into an unfathomable abyss he knew he would never escape if he turned himself over to it.

'You can't run, Iridia. Not from this.' The horse reared and slammed its enormous hooves into the ground. Everything shook, right down to Ran's teeth, and Iridia pulled harder on his shirt. 'I will always be here. I will always be waiting.'

'Ran, we need to go NOW!' she screamed, and the horse lurched forward, its great hooves thundering against the ground.

Ran broke free of the man's gaze and turned. He wrapped an arm around Iridia and fired his magic.

Blinding white blinked out, smothered by crushing darkness, and a close, hot night enveloped them.

The craw launched itself at the woman's face and Lidan rolled away.

The white place vanished, and she fell onto the bedroll in the wagon, the timbers creaking as she gasped at the pain spearing through her chest. Loge groaned beside her but didn't wake as she sucked air back into her lungs. Above the roof of the wagon, a craw cried out and Lidan shuddered.

'Liddy?'

She turned toward the voice and saw Farah blinking at her from the front of the wagon, her children sleeping soundly either side of her.

'You all right?'

'Just a dream,' Lidan croaked, and her half-mother nodded. Farah folded back down to her bed and Lidan stared straight up at the ceiling.

The craw called in the night.

At least she hadn't woken Loge. She didn't want to see the worry in his eyes, or face questions for which she had no answers. She would have to tell him she was fine, and he would know she was lying. Shivering, she pulled a thin blanket up to her chin.

None of it made any sense—the craw or its insistence on dragging her off to the white place where she could no longer be seen or heard by the living. She tried to unravel the words the woman had screeched in heavily accented common, demands about witches echoing in the emptiness of the abyss. Lidan had a vague understanding of the term—a northern name for a woman who did magic.

Then there was the man with eyes the colour of the early morning sky. He'd just stood there, staring, as stunned as she was, a thousand questions waiting to be spoken. And the rider approaching from behind, hooves of a huge horse flashing against brilliant white. She knew him from her people's stories—Dennawal, the Shadow Rider; and knew of the horse with hooves of starlight, giving it the strength to bridge time and space, collecting the dead and escorting them to the place where the ancestors watched.

She rolled over and curled into a ball around her churning stomach, squeezing her eyes shut. What was the craw playing at? It had brought her back as soon as the woman attacked, the bird touching her to take her through to the white place and flying free to let her leave. But *why*?

Lidan shivered despite the blanket and the warm summer air, exhaustion washing through her. She was so utterly bone tired. Whatever the strange dead bird wanted, it would have to wait until she had more than a speck of energy to her name, and the fortitude to rope her mind into working properly. As she wove her fingers through Loge's, sleep reached for her, ignorant of her anxiety, uninterested in her worry, and dragged her into the darkness again.

Ran hit the ground first, Iridia held tight to his chest as they rolled away from the line of magic shimmering above them. She ended up pinned beneath him, and her solid form began to collapse under his weight. She trembled, her body wracked with convulsions and he pushed himself off and landed on the grass. Without thinking he reached for her hand and caught it before it lost its form, pushing his magic against her.

Her eyes opened and her fingers clenched around his. 'I can't stay here. He's pulling me back.'

'Wait, no!' Ran tightened his grip and willed his magic to encircle them until they lay on the ground surrounded by oscillating blue light. 'Who is he?'

'The Rider.'

'*The* Rider?' Ran couldn't believe what he was hearing. He could barely believe what he had seen, but this was a whole new level of insanity. 'The Dark Rider? Messenger of Death, Master of the Underworld, *that* Dark Rider?'

Iridia screwed her eyes shut and shuddered, her body responding to a force Ran could only barely feel, an insistent pull dragging her from his grasp and the cocoon of his magic.

'You have to let me go. He won't stop until he has answers.'

'I am *not* letting go! Take me with—'

She put a cold hand on his chest, heavy as stone, and almost stopped his heart. His pulse slowed and he shivered as his blood turned to ice.

'If you go back, he'll take you. Things aren't as they should be there, and he's desperate. You need to live, Ran. It's not your time. We have things to do, work to finish. I swear I'll come back. He can't keep me there forever. I'm bound to you, remember?'

She turned his power back on him. The circle of magic cracked like an egg. He gasped and his hand flexed, searching the air where she had been, but Iridia was gone.

CHAPTER THIRTY-FIVE

The Western Reaches, Tolak Range, the South Lands

Lidan's craw sat perched on the pommel of her sword for the remainder of the journey to Tingalla, invisible to the clan folk around her. It made a point never to touch her, the sword far enough removed from her skin that it could stay close without dragging her into the abyss.

The face of the man in the white place haunted her, and days crawled past while she wondered if *he* was who the craw had taken her to see. She turned the memory over as she escorted Ehran's wagon with Loge, who insisted on riding the rest of the way—against her advice. She did her best to ignore the way he watched her as she swam silently through her thoughts. She knew he had questions, but he had enough manners not to ask. Lidan hadn't intended to keep it from him, she just couldn't find the words.

The frenetic activity of the caravan didn't afford many opportunities for privacy, where curious eyes were occupied elsewhere. She barely had enough time to wash, let alone undertake a deep and possibly awkward conversation with Loge. The brief moments they found themselves alone were filled with something altogether more urgent than discussing her strange dreams or the white place—things her youngest sister kept interrupting. Lucija had a frustrating habit of appearing around the back of a wagon, or from behind a tree, right when Loge had his hands somewhere they probably shouldn't have been.

She shooed her sister away to find some supper and turned back to Loge as he tucked his shirt back into his trousers.

'We can't keep doing this,' he said, glancing around the side of a rocky outcrop they hid behind under the pretence of collecting firewood.

'I doubt Lucija is going to tell anyone,' Lidan replied with a roll of her eyes.

'You seriously think she's following us out here on her own?' he countered and raised a brow, fastening his belts.

Lidan frowned and laced her jerkin. She *had* begun to wonder if Bridie and Elva weren't sending Lucija to find them. Neither of the older girls had said anything, but their quickly disguised sideward glances at Lidan and Loge had given them away. They knew, and they were unleashing their youngest sister to ambush Lidan whenever she slipped away.

'What if she says something to your father?' Loge pressed. He picked up his hatchets from beside Lidan's tangled pile of weapons and leathers and dropped them back into the loops on his belt.

She sighed. 'If I'm honest, my father isn't the one I'm worried about.'

If Erlon did stumble upon them, he was just as likely to give Loge a manly slap on the back as he was to admonish them. If they were to fear discovery by anyone, it was Sellan.

'I'm not saying I want to stop,' said Loge softly. So far, Lucija's constant interruptions had prevented them from fully embracing their desires, and that need simmered between them like a brewing storm. He handed her the knife belt, then gently tucked a stray lock of her hair behind her ear. 'But maybe it's safer. They've doubled the perimeter patrols. Everyone is on edge. I'd rather not get shot coming back to camp because some apprentice with itchy fingers decided we were raiders.'

Lidan sighed again and nodded. 'All right, but only because I don't want you to get shot again.'

He grinned and they turned back to the camp, collecting an arm-full each of firewood along the way. It was then, when her mind emptied and silence fell between them, that her thoughts returned to the white place.

Everything around her seemed to be spinning, moving so fast it became a blur. She had barely come to terms with these new emotions that shot through her whenever she looked at Loge, or when he walked past, or when he touched her. Now, the memory of this other man's face burned in her as though she'd swallowed a glowing coal from the fire. How in the world could she explain that? It felt like a betrayal, and her stomach clenched every time his light blue eyes flashed in her mind.

He had the same pale skin as her mother and the Crone, but darker brown hair than Forge Master Rick. He could only have been a couple years older than her, armed with a sword similar to her father's, hanging in a scabbard at his side as he towered over her. He'd frowned as though he'd seen something he recognised, but then the woman with hair the colour of moonlight cut across her vision. It was there the memory shuddered to a stop, and Lidan locked it tight in a corner of her mind until her defences crumbled and it slipped free again. This was how she kept it hidden from Loge and her sisters and her mothers, and most of all from herself, hoping the distraction of arriving at Tingalla would suffocate it from her mind altogether.

The bush along the trail thinned and the caravan wound through a line of hills until a wide flood plain opened before them. Across the flats dotted with trees and lagoons edged with reeds, Tingalla rose to greet them. An island dominated the centre of the wide brown river, and from its southern end an incline grew. The hill rose northward across the island like a wedge of stone, interrupted at intervals by earthworks, ditches, and walls until at its highest point, it ended in a cliff that plunged down to the river below.

Atop that high ground, a walled village stood proudly overlooking the river-lands. To the north-west of the island, across the river on the far side, a high tableland stretched away, marking the western edge of the Tolak Range and the border with Daylin territory. How much of that tableland was still in Tolak or Daylin control was yet to be seen, given the area north of the river was apparently crawling with Namjin and Wolban raiders.

Loge arrived beside her and pulled Striker up from a trot. 'I'd heard stories about this place, but they don't really do it justice.'

'You haven't been here before?' she asked, then let the question fall away, wondering if that memory was an old wound she shouldn't pick at.

'Before the ngaru?' He shook his head and adjusted his grip on the reins. 'We kept to the north mostly—the hills east of Namjin or the high country. We never got much trouble from the Daylin.' He'd only been an apprentice then, the same age she was now, still learning to navigate the bush and its dangers.

Their horses followed the wagons along a raised trackway that wound through the lagoons and marshes before terminating at a small riverside outpost. Every single building here stood on stilts at least ten feet high, and Lidan craned her head back to look at the people on the verandas above them. Siman had gone ahead with a small group to announce the daari's arrival and over the heads of the rangers in front of the wagons, a huge timber gangway creaked toward the ground. She urged Theus through the crowd and halted a few lengths behind Titon while her father sat chatting with Siman and another man she didn't recognise.

'They arrived yesterday, sir. Signal fires were lit on the bank.' The man pointed along the riverbank and Lidan shifted to follow his gesture. A dark, fuzzy collection of what looked to be buildings stood on a promontory facing northward from Daylin territory. Languid wisps of smoke rose from the cluster of buildings, and a thicker column plumed from a much larger fire beside two enormous timber posts.

The gangway boomed as it settled in the ground and Erlon nodded at the man Lidan assumed was the bridge master. 'At sundown signal them that the bridge will be lowered in the morning. That will give them the night to prepare, and us time to get settled.'

The bridge master nodded and Erlon gave Siman a wave before a loud whistle cut the air and the caravan moved onto the gangway. The ramp angled gently up from the riverbank to a height of about ten feet again from the water's surface. From there, the wide timber bridge stretched across to the island. Huge posts the width of tree trunks supported the bridge, each surrounded at the base by boulders piled up to divert the power of the flowing river.

The water was angry today; a dark brown churn of eddies littered with branches, logs and debris from upstream, carried in a surging torrent toward the coast through this swollen channel. The river split at the promontory to the south, sending half the water directly west and the remainder continuing southward. It was little wonder the buildings at the bridge stood so high from the ground, and Lidan wondered, as she looked down at the churning depths, if hosting a matching at Tingalla in the wet season was an entirely wise endeavour.

The horses and wagons made the crossing without incident and skirted the base of the incline. The trackway took them to the southern end of the island, then embarked on a winding ascent of the hill. Even with forward riders announcing the caravan and ensuring gates stood open, the procession took the remainder of the day to trundle to the plateau at the top of the cliff.

Lidan could hardly speak as they made the climb, struck dumb by the magnificent vista opening around her. Verdant green blanketed the flood plain; streams, lagoons and pools swollen with wet-season rain glistened in the afternoon sun. Each earthwork they crossed, each gateway they passed under, took them higher until they finally made it to the wall circling the complex at the very top of the hill. The wall was carefully stacked stone at the base, with a tall timber palisade atop. It ran across the width of the hill, then around the perimeter of the cliff, ensuring a defensible position that was close to impossible to scale. A deep ditch preceded the wall, and the only access to the gate was via a thick timber gangway controlled from the gatehouse on the far side. The bridge was in place by the time the caravan made it to the lip of the ditch, and they crossed under the lintel and into the confines of Tingalla.

Night took its time to arrive, the sun lingering on the western horizon. Midsummer was close at hand, the hours of darkness growing ever shorter as the steamy days stretched on. Lidan followed the rangers through the hazy heat of the evening to the stables at the left-hand side of the gatehouse, breathing in the rich, earthy scent of the large bustling space.

A boy appeared from a tack room and took Theus by the bridle as she dismounted. Before she could protest, the boy led her horse away to be tended by a stable hand, leaving her standing with empty hands and no idea what to do. A young man, closer to her own age, slipped through the crowd, bowed and indicated to the door at the far end of the building.

'Your rooms have been prepared, Witness Lidan. You will find your things there.'

'Ah,' Lidan began. She stared at him, then glanced out the door. Was he pointing at the hall or the stone and timber buildings arrayed beside it? Tines hurried across the common, carrying trunks into the huts clustered to the left of the hall. Rangers had begun to set up their tents and pavilions around the buildings, so Lidan ventured a guess and left the bowing young man in the stable.

All the activity was concentrated to the left side of the hall, while the identical buildings to the right, including a full-size stable, stood empty. Realisation hit her. The entire settlement had been built for meetings such as this matching. Those buildings were for the Daylin clan, who were at this moment waiting beyond the river to the south. They would cross in the morning and traverse the hillside, then set themselves up in the area opposite her family's quarters. The Tolak rangers positioned themselves around the back of the buildings, nearest the wall, and in the open area near the stables, rather than in the middle of the common. Appearances were important at these sorts of things, and her father wouldn't want the Daylin to suspect aggression on the part of the Tolak.

A tine-woman approached Lidan, her flaxen head bowed, and her pale hands folded in front of her. Lidan hadn't seen her among her family's women, and quickly assumed she was one of the caretakers of Tingalla.

'Witness,' the woman greeted her. Lidan cringed, not entirely comfortable with the way the title was being thrown around but said nothing as the woman opened her hand toward the cluster of buildings. 'I will show you to your quarters.'

Lidan bit down on a small shiver of anxiety. They all seemed to know her, unfamiliar eyes tracking her across the common as she followed the tine-woman. She caught Loge's gaze as she passed the ranger's tents and raised a questioning brow at him. He looked at her, then at the blonde tine-woman, and shrugged. They had an army of tines tending their needs at home, but they remained at the periphery, and Lidan had grown up with tasks that were her own, especially as they pertained to her horse. No ranger let another care for their horse unless they were too sick or injured to do it themselves. It was unheard of to do otherwise. Except here it seemed entirely proper and expected that she would leave the work to someone else.

It took her a moment to realise what it all meant, and her heart sank. None of this was unusual or unique to Tingalla. She wasn't expected to tend to her horse because she wasn't a ranger anymore. She wasn't even an apprentice. She was a witness of the blood, and apparently that came with a whole raft of privileges, possibly intended to ease the burden the title carried. The weight of expectation settled on her shoulders like quern stones and each step she took seemed all the harder.

She followed the woman between the buildings, walking along a pathway of duckboards fixed half a foot above the ground. Deep channels ran either side of the boardwalks, and timber accesses bridged wide drains, reaching across to the stone steps of the entryways. At the centre of the cluster was an open area and a building close to the size of her mother's private hall in Hummel.

The tine-woman opened a hand toward it. 'This is where Daari Erlon will reside. Your mothers and the children are on either side.'

Lidan bit down on a groan. *Please don't say I'll be quartered with my mother. Please…*

Above, her craw called, a chattering kind of noise that reminded her of the Crone's laugh.

'As your title requires, you have been assigned quarters near the heir and Mother Farah.' The tine turned and led her to a nondescript building beside the others, halfway between the hall and her father's quarters. The timber door eased open, revealing a bright interior already furnished with Lidan's trunks and saddlebags. There was a large bed, much like her father had at home, with a sturdy timber frame, a thick mattress and a pile of soft looking cushions Lidan ached to fall into. A fire pit divided the room under a vent in the roof, while a table and some chairs stood to one side near a stand with a bowl and water jug. A frame draped with a linen cover stood in the far righthand corner of the room, near her trunks.

The woman pulled the cover on the frame to one side. 'The gowns the dana has arranged for the ceremonies will be in here, and the other items will be in the drawer of the table.' She bowed again. 'I am to attend to any wish you may have during your time at Tingalla.'

Lidan smoothed clammy hands down the front of her dusty trousers and stared. She'd never had her own room. The closest she'd come was the tent she'd occupied before her father ordered her to guard Ehran's wagon, and even then Loge had spent a decent amount of time sleeping inside the door. This was a lot bigger than the tent, or the room she shared with Marrit, almost cavernous and eerily empty for all its fine furnishings, as if she could get lost in here and never be found. Surely this was some sort of mistake. 'Who else is staying here?'

The tine-woman frowned, and for the first time, looked at Lidan directly with her chestnut-brown eyes. She had a round face with full cheeks, and a smattering of sun-kissed freckles across her nose. 'No one, Witness. This is your room alone. I have a cot in the back room, but I can sleep in the tine-quarters if you prefer.'

Lidan stifled a laugh, and creases of worry furrowed the woman's brow. 'Is it not to your liking, Witness?'

'Oh!' Lidan brought her hands up and shook her head. 'No, it's fine. I just... Thank you. I meant to say thank you.' Bright red spots of colour bloomed on the woman's face, and Lidan wondered how long it had been since anyone had thanked her for anything she'd done. 'I'll make sure to tell my father how perfect everything is when I see him.'

A small smile twitched at the sides of the woman's mouth and she instantly seemed younger. An ache pinched at the muscles behind Lidan's shoulders and she reached to unbuckle her knives and the harness holding her sword scabbard to her back.

In a smooth, cat-like movement, the tine-woman darted forward and Lidan slid backward, a knife whipping free of its sheath, spinning in her hand to point at the woman's chest. It hovered there, poised between them, and Lidan froze.

The woman jolted to a stop and her wide-eyed gaze flicked to the glinting curve of the blade. 'Would you rather I didn't assist you?'

Lidan's stomach flipped and heat rose in her cheeks. She'd moved on instinct, primed to fight at the slightest hint of threat, even when there was none to be found, as much a finely-honed weapon as her knives. Or had she become something else? An animal, driven by base reactions, unable to think before acting, unable to discern friend from foe and all too quick to bare her teeth?

She straightened and put the knife on the table, taking a slow, steady step away from it and showing the tine-woman her empty hand. 'I'm sorry, I... I've not had an assistant before.' Turning, she offered the woman her back, and let her take the leather harness from her shoulders.

'You're a witness of the blood, yes?' she asked, stepping away to take the harness to the hanging frame.

'I am,' replied Lidan. She managed to get her knife belt off before the woman came back.

'Don't you have tines in Hummel?'

'We do, but… I haven't been a witness for long.' She smiled and the tine-woman returned the gesture, as if that was explanation enough for her awkward response. 'What's your name?' Lidan asked, and the woman glanced up in surprise.

'You may call me whatever you like, Witness.'

'I'd like your name, if you'll give it to me.'

The woman ran her long pale fingers down the front of her apron, smoothing the linen and perhaps soothing her nerves. 'My masters call me Twelve.'

Lidan almost choked on a cough. 'Pardon me?'

'I was the twelfth child born to my mother, so that's what they called me. They sometimes call me Vee. Or whatever they feel like at the time.' She said it with a nonchalance that stunned Lidan. They called her a number? The number of the order she'd left her mother's womb?

'May I call you Vee?' Lidan asked, wishing she could spit out the bitterness the name left in her mouth.

'Of course, Witness.' Vee indicated to the bowl of water on the side stand near the bed. 'I'll leave you to wash and change, if you wish. Unless you want me—'

'It's all right. I can manage.' Lidan slowly curled her fingers into a fist. For some reason, her hands were shaking. 'What am I to wear tonight?'

'Supper will be served in quarters this evening. The daari decreed that the travellers are to rest tonight before the ceremonies begin tomorrow. I'll be back soon with your tray.'

Vee disappeared out the door and pulled it shut behind her, leaving Lidan in the centre of the room, wondering if she hadn't fallen into another world.

CHAPTER THIRTY-SIX

Tingalla, Tolak Range, the South Lands

Vee collected the breakfast dishes onto a tray, and Lidan's mother swept through the door without so much as a knock. Sellan came alone, and the craw squawked and snapped at her from the windowsill.

'Good morning, Mother,' Lidan said dryly, placing her steaming cup on the table. 'Tea?'

Vee paused, waiting to see if Sellan accepted the offer, but the dana waved the idea away.

'I haven't time to stay. The Daylin are crossing the bridge and will be here in a few hours, and I'm currently at war with your sister over a specific colour of red she refuses to wear. Thanie is no help at all. I honestly don't know why I bother.' She flicked open the cover of the hanging frame. 'This one,' she said, pointing to a deep blue gown in the depths of the hanger.

Vee carefully retrieved the dress and Lidan eyed the thing with dubious concern. The skirt was spilt into four panels from the mid-thigh and a fine white shift peeked between the dark lengths of ridiculously expensive fabric. It was lovely to look at, but she wondered how long she could keep it clean.

'And her hair, Dana?' Vee asked, laying the gown on the bed and turning back, her eyes downcast and her hands folded in front of her apron.

'Up, with lots of braids. Make sure to put in a few of those metal rings, too. Not many, mind. The other girl is the show piece this week, and I won't be accused of fashioning my daughter to outshine her.' Sellan strode across the room and put a pale hand on her daughter's cheek. 'Chin up. Won't be long until it's your turn, blossom.'

Despite the humidity building in the morning air, her mother's finger-tips were as cold as a mountain stream. The chill ran straight through

Lidan's heart and her stomach tightened. Did her mother know about Loge, or was she simply stating fact?

She shivered and Sellan's hand slipped away. Every passing day felt like time lost, falling through her grasping fingers like coarse sand, pulled by an unrelenting wind that drew her ever closer to an inescapable future. Every day she was a little older and a little more vulnerable to her father's whims, but at this very moment, in the still silence hovering between her and her mother, all she could think of was Loge. Sellan left without another word, a mirthless smiling dancing on her lips, the door standing open in her wake. If the dana knew, she wasn't putting all her tokens on the table just yet.

Vee wrestled Lidan into her ridiculous dress and, with the help of another tine-girl, Havuli, went to work on her hair. Close to midday, the daari arrived, stepping through the door just as Havuli slipped the elaborate bronze comb into the side of Lidan's braids.

'Da?'

'Are you ready?'

'I think so.' She glanced around at Vee, who nodded. 'Am I late?'

'No, their advanced riders have just made the gate. The rest aren't far behind.'

'All right, let me just—' She reached for her ornate ceremonial knife belt, but her father moved to stop her.

'Leave that for a moment,' Erlon said in a tone that set her heart thumping a little harder. Vee and Havuli melted into the shadows as the daari stepped closer, and Lidan suddenly saw her father as the tines did; a distant and unknowable force that had become very big and very real.

Erlon put his hands on his hips, his new leathers creaking gently in the silence. He had a bouncer pelt draped over one shoulder and it shifted as he rubbed the pads of his fingers across his lips, as he was wont to do when his thoughts refused to order themselves.

'I just want to... I wish I could tell you to rest now we're here, to take some time and enjoy yourself, but I need you to be ready. I need you to be my eyes when I have to be looking elsewhere. I know Horice and his boy Harran, but the rest of them...' He looked at her and released an unsteady sigh through his nose. 'Will you stay close to Ehran?'

Lidan watched him for a moment, then squared her shoulders, reaching for the knife belt and laying it over her hips before securing the clasp. One of her knives rested in the small of her back, and the leather-smith had added a scabbard so her sword hung at her hip. She took a deep breath and tapped her fingernail absently on the tabletop.

Erlon's words swirled in her head. How well did he really know Horice Daylin? As well as he thought he knew Yorrell Namjin? He had embraced Yorrell as he might a once estranged brother, in the spirit of building an alliance, not moments before the man's eyes roved all over Lidan's young body as though she were a prize mare. He'd professed to know Yorrell's intentions, and he'd almost matched her off to his son Cole without a second thought, years before the Law allowed a first daughter to match. She remembered it all through the haze of years past and tried not to let any of it show in the lines of her face or the set of her jaw as she met his eyes.

'I took an oath, Father. I kept it on the journey here and I don't intend to disregard it now. I'll be with Ehran as often as I'm able.' But she would do more than watch Ehran. She would survey Horice and Harran at every available opportunity, and if at any point she suspected something amiss, she would make her thoughts known to her father. If he failed to act, then she would.

She kept all this locked firmly behind her lips as her father's shoulders lifted and he smiled. His enormous, scarred hand reached to touch the top of her arm, and with a slight squeeze, their eyes met. It was a gesture that said more than mere words ever could—it was trust and forgiveness and gratitude, and it was also acknowledgement that he needed her, and he knew it. He may never say it aloud, but for now, this would be enough.

'Thank you,' he murmured. 'Now, we'd better get a move on or your mothers will have my hide.'

Lidan's family arranged themselves on the hall's stone steps; her father and his wives two steps up from ground level, while Lidan and her siblings stood on the step below, split into two groups. She stood with Ehran at the head of one, directly across a small gap from Bridie.

The younger girl's hair shone with metal trinkets, and chains adorned with gemstones hung around her neck. Her gown was a similar deep blue to Lidan's but worked with a thread that gleamed so brightly Lidan wondered if it wasn't metal as well. The dana's concern about Lidan outshining Bridie was entirely unfounded. The only way Lidan could possibly outdo her sister today was in a fight, and today was not about fighting. Today was about matching, and matching was all about impressions.

The Daylin caravan trundled through the gate, riders flanking the wagons and trotting into the common before the hall's steps. Tolak rangers stood ready but relaxed, their weapons stowed to limit the approaching clan's view of them. Lidan tried to keep her eyes off Loge, but every time her gaze wandered to where he stood at Siman's left, she found him glancing back. He winked at her after a while, and she bit the inside of her lip to stifle a laugh.

A man perhaps a decade her father's senior swung down from his saddle, followed by a younger man closer to Loge's age, with hair as blond as Vee's and smooth brown skin that Lidan instantly recalled from the Corron. Harran had grown in the four years since, taller and broader than his father until he stood at a height equal to Erlon. He was an absolute weapon of a man and Lidan threw a glance at her much slighter sister. Bridie's eyes widened considerably as Harran approached. The girl would be lucky if he didn't crush her to dust on their matching night.

Four women emerged from the leading wagon and Lidan picked Harran's mother from their number; a tall wisp of a woman with skin closer to Lidan's colouring and the same pale hair as her son. A number of younger men and boys alighted from horses and came to stand at Horice's back, and as Lidan scanned the assembled Daylin family, her eyes narrowed.

Other than the daari's wives, she saw not one girl or woman among them. There were at least fifteen sons, not including Harran, who stood apart with his father. The apparent lack of any daughters seemed somewhat odd until she glanced at her own family, flushed as they were with girls, and she wondered what a sight they must make by comparison.

Horice stopped at the foot of the stairs and pressed a closed fist to his chest. 'Daari Erlon, it has been too long.'

Erlon descended to stand level with Horice. He returned the gesture and she thought she heard a smile in his voice. 'That it has. A happier occasion brings us together this time.' They gipped each other's forearms in the less formal greeting shared between friends.

Horice turned to his son. 'You've met Harran, albeit all those years ago. Sometimes I hardly recognise him myself.' The younger man flashed a smile as he gripped Erlon's arm and Lidan was sure someone nearby gasped.

When Erlon turned he raised a brow at his wives, ascending to stand beside Bridie and suppressing a smile as he did. He seemed rather impressed with the man Harran Daylin had become. 'This is Bridie, my second eldest.'

Harran gave Bridie a bow, which she returned, the metal rings in her hair tinkling gently together. Harran's gaze darted over Bridie as though he struggled to take in all of her glistening splendour at once, and Lidan looked down to hide a smile of her own.

Before Erlon could introduce anyone else, a cluster of riders emerged through the gates at a canter.

The Tolak rangers braced, hands reaching for weapons. Lidan shoved Ehran behind her and took a step forward, her sword half drawn before her father caught her arm. She half expected to see Yorrell's face material-ise from the dust left by the Daylin wagons, and she shot a glance at Loge and Siman. They stood ready, hands on their weapons, angling their bodies toward where Erlon stood. Her father's grip did not loosen as the riders halted.

A man dressed as finely as Horice and Erlon swung down, followed closely by a young man about Lidan's age. They strode across the common and in their haste, forced Horice's wives to scramble from their path. The grip on Lidan's arm tightened.

'You didn't start the introductions without me, did you?' asked the man, who Lidan vaguely recognised. He grinned and opened his arms wide. 'Very unlike you to forget a friend, Tolak!'

'Merk,' said Erlon. Lidan saw the corners of his mouth twitch upwards stiffly, as if drawn by water-logged ropes. 'No offence intended, friend. We weren't expecting you so soon.'

Merk Marsaw waved Erlon's comment away. 'Thought we'd come down early to see our good friends the Daylin before the Corron. Then blow me down like grass in the wind, old Horice tells me they're on their way to a matching.' Merk gave Erlon a smile that Lidan did not think was reflected in his dark, flinty eyes. 'We decided we'd join you, seeing as how our invi-tation must've been eaten by a ngaru.'

Slowly, Erlon released Lidan's sword arm, and she let the blade slide back into its scabbard. She put her left hand behind her back, flicked away the thin leather band securing the knife to its sheath and rested her fingers on the hilt. Her father held his shoulders square and clenched one hand into a fist at his side.

Of course, to anyone who hadn't spent a lifetime studying him, watching his every move as she had since she was a child, her father's demeanour appeared relaxed, if a little surprised. For all intents and purposes, the Marsaw's invitation might well have been eaten by a ngaru on its long journey up the coast.

Except it hadn't.

Marsaw hadn't been invited to the matching, her father intending to use the time alone with Horice to discuss the terms they would offer Merk in an alliance. Merk's early arrival had thrown that plan straight out of the window.

Erlon rolled his shoulders and swept his arm toward the hall. 'An unexpected surprise warrants a drink, I think. The reunion of old friends should be celebrated!'

'Yes! Inside to drink!' Merk grinned. He turned and waved to his men, then bustled up the steps.

Lidan herded her brother toward the hall door while her father addressed his wives. He sent Farah and Kelill away with the other girls, assuring Farah that Ehran would be perfectly safe with his sister. Sellan would accompany him as the dana and Raeh as Bridie's mother. A similar conversation occurred behind them as Horice sorted his family into order and hurried to follow with Harran and the young man's mother.

Loge appeared at Lidan's elbow as she made it to the doors. 'I don't like this,' he muttered in her ear.

He made a show of escorting her across the hall to one of the seats nearest the two large audience chairs reserved for the daaris, and she accepted his "assistance" as if it was a matter of course rather than a stolen moment of hurried conversation.

'I don't either,' she replied as he gestured to her seat. 'But at least it's not Yorrell.'

He shot her a knowing glance and helped Ehran into the seat beside Lidan.

'You know,' Loge said to Ehran in his cheeriest voice. 'I've heard these things can be really boring. *But*, if you can sit here, very still until your da says you can go with Liddy, there might be a very special prize for you.'

The little boy's eyes grew wide. 'What is it?' he whispered urgently.

'I can't tell you that! Wouldn't be a surprise, then would it?' Loge grinned and smoothed the boy's hair.

A troop of rangers thumped in and arrayed themselves at the edges of the room. Loge gave Lidan's hand a small squeeze as he left to join them, and she held onto the sensation for as long as she could. The ancestors knew she needed something to get her through today. No one had expected Merk to ride through that gate. Nothing had been prepared for him, and tines hurried to rectify the situation before the daari took insult.

Siman led Erlon, Raeh and Sellan to the audience chairs, then stood behind them with Loge, both of them consciously folding their hands in front of them, rather than resting them on their weapons. Bridie followed with Harran and they settled into the seats between their father's chairs. A new cluster of seats appeared opposite the matching couple, just offset so to not block access to the doors, and Merk apparently found them suitably grand that he didn't complain as he sat.

Silence fell on the gathering and tines moved among the family groups with urns of wine and ale. Lidan took her cup and pressed it to her lips, making a show of drinking but allowing none of the wine pass. Erlon, on the other hand, drained two cups before turning to Horice. 'Horice, please meet my son and heir, Ehran.'

Horice bowed his head toward the boy and Merk snorted. 'He's still a pup! Whatever happened to that vicious little thing you had at the Namjin Corron? Or have you matched her off already?'

Erlon flinched and Sellan snarled something vulgar under her breath. Lidan turned slowly to meet Merk's eyes. He grinned, casually leaning forward and scanning the group. He hadn't seen her, or recognised her among the seated guests, and she realised he thought his comment terribly witty. She stared at him with as much demure passivity as she could muster, understanding now why her father had knocked back his drink the moment it had been poured.

She funnelled her anger at Merk's insult into one hand, her fingers strangling the wine cup, the contents rippling in response. If Merk was fishing for a bite, he wouldn't get one from her. At least not here, not in front of all these people. She was prescient enough to know how the politics of the clans worked. A daari could say and do a great deal that other clan folk could not, and if her father chose to take insult here, that was up to him. If not, then she would have to wait. She was good at waiting.

Loge, on the other hand, was not. It was only thanks to the width of Erlon's audience chair that Merk didn't see Siman's hand snap out and catch Loge before he darted forward to defend Lidan's name.

A smile played across Erlon's lips as he eyed Merk. 'Lidan is here. She now stands as witness of the blood.'

A gentle murmur flowed through the hall and Lidan shifted in her seat as the eyes of the assembled guests swivelled around to examine her. Horice and Harran stood and pressed their fists into their chests, bowing at her in a manner she had not at all expected. Merk followed suit, his gaze flickering between Lidan, Ehran and their father.

'It is an honour, Witness Lidan. May the will of the ancestors always be yours,' Horice intoned, then returned to his seat. Harran's eyes lingered on Lidan for longer than she thought polite, given he was sitting beside his betrothed, before he glanced back at Bridie and smiled. If he hadn't recognised Lidan before, he knew exactly who she was now. Lidan nodded stiffly at the daaris and let out a relieved sigh as the rest of her father's introductions drew their attention elsewhere, and the proceedings moved on to the planned events.

There would be day-long feasts, gift exchange ceremonies the day after that, followed by a day of games and competitions. Finally, the matching day would dawn and after lengthy rituals, the deed would be done by sundown.

Erlon smiled, the volume of drink he'd consumed lending a gleaming shimmer to his eyes. 'Then, we shall know a real feast!'

Grunts and nodded agreement filled the hall, cups were hammered on the arms of chairs and the women whispered excitedly to each other. Harran gave Bridie a half smile and two bright spots of colour glowed in her cheeks. The girl shot a glance at Lidan, her deep blue eyes full of uncertainty.

Lidan gestured subtly as she lifted her chin and squared her shoulders. *This is not a time for fear.* Bridie responded immediately, lifting her shoulders and turning her eyes on Harran. It was his turn to blush, his paler skin betraying him under the scrutiny of Bridie's unwavering gaze. He looked away, suddenly finding the inside of his ale cup extremely engrossing, and a slow smile spread across Lidan's lips.

Beside her, Ehran began twitching in his seat and Lidan glanced down. She recognised a desperate need in his eyes, his small legs crossed tight where he sat, and she cleared her throat. Erlon snapped around at the sound.

'Father, Ehran and I have some business to attend to in preparation for the ceremonies over the coming days. May we be excused?'

He frowned and she tilted her head slightly at Ehran, then toward the door. He caught her meaning rather faster than she anticipated and nodded quickly.

'Please excuse us.' Lidan bowed to Horice, and after a delay edging toward rudeness, repeated the gesture to Merk. She caught Loge's eye and he snapped the heels of his boots together, bowed, then escorted her to the door as if such a task were part of his everyday routine. Ehran gripped her hand and they hurried behind Loge into the sunlight beyond the door.

CHAPTER THIRTY-SEVEN

Tingalla, Tolak Range, the South Lands

For the first day and night Lidan saw nothing of Erlon, Horice and Merk, or their sons and male attendants. Similarly, they saw nothing of their wives and Erlon's daughters. Merk had notably failed to bring any women with him, leaving Horice's four wives starkly outnumbered by the Tolak women. Still, her mothers and the women of Tingalla were intent on showing the Daylin women the very best hospitality Tolak had to offer.

A massive pavilion had been erected in the middle of the open area on the Tolak side of the compound, and under it, the women of the two families lounged on cushions and artfully-woven ground covers, with swarms of tines hovering nearby to attend their every need. Tines wandered by with platters of roasted meats and bright seasonal fruits cut into bite-sized pieces, or fragrant flat bread strips and tiny dishes of preserves and pickles for dipping, all designed to be consumed with a single hand while a guest reclined and nursed a cup.

Lidan began the feast with every intention of pacing herself, but very quickly found the small servings of food were unable to keep up with the volume of wine passing her lips. Useless and idle at the periphery of her sister's feast, she felt almost bereft without Ehran's presence. He was like an intense ball of light, his fires always stoked, his tiny body close to bursting with the energy of it. After weeks at his side, his absence left her cold, as though a dark cloud had cut across the warmth of the sun.

At least with Ehran around she had something to do, somewhere to focus her mind. Without him providing endless distraction, her thoughts wandered, cycling back to the white place and the face of the man she had seen. He lingered before her eyes as she stared into the middle ground, uninterested in the murmuring chatter around her. She'd never seen him before—of that she was sure. No doubt she would have recognised his vivid blue eyes, shocking as they were against his dark hair and brows. The way he'd gaped at her settled heavily on her mind, and the reaction of the woman with the moonlight hair still sent a shiver up her spine.

When she did manage to drag her mind free of the circling memory, her eyes wandered to the edge of the pavilion. Rangers patrolled beyond the shade of the canopy, among the tents and buildings, discreet and silent, unnoticed by the gathered women. Lidan watched, waiting for the moment she would catch Loge's eye in the shadowy lee of a nearby building. He didn't appear, though she continued to watch, her wine cup never empty for more than a few moments.

She had to tell Loge what she'd seen. The strangeness of it was becoming too much to bear alone.

By sunset her face and hands were flush with a numb warmth, and as the light of the long day faded and the sky deepened with shades of lilac and burnt orange, a strange woman was ushered inside. Lidan sat up, blinking the fog of drunkenness from her eyes as tines guided the woman through the gathering toward Bridie. The girl sat perched on a dais, surrounded by platters and cushions, looking more and more like a sacrifice on an altar as the evening wore on. Lidan shoved the thought away and watched her mother and half-mothers greet the newcomer, who for all the sun and stars looked like she'd just stumbled out of the wilderness.

Her appearance reminded Lidan of the Crone, who sat off to the side of the dais, gumming some delicacy into submission and watching the proceedings carry on about her. The newcomer had long hair pulled back into a half knot, matted in places and streaked with a white powder that might be wood ash. Deep creases wrinkled the warm brown skin around her eyes, as though she'd spent decades squinting into the sun. She didn't walk with a limp or a stoop but stood with a straight back and the easy confidence of someone used to commanding the eyes of a room. The woman's clothes were worn and dulled with dust, but the boots that peeked from under her old linen skirt were sturdy and well soled.

A tale-keeper...

The memory of Abbi's mourning ceremony slammed into Lidan, and something tightened at the centre of her chest. Vines of long-confined grief slipped from the darkness to wind their gnarled lengths around her heart. It had been four years since a tale-keeper had walked among her people. But it had not been this woman speaking the words over Abbi's tiny, linen-wrapped body before it was consigned to the depths of the tumal. The dull haze of Lidan's drunkenness peeled away and she saw the man muttering and gesturing, little white bones woven at the ends of his plaited beard gleaming in the torch light.

Lidan clenched her hand, digging her nails into her palm. The pain tore through the memory and she buried it, blinking away stinging tears to focus on the tale-keeper. Horice's wives and Lidan's half-mothers hurried to greet the woman, offering their hands and gently touching her fingers to their lips and foreheads. The dana was less enthused, and hung back, waiting for the others to finish before offering the bedraggled woman *her* hand.

The women in the pavilion stood enamoured as the tale-keeper addressed Bridie with words Lidan could not hear. She drew lines on Bridie's face with chalky paint and muttered while everyone except Sellan looked on solemnly. Her mother watched with vague curiosity, more interested in the contents of her cup than the tale-keeper's blessings. Sometimes it was easy to forget her mother was a northerner, and sometimes the difference was so stark it hit Lidan like a slap in the face.

Darkness fell and the group under the pavilion shrank. Tines quietly herded the younger Tolak girls into their beds, and left Lidan with the eight wives, her sisters Bridie, Elva and Marrit, as she swirled the dark wine in her cup, intrigued that it never seemed to empty, despite her best efforts to reach the bottom. She never stopped the tines from refilling it.

Elva sat with a deep scowl on her face and her arms crossed over her chest while Kelill whispered something into her daughter's ear, her hand jerking out at intervals, pointing and sweeping through the air as she tried to emphasise her point. Elva's scowl only deepened, and Lidan suspected the girl was unimpressed by the need for all this ceremonial nonsense. Bridie suddenly appeared in front of Lidan and slumped on the cushions beside her sister. She had a glow about her that spoke of too much wine and the fuzzy kind of happiness one might expect after a day at the centre of everyone's attention.

'You look pleased with yourself,' Lidan observed dryly, taking a sip of wine. She could hardly taste it now. She rested her chin in the palm of her hand and leaned toward her sister. 'Or is that just the wine?'

Bridie settled into the cushions and squinted into her cup. 'Probably the wine. They just keep bringing it, don't they?'

A shout echoed from somewhere across the compound, followed by loud whooping laugher. Shadows danced through the orange glow of the fires at the men's feast.

'You think any of them will surface before midday tomorrow?' Lidan asked.

Bridie snorted. 'I'll be lucky if *I* surface before midday tomorrow!'

'Ne'er have truer words been spoken.' Lidan slapped her cup clumsily into the side of Bridie's, and they drank deeply. She put her cup aside and ignored it even after a woman slipped from the darkness to refill it. 'Have you been to the privy lately?'

Bridie turned wide eyes on Lidan, as if the thought had only just occurred to her. 'No, but I'm absolutely busting!'

Lidan climbed to her feet, alcohol and too many hours of lounging conspiring to make her fight for every step. She pulled Bridie up after her and they linked arms. Together the girls slipped from the pavilion and into the warm night air of the common, Lidan vaguely aware of a ranger shadowing them at a distance, but she paid them little mind.

'Did you see him, Liddy?' Bridie hissed into her ear as they skirted the stables and angled toward the back where the outhouses stood in a line.

'Who?' Lidan glanced around, but Bridie giggled.

'Harran!' she said in a very audible whisper. 'Did you *see* him?'

'Pretty hard not to, really. He's like a big ol' man mountain.' Lidan realised then just how stunningly drunk her sister was, and sobriety crept toward her. It always happened when she found herself in the company of someone a little bit more hammered than she was—her instincts flared back to life, preparing her to be their nursemaid. 'Question is, did *you* see *him*?'

Bridie unwound her arm from Lidan's and walked backward toward an empty outhouse, her eyebrow arching suggestively. 'You can bet your arse I did.'

Lidan rolled her eyes and stepped into an empty outhouse. She fought with her skirts until she could be sure they were out of range and got on with her business.

'That's what I wanted to talk to you about...' Bridie's voice drifted over from the neighbouring privy. Lidan frowned, adjusted her dress and stepped back into the fresh night air, the gentle southern breeze a relief after the fetid stillness of the outhouse. She hated those things.

'What are you talking about?' The warm glow of the wine had all but abandoned her now, leaving behind the first scratchings of a headache that would surely rip her skull open by morning.

Bridie emerged and stumbled toward her, whisking her hands suggestively through the air. 'The matching night.'

Lidan blanched and hooked Bridie's arm again, hoping the younger girl hadn't seen the look of nervous horror on her face. 'That's really something your mother should—'

'I don't want to talk to *her* about it!' Bridie smiled sweetly at someone passing by and leaned closer to Lidan as they walked slowly back to the pavilion. 'I know what's supposed to happen, how it all works, but I wanted to ask you what it's like.'

Lidan almost choked. 'Excuse me?!'

Bridie's laugh echoed off the walls nearby, and a few rangers glanced their way. Lidan pulled Bridie to a stop in the shadow of a building and glared at the ranger shadowing them until she backed away and turned to admire the stars.

'I'm serious,' Lidan hissed. 'What the fuck are you talking about?'

'You and Loge,' replied Bridie, her brows arching again, urging Lidan's mind to catch up.

She forced out a disbelieving laugh. 'Loge's my friend. There's nothing—'

Bridie gave Lidan a dead stare. 'Don't feed me that horse shit. I know.'

'You know?' Lidan folded her arms. 'And what is it precisely that you *think* you know?'

'I know you've been sneaking off. I've seen how you look at him—it's so obvious!' Her sister waved a hand toward the stables. 'I reckon the only reason your mother hasn't cut his balls off is because she spent the whole trip inside that bloody wagon. A blind man could see it from the peaks of the Malapa!'

A shiver of fear rushed across Lidan's skin. 'It's not what you think,' she countered, wondering if her voice sounded as meek to her sister's ears as it did to hers.

'Fine then! Keep your secrets.' Bridie rolled her eyes. 'So much for sisterly confidence.'

A horn blast ripped through the night from Tingalla's wall and Lidan reached for her knife at her hip. Her fingers closed over empty air as Bridie's hands clamped around her arm.

'What the fuck was that?' Bridie demanded, her wide eyes scanning the sky. Rangers hurried by, hands on weapons as they ran to their posts. The ranger trailing them appeared from the shadows and put her hand on Lidan's elbow.

'Please come with me, Witness Lidan.' The ranger wasn't asking, and gave Lidan no time to respond before rushing her into the chaos. Lidan dragged Bridie with her and allowed the ranger to lead them both toward the hall.

Shouts from wall guards echoed overhead and Erlon materialised from the confusion with Merk and Horice at his heels. The ranger delivered Lidan to her father's side and stepped back as a breathless wall guard ran up to the daaris and gulped air while giving a salute.

'Scouts from the east, sir.'

'Ours?' Erlon asked, and the guard nodded. 'For fuck's sake, can't a man have a drink in peace?'

Lidan prised Bridie's fingers off her arm and spun to face the ranger. 'Take her back to her mother and stay with them.' The ranger gave a sharp nod and Lidan turned to follow her father marching to the gate.

The scout was in the guard house when they arrived, his exhausted horse sucking water from a trough outside as Lidan followed her father through the door. It was a decent sized room, plenty big enough for several guards to take a rest from duties on the wall. A fire burned in a hearth to the left with a large clay pot hanging just out of reach of the flames, and the scout sat at a table in the centre of the room, greedily shovelling stew into his mouth from a steaming bowl. He looked up at the daari's arrival and started to his feet, but Erlon waved him back.

'This better be worth interrupting my daughter's arrival feast,' said Erlon in a low voice that reminded Lidan of distant thunder.

The scout wiped his hand across his mouth. 'We've seen travellers.'

'Travellers?' the daari repeated flatly and Lidan grimaced on the scout's behalf.

To his credit, the scout read the meaning in the daari's dead pan stare and hurried to elaborate. 'They aren't southerners, sir.'

Erlon tilted his head and frowned, his ale cup dangling precariously between his fingers. 'You're sure?'

'Wouldn't have bothered you otherwise. They're not from south of the Malapa, that's for certain.'

'Isordian traders?' Erlon asked, his earlier anger dissipating as he absorbed the news.

'One is, by her clothes. The others we're not so sure. Our captain is shadowing them with the rest of our party. They're tracking toward Tingalla.'

The daari nodded. 'How many?'

'One woman and four men; all on horses, all armed.'

Erlon ran a hand through his hair and set his cup on the table, his face contorting with the effort of thinking after so many hours of drinking. Lidan watched the exchange from beside the door, her mind racing with a thousand thoughts.

'How far out?' Erlon asked.

The scout sucked meat from his teeth. 'Two days steady ride, unless they get swarmed by ngaru or a raiding party.'

Somewhere in the distance the craw called and Lidan's heart thumped harder. Northerners never came this far south. They always tracked straight to Hummel, traded there, then turned for home. Fracture Pass wasn't open long enough for them to venture farther into clan territory, which meant these travellers weren't here to trade.

'Have they got wagons?' Lidan asked. The scout and her father whipped around, only now realising she was there.

The scout recovered first. 'No, only horses. One of the other rangers reckons she's seen the woman before, but she couldn't put a name to the face. And the saddle on one of the mounts looks suspiciously like the work of Hender Hide.'

'They aren't coming here to trade. If they were, there'd be a score of them and wagons to boot.' Lidan turned to her father. 'And if one of the horses is carrying a saddle by Hender, that could mean they've already been to Hummel.'

Erlon bit his lip and put his hands on his hips, his eyes bright with light from the fire but his reactions dulled by drink. He was taking too long to find a solution, too long to make a decision.

'There's something not right about this, Da. Northern traders never come this far south. Not ever.' When he didn't reply, Lidan continued, questioning the words as they fell from her lips, wondering if she'd thought any of this through or if it was just wine-fuelled bravado talking. 'I'll take a party out to meet them.'

Erlon opened his mouth to deny her, but she hurried on. 'If they mean us no ill will, then I'll escort them here and you can deal with them yourself. If not, we'll sort it and take their horses.' Her father shook his head as if it was all too much for him to take in at once. She pressed her advantage. 'Five northerners against two ranging parties? That's better odds than we ever get against ngaru or the Namjin.'

He softened, the muscles in his shoulders relaxing. He watched her from the sides of his eyes, weighing her demands.

'We'll be out and back in two days. I won't even miss the matching.'

'I need you here. I need you to watch Ehran—' he started.

'You don't, Da. You need me to go and find out what these people want before they reach a settlement.' She waited, her heart still pounding, but she knew she'd won. He couldn't send Siman or any of the high-ranking rangers—he needed them here—and if they were northern traders, it was customary that they should be met by someone with a title. He didn't have anyone else to send *but* her.

Erlon raised two fingers and fixed her gaze over them. 'Out and back in two days. Any longer and I'm sending a full troop after you, understand?'

Lidan nodded quickly and tried not to grin like an idiot. She turned to the scout instead, heady, irrational excitement singing in her veins. 'Will you be ready to leave at dawn?'

'As sure as the sun rises, ma'am.'

Chapter Thirty-eight

Tolak Range, the South Lands

They led their horses along the track, resting their backs and legs after a fast ride out of Tingalla before dawn. Lidan had drained two water bladders and several cups of strong tea in an effort to wash away the sticky dryness left in her mouth by the wine, and she couldn't thank Torren—the scout from the previous night—enough for interrupting the evening when he did. Without the distraction and the excuse to head for bed, she'd probably be nursing a screaming hangover and throwing her guts up right about now.

'What do you think Merk's up to?' Loge's question jolted Lidan from her thoughts and she turned around.

She blew out a sigh and looked up at the trees. 'I'm not really sure,' she admitted. 'I hope he just wants to make an alliance against Yorrell, but...'

'Seems too good to be true if you ask me,' Loge said bitterly.

Lidan frowned at him. 'Did you see something at the feast yesterday?'

He shrugged a shoulder. 'Yes and no...'

She eyed him until he continued.

'He's just too friendly, too engaged. I can't put my finger on it.'

Lidan nodded, watching the other rangers leading their horses ahead. 'I want to know what he wants in return for betraying Yorrell.'

'That's it, isn't it? He's not going to sell out the Namjin without asking for something valuable in return, is he?' Loge absently scratched Striker's nose and Lidan tensed. She stopped in the middle of the track, the other rangers disappearing around a bend up ahead, leaving her alone with Loge among the whispering trees. Insects whirred and chirped in the rising heat of the morning, humidity steaming from the damp soil around them.

Loge stopped beside her, a frown darkening his features. 'What is it?'

Lidan met his questioning gaze. 'What if...' The words caught in her throat as though they were barbed, her heart hammering against the wall of her chest. She leaned forward and whispered past dry lips. 'What if it's me?'

Eyes narrowing, Loge stepped closer. 'Excuse me?'

She barely heard him over the thud of her pulse. 'What if *I'm* the price he demands? What if he wants a matching to secure the alliance?'

'Lidan, that is absurd.'

'Is it?' she hissed. 'Yorrell demanded it four years ago, and he almost got it. What else could Merk possibly ask for in exchange for turning against the Namjin?'

'Weapons? Horses? Land? I don't know. You're not old enough to match yet.' Loge's assertion lacked a certain conviction. His eyes searched her face, as if looking for a reason not to believe her.

'Things have changed, Loge. My father was playing for time at the last Corron. We all were. Hoping the ngaru were a passing threat, hoping things would go back to the way they were.' Lidan chewed the inside of her lip, her hands tightening around Theus' reins.

'You think things have changed so much that Erlon would defy the Law?'

'Maybe...' she said. 'He thinks an alliance with the Marsaw will end the war with Yorrell. He thinks this is the turning point. I have no idea what he'd do to make sure that happens...'

Realisation flickered in his features. He knew she was right.

'This war started because we refused Yorrell's proposal. But what if that's the only way to end it? My father's getting desperate. He needs to end it.'

'You can't be serious?' Loge countered, a muscle jumping in his jaw as he shook his head and shifted his feet. It was as though his entire body railed against the idea, despite the obvious. Silence fell between them and Lidan hurried to fill it.

'I could be wrong—'

'He wouldn't dare,' Loge growled under his breath.

'Pardon me?' Lidan stared at him in unveiled astonishment.

'There's no way he'd do it, Lidan. He'd be mad...' He shook his head as if to rid himself of the thought. The anger in his voice, the fury he held prisoner behind his teeth, stunned her. It simmered in him, held back by sheer concentrated will.

Lidan looped her reins around the saddle pommel, leaving Theus to crop at the shrubs and grasses beside the trail. She balled her hands into fists to stop them shaking. 'Since when have you been an expert on the politics of clan matches?'

He looked at the sky, as if asking his ancestors for help, then rubbed the bridge of his nose.

'Look, I'm not.' Loge stepped toward her, leaving Striker to feed by the track. Barely a foot of space separated them now. 'I know, in your mind, it makes sense that he would do this. It makes sense that he would sacrifice you to save everyone else, even if it defied the Law and everything that's held the clans together since the beginning of time. He might just be able to pull it off, despite the legal mess it would cause. He might even be able to convince your mother to agree, though, if I'm honest, I think the sky is more likely to fall in. But it makes no sense, that after four years of protecting you, of keeping you away from Yorrell and his rangers, of defending his border against two separate foes, that he would just roll over and give you up. It boggles the mind! There's been too much bloodshed for your father to simply throw his hands in the air and give in now.'

'What are you talking about?' Lidan demanded. 'He hasn't protected me from anything!'

'That's horse shit and you know it.' Loge stabbed a finger back in the direction of Tingalla. 'You think he's had his chief ranger, his most trusted advisor, out here hunting ngaru for fun? Of course not! Siman should have been at the border running a garrison or something, but instead he was under orders to protect you. His orders, *all* of our orders, were to keep you as far away from Yorrell Namjin as physically fucking possible, because he refused to give you up.'

Lidan's mouth ran dry and it was all she could do to stop herself taking a wary step back from the hot anger rolling off Loge. When she opened her mouth to speak, nothing came out—no snappy retort or withering counterargument. All she could do was stare and wonder how in the world she hadn't realised this before.

How had she not known? How had she not seen it?

She'd been so focused on her mother's demands and her own goals that she'd missed the wall of hands her father had built to keep her safe. Still, despite all that, things had changed.

'It makes no sense for your father to trade you off now, because if he did, he'd lose the respect and loyalty of every ranger in this clan. If he even suggested such a thing, Siman would have fucking kittens, and I dare say your mothers would exile him from his own hall. And—' his tirade stumbled, as if his throat had tightened around the words and he fought to release them. 'Do you think for a second I'd let that happen to you?'

She blinked at him, stunned into silence. She wanted to touch him, to anchor herself in the storm of emotion swirling around her, but she just stared. The worry and pain etched in his features hurt her heart more than any wound she'd ever worn in her skin. Her vision blurred and she bit down on her quivering lip. 'What if we don't have a choice?'

'There's always a choice, Liddy.'

They caught up to the other rangers and stopped to eat as the sun reached its scorching zenith. Lidan ate in silence, and the food tasted of dust. Her mind replayed her exchange with Loge over and again, burning the image of his anger into her memory, her thoughts tearing each other apart as they vied for supremacy of reason.

One half of her accepted Loge was right—her father would lose an immense amount of respect among her people if he broke the Law and matched her off before she was old enough. But she was less than a year shy of her eighteenth birthday, and what Erlon lost by breaking the Law he might regain if it proved to be the decision that ended the war with Yorrell. If it turned the tide, if Merk's rangers were pitted against Yorrell's, in combination with Horice's and her father's forces, it could just be enough to put the Namjin back in their place. How could she refuse if it saved countless lives? Surely it was a sacrifice worth making.

She rode in the centre of the group for the rest of the afternoon, wary of the return of forward scouts searching for the rangers shadowing the travellers. They were close now, but she didn't want to stumble across them without some sort of plan. Lidan urged Theus into a trot and she drew level with Jessah.

'Any word?' she asked.

Her friend shook her head. 'I expect they'll be back by sundown. By Torren's estimates, we should run into the travellers in the morning.'

Torren had been riding ahead, surveying the bush and the track as they went, watching for a sign of the rangers he'd left trailing the travellers.

'We need to find somewhere to camp off the track,' Lidan said. 'We can set up a soft ambush. Let them come to us?'

Jessah glanced up at the sun edging toward the western horizon, beams of warm light angling through the trees. 'A few more hours and we'll be near that ridge we passed on the way in. Two outcrops of rock on either side will funnel them through and you can do your worst.' The ranger winked at Lidan and she smiled.

It was the first time since the raider attack that she'd had a chance to speak with Jessah, and she noticed the dark circles under her friend's eyes, a drawn look that spoke of sleepless nights and too many tears shed. Jessah had lost more than a friend and companion when Iema died—she'd lost a fledging love that had shattered her heart. The thought made Lidan's heart ache and she reached over to squeeze Jessah's arm. 'Thanks, Jess. Let me know what you want me to do.'

Jessah looked down at her hands. 'I want everyone home safe, Liddy. I don't want anyone else to die.'

She gave Jessah's arm another gentle squeeze. 'I know... Let's get to this valley and set up. Then we can sort out a plan.'

Night descended around their camp and the scouts emerged from the darkness. They met Torren at the perimeter and hurried over to Lidan and Jessah by the small cooking fire. The scouts crouched, breathless and sweating, and nodded a wordless greeting.

'This is Nevis,' said Torren, gesturing with his thumb at the man beside him.

'What can you tell us?' Lidan dispensed with any small talk.

'They'll be on you just after sunup,' Nevis replied in a low voice. 'My party is circling in behind them to make sure they don't diverge from the track. They don't ride after dark, so I doubt they'll try and get the jump on you before dawn.'

'They're armed?' asked Jessah.

Nevis nodded. 'Steel blades by the looks. A few bows.'

'Right,' Lidan began, leaning forward to draw a map of the valley in the dirt by the fire. Jessah watched over her shoulder, and she was aware of Loge sitting at the edge of the light behind her. 'Nevis, we need your group to hold where they are. Don't get too close if you can avoid it. Hang back and be ready to turn them around if they make a run for it. I want them to come to us quietly, so no surprising them. I don't want anyone getting killed over this. We need them to cooperate, if we can manage it. Jess, can you get our party to fan out through bush at either side, like this, in case they split up? I'll wait for them down here.' She pointed at a spot beside the winding track with her drawing stick.

'You sure that's a good idea?' Jessah asked dubiously. 'You'll be pretty exposed.'

'They're less likely to panic if they can only see me. If we jump out armed to the teeth, they'll fight.' Lidan stood and looked at the gathered rangers. She took a deep breath to steady herself and hoped they couldn't hear the uncertainty in her voice. 'I don't think I need to remind any of you we're in the middle of a war. The Namjin border isn't far from here and we can't take any chances. We know they aren't traders, but we need to find out what they're doing here. Make sure everyone knows we need these people alive. They aren't going to tell us anything if they're dead.'

Jessah, Torren and Nevis nodded, and the group broke up. Torren and Nevis vanished into the night beyond the clearing and Jessah moved around the camp, assigning tasks to the other rangers. Lidan turned away from the fire to face Loge, reclining on his bedroll, idly twirling a twig between his fingers.

'What do you think?' she asked, rubbing her hands together and hoping he hadn't seen the ghost of a tremor in her fingers.

'Jess is right—you'll be exposed down by the track.' He glanced up, his hazel eyes reflecting the light of the fire.

'Will you come with me?'

'As if you had to ask,' he smirked. He'd been on edge since their conversation that morning, his demeanour cooling as the day wore on. They hadn't had a chance to talk much afterward, and Lidan had admittedly been avoiding him. She had to tell him about the things she'd seen in the white place, and in light of what they might face in the morning, this was probably the last chance she'd get. She shoved her fear of his reaction to one side and licked her lips.

'Can we go for a walk? I... I need to talk to you.' She folded her arms and shifted where she stood. Loge studied her and for a moment she thought he might refuse. Then he climbed to his feet.

'Probably need some more firewood, don't you think?' He tilted his head toward the edge of the clearing and the hill above the camp. She let out a shaky breath and nodded, then followed him away from the fire.

They wove through the trees in silence and when they reached the farthest edge of the fire light, she cleared her throat. 'I need to tell you something...'

'Sounds ominous,' he muttered without stopping.

'Loge, please.' Lidan grabbed his elbow and forced him to stop. He put his hands on his hips and refused to meet her eyes. Instead, he looked back down the slope toward the glow of the campsite. 'Remember the blue craw?'

He looked at her and nodded slowly. 'Haven't seen it in a while.'

'It's been keeping to itself...' She scanned the bush around them for no other reason than to delay. 'You know how I disappeared when it touched me? It, um, took me somewhere—a white place—a huge expanse of white emptiness. It's a void, but it feels full at the same time. Like crowded air.'

His eyes narrowed and he folded his arms but didn't speak as she searched for the words to explain what she'd seen.

'I don't know why, but the night after the raiders attacked us, it took me there again.'

His jaw dropped and he leaned forward. 'It did *what?*'

'Don't give me that look!' Lidan hissed, glancing around to make sure they weren't being overhead. 'I didn't ask it to!'

'You didn't think to say something?'

'I wanted to, but I just... I couldn't find the words. There was so much going on and time slipped away and...' She opened her hands toward him. 'The first time, when I burned the priggin doll, there was nothing there but me and the bird. The second time...'

'What happened?' His stance shifted and he stepped closer. 'Did it hurt you?'

She shook her head. 'The bird? No, I don't think it's dangerous. It's actually saved my life more than once, if that counts for anything.' She ignored his disbelieving frown and ploughed on. 'The second time, we weren't alone. I don't know why, but I think it was trying to show me something.'

'What did you see?' By the grim set of his mouth, she could tell he held a torrent of questions behind his lips.

'A man… and a woman. I've never seen either of them before, but the woman came at me like she knew me. She *screamed* at me. I don't know why. I don't know what it means!' Panic rose in her voice, shaking loose tears that threatened to fall from her eyes. 'It's been haunting me ever since. I can't get them out of my head, Loge. They're always there, whenever I close my eyes, whenever I'm alone with my thoughts for more than a few moments. He's just *there*—staring at me like he's seen a ghost!'

Her body shook and Loge wrapped her in his arms. He pulled her against his chest and she folded into him, shivering with dread that ran down to her marrow.

'Why didn't you tell me?' he whispered, his head against hers, his voice rumbling in his chest.

'I don't know…' She choked on a sob and wound her trembling fingers into the fabric of his shirt, holding tight, afraid the churn of her thoughts would pull her away into a darkness deeper than any night. Her eyes closed and a tear slipped down her cheek. 'I'm sorry…'

Loge leaned back and took her face in his hands. His gaze locked with hers and the churn began to ease. He was a safe place to shelter in the storm, a rock against which the turmoil of her heart broke. 'You don't ever have to be sorry. Not with me. Not ever. Do you understand? Not ever.'

'I'm scared,' she admitted.

He shook his head slowly. 'I can't hope to understand all this, Liddy. It's beyond me why this is happening, but I can't help you if you don't tell me what's going on.'

Her eyes slid shut and she hung her head. 'I don't think you *can* help.'

'Maybe not, but you don't have to face any of this alone.' He eased her head back and she looked up at him. 'No matter how weird this shit gets, we fight it together, like we always have.'

Lidan nodded and let his kiss wash away the pain and confusion until she stood in a place where nothing could touch her but the warmth of his hands and the press of his body.

CHAPTER THIRTY-NINE

Tolak Range, the South Lands

Ran kept his eyes on the track and the reins loose between his fingers. His horse walked calmly enough, but its ears swivelled back and forth, searching the bushland for sounds Ran could not hear. Their tail couldn't be heard over the rustle of the wind through the trees or the whirring of insects. It was only thanks to Brit's eyes they'd known they were being shadowed at all.

'Are they still following us?' Ran asked in a low voice.

Brit waved a fly away from his face and sucked at his teeth. 'They've fallen back. I haven't seen anyone since we made camp last night.'

'Maybe we've crossed a border?' Ran looked up at the sky between the trees. The sun inched into the new day, humidity building, insects and birds singing around them.

'I don't know,' Brit muttered, looking over his shoulder. 'They've shadowed us for days and now they just vanish? Doesn't feel right.'

Ran conceded the point with a nod and chewed the inside of his lip. Aelish rode behind him with Zarad, and Eian followed at the rear. Their magic was useless for spotting the unseen threat in the trees, but that hadn't stopped Ran unfurling his power to search for the riders.

A few days back they'd passed what looked like a war zone along a nondescript section of the track, flies buzzing around corpses and the air thick with the eye-watering stink of burnt bodies and timber. The remains of a collection of scorched funeral pyres had confirmed his suspicions, and he'd warned the others to stay alert. It was Brit who spotted the first of the southerners that evening, and Ran had expected them to emerge from the trees as the others had at the tablelands. But these riders remained at a distance, observing him and his companions in utter silence, barely noticeable amongst the shadowy undergrowth.

A squall of thundery rain had washed through the shallow valley that morning, and the earth smelled rich with moisture and life. A few thaumalux trails wove along the track beside them, the most recent that of the magic-user he hoped was the witch. The trail had been a constant thread since they'd left the village, and Zarad swore a spell had been worked along the track no more than a few days ago. All of this left Ran with a creeping sense of anticipation and dread. He had no idea what to expect at the end of this trail but couldn't shake the certainty it wasn't anything good.

Something shifted in the undergrowth and he yanked back on the reins. A tall animal hopped from the trees, took the width of the track in a single bound and sailed off into the bushland. Brit had his sword half-drawn before they realised what the thing was, and Ran released a shaking breath as a few more of the bouncing animals crossed their path.

'For fuck's sake,' he muttered. He glanced at Brit, who shook his head and jammed his blade back into its scabbard.

'You two are a bit edgy this morning,' Aelish observed dryly from behind them.

Ran shifted in his saddle. 'This place gives me the creeps.'

Aelish snorted a laugh. 'Relax, your highness. There's nothing out here except—'

A shriek tore up the valley and Ran froze. Three more cries ripped through the air, followed by a chorus of others, answering the call of the first.

'Oh shit.' Ran pulled his horse around, scanning the trees as he did. 'Shit, shit, shit.'

Aelish glanced about frantically and Eian and Zarad drew their weapons, blades singing from their scabbards. Screams and howls burst from the shadows, surrounding them in a cocoon of noise that assaulted Ran's ears.

His heart pounded and he caught Brit's eye. 'Dradur!'

'Can we outrun them?' Zarad called, his horse wheeling and stamping.

'Not likely!' Ran shouted back. 'There's too many.'

Eian swung down from his horse and let it go. He whirled his sword in his hand and the familiar tang of magic filled the air. Zarad followed suit and Aelish rolled from her saddle, snatching her crossbow and quiver before her horse trotted off to the side of the track. Ran jumped down to the ground, yanked his sword free and released his horse. Flexing his fingers, he called his magic to the surface, balling the blue energy in his palm as Brit drew his blades. The screams closed in, trapping them on the track.

'Go for the neck,' he called to the others, turning his sword in his hand. 'Sever the head.'

Somewhere over the rippling screams and hungry howls he thought he heard shouting, but he shut it out and forced his mind to slow.

The first dradur burst from the trees and swung for him. He whirled, slicing his sword into the side of its head and following through with a blast of magic. The bush around the track exploded into chaos.

The second creature slammed into him and they rolled together into the trees. It came up swinging, blades scything over his head as he fought to regain his footing in the slippery undergrowth. He blocked the onslaught as best he could and drove the creature back, hacking wildly at where he thought its head should be. The steel connected with something and it yielded, spraying bright blue pus across the trees beside him. The creature slumped to the ground and he spun in time to fend off another attack.

A mace whooshed past his ear and thumped into the ground beside his feet. He called his magic again and punched it at the dradur's head. The monster's skull exploded under the force of the energy and the remains flopped beside the other corpse. A scream split his head and blade sliced down his back, pairing away the fabric of his shirt and gouging the skin beneath.

Ran roared and arched away from the pain, swinging his sword with two hands at the place the creature had been. It cut through something and he heard the thing wail. Another dradur loped toward him and he staggered, his energy failing.

He hauled his sword arm up and blocked a strike that shuddered down the length of the blade into his shoulder. He blocked again and again, the force of the assault driving him back and forcing him down. He called his magic, but it sputtered, his body failing under the weight of the attack. The flat of a blade whacked into the side of his head and the world tilted at a sickening angle.

Turning his steel, he hacked at the creature's legs, slicing though rotting muscle and bone, and the dradur collapsed onto its back, flailing its blade-riddled arms at him, desperate for a kill. Ran drove his sword down into its neck and it shuddered, blue fluid spurting across the ground.

He staggered back, blinking hard to clear his vision.

Then he saw it.

A dradur watched from the shadow of a tree, broken teeth bared in a rotting snarl. It hissed at him, spittle and pus spraying forward in a nauseating shower. Then it hefted an arm that ended in a warhammer and swung for his head. His sword came up and his magic flared, the last spark crackling a moment too late as the weapon slammed into his arm, bone snapping and his cry echoing through the trees as he fell.

The dradur collected itself and turned for the final swing as Ran blinked blood and sweat from his eyes. Slithering away from the dradur as fast as his broken body could manage, he dug deep for any power hidden in the darkest recesses of his soul.

The world spun and he fought the urge to vomit as his vision swam. He'd come so far, and yet this was how it would all end? Bludgeoned to death by an undead corpse in a foreign country? His shoulders bumped against the trunk of a tree and he realised he'd dropped his sword.

He had nothing; no magic, no weapon. His friends were probably all dead and he was out of options.

Black spots fizzed in his eyes and the dradur loped toward him, deciding he was spent and ready to die.

His vision faltered and the dradur screamed.

The day fractured around him, screeching and shouting tearing the fabric of his mind.

The dradur whirled and flailed and he blinked furiously, struggling to bring himself back to consciousness. Across the tiny space between the trees, someone fought the creature with furious intent, stabbing and slicing, kicking and punching until the dradur crumbled before them.

They spun behind the defeated dradur and ripped a blade across its throat, tearing the creature's neck apart and snapping the spinal cord in two. Foul blue ichor slopped down and a headless corpse flopped to the ground, twitching at the feet of the assailant like a fish out of water. The attacker spat and tossed the head aside.

Ran's gaze worked its way from their boots up to their torso. His brow creased in a brief frown.

It was a woman, but not Aelish. Someone else. The stignada on her arms glared at him and realisation shuddered through his chest.

'You…' he said in a hoarse whisper.

She turned from surveying the twitching corpse and froze, wide green eyes roving across his face.

'You?' she replied in accented common.

Breathless silence filled the void between them. He knew that face. He'd seen her in the place between, sleeping, then torn from her rest by the screaming raven. The image flared in his mind and he gasped, blinking it away. She lifted a long, wicked knife and pointed it at him as she caught her breath.

'*You're* the traveller?'

His face contorted and he winced at the pain coursing down the side of his head. His eyes stung, nausea roiling in his gut like a storm. 'What? What traveller?'

She moved closer, every step a careful calculation. 'It was you, in the white place. You?' She glanced around quickly. 'Where's the other one?'

Ran grimaced and wondered if she really was making no sense or if his mind was so scrambled by the blow to his head that he couldn't understand her meaning. 'The others? By the track… I…'

He rolled over and tried to stand. She didn't move to help him. She stood fixed to the spot by fear or dread or perhaps pure astonishment, and her expression darkened. She darted forward and snatched the front of his shirt, hauling him to standing and slamming him back against a tree.

'Where is she?' she snarled, barely an inch from his face.

His legs failed and the world spun. He was going to vomit on her if she didn't let him go. His hands shook and his stomach flipped, his head pounding like a beaten drum while his arm burned as though someone had set him alight.

'What? Who—'

The day collapsed into darkness.

The ground slid past, his head jolting and swaying. Someone dragged him through the bushland, his arm slung over their shoulder while his feet slid uselessly behind him. Daylight burst into his eyes and the undergrowth gave way to a bare track. The ground came up to meet him and he groaned, screwing his eyes shut to block out the blinding light above the trees. Someone shouted his name and boots thumped toward him.

'Is he alive? What did you do to him?' a voice demanded, and someone stepped back. Was that Aelish doing all the shouting?

She wasn't dead, then. That was nice. He liked Aelish.

'Nothing,' another voice insisted. 'Saved him, actually.'

That was probably true.

Memories flashed before his eyes; the snarling dradur, the snarling woman. Or girl. Was she a girl? She was tall and fast and strong so probably not a girl. Definitely a woman.

He groaned as hands started to work their way across his body, poking and prodding at parts that hurt. Fingers closed around his forearm and he jerked sideways. A wordless cry escaped him, and he whimpered away from the hands.

'That's definitely broken.' That was Zarad. He wasn't dead either. Bonus.

Two down, two to go.

Where were Brit and Eian? Today was already shaping up to be shithouse. He really didn't want either of them turning up dead.

'Better set it before it heals,' Eian called from somewhere in the distance. His friend let off a string of curses, sucking air between his teeth. Alive but injured. He'd take that. Could've been worse.

He waited for Brit's northern drawl to reach him, but there was nothing amongst the hurried chatter of folk he couldn't understand, their words dropping in and out of the common tongue. He rolled his head toward where he'd last heard Aelish.

'Brit?' he croaked.

Aelish's hand touched his face. 'He's alive. Stone cold unconscious, but alive. Got slammed into a tree trying to get one of those things away from me.'

'The fuck happened to you, Ran?' Zarad leaned over and blocked the sunlight from his face.

Ran peeled his eyes open. 'There was... I dunno, ten of them? Boiling out of the trees.' He hadn't kept count, really, but ten sounded like a nice round number to accurately convey what he'd faced.

'Here, bite down on this.' Zarad shoved a stick between Ran's teeth without giving him a moment to respond. Hands wrapped around his arm again and with a quick pull and a flick, the bones snapped back against each other.

Ran roared, jerking upright, his teeth crushing the stick as pain tore up his arm and down into his fingers. His roar became a sobbing whimper and Aelish pressed against his shoulders, easing him back onto the ground.

'There we go,' Zarad cooed like a father might to a child. 'We'll splint this, and your body will do the rest.' Heat swirled down his arm, bone deep pain throbbing through every fibre of the limb, consuming his thoughts. 'Chew on some of this.'

He opened his mouth and a pungent leaf touched his tongue. He started chewing and tried not to vomit. He knew this stuff. Sasha had fed it to him to ease his fever and quell the pain of his injuries after she'd found him at the bottom of that mine shaft. He also knew it was good. It did the job, and he'd be fucked if he was going anywhere in this amount of pain.

'We have to get moving,' a voice said. It was a voice he'd heard before, speaking again in accented common, with an educated lilt that was ever so slightly northern. That was weird. How could she have a northern accent? It was *her*—the one who'd found him in the trees at the mercy of the dradur! She sounded like she was drifting though, like a boat pulled away by the current of a river.

'Excuse me? Look at him! He's barely able to stand and Brit's out cold,' Aelish protested. He heard her stand and move away, but the sound was muffled at the edge of his awareness.

'We don't have time—'

'I won't let you—' Aelish began, cutting off the other woman.

'You don't get to decide what you will or won't do here!' The young woman he'd seen in the place between snarled at Aelish and he almost laughed. Aelish wouldn't take kindly to being ordered around like that. 'You're on my land, *my* father's territory and you'll do as you're told.'

That gave him pause, and the murmur of voices around him died away.

'Your father's territory?' Aelish repeated in a much smaller, more confused voice.

'Yes, Daari Erlon Tolak is my father,' the southern woman said coolly. 'I am Lidan, First Daughter of the Tolak and Witness of the Blood to Ehran,

First Son and Heir, and if you want to survive the next day you would do well to do as I say. If we don't get back to Tingalla by nightfall, my father's going to send out twice this number to find us. And trust me when I tell you, you don't want to face that wrath. Riders have gone ahead so they'll know to expect us, but I can't guarantee a warm welcome if we delay.'

'She's right, Aelish,' Zarad put in from beside Ran's head. 'Who knows if there are more of those things out here. I'd rather not wait around to find out.'

'What about Ran and Brit? They're hardly fit to ride!' Frustration rose in Aelish's voice. She wasn't going down without a fight. Ran's heart warmed with pride and—

No, wait, not pride. Powerful painkilling leaf juice warmed his heart, pouring through him like hot water from a kettle. This stuff was *good*.

'They can ride tandem,' the young woman—Lidan?—insisted. 'We'll tie them to the saddles if we have to.'

Ran chuckled and fell into a sweet pain-free abyss.

CHAPTER FORTY

Tolak Range, the South Lands

Lidan stood at the edge of the clearing, her eyes trained on the man fading in and out of consciousness beside the other northerners. The rest had minor injuries that had been easily tended, but he'd taken such a knock to the head that he'd been asking the same questions over and over with a handful of minutes between as they rode through the bush. His companions had almost given up trying to get their answers to stick in his mind. She'd have to hand him off to Marrit and the other healers at Tingalla unless he improved markedly in the next few hours. They still had some distance to travel, their progress slowed by the injured and the rising heat that seemed to drain the northerners more than her own people. She hoped her forward riders had reached Tingalla by now, and news of her imminent return had stopped her father sending half the clan out looking for them.

'Liddy?' Loge appeared at her shoulder and handed her some dried meat strips. 'What's eating at you?'

She ripped into one of the strips and looked back at the northerners, clustered together with their horses under the watchful gaze of the rangers.

'That's him,' she replied simply.

'Who?'

'The one with the head injury and the ridiculous blue eyes. That's the man I saw in the white place.'

'Are you fucking serious?' Loge hissed into the small space between them, his body tensing.

She glanced at him, sighed and shook her head, her hand resting on his arm as though her touch might calm him. 'It seems insane, but yes. I'd recognise that face anywhere.'

'What the fuck is he doing *here*? Did he recognise you?'

'I think so... yes.' She'd heard the others call him Ran, but none of them looked anything like the woman who had attacked her in the white place. She'd had moonlight hair and a gruesome wound at her neck that gaped when she moved, though it did not bleed. A dark rent in her otherwise unmarked, snow-white skin, an injury no one could have survived. The memory sent a shiver through Lidan and her skin tingled. Whoever that woman had been, she was not here, and Lidan wondered even more who she was.

Jessah waved at them from across the clearing, and the others began checking saddles and repacking bags. 'Time to move, or we won't be back at the village 'til well after dark.'

Lidan nodded, pushing thoughts of Ran and the mysterious woman away. 'Don't say anything, please,' she said to Loge quietly. 'He's not right in the head at the moment, and who knows how much of today he'll remember when he comes back to himself.'

'If he's forgotten you, he's going to get a mighty shock the next time he sees you.' Loge eyed the northerners over her shoulder, and she reached up to touch his face.

'We'll deal with that when it happens. For now, let's get them back to my father.'

He looked down at her, and for a moment, the lines of worry and anger in his brow eased. 'I don't like it. First that shit with Merk, and now this?'

'I know, but we'll get through. We have to. One step at a time.' She feigned calm, donning a mask to hide the creeping unease clawing at her gut.

The craw had taken her to the white place for a reason, and that reason was to see this man, this Ran. He was important somehow, but she couldn't say why. Not yet, at least. The craw called in the distance and banked unseen through the trees, but kept its secrets close, leaving her to wonder as she untethered Theus and led the rangers from the clearing.

The sole woman among the northern group found Lidan as the sun dipped low, long shafts of golden light slicing through the trees as somewhere in the distance, thunder rolled across the sky. Insects whirred and chirped over the gentle thud of hooves, the bush full of the rich, tangy scent of leaves and damp soil.

'I find myself in an awkward position, First Daughter.' The woman looked down at her hands, loose locks of flaxen hair falling over her face. 'I should have introduced us in accordance with your customs—'

'Please.' Lidan offered her a smile, albeit a forced one. 'I made the same mistake. I hardly greeted you with due respect.'

'I'm Aelish Yordam of the East Ruken Trading Company.' Aelish offered her hand and a smile in reply, light dancing in her green eyes. She wasn't an especially tall woman, but Lidan felt her strength when she shook her hand, absorbing a lance of pain from the not-quite-healed injury she'd sustained fighting the Namjin raider. 'We made our way to Hummel when we crossed the Malapa, but found it locked tight.'

'It's not like traders to travel so light,' Lidan observed. She glanced over her shoulder at the others on their horses, then looked down at Aelish's saddle, taking in the Tolak motifs and symbols worked into the leather. 'Or to come so far south.'

'We ran into some trouble at the Pass.'

Lidan caught Aelish's eye and saw a darkness there. *What kind of trouble?* She tilted her head as Aelish looked off into the trees. Ice serpents? Or something worse? She let the question flit away on the breeze, sensing a wound in the woman Lidan didn't want to poke at.

'Why didn't you stay at Hummel?' she asked quietly instead.

Aelish shrugged. 'Jac wouldn't let us in. Said the daari would feed him to the pigs if he did, so we moved on.'

Lidan snorted a laugh. That sounded like something Jac would say.

'And the Pass is more dangerous now than it's ever been. It wasn't safe to return. I suspect your father will want to speak with Ran?'

'Is he your leader?' Lidan frowned. The man she had saved from the ngaru didn't strike her as anymore senior than the others in the group. If anything, Aelish was the one to which the others deferred. Perhaps they were only doing so in his absence, injured as he was and unable to give them direction.

'He is, of a sort. He's from a nation far to the north where they've had trouble with the dradur.'

'The what?'

'My apologies,' Aelish inclined her head and brought her hand to her heart. 'That's what he and his people call those creatures who attacked us. They've been harassing the people of the north for some time apparently, but we haven't encountered them in Isord as yet.'

Lidan looked away down the track, her heart thudding uncomfortably in her chest. Ngaru were attacking people north of the Malapa? She had no idea they ranged so far from the South Lands, or that they were a problem anywhere but here. That might go some way to explaining Ran's arrival, but something didn't sit right. How could he have known the ngaru were a problem south of the Malapa? No traders had crossed the Pass in the years since they had first attacked her people. There was a missing piece in all this, a card someone was holding back, preventing her from seeing their hand.

'We call them ngaru,' she said into the silence, pocketing her disquiet to be examined at another time, and Aelish nodded. Lidan sighed. 'My father will certainly want to speak with him, but I'll be honest, Aelish Yordam; I can't predict how my father will react to all this. We're at war not only with the ngaru, but with other clans, and there is an urgent need to resolve both conflicts. My father may welcome you, but that will depend on what this Ran is bringing to our door.'

'I understand, First Daughter,' Aelish said and inclined her head again. She was polite, Lidan would give her that.

'Please, call me Lidan. I renounced that title to become my brother's protector.' She heard the bitter edge in her voice and cleared her throat. Now was not the time.

'Of course,' replied Aelish. 'I should get back and check on Ran. He was rambling on about something absurd earlier and I'm not entirely sure he's still got all his brains where they should be.'

'I'll have our healers see to him once we arrive. You might have to speak for him until he's well enough to address my father.'

'I hope that won't be the case.' Aelish almost grimaced and Lidan hid a smile. She wouldn't envy Aelish the task if it did fall to her. 'I'm hoping a night of rest will set him right again, and then he can speak to your father himself. I believe what he has to say will be better coming from him.'

Lidan nodded, wondering what it was bubbling under the surface of Aelish's polite charm that she couldn't quite unravel. 'I'll do my best to give you the night to gather yourselves before you face him.'

'Thank you, Lidan.' The relief was evident in Aelish's smile. 'I'll keep you informed of Ran's progress.'

Ran's mind wandered in incomprehensible circles as the group of riders led him and the others through the bushland, then out across a flat flood plain to a wide, churning river. The bridge and the buildings standing tall on timber stilts were a marvel, as if the trees themselves had become homes for people rather than birds. Beside his horse, Iridia walked—or floated, or shifted, or whatever it was she did to move from one place to another— hardly even present in this world but yet pressing in on his mind with an urgency he couldn't shift.

When they paused at the riverbank and waited for a gangway to be lowered, she stood still as stone, staring at the back of the young woman leading the southern riders. The last of the day's light lingered at the very edge of the horizon as the woman leaned down from her saddle to converse with a man.

Iridia folded her translucent arms. *That's her. For certain, that's her.*

Who? Ran asked, his thoughts stumbling over each other, struggling to order themselves.

Iridia turned and glared at him. *Pull yourself together, Ranoth, for fuck's sake. Her! The one from the place between. That's her. You saw her, you recognised her. I saw her. It's her!*

Ran narrowed his eyes at the woman as she waved her companions forward and urged her horse onto the bridge. *Oh. Yes. Right. I see now.*

He recognised that jet-black hair, her sharp, straight nose, and the green of her eyes, dampened by the long, deep shadows of the evening. Her gaze settled on him for a moment that might not have lasted as long as his scrambled thoughts imagined, but it did linger, and he saw a flicker of recognition in her eyes and a tightening around her mouth before she turned back to the path ahead. Eian clicked his tongue and pulled at the bridle of Ran's horse. Obviously, he was not to be trusted with the task of guiding the animal himself.

Fine then. He'd just sit here and watch the back of the southern woman and wonder why he'd been drawn across the length of Coraidin to stand in her presence. Not that he remembered meeting her. Not really. The memory was there, but it was as muddied and churned as the river below the bridge. The sensation remained, though; the shock of seeing her in the flesh, realising she was more than a sleeping girl in a strange white abyss, much more than a young woman protected by the ghost of a raven. There was fight and strength in her and a danger he couldn't put his finger on. Nor did he want to, lest he lose it.

The column of riders crossed the river and wove up an enormous hill that dominated an island in the centre of the rushing water, embankments and walls marked out in the creeping darkness by torches glowing along their length.

Ran didn't unveil his Sight. He couldn't even if he'd wanted to. His magic was concentrated solely on repairing the damage to his mind and the wounds in his flesh. Some part of him still functioning in the muddle hoped it would put him back as he was before. He didn't want to be like some of the soldiers he'd seen in the Disputed Territory, their minds broken, parts of them scattered like a puzzle broken apart by a child in a rage.

So many of those soldiers never found all their pieces, some of the parts so damaged they could never be put back together in a way that made them whole. Those soldiers didn't ever return home, at least, not as the people they had been. Part of them remained on the battlefield, lost amongst the mud and the blood and the screams and the gleaming bones under rotting uniforms. Ran didn't want that. He couldn't live like that.

The hill and its timber fortifications passed by and, before long, a tall gate loomed open before them, the path leading across a ditch and gangway. There was a hive of activity on the other side that he frowned at, riders dismounting and others running up to take control of the horses. He glanced around in the gloom, his sluggish realisation noting the ring of southern riders that remained around him and the others, neither dismounting nor riding on, but keeping curious onlookers at bay while the young woman and a slightly older man hurried toward a large hall.

'Does this feel right to you?' Brit murmured beside him. He turned to answer, and realised the watcher hadn't addressed him, but Aelish.

She shook her head, her hair shining in the torchlight. 'We're not supposed to be here. We're too far south and that's cause enough for questions, but these people are on a war footing. Gods know what they'll make of us, and I don't think Ran is in any state to speak for us right now.'

'Oi, now—' Ran began, then fell silent as Aelish turned and scowled at him.

'You aren't. You've barely said two sensible words all day and I can only bluff this for so long.' She turned to Eian. 'Can you see the trail?'

'It's here,' he replied, and Ran realised just how exhausted his friend looked in the evening shadows. He'd been tracking too long, and it showed in the gaunt planes of his face.

'So we're in the right place at least,' Zarad muttered from behind Ran, leather creaking as he shifted in his saddle.

Aelish eyed them all. 'Lidan said she would try and get us a reprieve for the night before her father sees us. Judging by the folk gathered here, something else is going on, but I'm sure he'll make time no matter the occasion. Let's just hope she can—'

Brit cleared his throat and Ran looked up, his eyes focusing on the woman returning from the hall, quickly crossing the open space stretched between two separate clusters of buildings. Lidan? Was that her? Riders moved aside to allow her into the protective circle, and the man stopped a few paces behind, fixing Ran with a baleful glare he wasn't quite sure he deserved.

Lidan nodded at Aelish, then at Ran after a brief moment's pause. 'Welcome to Tingalla. We're on the far western border of my people's range, and my father, Daari Erlon, is leader here. You should know that his word is law. I explained to him that you're exhausted from your journey and the run-in with the ngaru left you with injuries needing attention. He's agreed to speak to you in the morning, before the matching.'

'Matching?' Aelish ventured, as if that was the most important question to be asked. Had Ran been able to wrangle his tongue into working, he would have asked where the magic-user was hiding, but a pressure on his throat stayed his words. He looked toward the shadows between some buildings to see Iridia and the almost imperceptible shake of her head.

Leave it, she said. *Not yet.*

309

'My family travelled here for a matching between our clan and others on our border. The final ceremony is tomorrow, but he'll want to talk to you before.' Lidan gestured toward a nondescript building among all the other nondescript buildings. 'Jessah will show you to your lodgings. You'll be under guard and escorted by a ranger until the daari decides otherwise.'

Lidan looked at Ran as if she had more to say, but instead she nodded at one of the other women in the group of riders, before she turned on her heel and vanished into the twilight swirl of people and horses.

Chapter Forty-one

Tingalla, Tolak Range, the South Lands

Morning found Ran with a clearer head and a mind no longer whirling with disordered thoughts; a breaking dawn after a violent storm. The evidence of the tempest remained littered through him—the fatigue and the ache in his limbs—but all else was calm, the clouds of confusion blown away. He glanced around the small hut where they had been housed, bedrolls arrayed across a packed-earth floor, with a single bed pushed up against one wall. This was where he'd spent the night, Aelish and a southern healer insisting he take it, with its thicker mattress and cluster of light furs.

He'd fallen asleep as soon as the healer had let him lay down his head, exhaustion dragging him off to an empty darkness that held neither thought nor dreams. She'd checked him over thoroughly beforehand, waving a lit taper in front of his eyes and asking him a collection of questions while Brit verified the accuracy of his answers. It was an effort to keep to half-truths and misdirection, Iridia watching from the shadows, her gaze pinning him to the spot, a silent warning dancing in her eyes to not give too much away. The healer spoke excellent common, with the same slight northern lilt as Lidan, and she could have only been a handful of years younger. Their features were a close copy, giving Ran the distinct impression they might be sisters.

He swung his feet down to the floor and found his boots by the door, shoving them on over socks that could do with a wash but probably needed to be burned. All his clothes stank of blood and sweat, a sour iron tang lingering in his nose for long enough to tell him he desperately needed a bath. He wondered if he'd get one before his audience with the clan's leader, this daari everyone kept mentioning, but he didn't like his chances. The door eased open without a sound and he slipped out into the morning.

It was still early, the sun not yet peeking over the walls of the compound, but the place was beginning to hum with activity. In the centre of a wide, open area before the hall, a large pavilion-like tent was in the process of being erected, folk fighting with poles and ropes while others tended to the roof, which appeared to be made of stitched hides rather than canvas. He took a deep breath, his magic pooling at the base of his spine, a throbbing energy that was recharged after a night of rest. There wasn't much, but he reckoned he had enough in him to unveil his Sight and search the compound for the thaumalux of the witch.

Someone cleared their throat beside his ear and his hand went for a weapon. His memories sputtered to life and he stumbled back, his fingers grasping nothing but air, recalling too late that they'd given their weapons over to the riders. Magic rushed to the surface of his skin as he looked around to see a guard watching him from beside the door. The man's face was wrought with an expression somewhere between curiosity and indifference, and Ran crushed the surging magic back into his gut.

'Need something?' the guard asked in heavily accented common, leaning back against the wall of the hut, the crude bench he used as a seat creaking gently.

Ran collected himself, running his tingling hands down the front of his trousers then raking his fingers back through his lengthening hair. It felt slimy to the touch, and he had to stop himself glancing at his palm to see if it came away filthy. 'Anywhere to wash around here?'

The guard smirked and nodded at something behind Ran. 'Trough over there has water. The tines are too busy to draw a bath.'

'Tines?' Ran asked with a frown.

The man tilted his head at the people erecting the pavilion. 'I think you call them slaves.'

Ran narrowed his eyes against the glare of the rising sun. Many of the people working to build the tent had much lighter skin than the majority of folk moving around the compound, while others were as dark as midnight. They were all clearly foreign to this place and stood out amongst those he assumed were clan folk. His mind shuffled through the terms he had learned; tines were slaves, matchings were marriages, daaris were chiefs. It was as though he'd emerged from the Pass into another world, stepping into a place where even the plants and animals were markedly unfamiliar, while others remained remarkably the same.

He glanced back at the guard, taking in the leather of his boots, his light linen shirt and the weapons at his side. He could have been a guard or soldier from any nation in the north, if it weren't for the axe wrought of dark stone on the bench beside him, highly polished and sharpened to a wicked edge.

Wait. What? A stone axe?

He looked quickly back at the open area of the complex and realised with a start that hardly anyone he'd seen since arriving carried items wrought of metal. The few he had seen, were the riders, and then only some of them had a weapon or two made of steel or bronze. The buildings were, on the whole, of clay brick and timber, with very few constructed of cut stone, and the people wore simple yet serviceable garments, some with richer fabrics from the southern costal kingdoms scattered among them. It was as though he had not only stepped into another world, but back in time. He shivered, absorbing the oddity of the place.

He turned and held out his hand to the guard. 'I'm Ran, by the way.'

The guard hesitated, then leaned forward and grasped Ran's outstretched arm, squeezing his forearm with a strong hand. 'Torren Rainer. The daari wants to see you before things get too busy.'

Resigning himself to the unlikelihood of any kind of bath, Ran shrugged. 'Now's as good a time as any.'

Torren nodded and stood, letting off a sharp, high whistle. Ran started, the sound ringing in his ears and setting spots dancing across his vision, as if he'd been hit over the head again. Torren waved, and a woman jogged over, her face one Ran recognised vaguely from the previous day, and Torren asked her something in a language Ran couldn't understand. She nodded, listening to the guard and carefully running her gaze from Ran's face down to his boots. She moved to the door and leaned inside, and Ran wondered what she was looking for. After a pause, she gestured to the seat against the wall and spoke in her own tongue. Whatever she said drew a nod from Torren and he glanced at Ran.

'Jessah will take you to the daari. The others will remain here.'

'Of course,' Ran said, nodding at Jessah in case she didn't understand his agreement.

'Come,' she said, starting off for the hall. He stared at her back and watched the head of a hatchet at her hip gleam in the light. He'd crossed half the world to get here, yet he was suddenly overcome with a bone deep sense of dread, not entirely sure he wanted to follow the ranger, but knowing he had absolutely no choice but to obey.

The air inside the hall was already warmer than Ran cared for, his skin beading with sweat that might have had more to do with the nervous tension shivering in his limbs than he was willing to admit. Jessah led him in silence across the open room, reeds rustling under their boots as two dogs lifted their broad, brick-like heads to survey his passing with deep brown eyes. Neither of them growled, which he took as a good sign, but they raised their twitching noses in the air as if they smelled something intriguing.

Weeks of travel grime will do that, Iridia mused from a dark corner.

Reckon you can keep quiet for this? Ran asked without looking for her. He tried to ignore how the sound of her voice shifted something in his magic, dismissing it as the power responding to the tension of the moment. *I need to concentrate and I'm not sure I'm all back in one piece yet.*

You're not, which is why I'm here.

What? he snapped, fighting the urge to turn and confront her as a mountain of a man stood from a large, timber chair at the far end of the hall.

Beside and behind the man's chair, a small group of people were gathered, all of them watching Ran with steady eyes and unreadable expressions. Ran ignored them and focused on the man, taking in the breadth of his shoulders and the display of stignada ink drawings etched into his warm brown skin. He had a fine fur pelt of some kind draped over one shoulder, and tiny metal rings clipped into the braids that bound his long black hair, all of which paled in comparison to the enormous bronze axe hanging at his hip. The handle of the thing was easily as thick as Ran's wrist, and it looked to weigh more than even Quaid could lift.

Goosebumps coursed across Ran's skin and he almost baulked, catching himself before he did and painting a smile on his face as shiny and convincing as any he'd worn in the presence of his father. The man before him looked so remarkably like Quaid Greyling that Ran wondered if he wasn't staring at a predication of Quaid's future. Would he look like this in another decade—a little more grey at his temples and a few more lines of worry and laughter carved in his face? They were not so similar that Ran thought they could be brothers, but the likeness was so remarkable it made his stomach clench as he sketched a deep bow.

Jessah didn't introduce Ran, but then, he hadn't told her his name, or titles, or even where he was from. He wondered when he'd forgotten the manners his mother had so endlessly drilled into him.

'Daari,' Ran began, straightening and resting his hand on his chest above his heart. In another time and place his father's family crest would have been stitched into the breast of his tunic, but that was a long time ago and a whole world away, and he stood before the daari as plain as any traveller from a nation in the north. Hoping the others hadn't betrayed his true identity, he kept to his alias from the Keep. 'I am Ran Harroe.'

A slight man with a pale face and whisky-brown hair stepped from a shadow behind a thick timber column. 'Daari Erlon Tolak greets you, Ran Harroe. He wishes the blessings of the ancestors upon you and hopes that you and your companions had a restful night, despite your spare accommodations.'

Ran glanced at the man, who had an accent from the Archipelago, and he wondered if their entire conversation was about to be run through a translator. 'I thank the daari for his kind hospitality, especially at such short notice.'

The daari waved a hand. 'Think nothing of it. We treasure any visit from our northern neighbours.' The pale faced man was not a translator then, but merely there to offer a formal greeting. Daari Erlon gestured to a single chair a few feet in front of the larger seat. 'Please, sit and we will talk. My daughter, Lidan, you have already met. This is my chief ranger, Siman Jarrah, and Ranger Loge Baker. They are witnesses to our discussions.'

As Ran moved to the chair, he scanned the people behind the daari, recognising some faces while others were new. The tall, older man called Siman was possibly of an age with Daari Erlon, with an equally menacing collection of ink etchings on arms that were folded across his chest. Beside him stood the much younger man, Loge, who Ran had seen the day before. His piercing hazel eyes followed Ran's every move like the sharp glare of a raptor, his regard so unsettling that Ran glanced at the young woman, hoping to find a more welcoming expression. He knew her instantly, the unnerving realisation washing through him and settling heavily in his gut as he registered Lidan's cool stare.

There was no denying she was the girl from the place between—the one with the blue raven, the one who had saved him, in his vague, fractured memories, from the dradur. A sword hung from a belt across her hips, buckled over a green gown, and bright bronze comb shone amongst the ebony black of her braids. Her arms were folded not unlike Siman's, but she didn't glare at him quite as savagely as her eagle-eyed companion. Loge stood at her shoulder, angled toward her in a manner that was both protective and deferential, as if he'd jump at the chance to sink one of his steel hatchets into Ran's neck if she so much as nodded or Ran made any move to approach. Unsure of exactly what he'd done to warrant such a scathing glare, Ran sank into his seat, doing his level best to shake off the feeling that he was cornered prey.

Remember that feeling, Ran? Remember the rabbit? Iridia spoke from somewhere in the hall, dragging unwelcome memories of the past from the dark parts of his mind. *Remember. Remember what it was to be hunted.*

I remember, he replied, taking a deep breath and letting it out slowly.

These people are not our friends. They owe us nothing.

Us?

Yes, us! This is for both of us, and all those people in my village who were slaughtered—

'You've travelled far, Ran Harroe,' Daari Erlon began, his common as easily understood as his daughter's. 'Lidan tells me you've come from the deep north?'

How did she know that? Ran took the shock in his stride and tilted his head in a casual sort of nod. He'd been out cold for a good portion of the previous day and slipping between the planes of reality for the rest of it. It was impossible to know what truths had already been revealed by Aelish or the others. 'We have, sir.'

Don't tell him why, Iridia whispered. *Not yet.*

Lidan blinked and worked her jaw, rubbing at the base of her skull, right behind her ear. Was the conversation boring her already?

'It's unusual for northerners to come this far into the South Lands...'

Erlon paused and watched Ran as a woman poured some sort of drink for the daari and moved to hand Ran a cup.

For want of anything else to do, Ran accepted it with a nod. 'It is, according to our companion, Aelish Yordam. She's familiar with your people, as a trader from Isord.' He hoped Aelish's name might build some sort of bridge between them and whittle away the man's suspicions, but he seemed unperturbed.

'Even the traders don't come this far south,' the daari pressed the point then sipped at his drink. Ran did the same, letting the bitter taste of ale fill his mouth as he collected his thoughts.

'I'll speak plainly. My companions and I are seeking a fugitive. Their crimes are some years in the past, but they evaded Justice in my homeland and we believe they fled south.' He shrugged, taking in the glance of confusion Lidan shared with Loge and the deepening frown on Daari Erlon's brow.

Ran felt Iridia move behind him. *Nothing specific, not yet. They owe us nothing...*

'A fugitive?' the daari repeated, rolling the word across his tongue like an unfamiliar taste, while his daughter winced and worked her jaw, as if trying to clear her ears.

What's wrong with—

'They may have passed by Hummel, or they may have continued on without contacting you at all,' Ran lied through his teeth and hoped it didn't show on his face. He knew the witch had been at Hummel; knew they had left the village, most likely with the daari's caravan several weeks ago. He also knew, thanks to Eian, that the witch's thaumalux trail was here.

But Iridia was right—these people didn't owe him anything. Had his magic been in better condition, his Sight might have revealed the trail he sought before now. As it was, he hadn't the chance to seek it yet, and wondered what he would find when he did. That Eian had at least seen the trail gave him hope, but he had to position himself among these people before he started throwing accusations around. For now, he would bide his time and build his case.

He cleared his throat and smoothed out his lies. 'As for our group, we ask only for a few days shelter in a place of safety, away from those creatures in the forest, and then we'll be on our way.'

'Do you think this fugitive is among our people?' Lidan asked suddenly. Her father seemed unbothered by her interjection and Ran shrugged again.

'I have no evidence to suggest they are.'

'But you're looking for it. That's why you've come. Not because the ngaru, or dradur as you call them, are attacking your people.'

Ran reeled from the hit, scrambling for an answer. But it wasn't a question. She spoke as if she saw into his soul, stripping away his carefully constructed facades until he was nothing but bare bones and truth laid out before her. A darkness coiled in her voice, the lingering ghost of things she'd seen. She couldn't be much older than his sister Nerola would be now, but a weight of responsibility sat heavy on Lidan, and for a moment, he pitied her.

'I take it my companions told you of the dradur?' he asked, watching her face for a hint of a lie. Lidan nodded and he sighed. Had he known that, he could have used it as a diversion from his real purpose, but now he'd revealed himself, there was no way to undo those words. He would have to lie his way out as best he could. 'No. The dradur are a problem, I grant you that, but we are looking for someone.'

End this, Iridia demanded. *She's drawing you out.*

I have it under control!

You don't! She's squeezing information from you like pus from a wound. You have no idea what she already knows and she's laying a trap.

'We were merely passing by when your riders found us, and lucky they did, or those creatures would have made a meal of us!' He grinned at the daari, impressed with how smoothly he had changed the subject. An idea occurred to him as he spoke, a way of winning favour that might be the key to unlocking the identity of the magic-user in their midst. 'Your daughter saved my life, sir. I owe her a great debt.'

Loge flinched, albeit slightly, and if Ran hadn't been watching for it, he may not have seen it at all. He and Lidan were close, then. Closer than friends, most likely; closer than he and Sasha had ever been. Did Loge perceive him as a threat? He would have to watch that one.

'If my daughter is anything, she is fierce. And she gives no quarter to the ngaru or any other threat lurking in the bush.' Erlon whisked his hand in the air, a dismissive gesture, as if his daughter's bravery was a matter of course.

'Of course. But she arrived just in time—'

What are you doing? Iridia hissed in his mind.

'—to stop the dradur finishing me off. I would very much like a chance to repay such a selfless act. I should like to stay, along with my companions, until I can.' Ran's words fell away to silence.

For a moment, no one spoke. Lidan frowned at him as if he'd suddenly slipped into a language she didn't understand and the daari slowly nodded with what Ran thought might be understanding.

'Very well,' Erlon said. 'You are welcome to stay among us as long as you need. You will have guards, of course, and Lidan will be your liaison. Should you have need of anything, please speak with her.'

Lidan shot a glare at her father that could have melted steel, her disdain for his unilateral decision evident in her scowl. She didn't want this, but she obviously had no choice. Ran didn't care. This arrangement bought him precious days to seek out his quarry, no matter how well camouflaged they were amongst the people of the clan.

CHAPTER FORTY-TWO

Tingalla, Tolak Range, the South Lands

Bridie's matching passed in a blur. Music and dancing, ceremonies and entreaties to the ancestors, all shifting about Lidan like clouds over a mountaintop. People were aware of her, acknowledging her, but she remained unmoved by it all, trapped at the peripheries of the day, numb and drowning in her thoughts. Her craw remained nearby, quietly perched as close as it could manage without touching her, as if it knew something wasn't right, as if it sensed the nausea rolling in her stomach. She was thankful for its silent vigil, and wondered more than once if it might just be easier to reach out, touch the bird's smoky blue feathers and fall away into the white place.

Her mind was stuck back in the cool shadows of the hall, trying to unravel Ran's motivations, while her body stood outside in the hot, humid air, surrounded by the sound of pipes and drums mingling with murmuring voices. She replayed the morning over and over as her sister and her new husband spoke vows and oaths, bowed and walked their way through the complicated rituals of matching. But instead of seeing them and witnessing their joining, she saw only the slight smile on Ran Harroe's face as he secured permission to remain at Tingalla under the guise of repaying some sort of life-debt to Lidan. It was a ruse, albeit a clever one, but for the life of her, she couldn't understand why he'd done it. What did he want here? Why was he here at all? Whatever it was, she was fairly certain she wanted no part in it.

Bridie and Harran continued their matching, unaware of Lidan's turmoil, the tale-keeper painting them with goat's blood and sprinkling ash from sacred trees in their hair. Ran and the other northerners were somewhere at the back of the pavilion, invited to witness the ceremony, but under guard. Lidan didn't look their way. She couldn't. The mere sight of his face had dread clutching at her heart with a hard, unrelenting hand.

Bridie's voice jolted Lidan back to the present to see Erlon press his daughter's hand into Harran's, sealing the final stage of the matching before the last blessings were bestowed. It was then Lidan glanced at the sky beyond the tent's roof and realised evening was approaching swiftly, bathing the sky with pink and orange and deepening blue. Somewhere, beyond the reach of her sight, storm clouds gathered in the oppressive heat, and thunder rumbled at the edge of her hearing. Cloistered within her thoughts, she was only vaguely aware that Ehran held her by the hand and had followed her from one ritual to another all day. He gave her hand a tug and she looked down, blinking.

'Sorry, what was that?' she asked, her voice a hoarse whisper as the matching continued several paces away.

'My legs hurt,' Ehran groaned, shifting his weight, then leaning his head on the back of her hand. 'I want to go play.'

Lidan scooped the boy up, settling him on her hip and ignoring the glare her mother shot at her from across the large tent. 'We can play soon. This is the most important part. After this Bridie will go home with Harran and live with the Daylin. We have to be here to make sure the ancestors see them.'

'I can't see any ancestors.' The boy narrowed his eyes at the crowd.

'No, but they're here. Maybe when you're older, you'll be able to feel them.' Lidan certainly thought *she* could; their gaze boring into her like hot pokers pressed against soft flesh, their judgement weighing on her chest until she was sure she wouldn't be able to take another breath.

There was a sharp crack as someone gave a single clap of their hands, and Lidan looked at the tale-keeper, her hands outstretched over Bridie and Harran who knelt before her in the dust.

'Witness!' she cried.

'Witness!' the gathering replied, Lidan lending her voice, if not her heart, to the moment.

'Is it done?' Ehran asked, wiggling in her arms like an excited puppy.

Lidan glanced at the crowd as people moved forward to give the couple their congratulations, and she nodded. 'Yes, it's done.'

'Play time?'

'Not yet,' she chided. 'Go and see Bridie and give her a hug, then you can go and find the girls.'

She put him down and he took off, weaving through the cluster of people growing around Bridie and her husband, and leaving Lidan on a precipice. Distraction seemed a better option than wallowing, so she turned to a nearby table with a collection of wine urns and unreasonably ornate cups. They were fine things, enamelled and glistening in the afternoon light, the pottery a reassuring weight in her hand. It was enough to anchor her until later, when she could talk to Loge about what had happened in the hall that morning. He was somewhere in the compound, perhaps tending horses or guarding the wall. It didn't really matter where he was, it only mattered that he wasn't here, and once again they hadn't had time alone to discuss what Ran's arrival really meant.

She took a few hearty gulps of wine and hardly noticed when the tine-woman refilled her cup, her thoughts grasping for something to catch onto. When had she become so reliant on Loge? So caught in the current that moved around him that when he was gone, she felt like a fish gasping and abandoned on the shore. On one hand it unsettled her—she'd never thought of herself as dependant, as needing the presence of another person to prop her up or make her whole. But on the other, it felt utterly right, as though it was the way the world should be.

As the gathered folk followed Bridie and Harran toward the hall for the feast, Lidan drained her cup and handed it back to the serving woman, smiling her thanks. For her sister's sake, she would get through tonight and leave the trouble of the northerner and what he wanted for the morning.

People crammed into the hall, the clamour of chatter and footsteps echoing against the roof and walls as the thunderstorm rumbled closer. Lidan pushed through the tangle of bodies, moving to the farthest end of the hall where her family would be seated. Here she might find solace in food and drink, and distraction in conversation that went nowhere and meant nothing. She didn't want to listen to talk of alliances or the war, or matchings or the arrival of the northerners. She wanted to sink into empty silence, but that wasn't going to happen tonight. Tonight, she would grind her teeth, bear her frustration, and leave the hall as soon as polite.

She stepped around the edge of a table and reached for a wine urn. A man laughed, and she glanced up to see her father, deep in conversation with Merk Marsaw behind the most ornately decorated table in the room. This was where Bridie and Harran would sit with their parents, a place of honour usually reserved for daaris and danas, but they were not seated yet. Daari Merk was gesturing with a tankard in one hand, pointing back and forth between his chest and Erlon's, and Lidan paused. Erlon continued to talk, his head bowed to speak directly into the shorter man's ear, words passing between them that Lidan could not hear. Something about their stance, the way their heads leaned close as they spoke, set her heart to thumping.

Merk glanced up and caught sight of her across the room, and a grin broke across his face as he tilted his cup in her direction. Her mouth ran dry, her fingers fumbling to catch the wine urn as it slipped from her hand. Carefully, she put the urn down and threaded through the crowd, watching her father nod, her pulse drumming in her ears, drowning out voices and someone playing pipes. Within a few feet she caught the edge of their conversation and nervous fingers rested on the pommel of her sword.

'Yes, yes, my friend; all in good time!' Merk pulled back from Erlon and slapped him on the shoulder. 'We'll discuss this in the morning.'

Erlon made to say something else, but Merk stopped him, holding up his horn tankard and a single finger.

'It can all wait until tomorrow. Tonight, you must drink!' He clapped the side of his tankard into Erlon's and shuffled past Lidan, raising his brows as he gulped a mouthful and disappeared into the crowd.

'Da?' Lidan ventured.

Erlon looked around, caught sight of her and seemed to suppress a sigh. 'What is it, Liddy?'

'What were you...' she began, wondering if she had the guts to ask him outright. It was very likely none of her business, but something in Merk's grin and his lingering gaze told her differently. She cleared her throat. 'That looked serious.'

Erlon glanced after Merk and raised his brows. 'That? Just plans.'

'Plans? Shouldn't that wait for the Corron?'

'Not these plans.' He took a draw from his cup as Lidan frowned. 'If we get this done, we might not need a Corron at all.'

Heat rolled through Lidan's chest, a flush of foreboding. 'Why wouldn't you need a Corron, Da? We need to broker an alliance with the Marsaw.'

Erlon's gaze fixed on her then. 'There are other ways to secure an alliance that don't involve a Corron.'

The noise of the hall retreated, replaced by a loud ringing that filled Lidan's ears until she thought her head might split open.

No. Not again. This isn't happening. Not again.

Her fingers squeezed the hilt of her sword, strangling it, forcing the wave of emotion out of her body and into the steel beneath the leather grip.

'What?' she whispered. 'What did you promise him?'

'That we would consider his proposal.'

'His *proposal*?' Lidan hissed, leaning closer. 'What proposal?'

'He hasn't come here to simply raise his axe in agreement to a peace accord. He wants to confirm the alliance with a matching. You and Brandt.' Erlon said the words with such casual ease that he might have been remarking on the weather and Lidan reeled, locking her knees to stop herself from staggering back, her eyes burning and her vision blurring.

She'd been right. For all Loge's dismissals and assertions, she'd been right.

'No... what about the...' Her words stumbled over each other, catching in her throat. 'What about Ehran? What about my oaths? I'm a witness now, I can't—'

'If we don't need a Corron, you don't need to be a witness,' Erlon said, and she realised she was too late. Though it didn't look like it, he was well into his cups, a belligerent drawl taking over his voice and a vacant, glassy film covering his eyes as he scanned the crowd. Already he'd lost interest in their conversation, and his mind was made up.

'That's not how it works, Da! You said I was witness until Ehran is of age! That's fourteen years from now!'

'And you thought I wouldn't match you off *before* then?' He rounded on her, turning his back to the room and towering over her.

For the first time in her life, she shrank back from him in genuine, gut-clenching fear, her hand shaking on the sword she knew she could never use against him. 'You are only required as witness until Ehran is ten, and he will be perfectly safe within Hummel until then. There are ways around these things, Lidan, and you said it yourself—we need to end this war. There is no choice to be made here. This is the way it has to be.'

'That's not what I meant!' She fought to keep her voice down. 'I want to help, but not like this. This isn't—'

'Life isn't about getting what you want, Lidan. It never has been. I thought you would have learned that by now. We get what we're given, and it's up to us to navigate the river or let it drown us.' He eased away from her, his anger cooling to simmering disappointment as the sound of rain began to hiss on the roof above, cool wind swirling through the windows and roof hatches, dancing with the flames in the fire pit.

'Da, please!'

'No!' he snapped, then looked around as if worried someone had overheard him. 'This is how it has to be. These are his terms. I don't have a choice. This is how we end the war—with sacrifices we don't want to make, understand?'

He didn't give her a chance to respond, stalking off into the crowd and shouting a greeting at someone she couldn't see through the blur of her tears. Her pulse thundered, her heart hammering hard, knocking the air from her chest as if she'd been kicked by a horse. She stood there, staring at the fire, until Vee appeared at her shoulder and pushed a bone tankard into her hand.

'Are you all right, Witness?'

Lidan's fingers trembled as she wrapped them around the cup. 'Did you hear any of that?'

Vee shook her head, watching the hall. 'No, Witness. I bring news of the northerner you asked me to watch.'

Lidan had set Vee the task of shadowing the northern travellers, serving them with the other tines in an effort to glean information from overheard conversations. People would say all manner of things in your presence when they thought of you as nothing more than an animated piece of furniture, but all of that seemed so petty and insignificant now. She didn't care anymore why Ran was here. It didn't matter. None of it mattered.

'Anything of interest?' she asked, pretending to care, pretending to hear as her head spun and her stomach churned.

This was it.

She'd failed.

Her father had chosen to send her away. He didn't care that she was a sworn witness—ending the war was more important. More important than the Law or the oaths she'd taken.

What would her mother say about it all? Lidan glanced at Sellan, seated near the top-most table, leaning back in her chair and staring vacantly into the gathering. She could almost hear the rage her mother would spew, but worse was the silence as Sellan inevitably took the matter of the succession in hand, and the knowledge of what her father's decision meant wrapped a cold hand around Lidan's heart.

Vee tilted her head to the shadows on the other side of the hall, near where tines carried platters of meats and roasted root vegetables from the kitchens. 'He's been nursing a cup over there since the end of the ceremony. They haven't spoken to each other much. I don't think the woman is happy with him for some reason.'

'And the others?' Lidan asked, scanning the crowd.

Her mothers were herding their children into seats and attempting to get them to eat, but one by one they gave up and nodded wearily at tine-women to take the youngest ones away to settle them for bed. Harran's many siblings took up an entire table on their own, and everyone else found space where they could, falling hungrily on the steaming food and abundant drink. Laughter and chatter echoed around them, and a headache began to scratch behind her eyes. She wasn't going to last long here. The noise was already setting her teeth on edge and her heart was pounding. She felt sick to her stomach.

'They're at a table near the door. They keep mentioning something about some sort of light.' Vee's face contorted as if struggling to find the words to explain herself. 'I don't know. Perhaps I'm not hearing them right.'

Lidan's terror and anger took a breath then, and she looked at Vee in the lull, as if a curtain had been drawn back just long enough for her to see through. 'A light?'

Vee nodded in their direction, lightning flashing through the entry. 'The small catches I've heard make little sense, but they keep mentioning light.'

Light? Lidan wondered. Were they talking about the white place? It was blinding to the eye at first, and unmarked as newly fallen snow, but was it a light? Was that what they meant?

'Is there anything I can do for you?' Vee asked, keeping her voice between them as best she could in the noise of the hall.

'Keep an eye on them for me. See if any of the other tines have interesting news, and we'll talk it through in the morning.' Lidan gave Vee the best smile she could manage. 'Otherwise, try and enjoy yourself. I'll manage on my own tonight.'

'As you wish, Witness.' Vee bowed her head and returned the smile; a sly, knowing sort of expression that suggested she was quite looking forward to a bit of spying.

Lidan tucked her fury at her father into a dark place in her chest and returned her attention to the problem she had begun the day with. She strode away from Vee, weaving through the shifting crowd to the opposite side of the hall. She might not be able to control her father or accept that he was playing with her future like a game piece on a board, but she could find out what Ran was up to, and why he was here. They had business to settle.

CHAPTER FORTY-THREE

Tingalla, Tolak Range, the South Lands

Can you see them?

Ran sipped his drink and licked the ale from his stubbled top lip. *No. I've seen one trail, but not the person it belongs to.*

You haven't followed it? Iridia scowled at him, her arms folded tightly across her chest. She stood beside a timber roof support with one hip cocked, untouched and unbothered by the people walking through her transparent form.

We've been under guard and shuffled around since we got here! There's literally been no time to try. It took all of Ran's waning energy to stop himself shouting at her. They were grating at each other now, frustrated by the proximity of what they sought but thwarted by time and circumstance. He wanted to find the magic-user as much as she did; wanted to openly accuse them, take them into custody and get on with returning home, but going about his objective in that fashion seemed a good way of ending up with his head on a pike.

Home? Iridia snorted a laugh, reading his thoughts and his heart. *You're not going home anytime soon, Ranoth. Not now you've made yourself a body-slave.*

He glared at her. *It's a means to an end, nothing more. I owe her a debt for saving my life and it's an excellent excuse to stay here until we find what we need. I won't linger a moment longer.*

Whatever you reckon.

He looked toward the door and wondered if he could escape into the night and the rain falling beyond. Iridia would follow him into the storm, but at least he'd be free of the clan folk's stares and hushed whispers. Aelish had lost her shit when she'd found out he'd spoken with Daari Erlon without her, while Brit, Zarad and Eian had just stared in open disbelief while Ran explained the method behind his debt to the southern princess. The five of them had hardly spoken in the hours since, dragged from ceremony to ceremony, guarded and watched. This dark little corner behind a series of thick, timber columns was his only refuge from curious onlookers and none-to-subtle glances.

You've got company, Iridia whispered and slipped away as Ran turned and saw Lidan in her green gown and finery.

'Ran,' she began, nodding at him then glancing away, her face an unreadable mask.

He sketched a small, half-hearted bow. 'Lidan. Or is there a title I should call you by?'

She narrowed her eyes at him for a moment, then shook her head. 'No. You could call me Witness or First Daughter, but I'd rather you didn't.'

She paused as if to say more but a rumble of thunder filled the silence, and Lidan glanced into her tankard before deciding to drain whatever was in there. Someone walked past with a tray of brimming wine cups, and she snatched one away, replacing the full cup with her empty before the server moved on.

He eyed her, and realised her blank expression was not born of disinterest, but likely the result of the same fear or anxiety that caused her hand to tremble as she held the cup. She was about as unsettled as a spooked alley-cat, her gaze darting among the merrymakers, scanning faces without seeming to see any of them at all. How many drinks had she had before she'd found him? How many had she *needed*?

'What are you doing here?' she asked suddenly, pinning him with a sharp look that sent of jolt of panic down his limbs.

He stifled a shiver. 'I told you. We're looking for a fugitive.'

'Horse shit,' she hissed, barely louder than a whisper. 'What were you doing in the white place?'

'The what?' he frowned, his thoughts scrambling, his palms tingling with a familiar heat.

The place between... Iridia said quietly.

Lidan flinched and glanced around before locking onto him again with the unwavering force of her glare.

Iridia... I think she can hear you. Not fully, but enough. Let me handle this...

He wasn't sure he wanted to have this conversation—not here and not with her. Admitting anything about the place between meant admitting to magic, and he had no idea what these people thought of such power. It meant opening the door to questions about Iridia, and the type of person they were pursuing. He wasn't ready to give her any of that information yet, if at all. He needed to keep his mouth shut and his wits about him, lest he dig his grave deeper than he already had.

'Don't give me that nonsense. I know you were there. I saw you with a woman who isn't among your companions. I *know* you recognised me in the bush, and I know you aren't just hunting a fugitive.' She stepped closer, anger and the scent of wine radiating off her. 'I know you aren't just a traveller with a sword. I saw that light in your hands when you were fighting the ngaru. I *saw* it.'

Oh fuck, he breathed toward Iridia, but she did not respond. He gave Lidan his best attempt at a casual shrug and sucked loudly on his ale, taking a moment to vaguely cover a burp with the back of his hand. 'I honestly have no idea what you're talking about.'

'Horse. Shit.' Her words were venom and spite, anger and betrayal, drunkenness and pain. He had no idea where it stemmed from, but his denials were cutting at something raw and exposed, and she clearly hated him for it. She pointed a single accusing finger at him. 'I saw you. I know what you are.'

He fought the urge to step away, scowling at her to mask his fear. 'I'm an agent of the duke in my homeland. I'm seeking a fugitive. Nothing more.'

Lidan's lip curled in a snarl, but she drew back, looking him up and down. 'Whoever you're seeking isn't here. No one from the north has arrived and stayed in almost twenty years. The sooner you realise that and leave, the better.'

Twenty years?

Ran glanced at Iridia, who stood rigid in a shadow, staring wide-eyed at Lidan.

Lidan flinched again, the pale scars on her hand catching the light as she reached up to scratch at the back of her ear. The magic swirling between him and Iridia seemed to bother her more each time he spoke to his ghost, but Lidan said nothing, and he offered no further fuel for her inner inferno. With a final, disgusted glance, Lidan stalked away into the milling crowd, and Ran let her go, his heart pounding.

She knew so much more than he'd guessed, and much of it drawn from nothing more than her own observations. She'd sensed a crack in his facade and had begun to pick at the thin veneer he'd cloaked himself in, but how long did he have until she peeled it away and revealed what lay beneath? Who and what he truly was. Would he have time to finish his work here, time enough to find who he sought before she exposed him to the glares and wicked weapons of her people? The veil on his Sight slipped and he let it fall, registering the slightest flicker of light in the air where she had been.

What the fuck is that? Iridia pointed at the faint oscillating glint.

He blinked, wondering if it was nothing more than a trick of the torches and the lightning flashing outside. It was hardly enough to trace, and it faded as they watched, as if Lidan's fury alone had disrupted the air, but there was no mistaking what it was.

Thaumalux, Ran replied, staring in the direction the daari's daughter had gone. *She's not who we're looking for, but she can sense you and she's been to the place between. She's more than she appears, and I fear underestimating her would be a colossal mistake.*

Lidan swiped a wine urn from a table and pushed past a knot of people crowding at a side door. Thunder rumbled overhead and rain streamed down from the hall's roof, the hard-packed soil of the pathways turning slick with mud, and she skidded and wavered her way out into the downpour.

'Liddy?'

She spun and staggered, peering through the half-light and the rain. Loge sat on a bench near the door, dark circles of fatigue bordering the underside of his eyes, one hand rubbing absently at the side of his knee. It felt like an age since she'd seen him, when it had been only a handful of hours, each one dragging until they felt like years. He'd likely been on his feet all day, weight pressing down on the joint in his leg and aggravating the injury she'd hoped had healed by now. For a moment, her tangle of problems faded, and a pang of worry ignited in her chest.

'You all right?' he asked, his gaze falling on the wine urn.

'Yes. I mean… I don't know.' Lidan looked down and shrugged. 'Just the usual. Forced to do things I don't want, with no choice but to obey.'

'The northerner?'

She nodded and levered the stopper from the neck of the urn. 'He's part of it.'

She still had her tankard and some dignity, so she poured a good portion off into the cup and took a few long draws. When had she become so reckless with this stuff? She looked into the cup and all she saw was oblivion, which didn't seem so bad compared to the reality she faced. Rain poured down, drenching her hair and clothes, soaking through the fine fabric of the dress until it clung to her body. But she didn't move into the shelter of the eves where Loge sat. She didn't care anymore.

'I can't work him out, Loge. There's something about him that I can't unravel.'

'Did you talk to him? Ask him about…?' He whisked his hand in the air, unwilling to utter "the white place".

'I did, and he denied it. I sounded like a mad woman. Like a spoiled child demanding to be given something that doesn't exist.' She narrowed her eyes against the rain and looked out into the night beyond the reach of the torches. 'Maybe I dreamed it all.'

'I'm sure you didn't, Liddy.' He stood and moved closer, trying his best to reach her through the walls she was frantically building. 'You'll wear him down, I know you will. We'll get to the bottom of this.'

Lidan sighed and shook her head. 'I'm done,' she said, turning and walking away down a path.

'Done with what?' Loge called after her.

'That.' She waved her tankard back at the hall. 'All of *that*.'

Running footsteps splashed in her wake. 'How much have you had to drink?'

Lidan spun and stumbled, blinking away the rain and waving a finger in his direction. 'Not enough.'

She kept walking, listening to his footsteps shadowing her through the mud before stomping onto the timber boardwalks. They wove through the living quarters in silence, neither of them dressed for the downpour, but neither of them making any haste to escape it.

'Liddy, what else happened?'

There he was again, digging down into her mood and prodding at the cause. Forcing her to admit things to herself, to face what she'd rather hide from, and for a small beat of time, she hated him for it.

'Da wants to match me to Marsaw.'

Loge stopped, his footsteps falling away as she continued through the rain. 'He *what*?'

She turned and opened her arms wide, taking a few wavering backward steps, wine slopping down onto the boards. 'He says it's Merk's price for peace. Says it's how we end the war, exactly like I knew he would.'

'But you're a witness of the blood now. You can't...' Rain streamed down his face, dark tendrils of his hair caught in tiny rivers, his clothes as soaked as her own.

'I said the same thing,' Lidan replied quietly, taking another drink. Their eyes met across the path, and she started to shiver. She probably looked like a drowned rat. She certainly felt like one.

'He doesn't care? Surely he can't send you away now you've sworn an oath to protect Ehran?' Even as he said it, she saw the flicker of doubt in his eyes, heard the slight waver as his throat tightened around the words.

He knew what this meant, what matching to Marsaw *really* meant, and it had nothing to do with Ehran. Erlon would send her away, and Loge would remain, returning to patrols with the other rangers, away from Hummel for months on end. His time as her mentor and protector was over, and worse, neither of them could admit what they felt for each other to the world. All that would lead to was misery and strife. The daari would never let Lidan match to Loge—she was too valuable a commodity to trade off to a ranger, even one who was the first son of a well-thought of trades-man. Nor could she justify, or risk, taking Loge with her to Marsaw as some sort of bodyguard.

There was nothing to be done. She would go, and he would stay, and there was no telling if they would ever see each other again. And when Lidan truly dug down, that was what sat at the root of her anger and her sadness. She was losing him, and it was tearing her apart.

'He said I was a fool to think he wouldn't match me off before Ehran comes of age. And I was.' She looked around and realised she was opposite the door to her little hut. The common and walkways were devoid of life in the pouring rain, as thunder grumbled across the sky.

Loge's eyes narrowed. 'He wouldn't dare...'

'He would. He's desperate. And why wouldn't he give me up to end the war? It's not like I'm not old enough now.'

'You aren't old enough! We've been through this!'

'I'm close enough, and the Law seems to be getting thinner and thinner with every passing year this conflict goes on.' Shivers wracked her body as she waved her wine urn toward the hall, lightning sheeting along the belly of the clouds, still some distance off, but drawing closer with each passing minute. 'He doesn't care if he breaks the Law. He cares if he defeats Yorrell, and what's one life sacrificed for the sake of many? Isn't that my job? Isn't that what I was born to do? What *I* want doesn't matter in the face of that. What *I* want isn't even on the table.'

Lidan sniffed and realised she was crying, her tears mingling with the rain cascading down her face, and she let out a heavy sigh. The sounds of the hall and its celebrations had long since faded, and there were no insects calling in the wet. They had vanished at the emergence of the croaking frogs and chattering tree dragons huddled under the eaves of the buildings. She shook the wine urn. It sounded depressingly empty.

'What *do* you want?' His question hit her like a punch to the chest. It ripped away the shield she'd built of drunkenness and anger, and left her exposed, defenceless and unable to form thoughts into words.

She stared at him.

There were so many answers to that question.

She wanted to go back to when she was small, before the ngaru came to rip her people apart. She wanted to go back to when her world revolved around her family and her horse. She wanted to reclaim her future, the promise of security that came with her title, to flee to an imagined time when her mother was happy, and her parents weren't at war with each other. There were so many things she wanted, but not one of those answers tasted right on her tongue. They were all bitter and selfish and warped by years of looking over her shoulder. The only thing that made any sense, was standing right in front of her.

'You,' she whispered through the rain. Her heart skipped and her chest tightened at the look on his face. She stepped over to the door of her quarters, eased it open, and moved inside.

It was warm and quiet here, the hissing fall of rain and the song of the night creatures muffled behind walls of timber and clay. The air smelled of the smouldering herbs Vee had set to banish biting insects from the room, and all stood still. It was a sanctuary from the outside world, a place no one could touch. She stood behind the panel of the door, her forehead against its rough grain, her nails sinking into the timber.

She waited.

Loge finally stepped through the threshold, and they stood there, dripping pools onto floor.

Lidan shut the door.

Her pulse hammered in her throat and she put her back to it, dropping the latch into place with a flick of her wrist.

Loge stepped forward and she met him, his hands at her waist, her arms wrapping around his neck. She kissed him hard, pressing her body along the length of his, feeling every inch of him against her. Her trembling fingers danced down the length of his neck, feeling the muscles underneath as his hand cupped her cheek, his thumb brushing back slick tendrils of hair from her face. She traced her hands across his chest and pulled at his shirt, fighting to unbuckle weapon belts until they dropped heavily to the floor, discarded in the fever of questing hands and hungry lips.

She stripped off his saturated shirt while he fought the laces on the front of a gown not made to come off quickly. He soon abandoned any semblance of care and broke them, snapping the threads and releasing her from the heavy fabric. The dress fell away, leaving a thin shift, and he faltered, his eyes darting, as if suddenly unsure and unable to take her all in, hesitating on the brink.

Lidan didn't pause. She stepped forward and kissed him again, pushing him backward to the bed, step by step, until he sat on its edge, wide eyes watching her as she climbed into his lap. Uncertain hands became sure again as they lifted the skirt of her shift, his fingers running over her thigh as she unfastened his trousers.

'You sure?' he whispered.

'Yes.' She moaned as he pulled her closer and gasped when he brought her down to him. Their bodies met, and short, shallow breaths mixed with desperate, urgent need, drowning everything else out. Then Loge shifted, picking her up and rolling her onto her back, moving between her legs, strong but trembling, his movements cautious but certain, somehow still in control while her grip on herself slipped.

He wanted this as much as she did, despite the risks and a terrible, deep-seated knowledge that they were running out of time. She wound her fingers through his hair and pressed her lips against his, demanding more without saying a word, pulling him closer, consumed by need. Lidan didn't care about the future, she didn't even care about tomorrow; all she wanted was now, and for this moment to last forever.

Nothing mattered but this. The world shrank until nothing else existed but the tiny space between them, everything beyond vanishing into insignificance. She committed it all to memory—his smell, his hands sliding across her skin and his body moving with hers, how the muscles in his shoulders flexed as he leaned down to kiss her, the tiny sounds he made against her lips, taking the very breath from her lungs.

She bound it all up and fell, holding it to her, so no matter the colour of the coming dawn, she would always have this moment scored in her heart. The world beyond that door could crumble and burn, as long as she had this.

CHAPTER FORTY-FOUR

Tingalla, Tolak Range, the South Lands

Morning broke with a shaft of warm light stretching across the bed, and Lidan curled against Loge's chest as he slept. She didn't dare move. She didn't want to break the spell holding the small room in this single place in time. This was a moment she had to keep sheltered, held close where it could not be touched or changed, could not be lost or broken. This was another moment she would hold for as long as her memory allowed, because the world outside was full of people who wanted to tear it all away.

The storm had passed long ago, washing Tingalla clean, leaving dripping eaves and chittering birds in its wake. She listened to the small sounds of the morning and relished the newest of them; the steady beat of Loge's heart.

For a breath she wondered if they'd made a terrible mistake, and her heart gave an uncomfortable, heavy thud. There might yet be unseen consequences to this, but no matter how she turned it, she couldn't bring herself to think it a wrong to be set right or and evil to be cast out. It was right. This was where she was meant to be, where she felt safe and strong. Not with Loge standing in front of her, shielding her from the world, but with him at her side, like two halves of an indivisible whole.

But they weren't whole. They weren't joined, at least not in the eyes of the clan or her father. She let out a slow breath and sat up, glancing at the door as though Erlon might burst through at any moment.

Her father might send her away. He might divorce her from her people and sentence her to a life in a strange land with a man she didn't know, but for now, this moment was hers, and he would never take that from her. Not for as long as she drew breath.

A hand pressed gently against her back, fingers sliding up her spine. Lidan tucked her knees into her chest and looked over her shoulder, smiling at Loge.

'Morning,' he murmured.

'Morning,' she replied. 'You didn't talk in your sleep.'

'I was very tired.' His knowing smile mirrored hers.

'Oh really?'

'Really. I only talk when I'm restless, and I had no need to be restless.'

She turned and lay on her stomach, one arm draped across his chest, her chin resting on her hand. She was mere inches from his lips, and a burning fire in her belly urged her to kiss him. 'And here I was thinking something was wrong.'

'No, everything is very right.' Loge's hand shifted from stoking her back to drawing her into the kiss she wanted so badly, needed so viscerally. Her body responded, and she moved closer, skin against skin, legs entwining—

A door banged against a wall.

Lidan screamed, Loge swore, and someone began talking so quickly their words strung into an incomprehensible ramble.

'Oh my goodness! Witness, I'm so sorry, I should have checked but there's—something's happening, oh my—I'm so sorry, I don't know— Witness, I need you, please, I'm *so* sorry!'

Lidan whipped around as Loge slipped off the far side of the bed, down into the gap between the frame and the wall, snatching at his discarded trousers and fighting his way into them. Vee stood near the back door, the one she used to bring food and take away laundry, her eyes averted and her whole body shaking as if she'd seen a dead man walking.

'Vee?' Lidan had expected to see one of her parents, or perhaps even Siman, come to reprimand one of his rangers for bedding the daari's daughter.

'I'm sorry, Witness. I need you to come with me.'

Loge emerged from behind the bed and began scooping weapons and clothes from the floor while Lidan collected a blanket and attempted to wrap herself.

'What is it, Vee? What's happened? Who sent you?'

'No one. You just need to come. Please. It's very bad.' Vee glanced at Lidan then, her eyes wide with fear, her fingers clutching at her apron and holding it up in front of her belly as though it might shield her from whatever had frightened her.

'Can you—' Lidan looked around herself. None of her discarded clothes would do. Last night's dress was a ripped ruin dangling in Loge's hands, the fabric caked in mud to the knees. 'Can you throw me some clothes, Vee?'

The tine-woman snapped into action, as if the request triggered an instinct that even her fear couldn't override. She hurried to Lidan's chest and hanging frame, collecting trousers, a shirt, a jerkin, and Lidan's usual leather harness for her knives and sword. Lidan frowned and threw a questioning glance at Loge, registering the tension in his face as he shrugged on his shirt then extracted her knife and sword from the scabbard and belt sheath he'd gathered from the floor. Evidently, she was going to need them.

She slid off the bed and hurried into the clothes Vee pushed toward her, the woman turning to collect the soiled dress from Loge, before hurrying away without a word. When Vee emerged again, she stood trembling in the centre of the room, her eyes darting as if she didn't know where to look.

'What's happened, Vee?' Lidan pressed.

'Best you see for yourself, Witness. I've not got the words to describe it.'

Lidan and Loge hurried out the front door as soon as they were dressed, following the frantic tine-woman along the timber boards toward the open area near Daari Erlon's accommodations.

The screams reached Lidan's ears before her eyes found their source—Farah leaned against Erlon for a moment, then whirled around, crying, keening, fists balled at her side before she turned to beat them against her husband's chest.

'Ehran!' she screamed, wild eyes searching, her back bowing as she choked on a sob and railed against Erlon's arms. 'Where *is* he? EHRAN!'

Lidan's heart jumped, her fingers trembling as she slowed her steps and absorbed the chaos in the common area. People ran frantically from one building to another—rangers, tines, trades people, her half-mothers, the older girls—muttering and shouting, pointing and shaking their heads. They were searching, desperately hunting through the living quarters. The same frenetic activity pulsed through the larger common in front of the hall, and beyond, people shouted about horses and gathering riders.

'Vee?' Lidan breathed, Loge at her shoulder running his hand through his hair as he always did when he was uncertain and anxious.

'Your father needs you, Witness. Please, come.'

They followed Vee across the small common and Erlon spotted them, fighting to hold Farah upright as he turned. 'Liddy! Have you seen him?'

'Who, Da?' she asked, the throat tightening around the question to which she already knew the answer.

'Ehran. Have you seen him? Was he with you?'

'No, I haven't seen him since he went to bed last night... I... what's happened?' She struggled to put thoughts into words, questions lost before she could get them out of her mouth.

'He's gone,' Farah said, and while she stared at Lidan, she wasn't sure her half-mother actually saw her with those stricken, unfocused eyes. 'Ehran is gone.'

'Daari, sir.' Harran Daylin appeared with Bridie at his side, a shawl around her shoulders and her face wan with worry. 'We've searched the hall and our side of the village. No one has seen him.'

'Da!' Elva shouted from across the common, running toward them. 'Da, Lucija is gone too.'

'Fucking *what*?' Erlon staggered as Farah fell into him.

Both children were gone? Lidan didn't know where to turn first, what to do, what to say. What could she say? Her lips moved, but nothing came out as Loge's hand moved from the head of one of his hatchets to the small of her back, worry creasing his face.

'I can't find her at all,' Elva continued, throwing her arms wide, exasperated, and Bridie curled her arm around the girl's shoulders. 'All the other girls are counted and in your rooms. She could be hiding but I looked all the usual places she might go. Marrit is checking the stables with Jessah but I don't think—'

'I'm sure they are just off playing somewhere,' Sellan said, her voice cutting the confusion, calm and unfazed, almost nonchalant.

Lidan spun to her mother's voice and found her standing near the door to her quarters with her arms folded loosely. She didn't seem concerned, she seemed irritated, as though all the noise had interrupted her morning for no good reason at all.

'Mam, if they were playing, someone would have found them by now,' Lidan countered, finding her voice.

Her mother shrugged. 'Children are crafty creatures. I'm sure this fuss is all for nothing. They will appear.'

How could she know that? Lidan narrowed her eyes, but before she could speak, someone came running from the direction of the gatehouse.

'Sir!' It was Torren, breathless and sweating in the humid morning. The sun was already cresting the walls, and the saturated ground steamed around them. 'I've had news from the gates. Riders left last night. Seems the guards were either paid off or overcome by force.'

'What riders?' Erlon shifted Farah in his arms, and Bridie moved to collect her half-mother against her chest. Lidan marvelled at the girl, who seemed to morph into a woman who stood strong in the face of the turmoil around them. Erlon motioned to Kaito, his tine-man, who ran toward the large hut where the daari had been sleeping. 'Which way did they go?'

Torren shook his head. 'We don't know, but we're finding out.'

Lidan surveyed the people hurrying past, her mother's dismissive words forgotten. She stepped closer to Loge. 'If riders left last night, then someone is missing.'

Loge nodded and they headed toward the large common space between the hall and the gates. 'We can call everyone into the common for a head count,' he suggested, 'but the stables might give us a faster answer.'

They jogged toward the large building, dodging running people as they went. The stables were bursting with life, hands and rangers shouting and pointing, looking under blanket piles and in cupboards, raking out hay from stalls and climbing into the lofts high above to search the stacks.

Lidan snagged the arm of a senior hand jogging past her. 'Do you know where we can find the stable master?'

'You've found him,' replied the man. He was shorter than her, and well built, like a stout pony rather than a rangy high-country steed. 'Stable Master Omarn. How can I help you?'

He raised his brows and drew out the final word, giving Lidan a moment to realise she hadn't introduced herself. Not everyone here recognised her on sight.

'I'm Lidan Tolak, Witness of the Blood to the Tolak heir.' She pointed up the length of the stable building. 'Can you tell me which horses are missing? Riders left last night, so there will have been empty stalls this morning.'

Omarn sucked at his teeth, as if the answer weren't as easily given as she had hoped. 'Witness, I need to check.'

They followed the stable master, weaving through a press of bodies and stamping horses. It wasn't until she turned to suggest to Loge they should search the Daylin stables that she realised he had fallen behind. She craned to see him through the crowd, shuffling past a stable hand with a saddle to find him standing still outside a line of empty stalls.

He pointed at the open door in front of him. 'Who had their horses stabled here?'

Omarn whistled and shouted, and a young girl appeared, no older than Elva and Marrit. 'Pria, who was in this part of the block?'

Pria whipped a small bound volume from her back trouser pocket and leafed through pages. 'Daari Merk Marsaw and his company. They were here last night when I finished my shift, but they were gone by the time I got in this morning.'

'That motherfucker...' Loge growled.

Burning heat rose in Lidan's chest, and her vision began to swim. 'Are you sure? The horses haven't just been moved?'

'No, I'm sure. See this?' Pria pointed to a small disk of fired clay hanging from a hook on the door of the stall. 'It marks groups of horses who belong together, so they don't get confused or given to the wrong rider. This symbol was assigned to Daari Merk in the register, and the others here match his companions. Five horses all up.'

Lidan didn't know what she'd expected to find in the stables, but it wasn't this. In truth, she had thought to find the northern travellers and their horses missing, not Merk, who had just last night suggested a matching proposal for her and his son.

Or had he?

She had seen him talking to her father, but Merk had put Erlon off, deferring the conversation until today. All in good time, he had said. He hadn't seemed overly excited by the prospect of a deal… in fact, he'd appeared a little exasperated by Erlon's enthusiasm. Had he just been playing for time?

'Liddy, we need to tell your father and check the Daylin stables,' Loge pressed, his hand on her elbow, eyes scanning the stable.

'Pria, can you tell me where the northern trader's horses are?' Lidan asked quickly, before other thoughts crowded her mind and panic stole her words. Had Merk taken Ehran? Why? What was he doing?

'They're up in the northern end of this stable block. I just came back from checking that end. No mounts unaccounted for there.'

'Thank you, Pria. Stable Master, I need some hands to check across…' Loge's words washed over Lidan and faded into the noise pulsing around her. She heard them, but she didn't feel them, barely registering what he was saying. 'Liddy, we have to go…'

She nodded and followed him into the morning, unsure how in the name of the ancestors she would break this news without ruining her father completely.

Lidan and Loge crossed the common toward a knot of people and horses. Ran and his northern companions were there, watching at a distance while Aelish muttered to them, very likely translating what was said in the southern tongue. Each of them wore deep frowns of concern and as Lidan approached, she locked eyes with Ran, wondering what thoughts were spinning in his head. She hoped he'd stay out of the way and keep to himself, but something in his pale blue eyes told her she wouldn't be so lucky.

'Lidan,' her mother hissed suddenly from behind her shoulder. Sellan wrapped a hand around her daughter's arm before she reached Erlon, pulling her back from the group while Loge kept moving.

'What?' Lidan snarled. She didn't have time for this. She needed to speak with her father and find out what he knew. She didn't want to tell him about Merk, but she had no choice, and the mere thought of giving voice to that knowledge ignited a headache behind her eyes.

'If the boy is gone, perhaps it's for the best.' Sellan glanced around.

Was she nervous? Lidan frowned and waited.

'Let him go,' her mother growled through clenched teeth.

Lidan leaned away as the words sunk in. 'You can't be serious? I made an oath to protect him!'

'And now he's gone, he's no longer your responsibility!'

'That's not how it works, Mam! He's barely older than a baby—he doesn't deserve this.' Lidan's top lip curled in disgust. 'And neither do I.'

'Lidan—'

'Back off!' Lidan snapped and yanked her arm free of Sellan's grasp, pulling the woman into an awkward stumble. The shock on Sellan's face was momentary, a blink and she would have missed it, before it was masked by a perfectly passive expression and a dead, emotionless gaze.

'Very well. Have it your way.' Sellan looked her up and down. 'I had thought you stronger than that.'

Lidan buried her mother's acidic words and spun back to where Loge stood just shy of Erlon's shoulder. 'Da! I have to go after Ehran. I think I know what's happened.'

Erlon turned away from Siman, their discussion falling to silence. It was almost as if he didn't recognise her at first, grief and worry blinding him to the sight of his own daughter's face. 'What do you know?'

Lidan gestured with an open hand at the crowd gathered around them, ignoring how her fingers trembled. 'Who's missing? Who isn't here, offering his men to help in the search?'

Erlon scowled and scanned the common. 'Merk.'

'He didn't come here to build an alliance. He came here to rip the heart out of our clan. He got close to you, offering friendship and answers to the war, then stole the thing you hold most dear.' She forced those last words out. They hurt to say, but it didn't make them any less true. 'He's taken Ehran.'

'But why?' Erlon's brow creased, anguish deepening the lines of his face to canyons that might have been carved by rivers of tears. Did he realise how easily he'd been played? He'd been so quick to grasp at any offer of friendship, any opportunity to end the war, even one offered by the hand of an enemy, that he'd failed to notice the knife before it slipped past his guard and cut straight into his heart.

'For Yorrell,' Lidan replied, her heart thumping hard and fast in her throat. She ached to put her hand in Loge's, to take comfort in his presence, but instead she gripped her knives and squeezed, strangling the handles until her palms burned with the pressure. Confusion transformed into fury and Erlon clenched his shaking fingers into huge fists.

'Siman,' he began, and Lidan put a hand on his arm.

'I'm going after them—'

Erlon took her hand in his, his grip like steel bands, squeezing until her bones ground together. 'The other rangers will handle this.'

She twisted away from her father's grip, just as she had with her mother. 'No!' Her shout echoed across the common, and those nearest stopped and stared. Aelish fell silent, as did the cluster of rangers behind Siman.

Her father glared, barely controlled rage simmering behind a wall of affected calm. She was provoking a beast, but she had no choice. He would hear her, and he would listen.

'I will not sit by and let others do the thing I swore to. This is *my* oath, *my* responsibility. I will find him, and Lucija, and I *will* bring them back.'

CHAPTER FORTY-FIVE

Tingalla, Tolak Range, the South Lands

'Who's she talking about?' Ran muttered from the corner of his mouth, holding his hand over his lips, hoping to direct his words toward Aelish without attracting attention from the southerners.

'Merk Marsaw, one of the other clan leaders. He was here last night but he's vanished apparently. Lidan thinks he's taken the children on behalf of someone called Yorrell.'

'Who's Yorrell?' he asked.

'I don't fucking know!' Aelish growled, her face twisting with frustration. 'I'm not an expert on the South Lands! I only trade with the Tolak.'

'Sorry,' Ran muttered and eyed the gathering. Iridia's presence sat heavy in the back of his mind, waiting in a dark corner since last night when Lidan had reacted to her speaking into his mind.

Waking up to the chaotic search for the daari's youngest children had done nothing to help his hangover, and he was relying on Aelish more than he would have liked to make sense of the South Land clans and their politics. He blinked and turned his face from the rising sun, pretending the light didn't make his head ache like it had been hit by a forge hammer, or that his mouth didn't taste like he'd been eating horse shit in his sleep.

Despite the evident anguish on the faces of the southerners and the very real grief of the daari's wife, Ran's mind swirled with ideas. Thoughts began to coalesce into plans as soon as he'd realised something terrible had taken place in the night, all of them leading to a point where he could use this awful event to his advantage.

As much as it pained him to admit it, at the end of the day, he didn't care about these people. As Iridia had said, they owed him nothing. They had, he would admit, given him and his companions shelter and refrained from interrogating them too heavily, but he knew that was only thanks to circumstance, not some altruistic goodwill or customary hospitality. Had Erlon not been distracted by the marriage of his daughter, Ran doubted they would have been afforded such a reprieve.

Ran leaned toward Brit. 'Do you trust me?'

The watcher studied him for a moment. 'Not as far as I could throw you.'

'Bullshit.' Ran smirked. 'Play along, then?'

Brit nodded, exchanging a glance with Aelish that said a thousand things Ran couldn't hear. He didn't care much about that either. He had a goal to achieve, and fussing over what people thought of him wasn't going to help him get there. To that end, he had to give these people a reason to not only trust him, but to be in his debt.

Ran took a step forward and cleared his throat. 'Daari, please excuse my intrusion, but one of my companions is an excellent tracker—one of the best I've ever known. And we have trained fighters among us. We'd be happy to help the search.'

He heard Eian mutter something under his breath, and Brit shifted his weight as if suddenly uncomfortable. Erlon turned, scanning the northerners through the fog of his emotions before carefully studying Ran for what felt like an age.

Come on. Take it. Let me help you... he whispered to himself, sensing Iridia's approval as a warm shift in his mind. She knew where he was going with this, even if the others didn't.

'I'm not sure...' Erlon began, looking back at Lidan. For a moment Ran was certain he would refuse. Panic rose in his chest like a hot wave and he scrambled.

'At the very least let us accompany the Witness in her search. The more eyes you have out there, the better, especially if this gets nasty.' He gestured to the common and the people around them. 'There's a conflict here I can't begin to understand, and if what Lidan says is true, these men have taken your children as a part of it. What if this is all some elaborate ruse designed to leave you exposed? What if they anticipate you emptying this compound of every rider you have and scattering them across the countryside in the search, only to attack while you wait for news? You can't spare warriors from the defence of this village. Maintaining a garrison here is as important as searching for the children, and we are more use to you out there than in here. Think of it as my way of repaying Witness Lidan for saving my life.'

There. He'd dropped the lure.

Now to see if they would take the bait.

'Da,' Lidan began, addressing her father without glancing at Ran for more than a heartbeat, disappointing and intriguing him in the same moment. 'Did you give me this sword to defend your heir, or is it nothing more than a pretty plaything?'

There was a sharp intake of breath from a woman behind Lidan, a woman who looked remarkably like her but with milk-pale skin and auburn hair. They shared the same green eyes, and Iridia's presence shivered as the woman glared at Lidan's back.

'Every second we stand here debating is another second Ehran is closer to Yorrell.' Lidan looked at Ran with a gaze full of doubt before continuing. 'And if the northerners think they can help, then let them try.'

That was true, Ran conceded. The longer they waited, the harder it would be to pick up the trail, and so much of his plan relied on finding these children that even he saw the folly in delaying.

'Let me do this, Da. Let me bring Ehran and Lucija home.'

When Erlon finally nodded, Ran tried not to sigh out the breath he'd been holding or let his shoulders drop with relief. Instead, he turned to Brit and nodded. 'Watcher Doon, if you would be so kind?'

Brit shot another glance at the others, cleared his throat and nodded at Lidan. 'You reckon he's gone on horseback?'

'I do,' she pointed at the stables. 'His horses are gone, and riders left in the night. They'll make for friendly territory, so either west to the Marsaw coast, or north toward Namjin.'

Ran had no clue what she was talking about, but he assumed they were clan lands that bordered this village. He saw Brit nod again and the watcher pointed at the wall around the compound. 'I need to get up there.'

They set off for the gatehouse at a jog; Brit, Ran and the one called Loge, following Lidan up the timber stairs inside. Ran emerged into daylight to find Loge staring at him, not quite with the baleful glare he'd pinned him with previously, but a distinct distaste that wasn't even barely disguised.

Unsure of what else to do, Ran stuck out his hand. 'We haven't officially met. Ran Harroe.'

The man looked slowly down at Ran's outstretched hand, then back up at his face. There was suspicion there, deep seated and smouldering, and Ran tried to ignore the gleam along the sharp edges of Loge's hatchets. Had Lidan told him about their encounter in the place between? Or was he just a naturally cautious, if not slightly intimidating man who saw Ran as a threat or a nuisance?

'Loge Baker,' he replied, clasping Ran by the forearm. 'You think you can help?'

'We'll do all we can. It's the least we *can* do, after everything Lidan and her father have offered us since we arrived.'

Loge gave a sort of grunt and released his arm, turning to where Lidan stood with Brit a few feet away at the edge of the rampart. She was pointing off to the west, but Brit shook his head.

'Unless they got that bridge up and down on their own, or had someone to help them, they didn't go that way,' said the watcher, narrowing his eyes at the river far below. Brit shifted his gaze, his eyes scanning along the water to another bridge that crossed the angry brown churn to the north. 'But that bridge is still down.'

'How can you…?' Lidan began, squinting and leaning over the railing, trying to make out what Brit had seen. She turned a questioning gaze on Ran, and he shrugged.

'Told you he was good. Best eyes in—' He caught himself before he said the word "Usmein". '—our town guard.'

If Lidan noticed his stumble, she didn't remark on it, instead gesturing to the bridge below. 'If they went that way, the trails lead into the tablelands and contested territory with the Namjin. That's Yorrell's clan. If they've taken Ehran and Lucija that way, they're going to meet someone.'

'How long ago did they leave?' Brit asked as Ran began to calculate distance and travel time across terrain that looked much the same as that south of the Ice Towers. He didn't fancy heading back into the bushland or endless gorges full of shadows and dark places for the dradur to hide, but if the payoff was as he anticipated, the risk was worth the reward. A part of him recoiled at the cold, heartless bastard he had become, the person who was willing to use the abduction of children for his own ends, but at least he wasn't the arsehole who'd stolen the children in the first place.

'Some time in the deep dark before dawn,' Loge replied. He nodded at the tablelands, shrouded in a blanket of low cloud that hung over its sharp cliffs like a soft, white cloth. 'They would've moved fast across the grasslands, but it'll be slow going in there, even if they have a map or a guide.'

Brit chewed his lip in thought. 'We need to go now, or risk losing them in there. If we get a rain like last night, it'll wash the tracks out of the mud.'

Lidan and Loge shared a look Ran couldn't read, and the man nodded. 'I'll get Jessah and the others.' Then he looked at Ran, his mouth set in a grim line of grudging acceptance. 'Get your people ready. We won't be waiting for stragglers.'

They left the village without ceremony or fuss. The only recognition of their departure the solemn presence of Daari Erlon watching from the entry to the hall; his lone, broad frame filling the doorway in stoic silence that Ran found deeply unnerving. There was something in this man that reminded him of his own father—undeniably wedded to tradition and duty, preferring a small boy as his heir rather than the capable, determined daughter standing right in front of him.

Aelish whispered snippets of what she'd learned from overheard conversations the night before; tales of Lidan's fight against the dradur, and her defiance of her mother, who Ran guessed was the woman he'd seen in the open yard of the compound. There was something about that woman too, something he couldn't place. His sense of Iridia had changed when she had appeared, shifting from calm observation to fearful, anxious shivering for a reason he could not name.

It frustrated him no end that he couldn't ask Iridia about it. The risk was too high, given Lidan seemed to detect his conversations with the ghost, even more strongly than Aelish had—as if she heard something at the edge of her consciousness but could not make out the words. Ran reasoned both women had to have some sort of magic in them, buried deep and likely very weak, but present enough that they sensed his magic moving in the air.

Brit and Torren led the search, scouting ahead and watching the trail. There were fifteen in all—ten southerners and Ran's group of five from the north—and after crossing the river, they fanned out into the grasslands, searching for any sign the abductors had changed course or doubled back.

He felt a familiar tingle on his skin as Eian unfurled his Sight, and wondered what good it would do them other than to discover the trails of any dradur or unidentified magic users among the abductors, but Eian said nothing of what he saw as the day wore on, keeping his thoughts to himself and quiet, murmured conversations with his partner. His own Sight revealed nothing, and Zarad made no mention of any frequency magic present in the air. For all their power, the three of them were next to useless. As they moved into the mouth of a great, soaring canyon, he pulled his magic in and watched Lidan's back as she rode ahead on her rangy black horse, staring for long enough that she turned and glared at him over her shoulder.

'Are you sure?' Loge asked, his voice harsh in the anxious silence that had fallen over the searchers.

Brit nodded and threw a questioning look at Torren, who echoed the gesture. 'Aye, they passed this way.' The watcher tilted his head toward the canyon. 'Five horses in single file.'

'We're a good half day behind, maybe more, but they're in there,' Torren agreed. He sat on his horse with the ease of a man born in the saddle. Ran envied him that. He'd enjoyed riding in his childhood but four years in the Keep had stripped him of his conditioning, leaving him saddle-sore and aching after weeks of travel. He'd never admit it out loud, but he'd gladly never climb into a saddle again if given a choice.

Lidan glanced around and took a deep breath, the leather of her saddle creaking as she shifted her weight. For all her outward strength, she seemed deeply afraid. 'We need to make up time if we're going to catch them. We'll have to travel through the night, but how we'll manage that without torches, I have no idea.'

Silence fell on the group, none of them with anything to offer as a suggestion or alternative. Then Zarad cleared his throat beside Ran, and he glanced over his shoulder.

'We have a way of making light,' he whispered, and Ran's heart gave a heavy, uncomfortable thud against his ribs.

'I'm not sure that's a good idea...'

'Give trust to receive it, mate.' Zarad nodded at Lidan and the southern riders emerging from the trees. 'You want them to trust you, you have to give a little to them.'

Fuck... Ran sighed and licked his lips. His mouth was suddenly very dry, and it had nothing to do with the sapping humidity. He was absolutely sure Zarad was right and absolutely sure this could only go one of two ways. These people would either lose their minds as soon as his magic flared to life, or they would accept it with ease and possibly a little awe. There would be no in-between. *Shit, shit, shit...*

Do it, Iridia said, pressing her will and giving him a confidence he couldn't muster from within. Lidan's gaze snapped to him immediately and he shrugged.

'We may have a solution to that particular problem...'

Her eyes narrowed and Loge's hand went to the head of his gleaming axe. Ran sighed again. *Fuck it...*

He drew his magic up and pooled it in his hand, letting it seep through his skin until a ball of oscillating blue light swirled above his palm. Someone swore, and weapons appeared in ready hands, horses stamping and snorting as their riders squeezed their thighs against their flanks, feeding anxiety and fear into their mounts.

Ran looked up from his ball of energy and stared straight at Lidan. 'We'll light the way if it helps you find your siblings.' It was all he could do to ignore the collection of arrows trained at his head.

Lidan, however, hardly flinched. She'd known, of course. She'd seen him use his power the day they'd met. She'd seen him in the place between and knew he wasn't ordinary. She'd said as much the night before, an accusation he had denied only to admit it in the light of day. She'd known he had secrets and he could almost taste her fury at being unable to unpick them from the tapestry of lies he'd woven around himself. They stared at each other for what felt like an eternity, her emerald gaze bearing down on him with a weight he could not see or shake.

With a slow, steady hand, she waved the rider's weapons away, and gradually the stone tipped arrows lowered, and the knives and axes rested against the rider's knees. Still, Ran's magic throbbed and swirled in his hand, cold as ice and burning. Lidan nudged her horse forward until their mounts stood together, his leg mere inches from hers, her face a mask carved from stone.

'How many of you can do this?' she asked, her voice low and steady, only the slightest waver betraying her tightly controlled emotions.

'Three. Myself, Zarad and Eian. We each have skills the others do not, but we can all light the way and bring you closer to your brother and sister. *If* you'll let us...' He let that last statement hang in the air, full of promise and threat.

Without them, she was cooked. Without their magic, there was no way they would ever catch the abductors before they reached safe harbour, and no way this ended in anything but failure. But he needed this to succeed as much as she did. They were relying on each other, a reality neither of them was comfortable with, but there was nothing to be done.

'When full dark falls, one of you will lead the way. The others will be guarded.' She had measured him and decided in that moment that she would trust him, despite his deceptions. He knew he would answer for them when this was over, but for now she would let him run. 'A single misstep, and you're all dead—we won't hesitate, understood?'

'Understood.' He spooled his power back as she turned her horse away.

CHAPTER FORTY-SIX

Western Tablelands, Namjin range, the South Lands

The smell hit Lidan first, stinging her nose and making her eyes stream as she held her hand over her mouth and gagged. The vile, acrid stench coated the inside of her mouth, clinging like the flesh of an over-ripe fruit.

'Oh, fuck that,' Brit cursed, leaning over the side of the track and retching.

They'd been walking the horses, with Brit, Ran and Lidan at the head of the group, the way forward lit by the cold blue fire of Ran's magic. The others followed behind in a tight cluster, Zarad and Eian lending their own faint light to the journey. The air in the canyon was still and hot, sweat beading on Lidan's brow and the palms of her hands, with not a wisp of breeze to cool her skin or dispel the foul odour wafting from nearby.

The sweet, putrid, reek of death turned her stomach as she peered through the gloom. The track ahead seemed clear, but only as far as Ran's light reached. She shuffled past the northern watcher and handed him Theus's reins.

'Stay here. Get the others to set a watch.' She turned to Ran; his face was lit from below, and the deep shadows drew his features into a gaunt mask of concern. She buried her immediate instinct to care what he was thinking. He'd chosen to come on this search, something she wouldn't have allowed had she felt she had a choice. He still hadn't come clean about his appearance in the white place, and it irked her that he held fast to his lie. So, if she had to suffer his presence here, he could earn his keep. 'Come with me.'

Ran didn't nod or reply, but he passed his reins to Brit and left the man with the others gathered behind him in a wary knot, lit by a weird blue glow. Lidan's hand found her knife and she stepped up the track, her breath loud in her ears, the sounds of the night falling away as if the small creatures didn't dare move any closer to the source of the smell.

'I know that smell,' Ran whispered.

She did too, but as his light expanded beside her, the ball of magic growing larger, she glanced away before it blinded her. A burning sting bloomed at the edge of her awareness as his magic moved. She'd seen magic before, heard it cut the air when the Crone snapped blue lightning from her fingers, but she'd never felt it coiled in her gut like a snake slowly waking from the cold.

Ran was different to the old woman in ways Lidan couldn't quite unravel, yet filled with the same self-assured confidence in his abilities. She was sure if given half a chance he could conquer the world.

But now was not the time.

Ehran and Lucija needed her. They were lost, probably terrified. She squeezed the hilt of her knife and closed herself from the images flickering to life in her mind. She didn't want to think on what awaited when they finally found them. She didn't dare.

They had to get out alive—all of them. She had to get them back to her father. She couldn't let what happened to Abbi happen to Ehran or Lucija. That could not and *would not* be their fate, not while she had breath left to fight.

'Not too much,' she hissed as his magic illuminated the bush further, pushing back the shadows. 'You want us to be seen?'

'No, I don't—'

She glared over her shoulder, then lowered her hand toward the ground. His light receded and together they sank into a crouch and continued up the track. 'When are you going to tell me the truth?'

'Is this really the best time?' he snarled through his teeth.

'Oh? Would you rather have this conversation back there, with an audience?'

Ran gave a half shrug. 'I suppose not, but I don't know what else I can tell you.'

Lidan rolled her eyes. 'Who you really are would be a start.'

He growled, fatigue and the heat wearing at his patience, as it had been chipping away at hers all day. She was on edge and ready to snap, like a bow string drawn taught and held for far too long. She would break soon, if something didn't change.

'I've told you and your father all you need to know. Anything more would put my mission at risk, and I'm not going to keep repeating myself.'

Something crashed through the bush and they whirled to face the noise, a bright lightning bolt of magic crackling between Ran's fingers as Lidan's knives sang from their sheaths and spun in her hands. The sound thumped away from them through the undergrowth, up the canyon, and into the night.

Lidan willed her heart to slow, and reached out to touch Ran's forearm. His skin was clammy and hot where he had rolled the sleeves of his shirt back to his elbows.

'It's just a bouncer,' she whispered.

Slowly, the muscles in his arm relaxed and the magic faded. He'd stepped forward, angling himself to the side with both hands up, ready to attack or defend. He returned his power to the ball of light and she thought she saw him wince. How long could he keep this up? What toll was it taking on him and the other two lighting the way for the group on the track?

'Are you all right?' she asked quietly, the question a step toward familiarity she wasn't sure she was ready to take.

'I'm fine,' he muttered. 'Fuck, it's hot. Is it always this hot? How do you stand it?'

She shrugged and turned back to the track, hiding the smile playing on her lips. 'I suppose I'm just used to it. But it's disgusting in here with no breeze. This heat will drain you faster than a fist fight with ten men at midday.'

'It never gets this hot at home,' he murmured, lifting his hand higher to throw the light further.

'Ugh.' Lidan's throat contracted and she bit down on the urge to vomit. The smell was infinitely worse here, and she blinked hard, her eyes stinging. 'Over here.'

'Is that…?'

'Ngaru…' she ground out.

The corpse lay crumpled at the base of a tree just off the side of the track, dark ichor staining the sandy soil at her feet.

Ran nodded. 'I thought I recognised it. The burn at the edge of the stink.'

'I was hoping I was wrong.' She hadn't been though. That smell was one that never left, never really washed off, never faded from dreams or nightmares or the silent moments of wandering thought in the bright light of day.

Lidan crouched and poked at the body with her knife, turning its head to reveal the wide, seeping wound that had torn the thing's spine apart and almost severed the head completely.

'Was it the folk we're chasing?' Ran asked, standing at her back with his light orb shifting the shadows around them.

'I'd say so.' The wounds were made by a weapon, not another beast—that much was certain. 'There aren't any big predators around here that'd kill a beast like this and leave the corpse. Serpents take their kills back to their dens.'

'Serpents?' Ran's voice rose with panic that he caught with a cough. 'You mean snakes?'

Lidan snorted. 'Sometimes. A big python will take down prey this size, but it'd still be here trying to swallow it. A dragon would carry it home, but there aren't any around here big enough to do that. And they don't generally carry knives or axes.'

She stood and scanned the night.

'Dragons. There are dragons down here too?'

She eyed him. So, he'd had an encounter with a dragon? She wondered for a moment if that was the trouble in the Pass Aelish had mentioned, then let it go. 'There'll be beaded rock dragons and some leafy tree dragons, but they won't be any bigger than my da's dogs. And they won't come near something that stinks this badly. This—' she pointed her knife at the body of the ngaru, '—was the work of people. Merk's party, I'd wager.'

'They must be close then,' he nodded, chewing his lip and glancing around as if their mere mention might draw them from the shadows.

'A few hours ahead, I think. They'll have stopped for the night.' Lidan sheathed her blades, ignoring the anxious hammer of her heart.

The lack of other bodies in the area was a good sign; they were unlikely to have been attacked by more than one ngaru and the children were probably perfectly safe, but how long that would remain the case, she couldn't tell. She couldn't afford to let Merk met up with Yorrell or any other rangers who might be waiting in the depths of the tablelands. With only fifteen in their group, they would lose the advantage of numbers quickly and stand little chance of rescuing Ehran or Lucija. She banished the lump of fear from her throat and turned back down the track.

'Should we make camp, too?' Ran asked, stumbling in a shadow and following behind.

Lidan shook her head, glancing back as she did. He was exhausted, that much was obvious in the dark smudges under his eyes. 'We can't. We need to get as close as we can and scout the camp before dawn. That's our best chance of breaking in and getting the little ones out. If we wait, we lose the advantage of early morning darkness.'

'I wish I could disagree with that,' he murmured. 'Fuck, it's hot.'

She stifled a smile, the part of her that despised him for a liar taking a step back for a moment in the close, steamy night. If he wasn't such a deceitful shit, she might actually learn to like him.

Lidan and Loge crept through the bush, careful footsteps placed lightly amongst the undergrowth. It was dark, the only light filtering through the trees from the moon above and a low burning cooking fire up ahead. They kept clear of the track, circling to the west of the little creek-side camp and quietly picking their way around tumbled piles of boulders. The others waited back down the trail, huddled in tight amongst the trees in case the Marsaw captors took fright and decided to make an escape to the south. If they made a break northward, Lidan knew she was fucked.

Somewhere on the eastern side of the gorge, Jessah and Torren mirrored them, the four of them scouting to see how easily they might creep in and snatch Ehran and Lucija from Merk's clutches. If it all went to plan, Lidan would sneak in with Loge, extract the children and slip away into the darkness leaving no more trace than the night wind, but she couldn't do that without knowing what she faced.

'Shit,' Loge hissed in front of her, stopping dead and sinking into a low crouch.

Lidan hurried quietly to his side and peered through the trees. 'Please don't tell me...'

'There are more than five horses.' He threw a frustrated glare at the sky, his face illuminated by fire and moonlight. 'We're too late.'

Lidan's hand shook where it held her knife. Her eyes felt like they were made of sand, and she itched to rub at them, ached to lay down in the undergrowth, curl into Loge's arms and sleep, but she could do none of those things. She rammed her fatigue down and dragged up what strength she had left.

'No... we're not too late,' she said, scanning the camp through narrowed eyes. 'Whoever they met is still here, which means so are the children.' She turned from the camp and sat against a log, watching Loge as he scowled through the trees.

'I count five extra horses,' he whispered.

Ten rangers, then. That wasn't so bad. It wasn't brilliant, but they weren't outnumbered. They were fatigued though, all of them weary from a day and a night in the saddle. Ran had insisted he, Zarad and Eian needed rest, and Lidan had agreed, preferring to extinguish the eldritch lights the closer they got to the Marsaw camp. And there was no point exhausting the three of them.

'Do you think we can get in and out without a fight?' she asked.

Her chest felt tight, her breathing laboured. She'd never been this anxious before a fight, never been so strung out that she couldn't think straight or form a coherent plan. But her mind was all over the place, ripping back and forth between memories of the white place, thoughts of home, flashes of the ngaru and her father's pained expression as they had ridden out the gate. If she didn't bring Ehran and Lucija home to their parents, there would be nothing left of them but broken shells and a gaping emptiness that could never be filled.

Amongst all of it stood her mother, that cold expression on her face. "Let him go," she'd said, and the words haunted Lidan. A worse person would have followed her mother's advice. A better person wouldn't have been tempted. But had she stepped down that road, she would have lived every day knowing what she'd done, woken every morning to face the empty, soundless space left behind by children who no longer existed. She would know, as would her father and her mother and her half-mother and the guilt would have crushed her. At least this way, even if she failed, she could live whatever days she had left knowing she tried.

She had to try.

Loge shook his head and sat back on his heels. 'We need a better plan, a back-up at least.'

'There's fifteen of us and ten of them, which is a pretty even match when two of us are weighed down by the children.' She licked her chapped lips as her thoughts wound around a point she hadn't yet considered. 'But we have something they don't.'

Loge frowned, watching her eyes until he saw the plan dancing there. 'Are you sure that's a good idea? I'm really not sure that's a good idea. What if—'

Her hand touched his. 'We don't have a choice. We have to use them as a weapon, because it's our only advantage. We're guaranteed to fail otherwise. They must have known we'd follow them. They're going to be watching. This is the only chance we have.'

His lips pressed into a grim line and he looked back through the trees to the camp, then up into the sliver of sky and the dusty river of stars visible above the edges of the cliff faces. 'I don't like it.'

'Neither do I, but I can't think of anything else.'

He gave a resigned sigh. 'Right then, let's get back and sort this out before dawn gets much closer.'

Only the ancestors knew if she could convince Ran to go along with her plan, but he had inserted himself into this rescue with the supposed intention of repaying his debt to her, so he owed her one.

CHAPTER FORTY-SEVEN

Western Tablelands, Namjin range, the South Lands

Lidan laid out her plan in whispered words, drawing a faint map in the sandy soil, her work illuminated by the light of a small glowing orb in Eian's hand. They didn't dare light a fire while she was away, Nevis scowling at them when Aelish had translated Eian's suggestion that they should cook some food. Aelish had carefully translated back Nevis's opinion that it was a fucking stupid idea that would only alert the captors to their presence. Ran found he agreed with that sentiment, handing out some dried meat, flat bread and hard cheese from the saddle bags.

And so, they had waited, the southern princess eventually returning to tell them the gravity of the situation. At the sound of her wavering voice, Ran had sat up, watching her carefully, noting how the fear had changed her, and finding he rather disliked the effect. She squeezed the handles of her knives and repeatedly tucked a stray band of black hair behind her ear, her hand trembling ever so slightly. This was not the Lidan he'd seen before. But he listened to her plan, trying to ignore the strain in her voice, and glanced at Brit as she came to the end of it. The watcher shrugged, a vague gesture that told Ran nothing of what the man really thought, and he looked back at the map in the dirt. He supposed it might work, but it needed something else.

He leaned over and pointed at the edges of the gorge on either side of the camp. 'How wide is the ravine here?'

Lidan looked up and shrugged a shoulder. 'I couldn't say for sure. Why?'

'It's just...' he began, then paused, sitting back and studying the drawing. 'What if they follow us?'

'Away from the camp?' Loge asked. He stood behind Lidan with his hands on his hips, his sharp eyes trained on Ran's face.

'Yes.' Ran looked at the man then pointed up the gorge. 'If we break into the camp, then fight their warriors while someone beats a retreat with the children, we're left with one option—kill the lot of them before we can leave, or risk someone pursuing us, correct?'

Lidan's lips flattened into a frustrated line and she sat back heavily on the ground, her fingers rubbing at the bridge of her nose. 'Yes. If any of them survive the fight, they'll very likely follow us to try and reclaim the children.'

'So, you need a back-up. Something to make sure they won't follow.'

'Or we could just kill them where they stand,' the ranger named Jessah growled from where she stood watch at the edge of the light, not turning to look at them.

'You could try,' Ran conceded with a nod, 'but as Lidan said, there are more of them. And that's the ones we can see, I might add. There's no way to know if there are more nearby and no time to go looking. At least two of us will be out of the fight once we get to the little ones. Now, I don't know about you, but the last time I tried to run anywhere while carrying someone, it was quite the workout. We won't be making a fast escape.'

'If they come after us, we need some way of cutting them off,' Loge put in with a nod. 'An ambush?'

'Might work if you set something up here,' Brit pointed at a spot in the gorge, just south of the rock that marked the camp. 'It means you go in with smaller numbers, though.'

'I've got a better idea.' Zarad cleared his throat and leaned forward, a lock of his hair falling over his face. 'Ran, you remember what we did at the Pass? How we stopped the ice dragon?'

'Aye,' Ran replied, a cold shudder rippling through his body at the thought of it. Eian groaned and rolled his eyes, as if he knew exactly what his partner was about to suggest and despised the very notion. He turned away in frustration, taking his light with him, and forcing Ran to illuminate the map.

Zarad tapped a finger beside the line that indicated the western cliff face. 'There's a bend in the ravine here, where it narrows quite a bit. If I can get up the top, near the edge, and you run like dogs after a rabbit, I reckon I could bring it down behind you. We could cut them off. They wouldn't be able to get through for days, if at all.'

Ran leaned back and glanced at Lidan. She was looking up at Loge, who had his eyes trained on the sand map.

'You cannot be fucking serious...' Eian hissed, pacing the sand and staring daggers at Zarad.

'How would you bring down the cliff?' Loge asked quietly.

'Magic, mate,' Zarad smirked.

'As if I'm letting you climb up there on your own. You can barely get up a ladder without breaking something.' Eian scowled at Zarad across the group. 'And you won't have enough power to crack the rock without a loan.'

'I really have no idea what you three are talking about,' Lidan cut in. 'But if you have a way to block the gorge and stop them chasing us down, then that's better than any ambush we can mount from behind a pile of rocks.'

Jessah snorted her disapproval but Lidan didn't respond. Instead, she stared Ran and Zarad down, green eyes shimmering in the oscillating light.

'We can't do it in the dark, though,' Zarad conceded. 'I'd recommend we get in position for daybreak. Once there's light enough to see, we can put all this into motion.'

He wished he had something else to suggest, but Ran was fresh out of ideas. He liked it about as much as Lidan seemed to, her reluctance showing in the way she chewed at her thumb, staring at the map in the sand while she thought.

'This has to work,' she murmured, almost too quietly to be heard. She looked up again, glancing at each of them in turn. 'I need to know you can do this, that it *will* work, or this will all be for nothing.'

'We can do this.' Ran nodded slowly, discarding the uncertainty threatening to choke him. 'This will work, I swear. We *will* get your brother and sister back.'

'This is *not* going to work! What were you *thinking*?' Ran hissed at Zarad, following him and Eian through the darkness and the trees, several feet behind Nevis. The ranger was leading them to a steep fissure he'd found scouting the rock wall. Here, Eian and Zarad could climb to the top of the cliff and work their way north to where the gorge kicked around in a dog-leg bend. 'Eian, tell him this is never going to work.'

363

'As if he's going to listen to me,' Eian whispered. 'I've already told him. He's my partner, not my puppy.'

'You think you can pull this off then?' Ran shot back over his shoulder, thankful Nevis couldn't understand a word of common.

'Fuck no,' Eian replied sharply. 'But it's a better plan than waiting in the trees and hoping we can outfight whatever comes down the trail. Did you see those southerners against the dradur? I do *not* want to face off against someone who can fight like that. I might be good, but I'm not that good.'

'So you're going to drop a cliff on them instead?'

Nevis had paused at the foot of the cliff and stood waiting for them. By the look on his face, he thought them nothing more than loud, northern idiots, and at this moment, Ran wasn't sure he disagreed.

'This is madness!' he hissed as Eian and Zarad took ropes that had been looped over their shoulders and started preparing.

They were a good distance to the south of the camp, and unless a scout happened upon them, they would escape the notice of the Marsaw rangers. Dawn was just beginning to turn the sky to a pale grey, low cloud blotting out the sunrise, and Ran shivered. The night had been stifling, but now a breeze cut through the morning, chilling the sweat in his shirt and raising the hairs on his skin. Nevis made a sharp *shhh* sound and jabbed his finger at the fissure.

'We'd best get going.' Zarad gave Ran's shoulder a slap and moved away. Eian followed, leaving Ran alone with Nevis, staring after them as they disappeared into the shadowy cleft in the rock.

'Fuck,' Ran breathed.

Nevis made a clicking noise with his tongue, something akin to the sound one makes to get a horse moving, then pointed back down the slight slope they had just climbed.

'Right. Fuck. Well then,' Ran cleared his throat and nodded down the hill. 'You start back. I've got business to see to.'

He didn't, but he wanted to be alone, even for the short hike back to where the others were moving into position around the Marsaw camp. But Nevis frowned and Ran suddenly felt very nervous. For lack of any other option, he made a gesture he hoped Nevis would understand, and the southern ranger nodded. He was sceptical as fuck—Ran could see that in his scowl and the way his eyes never left Ran's face—but he didn't seem all that keen on standing around while Ran took a piss behind a tree. With obvious reluctance, Nevis left him, and Ran sighed.

'She's there, Ran,' Iridia said beside his ear.

'What the FUCK?' He spun and jerked away from her. 'What are you doing here?'

'You got rid of him so you could talk to me, didn't you?' She tilted her head and the curtain of her white-blonde hair shifted over her shoulder, her old neck wound opening in a macabre grin that didn't belong.

'I might have. Or I might have wanted five minutes to myself before I throw my life away trying to rescue a pair of kids I don't even know!' He started back down the hill after Nevis, keeping his voice low, knowing that if he lingered any longer, someone would come looking. In any case, they couldn't afford to delay. Dawn was breaking slowly in the east, and the moment had almost arrived to put their plan into action.

'Why are you helping then? Turn around and go back to the village.' She moved through the trees beside him, whispering her words into his ears and his mind. He hated how that made him feel, hated the heat it ignited and the way he couldn't keep his eyes off her face for more than a few moments. Their gazes met, mirror images of each other, the colour burned away by magic. He was sure she could see right through him—she always had.

'You know why. I need them to trust me when I tell them there's a witch in their midst.'

'Witches. There are two of them. I've already seen one, but not the other.'

'You *what*? When?'

'No time for that now, Ranoth. You have children to save.' She vanished in a gust of wind and Ran ground his teeth until he thought they might crack. His fingers balled into hard fists and it took three deep breaths to settle his anger, his magic barely contained and burning cold under his skin.

Maintaining the light orbs hadn't drained him as much as he thought it might, but he would have much preferred to face this day with a full night's sleep at his back and a decent breakfast in his belly. A soldier rarely got what he needed to fight the battles ahead, though. He knew that from his failed command in the Disputed Territory. If he had been given all he'd asked for, all he'd needed, countless lives would not have been wasted.

Today, he would have to muddle through with what he had; a terrible plan that was unlikely to work, exhausted comrades who would struggle to wield a weapon after more than a few moments of fighting, and an enemy who was well rested, fed and recently reinforced.

'Brilliant,' he muttered, then set off to catch up to the others. He spared a final glance at the lip of the cliff face before slipping back under the canopy of the trees. 'This better work, boys, or we're all dead...'

Lidan heard Ran creeping up behind where she lay on her belly beside Loge. He was quiet for someone who clearly had no idea how to move through the bush, but he was still distinct enough to hear coming from several feet away.

'Anything?' Ran asked, settling down beside Loge.

'Not yet,' he replied. 'No one is stirring.'

'Except the ranger on watch,' Lidan whispered. They both glanced over, frowning, and she pointed at the camp, the silhouettes of tents just visible through the dawn. The man sitting by the fire was well asleep, but as they watched, he moved, tilting, leaning, slowly but surely, until he slumped on the ground between the log he'd been leaning against and the fire. From this angle it was easy to see the arrow buried in the back of his neck, its shaft sticking out from between the bones of his spine.

Ran's eyebrows shot up and Lidan and Loge shared a grin.

'Jessah?' Loge asked, and Lidan nodded.

'That's the signal,' he said to Ran. 'Let's go.'

Arrayed around the southern side of camp in a half-circle, hidden in the undergrowth and behind trees and boulders, the rest of their group lay in wait, armed and ready for the inevitable break when the rangers in the camp realised the Tolak children had been liberated. Those precious silent moments between rescue and discovery would be the hardest to steal, and the more they had, the greater the chances of their plan succeeding. But doubt had been gnawing at Lidan's confidence all morning, until it was naught but discarded bones, picked clean of all hope.

She locked the doubt away and focused on her task. Climbing to her feet, she ran, bent low and with light steps behind Loge, who had his axe in one hand and his knife in the other. Ran followed, carrying a sword much like her own, albeit a little longer in the blade, unsheathed and held ready.

Tents came into full view as the trees fell away and they entered a small clearing by the chattering creek, birds beginning to warble and squawk at each other in the branches above, announcing the coming day. Of the five tents, three stood in a half-circle, curved around the fire, with two more set slightly apart, just to the northern side of the camp. None of them bore any insignia or markings, no tell-tale signs of who exactly they belonged to or who might be in them. Lidan fought the urge to growl. This would be so much easier if she knew where to start looking.

Loge turned and signalled with his axe, pointing at each tent in turn, and Lidan nodded. Ran fell back to the first, while she and Loge edged along behind the others, until she slipped into a crawl and moved alongside the one pitched in the centre of the line. She leaned her head against the side and listened.

Over the morning cacophony above, she heard nothing but a faint snore. No voices of children or sobbing cries; only the silence of sleep. She drew her knife, and laying on her side, began to pick away the stitching where the base of the tent wall was sewn to the floor, flicking the blade until there was a hole small enough to peer through.

It was dark inside, the light of the morning barely illuminating the space through the thickness of the hide walls. But it was just enough to see two bedrolls laid out on either side, one empty and the other lumpy with the form of a sleeping ranger. The empty bedroll most likely belonged to the dead ranger by the fire, and she leaned away from her peephole, looking down the length of her body to where Ran peered inside the first tent. He glanced up at her and shook his head.

No children in there either.

She craned her head back and looked for Loge. She frowned. *Where is he?*

He'd vanished, and she rolled over quickly and darted toward the tent, her heart thumping, her pulse drumming loudly in her ears. Quiet steps whispered across the ground behind her and a hand rested gently on her back.

She froze.

Turning slowly, she saw Ran in the corner of her vision and let a long, shaking breath escape between her lips. Crouching, Lidan found a hole in the back of the tent, a much larger portal than she had cut in hers.

Her breath caught in her throat.

Loge was already inside, crawling between two bedrolls. Again, one was empty, but the other held an odd form that she hoped was the shape of two small children sleeping together. She shuffled through the opening as Loge rose beside the entrance on the far side, his fingers gently easing back the flap that was tied shut from the outside. The smallest sliver of light cut across his face before he let it fall closed and stepped carefully away.

Lidan crawled across the floor of the tent and caught his eye as he held up one finger, then pointed at the left-hand side of the tent-flap.

One guard, this side.

She nodded and turned to the bed, her heart hammering fast, skipping beats with anxiety. Her chest tightened as she eased back the thin blanket and revealed her brother and sister; Lucija holding Ehran against her, the boy with his hands up over his face.

She almost burst into tears at the sight. They had found them, and they were alive!

Lucija began to stir and Lidan leaned back. The last thing she wanted was to startle the girl and set her off screaming. A pair of deep brown eyes blinked open, and Lidan put her finger to her lips. In the space of a heart-beat, Lucija's face morphed from a terrified, silent scream, up to a beaming smile and down again to a worried frown.

'Shh, little bird,' Lidan whispered as low as she could. 'We need to be very quiet.'

Loge went to the back of the tent and murmured something to Ran, then returned as Lucija shook Ehran, rolling the boy onto his back and waking him gently. He responded almost exactly as his sister had, then leapt up into Lidan's arms and crushed her neck with a hug that could have cracked stone. Fighting tears again, her eyes burning and blurring, she pulled him back and held up her finger. He calmed, if only to watch her face as she spoke.

'We're going to play Sleeping Possums, all right? You and Luci are the possums, and you need to keep your eyes shut and be very still, just like when you play with your mam at bedtime. Loge and I are going to carry you. But if you open your eyes even a little bit, you lose the game. Understand?'

They both nodded solemnly and closed their eyes as Loge shot her a glance. 'Eyes closed?' he whispered.

'I don't want them to see—'

'Sleeping on the job again? Typical Marsaw...' a voice called into the morning outside.

Lidan's heart almost stopped dead. She didn't take her eyes off Loge, not for a second.

'No...' she breathed.

'Can't be.' Loge shook his head.

'I'd recognise that voice anywhere.' Her skin crawled at the memory, her stomach twisting in knots as though she'd swallowed a snake, and she gaped at Loge. 'Yorrell is here.'

Chapter Forty-eight

Ran's face appeared through the hole in the tent and Lidan silently thanked the ancestors the children had listened to her. Their eyes were shut tight, Ehran's face pressed against her shoulder while Lucija let Loge scoop her into his arms. For certain they would have screamed at the sight of a pale northern man they didn't know from a hole in the ground shoving his head into their tent.

'We need to go,' Ran hissed.

Lidan nodded and shuffled after Loge, slipping out through the hole and into the cooler morning air. They stayed low, creeping along behind the tents as the splattering sound of urination ended and footsteps crunched across the sandy ground toward the campfire.

'The fuck is...' Yorrell's question trailed off and Lidan bit down on the inside of her cheek.

Loge and Ran paused in front of her, and she fought the instinct to bolt for the trees. There was a lull, a moment of silence so dreadful in its weight as Yorrell's half-woken mind processed what he was seeing.

Glancing around the corner of the last tent, Lidan watched him stare down at the body of the dead ranger, registering the arrow and the expanding pool of blood. At a distance the guard had seemed asleep, and he had been, right up until the arrow had dropped him cold. Now he was just dead, and Yorrell Namjin's sleep-addled mind was about a heartbeat away from understanding what that meant.

'Ready,' Loge asked.

She nodded while her mind screamed, *No!*

'UP!' Yorrell bellowed, and for a blink, nothing happened. 'All of you, UP! Get up!'

Then the rain began.

A faint whistle and a thump. Another, then another, falling heavily from the sky, from nowhere and everywhere, arrows slamming into the ground beside Yorrell as the Namjin daari scrambled and bolted for cover back between the tents on the far side of the camp.

Loge took off like a shot, sprinting hard for the tree line. Lidan hurried after him, Ehran bouncing against her chest, his tiny hands clinging to her shirt, his nails biting through the fabric, drawing blood. Running steps behind her announced Ran, and the three of them wove through the trees along a faint trail that wound up to the base of the western cliff face.

Lidan's breath rasped in her ears, her pulse drumming in her head as her thoughts darted to the others, who she hoped were drawing the Marsaw and Namjin ranger's attention away from the missing children. The plan had been for the Tolak rangers to harry the captors from the trees, picking them off one by one, but Lidan couldn't see any of it. All she saw was the distance left to travel to the narrowing of the gorge. They hadn't dared bring the horses in this close, leaving them down the track, saddled and ready to run.

They ran hard for what seemed like an age, but it could have only been a few moments before voices echoed through the trees behind them, shouts and orders, thumping hooves against soft ground, crashing through branches and thick undergrowth.

'Riders!' Ran shouted.

Two deafening cracks snapped through the air behind Lidan and she stumbled, her feet slipping as her stomach lurched. The atmosphere reeked of a foul metallic odour she knew from the forge at home, and the Crone's hut. She staggered and turned, her skin rushing with goose bumps.

Ran hurried up the trail, then turned and fired magic from his hands at two riders thundering toward them. A bright bolt arced away and tore through a tree trunk, the massive bole creaking and screaming as the timber gave way. The tree twisted as it fell, a slow inevitable collapse, until it slammed into the ground, crushing one rider and violently barricading the other.

The horse's shriek rent the air and Lidan whirled away, clutching Ehran's head to her shoulder and praying to anyone listening that the child hadn't seen a thing. Ran caught her up and pressed his hand against her back, steadying her, urging her on, while Loge kept up the pace ahead.

The trail began to arc back down toward the creek. She hoped the way through the narrow bend was clear. She hoped—

Loge stumbled.

She glanced around, then back at him. There was no arrow shaft or wound that she could see. He started running again. Perhaps she'd imagined—

He stumbled again, this time slipping on the loose stones of the downward sloping trail, almost losing his footing completely. He corrected himself, adjusting his grip on Lucija, and hurried on, ignorant to the frantic hammer of Lidan's heart. What was going on?

The distance between them closed as they reached the base of the slope, the game trail merging with the main track by the creek. They burst from the trees and skittered onto the path, ducking for cover as arrows whistled overhead, rangers and northerners shouting warnings and orders at each other.

'Lidan!' Jessah screamed, and a knot of protective bodies appeared around them and the children.

Lidan spun and launched Ehran at Jessah. 'Take him! Get to the horses!'

She turned back in time to see Aelish collect Lucija from Loge and then hand her off to Brit. The big man hurried after Jessah, and they vanished around a distant bend in the track as a score of mounted rangers from the camp barrelled toward them.

'Arrows!' Lidan screamed.

Aelish's weird sideways bow thunked back into action, ripping flesh from man and beast as they drew near. Nevis, Torren and the other Tolak rangers maintained their barrage from the sides of the track and Lidan whipped her knives from their sheaths as magic crackled in the air between Ran's tensed hands.

Nausea pulsed through her and she rammed her teeth together against the back of her lip, the pain pulling her back to the moment as a wounded rider reached her. She rolled away from the horse's thundering hooves and came back to her feet, raking a knife down the animal's flank in a merciless bid to unseat the ranger.

They went down screaming and flailing, legs and arms whirling as the injured animal rolled on its rider and crushed him, snapping his neck before she had the chance to slice it open. Yorrell was somewhere, bellowing orders over the top of Merk, and suddenly there were more rangers in the fray than she could count, her knives slashing and stabbing as they burst from the trees and fell upon her people.

Lidan whipped around and met an attacker leaping from the bush beside Loge, his axe scything through the air to cleave a leg from a horse bearing down on him. The space was too small for the horses to turn, and the unmounted Tolak and their northern allies took the advantage.

'Where the fuck did they come from?' Lidan demanded as she pulled her knife from the body of a ranger and flicked his blood across the trail.

'Must have been camped up the valley!' Loge shouted before the horse's rider dove from the saddle and slammed into him.

'We can't hold here!' Ran's harsh call reached over the lightning crack of his magic. He worked his sword more than his power now, carving into rangers and slashing at horses. There couldn't have been more than a dozen attackers, but in this tiny, narrow bend of the track, they might as well have been a horde surging against them.

Aelish's side-bow fell silent and Lidan glanced at her. The northerner slashed savagely at a ranger with a knife, but she missed her mark, unable to get inside his guard for a killing blow. Lidan kicked the ranger she was fighting in the gut and drew her sword. 'Aelish!'

She tossed the blade and Aelish snatched it up from where it fell, ducking below the ranger's knife, and slicing a ragged channel through his face.

'Ran!' Loge's shout echoed against the stone of the cliffs. 'Retreat!'

'Trying!' came the answer.

'Now!' Loge ordered. 'Run!'

Not needing to be told twice, Aelish turned and sprinted down the gorge, Lidan's sword snagging on a tree and disappearing into a bush. Lidan glanced at the cliff above, backing toward the narrow bend in the gorge as she did.

Time was almost up.

High above, Eian and Zarad would be ready; waiting, listening to the screams of dying rangers and horses. She started jogging, moving faster, her breath rasping, her mouth parchment dry, leaving the fight behind.

It took no more than a few heart beats to realise something was wrong. She turned back.

Wounded but still fighting, Nevis buried a club in the back of a ranger's skull, bodies strewn at his feet like fallen chips of wood from a timber-cutter's block. Torren lay on the ground nearby, blood gurgling from his mouth and pumping from a grisly wound in his gut, his fingers bright crimson, vainly trying to push his insides back where they belonged. Horses and rangers lay strewn about, some flailing, more often motionless, few still standing on the blood-soaked sand.

More enemy rangers hurried forward from behind a line of men standing in the distance. Merk and Yorrell, she guessed—too precious to get their hands dirty while they still had others to do the work for them.

An axe ended Nevis as he started back toward the fight, and Loge appeared where the other man had fallen. With a sharp, quick movement, he turned and shoved Ran toward Lidan.

'Take her and go!'

Lidan jolted to a stop. *What?*

Ran crashed into her, wrapping an arm around her to steady himself as she scrambled to push him off. They were directly below the bend in the gorge, right where the line in the sand had been drawn.

'Like fuck, Loge Baker!' she screamed as the last few rangers lurched toward the Tolak left standing. He was close enough to hear her but too far away to touch.

'Light the signal!' Loge shouted at Ran.

Hands grasped her shoulders and dragged her into a staggering backward jog, pulling her away from Loge, away from Nevis and Torren and Yorrell and Merk and the ancestors only knew who else on the other side of that narrow point in the track.

Loge carved his axe through another ranger, who kicked out as he fell, slamming a boot into the side of Loge's leg. His went down hard, roaring and swinging up, opening up the chest of an attacker.

'Loge!' Lidan screamed.

'Light it!' he bellowed at Ran, climbing painfully to his feet.

Desperation flared in her chest. She had to get him out of there, had to get him on a horse so they could retreat. The men in the distance did not move. They would wait for him to fall, wait for all who remained to fall, then they would ride over the dead and follow Lidan and her siblings south.

They would hunt them for a day and a night they would find them and—

Lightning ripped into the sky beside Lidan's head, and she ducked away.

Ran's signal shot upward into the overcast morning, up past the top of the cliffs, and Lidan froze.

No...

She looked up at Loge and watched him fight, time slipping slowly by as the rock wall beside them began to groan and shudder. Ran had told her what Zarad would do, how he would put his fist to the rock and send his power into the ground, drawing on Eian until his magic severed a slab of stone from the face of the cliff, releasing it into free-fall. She knew this, and she screamed as blue light broke through cracks in the cliff, the stone rumbling as it shifted.

She screamed again and raged against Ran, raged against him dragging her free of the tumbling rock, raged against him pulling her away. She screamed until there was no voice in her throat, nothing left but burning; no words, just strangled sound. Nothing left but horror and pain and awful knowing.

Loge cut a ranger down, punched another and glanced over his shoulder.

She locked her eyes on his.

He blinked once.

He gave her a sad smile.

And turned away.

The avalanche of rock and vegetation roared down and Loge vanished, the world shaking as the stone crashed into the gorge, a thunderous boom knocking Lidan back into Ran and sending them both flying. She hit the ground hard, bones snapping and stones tearing at her skin and clothes. Water surged up out of the creek and washed the two of them against the trees, slamming them into the trunks before rushing away down the gorge.

CHAPTER FORTY-NINE

Western Tablelands, Namjin range, the South Lands

No battle noise.

No birds calling.

Darkness and silence, broken only by the muffled sound of rasping breath.

Was she dead?

Someone called her name, and hands clamped down on her arms, setting her body on fire. She gasped and came up screaming, swinging wildly at her attacker, knocking them back and scrambling to her feet. Muddy ground slid out from under her boots and she stumbled, crawling and clawing her way back up again.

Blinking water and dirt and fuck knows what from her eyes, she searched, scanning the trees, scrutinising every lump and rock. The voice kept shouting, but it was distant, a dull annoyance that despite her efforts to ignore, was getting louder. She fell again and the hands collected her once more, pulling her to her feet and spinning her around.

'Lidan!' Ran shouted in her face, his features distorted by fury and blood. 'Stop and listen to me!'

'Can't.' Lidan shook her head. 'Need to search.'

Her words were broken things, all shards and coarse, ragged edges, ripping at her throat. Injuries screamed at her, limbs trembling, her chest struggling to fill with the air she desperately needed to continue.

'For what?' he asked, the fury fading, the frown on his brow softening. 'We have to get out of here, come on—'

'No! Get off me! Let me *go!*' she cried, jerking her arms from his grip and ramming her fist into his chest. Ran staggered back, clutching at his ribs and gasping, cursing and spitting, and Lidan took off. Unable to keep her feet for more than a few steps, she wavered toward the rock fall.

There was a colossal scar down the side of the canyon now, a discolouration that ended in a heaped mess of jagged boulders and splintered trees. She stared at it, and silent as a grave, the broken stones stared back.

She stopped.

Blood dripped across her vision, but she made no move to wipe it away.

'We have to leave, Lidan.' Ran's voice reached through the fog and she looked slowly over her shoulder. Their eyes met, so much truth in that one glance, more than she ever thought her whole heart could hold.

'No.' She shook her head and her lip trembled. Pain lanced down the side of her face, burning in her shoulder and leg. 'Not without him.'

Slow, limping steps brought Ran to stand before her again. His hands cupped her shoulders gently, and those unnerving blue eyes held her firmly in place. 'He's gone,' Ran murmured.

'No—'

'He's gone,' he repeated, grunting as Lidan began to fight his grip again, railing against the truth, fighting the cold, immovable, dreadful certainty filling her chest. 'He couldn't have survived that—no, Lidan, listen to me! *Listen* to me!'

She stopped thrashing and went rigid. Her glare darkened into a snarl. 'You're lying. You don't know that. You *can't* know that! You don't know him! He's strong and fast; he could have run, he could have got clear—'

Her thoughts stopped, her tirade collapsing into silence. An image stuttered before her eyes; Loge stumbling, staggering, his knee giving out.

He couldn't have run. He couldn't have made it away in time…

Sadness creased Ran's face, his voice breaking, like the words were as sharp as the rocks filling the gorge. 'He's dead, Lidan. He's gone.'

The truth hung in the air, seeping through her skin like poison, swirling through her veins toward her heart.

'No,' she whispered.

'Yes. I'm sorry.'

Something in her chest snapped and she doubled over, wrapping her arms around her body. A wordless sob tore from her mouth, a crack opening through her centre. The hands on her arms drew her close and she wept, squeezing her eyes shut, pretending the arms that held her were Loge's, knowing all along they were not.

They couldn't be.

He was buried under a mountain of rock that did not care for her cries and would not be washed away by her tears.

He was gone.

Theus stamped a hoof against the soft, sandy earth, snorting his impatience at the delay, or perhaps at his disdain for the stench of death clinging to Lidan's clothes. She couldn't tell which it might be, nor did she much care. She just stared into the middle distance, not really seeing the others moving around her, packing the camp and dousing the fire. The reins were coarse against her skin, but it was a distant sensation, brushing against her awareness from a world she no longer felt a part of.

Her body trembled; an imperceptible shiver the others could not see, but it shuddered through her limbs and chest all the same. She couldn't make it stop, nor could she banish the rolling nausea in her gut or bring herself to put food in her mouth. She barely wanted to breathe, but her body continued to do so despite her apathy.

Her left arm hung in a makeshift sling fashioned from a shirt. She didn't ask where Jessah found it; she knew the smell in the fabric well enough. The bones of her collar were broken, and her shoulder had dislocated when the wave of creek water had slammed her into a tree. The livid bruise down the side of her face seared every time she blinked, her left side a litany of scrapes and grazes where stones had torn through her clothes as she slid across the ground, raking her skin as if the earth had become a bed of knives.

Something small pressed against her leg and she looked down.

A head of dark hair leaned against her thigh, a thin arm wrapping around her leg. Ehran did not speak, he merely stood, his presence reaching through the fog to bring the world into focus again. The blue craw sat on Theus's saddle, tilting its head curiously, studying Ehran with its shiny eyes, but the boy did not see the bird; no one did. It had not revealed itself to any of them as it followed her through the fugue of her grief; quiet, save for a few mournful warbles and the gentle ruffle of its feathers.

Someone appeared in front of her and lifted a small child onto the horse beside Theus. Lidan glanced up as Brit settled Lucija on the seat, then turned to Ehran.

'Ready to go, wee man?' he asked the boy. Ehran nodded and held out his arms, allowing Brit to scoop him up and place him in front of his sister. 'Now you hold on tight, and I'll make sure we go nice and steady.'

Lidan stared at the saddle.

The loop for an axe hung empty beside Lucija's leg, and there were a set of bulging saddle bags, the leather dusty and creased from years of use. She knew that saddle.

She ground her teeth to banish the tremor from her jaw. Striker didn't protest the children taking Loge's place; he just stood with his head bowed, his reins loose in Lucija's hands. The girl had a look of determination on her face that was much too old for someone so young, and Lidan grimaced, the memory of a promise she'd made stabbing through her chest.

'Look at you two?' Her vision blurred and she blinked to clear it. 'Up on a big horse.'

This had been their dream, these two children she hardly knew at all, and it should have been a thing of laughter and joy, not a grief-stricken funeral march. But it wasn't a funeral march, was it? There were no bodies to mourn over, no graves to dig or pyres to build. The corpses of the lost were already buried deep, covered in a tumal of broken rock that would never be moved, a lonely tomb in a strange land.

'He's a good horse,' Lucija said quietly.

They had ridden Striker the day before, Lidan recalled. The day they had escaped south toward Tingalla, riding until night fell and they stopped to rest. Lidan had not slept, not really. Her body may have collapsed onto a bedroll, but her mind had been a storm of hate and pain, mourning something she had known for no more than a fleeting moment before it had been snatched from her grasp, never to return.

'He's a very good horse. Make sure to give him lots of pats, all right? He'll need them.' The last words pushed their way out through her tightening throat. Brit returned with his horse and reached to take up the lead rope tied to Striker's bridle, but Lidan stepped toward him. 'I should do that.'

The watcher looked down at her. He was only marginally taller, dark brows framing doubtful, worried eyes.

'Are you sure? It's no trouble,' he said. His rolling northern accent reminded her of Master Rick. Ran's was less pronounced, more clipped and cleaner, except for the curses that dropped from his mouth with every second word. He was a barely contained vessel of boiling fury since the fight, and they'd kept clear of each other as much as was reasonably possible.

'No, I can do it. I'm all right,' she assured Brit, hearing the lie and knowing he saw it for what it was. 'This was my task, Brit. I need to see it through.'

He nodded and handed her the lead, Striker snorting as she gave his nose a gentle scratch. She swung up onto Theus with a leg up and Brit's steadying hand on her back, sucking a pained breath through her teeth, and turned both horses in a wide arc until they faced south down the gorge.

'Let's go home,' she whispered.

The gates to Tingalla stood open, and as they approached the drawbridge, Lidan glanced back at the shattered remains of the group that had left only a few days before. She, Jessah and two others were all that remained of the Tolak rangers, and while Jessah had escaped with nothing more than a few cuts and bruises, every step Theus took was a lesson in agony for Lidan.

Ran's group of northerners had escaped relatively unscathed, he and Aelish bearing the worst of the injuries among them. The two magic-users, Zarad and Eian, were dead on their feet with exhaustion, and Jessah had murmured something about Zarad cracking a bone in his hand, but they were both still alive. Brit was the best among them, with hardly a scratch on him thanks to his early escape from the fight. She sensed something in the watcher though, a regret or guilt that he had left while the others fought, but in Lidan's opinion, his efforts to get Lucija clear of danger more than made up for his absence. Still, she saw him taking on more than his share of the tasks, fussing over the children and rushing to the others as soon as anyone moved to see to a chore.

The weary band rode slowly up the hill, wandering behind Theus and Striker with no real sense of urgency. Striker followed Theus, her siblings bobbing and swaying on his back, complaining of sore legs and backsides before midday. They brightened a little as they looked up and saw the lintel of the gate pass overhead, and Lidan might have smiled if her face hadn't been so swollen and her heart hadn't turned to stone.

The weight of it was almost too much to bear as a call rang out across the common and people burst from the doors of the hall, rushing the horses and riders. She dismounted into their midst, and those who moved to embrace her stopped short, taking in her immobile arm and the ruin of her face. They nodded at her instead, uttering words she didn't understand, then moved on to the others, passing by her like water around a stone.

She ignored their happiness and relief, and turned to unbuckle her bags from the back of her saddle. This was a task she knew by heart, that she could have done in her sleep, and managed it with one shaking hand before shrugging the straps over her good shoulder.

Lidan stumbled away from Theus, her legs trembling as she took a few unsteady steps, then stopped.

Striker.

The horse stood beside Theus, his lead rope still looped around a hook on her saddle. The children had been enveloped in a knot of weeping adults and half-siblings, and the horses stood alone, a solitary stable hand holding Theus by the bridle. Staring at Loge's bags, her good hand reached to touch the leather, the pads of her fingers tracing the buckle. She undid it without thinking, releasing the clasps and sliding the bags away, lifting them onto her shoulder with her own.

She turned and didn't look back, retracing the steps she had made a few days before.

The pathways were empty, abandoned by the people who would usually be here, distracted as they were by the arrival of the search party. She didn't want to see any of them. Someone might have called her name, but she kept walking, heaviness settling in her chest, pressing down until she was sure her next breath would be her last. Her hand flicked the latch on the door to her quarters and she shoved it aside, staggering into the room.

The bags fell from her shoulder and flopped to the floor, contents spilling from a pocket and clattering among the legs of the table and chairs. She almost fell with them, catching herself on the back of a chair. Slowly, inch by painful inch, she lowered herself to the ground.

The tears came then, tears she didn't think she had left to shed. Perhaps she'd held them back for the sake of the children, for the sake of her companions who could not possibly understand but would have tried to comfort her anyway.

She didn't want their comfort. She didn't want their kindness. She wanted oblivion. Her knees touched the floor and she broke, the crack inside her widening further than she thought possible until it was a gaping chasm of sorrow, a yawning abyss she longed to throw herself into and fall through forever. With her forehead on the cool timber of the chair back, she wept, great heaving sobs that choked her as though her grief had hands, squeezing the very air from her lungs, crushing her under its weight.

Opening her eyes and sitting back on her heels, Lidan looked up at the ceiling, letting the tears fall from the corners of her eyes and drawing in a deep, trembling breath. Eventually, the sobbing eased and the tears ran dry, but the gaping wound no one could see remained. She turned and leaned back against the chair, staring at the open door, watching the day pass outside. Her craw flew in through the opening, swooping to settle on the back of the chair above her head. She might have looked up if she had the strength to do so.

Slowly, she began to sift memories from the broken pieces of her mind, collecting them and stuffing them into the internal abyss. She filled it with all the things she and Loge had said and done, all the time they had shared. It seemed a pitifully small amount as she stacked it into the hole in her heart, but it was just enough to stem the flow, just enough to dam the river of pain. It was just enough to fill the void.

Darkness crept across the sky some hours later, and Lidan remained on the floor, staring out the door. A small timber figurine lay in her hand; a horse, not yet complete, but its form and shape familiar enough that she knew what it was. Loge had been carving a new Icewind for Ehran, a replacement for the priggin doll she had burned. It was almost done, tucked away in his saddle bag, waiting for the next time he could sit by the fire and whittle away at the wood with his belt knife. A few more hours work and it would have been, but those hours had been stolen. The toy would remain unfinished, its potential lost, just like Loge.

Ehran would never see it, she decided. She wouldn't ask anyone to complete it, because it was perfect as it was. Lidan reached over and slipped it under the flap of her saddlebag, sliding it down among her shirts and spare clothes. There it would stay, unseen by the world.

By the door, someone cleared their throat and Lidan looked up. Sellan stood at the threshold, her form filling the space in the fading light. Her hands were folded in front of her, her eyes trained carefully on Lidan, scanning her from head to foot as she sat exhausted on the ground. She couldn't have climbed to her feet without assistance even if she'd wanted to, so she stared back at her mother with a blank expression that didn't make the skin on her face burn.

'You're a mess,' Sellan said quietly.

Lidan shrugged her good shoulder and looked away. She was, so why argue?

'But you will take unnecessary risks.'

Slowly, Lidan's gaze tracked back to her mother's passive face. Her skin ached as her features contorted into a scowl. 'What did you just say to me?'

Sellan rolled her eyes. 'Running off after the boy. You could have gotten yourself killed. At least this time the other rangers bore the brunt of it. Where's that one who follows you around like a dog? I expected to find him here guarding your door, but I suppose he's off getting drunk with your father, celebrating the return of his beloved—'

'He's dead.'

The truth dropped between them like an untethered counterweight, and her mother's mouth snapped shut. For a moment, she said nothing, and Lidan sat in blessed, empty silence. Then the silence began to fill, Sellan leaning her head to the side, studying Lidan carefully, more carefully than she thought her mother had in many, many years.

Lidan stared at her, unable to think, unable to move, unable to care. She wanted to be alone, but all the woman seemed capable of doing was looking her up and down, until finally she leaned back and let a sharp sigh out through her nose.

'Well, that is unfortunate. Had you simply let Merk take the boy, none of this would have happened. Your friend would still be here, and you would be the heir once more. It was a golden opportunity to regain what was lost, Lidan, and what do you have to show for all this blood and pain?' Sellan gave her a look that she supposed was sympathetic, but Lidan hardly noticed. The words rung in her ears, the possibility of their meaning unfolding like a poisonous flower.

Had Sellan planned this? Was this whole abduction *her* doing?

No… That was absurd. Surely, she wasn't that stupid. Surely, the risk of discovery was too great, the chances of Merk revealing her betrayal almost certain…

Unless she'd offered him something to sweeten the deal? Some payment, some reward…

She glared up at her mother. 'Did you help Merk abduct Ehran in exchange for matching me to his son?'

'Excuse me?' The question hit the walls of the room and echoed back like a whip-crack.

Nauseous and reeling, Lidan blinked, her aching jaw beginning to clench. 'Did you help him? Was it you who—did you *do* this? Was that why you tried to stop me going?'

Sellan baulked as though the very idea disgusted her, and her face darkened into a scowl. 'How dare you accuse me—'

'DON'T FUCKING LIE TO ME!' Lidan's roar ripped through the air.

She reached for the nearest thing she could wrap her hand around, gripping the leg of a chair and flinging it at her mother. It tumbled across the floor and smashed against the edge of the wall, exploding in a shower of splinters and timber shards. Sellan ducked away, staggering backward into the evening with her arms over her head, a pathetic shield against the flying debris.

Lidan found her strength, hidden as it had been under her pain, and dragged herself to her feet. She lurched toward the door and caught herself on the frame, falling out into the pathway and limping after her mother. The woman stared, a mixture of shock, awe and anger rippling across her features. Every time Lidan moved, she flinched, tiny movements that betrayed her fear; a fear Lidan never thought she would return to the woman who had beaten her, screamed at her, shoved her into a black pit to punish her more cruelly than she could have ever rightly deserved. Lidan loomed over her mother, drawing her broken body up to its full, aching height, and grew very still.

'Did. You. Do. This?'

'*What*? You cannot seriously think me capable of such a thing?' Sellan glanced around and realised she was cowering. She quickly corrected herself, but Lidan still saw the terror shimmering in those green eyes.

'You're capable of so many things, Mother… *so* many things… why not this? Merk had to have had help from someone.'

Sellan's face contorted. 'Are you insane?'

'*Did* you, or did you *not*, arrange for my brother to be kidnapped by our enemies?!' Anyone within the compound would have heard her, her voice so painfully loud it hurt her own ears. People emerged from around the corners of buildings, pausing with their baskets or livestock to stare at the dana and the first daughter facing off on the pathway.

Lidan didn't care.

Let them watch. If this was what it took to be heard, then so be it.

'I have done no such thing!' Sellan ground out between clenched teeth, leaning into Lidan's threat and pushing it back. She was a cornered snake, prepared to strike at anything and everything that might be a danger to her.

It was all fear—Lidan saw that now. Fear of losing, fear of becoming something less. Lidan's inheritance was her mother's security, her shield and her weapon against the world. With that in hand, as the mother of the heir, she was nigh on untouchable; all powerful and malevolent. It was no wonder she fought against Ehran's existence so fiercely, no wonder she hated Farah with such a burning passion that she had struggled to hold herself back for so many years. It was only Lidan's promise that had kept her contained, the promise that she would do her mother's bidding and bring the succession back to its rightful place.

'You are a liar and a traitor.' Lidan spat at her mother's feet and leaned away. Had she the energy to spare, she might have been disgusted, but now she was simply empty, battling to hold herself upright as more people crept forward to gawk and listen. 'I warned you once to leave Ehran alone, and you ignored me. I give you this final chance, out of the love I somehow still hold for you…'

Lidan's voice shook with an involuntary, hysterical laugh. It was a black thing, mirthless and wicked, barely more than a misdirected sob. 'If you so much as speak a *word* against my sisters or my brother, I will kill you. If I see you regard them with anything but a smile on your face, I will kill you. There will be no Hearing. There will be no judgement but mine.' Lidan stabbed a finger at Sellan and the woman lurched backward, the crowd around them shifting in response. 'Ancestors, witness me—I will gut you where you stand if you lay a finger on them.'

Silence fell, and not a single person moved.

No one spoke.

They merely stared in wide-eyed disbelief at what must have seemed like a suicide attempt by the first daughter. Such a challenge could not go unanswered, and Lidan knew it would not. She had merely set the wheel turning. Where the spiral would stop, she could not say, but Sellan would have to step over Lidan's cold corpse to get to Ehran, and now she knew it.

Sellan collected herself, smoothing her shaking hands down the front of her skirt and sniffing, as if she'd been exposed to a foul odour. 'I can see you have suffered a loss, my dear. I will leave you alone with your thoughts. Perhaps you will see things more clearly in the morning.'

The dana turned and left, people hurrying quickly from her path. Most of them vanished back behind the buildings nearby, some whispering, others pointing, not one of them looking at her face.

It was then Lidan's legs gave out and a pair of hands caught her waist. She turned, craning around to see Vee, the woman's arms lifting her back to her feet and taking her weight. Lidan's mouth moved but no words came out. She lost all sense of herself and floundered; falling toward the abyss.

Where was her anchor now? Loge wasn't here anymore. She was cast adrift, a storm taking her under, drowning her beneath a torrent of tears.

'Come, Witness,' she heard Vee's voice through the churn. 'Let's get you inside.'

CHAPTER FIFTY

Tingalla, Tolak range, the South Lands

There weren't many things Ran could think of to be thankful for these days, but a belly full of breakfast before facing the leader of a warrior clan was certainly one of them. The tables had been cleared and scrubbed, the dogs lay dozing in a satisfied slumber near the door, and the inside of the hall was quiet. He was waiting, as instructed by the daari's second-in-command, who had promptly left after delivering him to the empty, cavernous room.

Iridia sat with her legs crossed on a nearby tabletop, her hands in her lap, her eyes downcast as she picked at her nails. 'Do you think she'll come?'

'Who?' he asked softly, turning from where he'd been watching a side door.

'Lidan; the one who can hear me.'

'Perhaps… I think she might. I've not seen her since we arrived yesterday.' He glanced back at the door. 'I'm not sure she can really hear you. She would have said so…'

'Possibly,' came her reply. 'But she can sense me, and that's something to take note of.'

'You're right on that score.' Ran looked at her again, hoping no one was eavesdropping on his one-way conversation with a ghost. 'She can sense my magic too. It makes her ill every time I use it.'

Iridia frowned and tilted her head. 'Have you ever met anyone like that? Anyone who didn't already have magic?'

Ran shook his head slowly, raking his teeth over his bottom lip. 'No, I haven't.'

It was a puzzle that had been worrying at him, in the few quiet moments he'd had to think on such things, ever since he'd noticed the faint residue of thaumalux in the wake of Lidan's anger. Surely by now she'd been exposed to enough raw power that if she had any of her own tucked away somewhere, it would be roaring to life, showing itself with the full force of her emotions. And she'd certainly had enough intense emotion ripping through her in the past few days to bring any latent magic to the surface.

Footsteps rustling through reeds on the floor announced someone's arrival, and Iridia looked up, Ran following her gaze to see Lidan crossing the hall from the side entrance. She limped heavily, her arm in a better made sling than it had been the last time he'd seen her, but her face was a ruin; bruised from well above her hair line, down her cheek and neck. Here it met with the livid discolouration around her collarbone and shoulder, and he winced at the sight. She must have been in incredible pain, and these were only the wounds he could see.

He cleared his throat and hurried over, looping his arm under Lidan's good shoulder and helping her to a chair near Iridia's table. Iridia began to fade as Lidan hissed through her teeth and eased herself down but Ran shook his head at the ghost. He wanted her here for this. He needed her.

He'd missed her on the journey to the gorge; missed her brutal counsel and whip-fast intellect. The journey had been empty without her, and even if she couldn't speak in Lidan's presence, she could be here, beside him. He knew now that was all he had ever wanted from her, just to know she was there, no matter what.

Ran looked down at Lidan and stepped back to give her some space. 'How are you?'

Iridia's brow rose at his question, and he searched himself, shocked to find he actually cared about the answer. It was a stupid question, really. She had never said so much in words, but it was quite obvious Lidan had loved Loge in a way he had never loved anyone, and she had lost him in a most cruel fashion; unable to say goodbye, unable to even return his body home.

'As good as can be expected, I suppose.' She strained to push the words out, her voice hoarse and croaking. 'You?'

She nodded at him, and he held up his arm. It was bandaged from wrist to elbow, more for show than anything else. What wounds he had were mostly healed before they reached Tingalla, and the rest had almost vanished overnight as his magic put his body back together. So, he lied. 'Ah, a few old injuries are playing up, and I've plenty of bruises you can't see. The healer says I probably cracked a few ribs.'

Lidan eyed him, then gave a single nod. He couldn't tell if she believed him.

'Good.' She leaned back in the chair and sighed. 'Do you know what this is about?'

'Not really. Your father's man came to fetch me after breakfast, and I've been here ever since. You?'

She titled her head slightly. 'A message came for me to attend. That's all I know.'

Awkward, heavy silence filled the hall, and seconds dragged into minutes as they waited for someone to show up and explain what was going on. Eventually, footsteps echoed from the stairs outside, and Erlon appeared with a woman Ran recognised as one of his wives.

'Master Ran! Thank you for joining us!' Erlon said, beaming, as if Ran had a choice in attending at all.

'My pleasure, sir. What can I do for you?'

The daari slowed as he caught sight of his daughter, ignoring Ran's question. He walked toward her as one might approach a terrified kitten and put one hand gently on her un-marked cheek. 'Liddy...'

'Da,' she managed to say, then leaned into his palm for a moment.

'I am so very sorry,' he murmured.

Had Ran not been so close he wouldn't have heard the exchange at all, but he'd been right beside Lidan when her father arrived, and shuffled back now, uncomfortable in the face of such raw emotion. Iridia gave him a sad, knowing smile. Public displays of such things weren't exactly his strong suit.

'Ran, is it?' the woman asked, stepping forward and reaching for his hand.

'Yes, ma'am,' he replied, glad for the distraction.

'I'm Farah; Ehran and Lucija's mother. I can't begin to thank you for what you did, for all you risked helping Lidan bring my children home.' Her warm hands wrapped around his and gave them a gentle squeeze, her deep brown eyes shimmering with unshed tears.

Ran's throat tightened, and he nodded in reply.

'That's why I called you here, in fact.' Erlon turned from his murmured conversation with his daughter. 'I should think your debt to Lidan has been well and truly repaid, but my debt to you has not.'

'Sir?' Ran's heart gave a hard thud. Was this it? Was this the moment he'd been chasing when he set off to search for the children, when he had offered himself up to the gods and hoped that he would make it out alive?

'You've done my family a great service. And your companions, too. Jessah briefed me last night, and it goes without saying this could not have succeeded without your help.'

The thudding in his chest quickened. What exactly had Jessah told him?

'Apparently your strategy and bravery won the day, despite the wounds you all now bear.' Erlon spared a fleeting glance at Lidan and did not elaborate, while Ran fought the urge to sigh with relief. It appeared Jessah hadn't told the daari *exactly* what he, Eian and Zarad had done, which was fortunate. He had been warned these people did not abide magic well, so if the ranger had given Erlon every last detail, he doubted he would be standing here without shackles on his wrists and ankles.

Ran inclined his head humbly. 'I only sought to repay what was owed, and to do what was right.'

'That may well be, but I cannot allow you to leave us empty handed. Name a price, a reward for your service, and it will be paid.'

He let out a nervous sigh, glancing briefly to where Iridia sat on the tabletop, unnoticed by the others and utterly silent. It was now or never, he supposed. 'I mentioned that we came to your lands seeking a fugitive. While I'm unsure if this person remains in your midst, I suspect they may have spent time with you in the past.'

Lidan slowly looked up, her eyes narrowing. She would have her truth now.

'I should like to ask you some questions, and to have you answer them as truthfully as possible. If I find evidence of the fugitive, I would like them turned over to my custody without dispute.'

'Is that all?' Erlon asked with a frown, as though he couldn't believe Ran would ask for something so small and insignificant.

'That's all,' Ran replied. 'I have come a long way in search of this person, and should I find they are not among you, I'll ask nothing more of you and your people, and we will move on from here.'

The daari looked at Lidan, who gave a small, pained nod, then the man gestured for Farah to take a seat beside his daughter. 'Please, ask your questions.'

'This person…' Ran began, ordering his thoughts into some sort of sensible sequence. 'They would have arrived at Hummel within the last twenty years, but no more. They would have come from north of the mountains, and would very likely have skin the same as my own. Are there any among you who fit this description?'

Erlon ran the pads of his fingers across his lips. 'Many have come from the north, but only a few have stayed within the past twenty years.'

'You may have noticed them behaving strangely. Perhaps, they could do things that others among you couldn't.'

'Such as?' Erlon pressed.

Ran looked up at the ceiling and wondered at an example. 'They may have had an affinity for fire. Or an uncanny ability to know the thoughts of others without hearing them spoken aloud. They may have been at the centre of strange events, things that were difficult to explain by conventional means.'

'An affinity for fire?' Lidan asked, her croaky voice breaking across the conversation. 'What would that look like?'

'Lighting a fire without the aid of flint, for one thing.'

She grew very still. 'How might they do that?'

He shifted his feet. 'The means may not have been visible to the naked eye, or there may have been a blue spark, or a small burst of energy, like a lightning strike, only much smaller.'

The muscles in Lidan's face tightened under her bruised skin and she blinked quickly. She knew something; he could see it in the way her eyes refused to settle in one place, in the way her finger began to pick at the embroidery on her skirt. He fought the urge to press harder, pulling back, waiting for her to ask another question and hoping as he did that she had more to say.

'What about curses?' she asked suddenly, and he stared at her for a long, dragging moment.

'Liddy?' Erlon asked, but she ignored him, her eyes locking on to Ran.

'Could they place curses—and I mean *real* curses—on people? Or in objects?'

'Yes.' Ran nodded, clearing his throat. 'Yes, they could. It would take a... a great deal of effort on their part, but yes.'

'Lidan, what are you—where is all this coming from?' Her father turned his attention to Lidan as she looked away into the shadows, her lips moving as if searching for words that would not come.

'The priggin doll,' she whispered finally. A tear slipped down her cheek. 'The priggin doll was a curse, Da. A curse set to effect Ehran, or any of your children, for that matter. It gave me a splitting headache and I believe it might have been the cause of Ehran's recent illnesses, the times he was unwell while I was away. You saw what happened when the thing was burned. That was magic. There's no other way to explain it.'

Ran had exactly no clue what she was talking about, but Erlon and Farah certainly did. Their eyes grew wide and they stared at Lidan as if she'd grown a second head, but neither of them dismissed her. Neither of them disputed the point, and that was liquid gold to Ran. There was a witch here—one at the very least. Where the other had gone, he had no idea, but one of them was here.

'But *who*?' Erlon pushed, harder than Ran thought fair given Lidan's current state, but the man was verging on a rage Ran didn't want to witness. 'Who would do that to my children?'

Lidan levelled a dark look at him that would have turned most men to water. 'Think about it! Who arrived here about twenty years ago, from the north? Who is the strangest and most secretive person among us, who I have personally seen light a fire with no flint, only a bright blue shot of light?'

No one said a word. Farah stared at Lidan, her mouth agape, her hands balled into tight fists while her husband stood rigid between Ran and his daughter.

'You saw *what*? Why didn't you tell—'

'Because I was a child! And you had more important things to worry about! What with the ngaru slicing our rangers to ribbons and Farah's pregnancy, then the fucking Corron! Ancestors, save me. You wouldn't have believed me even if I *had* told you. You wouldn't have believed half the things I'd seen, half the things that have been...' She faltered and collected herself. 'The things that were done to me, and the things I have borne

392

witness to would turn you to stone where you stand, Father. *That* is why I never told you.'

Erlon said nothing, but Ran wasn't sure the man had any words left in him. It seemed they had all been stripped away by Lidan's tirade.

'Lidan, can you tell me who did these things?' Ran asked in a low, careful voice.

Her gaze settled on him and his blood ran cold. There was hatred there; real, poisonous hatred, unmasked and raging in the woman's emerald eyes. 'We call her the Crone. My mother calls her Thanie.'

CHAPTER FIFTY-ONE

Tingalla, Tolak range, the South Lands

Erlon let off a high-pitched whistle and a man appeared from behind a screen of woven reeds.

'Sir?' he asked with a bow.

'Kaito, I need you to find Siman.' Erlon waved a hand at the village beyond the walls. 'Get him to take some rangers to the dana's quarters and bring the Crone to me.'

The order seemed simple enough, but the man blanched and gulped so hard Ran saw his throat contract.

'Of course, sir…' Kaito paused, a pleading look on his face.

'Don't let her scare you, man.' Erlon waved a hand in a frustrated swipe through the air. 'If she gives you any shit, have them bring her too.'

Kaito took off, out the door and into the morning, leaving a pall of silence so thick Ran thought he might choke on it. Iridia shifted uncomfortably, as if she wanted to run, and Ran couldn't blame her. The thought of finally facing the monster they had hunted for so long, the cause of so much angst and pain, was overwhelming. He forced the sensation down, smoothing it over and calming his magic as it rose in response.

Nearby, Lidan sat chewing on her thumbnail while Erlon stood with his hands on his hips, his mouth set in a hard, thin line. It seemed to Ran that neither of them were looking forward to this. He only wished he knew why—

Irate shouts announced the arrival of Siman and the other rangers before they appeared at the threshold. Ran turned and the sight that greeted him was not what he'd expected. There was a knot of rangers with their hands on their weapons, and between them, limped a woman of middle to late years with an awful hunch in her back and, as far as he could tell, very few teeth. She was well dressed and clean, but haggard; a crooked, bent thing who hardly looked capable of killing a fly without toppling over and snapping a bone.

Yet despite all of this, her thaumalux glowed like a freshly stoked fire; healthy, strong, and as powerful as he had ever witnessed. More powerful than Collan or Quaid, steadier than the slow, beating heart of a great beast at rest. It hummed; a low sound that vibrated in the cavity of his chest, the light vacillating as she breathed in and out. He felt it in his ribs, down his spine, his magic responding as he watched the woman slowly cross the room and pause a few feet away.

He knew this thaumalux. Had followed it halfway across the world, tracked it through the Pass, and fallen through its magic to the place between.

He had found her.

He had found the witch.

Iridia stiffened, recoiling and sliding off the table toward the shadows. Ran almost whirled around, instinct driving him to hold her, to catch her to him, but he balled his hands and waited. Now was not the time. He had to do this properly, ignoring the rapid thud of his heart, lest it all slip through his fingers like a handful of hot sand.

The shouting grew louder, and he cocked his head, realising that it wasn't the Crone protesting the order to attend the daari, but another woman who burst through the door in a rush of fury and indignation.

'What is the meaning of this insult?' she demanded, scowling at Erlon and hardly registering the others in the room. 'Sending rangers to drag an old woman from her rest? What kind of man—'

Her rant died on her lips as she looked around, taking in the faces of those gathered.

'What is this?' she asked, her voice dropping dangerously low.

Erlon whisked his hands at the rangers. 'Wait outside, please.'

They did as ordered, leaving the old woman while her defender glowered at Erlon, then Lidan.

'If you wish to stay, you will control your tongue, Sellan.' Erlon fixed her with a withering glare that would have locked Ran's mouth shut for a week, but Sellan only sneered.

'I will not take orders from you like some tine-woman,' she growled back.

The tension between them shook the air, and the hairs on Ran's arms stood on end as something shifted behind him. He shivered, glancing over his shoulder to Iridia, who stared with wide, pale eyes, her face a mask of terror.

It's her, Iridia whispered.

Who?

The second witch.

He spun back to look at the dana, the daari's wife... Lidan's mother... *But she has no thaumalux!*

I don't know how that's possible, but it's her! Iridia all but screamed in his head and Lidan grimaced, turning to glare at the empty air where Iridia stood. She looked slowly back to Ran, and he realised he'd broken out into an anxious sweat that made his palms clammy and the collar of his shirt feel like it was strangling him.

She can hear you, Iridia.

I don't fucking care! she shouted. *That woman! It's her. She did this. It. Was. Her!*

Sellan's eyes settled on him then, and he wondered if she too, like her daughter, could sense the conversation with his ghost. He didn't much care. She pinned him with a gaze that dripped with disdain.

'What is he doing here?' she asked the daari, as if Ran didn't have ears to hear her. 'I should like you to answer me, Husband, or I will return Thanie to her bed, rangers or no.'

Thanie... Iridia whispered. *I know that name...*

Fuck me... Ran breathed. What had he done? Completely certain he wasn't ready for what might happen next, he ground his teeth and let the daari address his wife.

'It's come to my attention that certain past events have escaped my notice, for one reason or another, and that I have been inadvertently harbouring a magic-user in my village.' Erlon opened a hand toward Thanie, who glanced nonchalantly around the room, as if she hadn't heard a word. 'Further to that, there is speculation that she has a criminal past. Master Ran has some questions for her.'

Ran opened his mouth before he knew what he was going to say, but he needn't have bothered.

'*Excuse* me?' Sellan demanded. 'A criminal past? I have never heard anything more preposterous in my life! She's an aged woman, not a criminal. What evidence could you possibly have against her? What crime has she committed?' She turned on her daughter, who sat rigid in her chair. 'Did you do this? Did you concoct these accusations as some sort of sick revenge, a distraction perhaps from the loss of your little friend?'

Ran staggered back as Lidan launched from her chair and took two steps toward her mother, before Erlon's thickly muscled arm arrested her attack.

'This has *nothing* to do with me, and everything to do with *her*. You know she can do magic. You know what she is. And you know she made that priggin doll. Ancestors only know what else she's done!' Lidan stabbed a finger at Ran. 'He came here looking for a fugitive, someone who arrived from the north in the last twenty years, who can do magic. And do you know who fits that description? Her!'

Sellan blanched momentarily then quickly covered her shock in a perfect mask of dismissal, turning jade eyes back to him. Terror rolled through him, his own fusing with Iridia's until he couldn't tell one from the other. This woman was danger and rage personified, a banked fire waiting to burst forth and engulf them all.

There was power in her, seeping out so thick that she wore it like a cloak, and Ran knew Iridia was right. But still, she had no thaumalux…

'And who are you, little boy? Who are you to come here and accuse my companion of crimes without so much as a fleck of evidence?'

'Where are you from, Dana Sellan?' The question shot out before he knew what he was doing, and he almost smiled at the twist in her features as it caught her off guard. No point beating around the bush. Eian would have been proud.

'The north,' she replied flatly.

'Where in the north,' he pressed.

'The north is a very big place. I'm sure you wouldn't know it.' There was fear in her now, or perhaps it had always been there, hidden by her masks and sharp, cutting words.

'Oh, I might,' he took a careful step forward. 'Have you ever been to Wodurin, the capital of the Empire?'

'No,' she said. Her eyes narrowed, as if she wanted to reach over and strangle him before he could say more.

'That's very interesting.' He folded his hands to hide his trembling fingers. 'You see, I noticed when I met Lidan that her common wasn't like the rest of the rangers. When she speaks, she sounds very much like the Woaden prisoners of war we've captured over the years. Which got me to thinking, where does a young woman from the southern side of the Ice Towers learn to speak common with a Woaden accent?'

The people in the room stood so still he thought his words had frozen them to their core, but as he glanced at Erlon and Lidan, he realised it was the first either of them had heard this. Neither had any idea where this woman came from, even after spending most, if not all of their lives with her. They stared at her, their features hardening, all sympathy and hope draining away. Ran had caught the edge of Sellan's lies and if he did this right, he could peel back the layers and expose her to the world.

Sellan glanced at them, then turned her darkening eyes on him. 'And where are you from, child, to have come so far with such great knowledge?'

'Orthia.'

Her hand clenched reactively, and she unfurled it, flexing her fingers in and out. 'I can't say I've heard of it.'

'Again, very interesting, because I think it has heard of your friend. She's rather famous there, actually. Have you ever visited a town called Lackmah, Thanie?'

Thanie glanced up and Iridia flinched, a whimper escaping her throat. Rage ignited in him, burning through his chest and threatening to consume his affected sense of calm. He'd never heard such a terrified sound pass Iridia's lips in all the years he'd known her, never seen her cower and shake the way she did now. It made his blood boil that all it had taken was one look from this woman to reduce Iridia to a quivering mess. He wanted to turn, to bring her into the world with his magic and hold her, wrap his arms around her shoulders and scream at them, to show them the ruin of her throat and the two decades she had spent trapped like this. She was his evidence, and though he couldn't present her to anyone, he would pursue this until either Sellan or her strangely silent companion revealed themselves for what they were.

'Honestly, this is the most preposterous thing I have ever—'

'Lackmah?' Thanie said, and every face in the room turned to study her with a mixture of shock and disgust. She chuckled, and Ran felt like she'd kicked him in the chest. 'What a silly name for a town. Surely no such place exists, my boy.'

He swallowed and collected himself. 'It did, once. Before a pair of Woaden witches descended upon it and massacred the town's folk one by one.'

'What?' Lidan whispered, turning to him within the protective circle of her father's arms. 'Why?'

He glanced back at Iridia and saw her move, saw her square her shoulders, saw her shift through the air to stand as near to Lidan as she could without actually moving through her.

Tell her. She looked at Lidan with more sadness than he thought any face should bear. Lidan screwed her eyes shut, as if she was at war with the worst headache of her life. *She needs to know what they did, no matter how much it hurts.*

'The witches used the bodies of the dead to create creatures they sought to control. For what purpose I can only speculate, but they were discovered when their work was almost done, and they fled. My people lost track of them, as far as I understand. This was a year or so before I was born, and all mention of the place was forbidden.'

'Creatures?' Lidan's voice was barely more than a whisper.

'You call them ngaru.'

'You cannot seriously—' Sellan's protest rose over the gathering.

'Silence!' Erlon bellowed. 'Ran will be heard and you will explain yourselves!'

'I will do no such thing!' she shrieked, swiping her hand through the air as if to kill the conversation right there. Her glare found Ran again. 'And who are you, that I should stand by and listen to these ridiculous accusations?'

Ran took a breath, filled his chest, and decided now was the time. 'I am Ranoth Olseta, Prince of Orthia, son of Duke Ronart, and I have come to serve the Duke's Justice on those who massacred the people of Lackmah.'

Sellan froze, and a dark cloud seemed to fall over her face, hollowing her features as she glared at him with unveiled revulsion.

'Thanie,' she said, in a cool, even voice. 'Come. We're leaving.'

The old woman gave Ran an almost apologetic shrug and turned to limp after the dana, who was by then at the doorway. Iridia growled, and Ran took off, hurrying to catch up as the women descended the stairs and made quick time across the open area outside.

'I am an agent of the duke and you will attend me!' he shouted after them, realising how stupid he sounded and not caring one bit as he jogged down the stairs. He didn't know what else to say to get her attention, but it did the job.

The dana turned, rage etched in her face, and stalked past Thanie, putting herself between Ran and the old woman. 'Attend you? *Attend* you! Little prince, I am no more obligated to attend you or your whims than I am to give you the time of day.'

'Sellan,' the daari's voice echoed in the clear morning air.

'What?' she snapped. 'I suppose you believe this lying little shit?'

'I cannot say either way, but I see no reason not to hear him out.' The man's words held all the promise of thunder, though they were evenly spoken. 'In private.'

Sellan glared at Ran, then spat on the dirt between them. 'I'll hear none of it. It is baseless accusation.'

Do it, Iridia said, her voice shaking but strong despite her fear. It stirred the air like a physical thing, the way the wind moves the leaves of a tree without being seen.

Sellan turned on her heel and took two steps before Ran had a chance to pool his power. It crackled across his fingers and he heard someone swear. Shouts echoed behind him and he aimed the energy at the ground behind the dana, blasting the dirt and sending a column of earth into the sky. She staggered and whipped around, fury flashing in her eyes as she found Ran through the shower of dust and falling clumps of soil.

It was a warning shot, nothing more, but he had her attention.

'Sellan,' the old woman said from across the common area.

The dana did not respond, and something shifted, like a bubble popping, and Ran's ears equalised as the air pressure changed.

'Sellan!' Thanie shouted, desperation shaking her voice. 'Don't! Remember yourself!'

Could she even hear the woman's cries? Ran doubted it. There was something changing in the dana, a tangible transformation that he couldn't believe he was seeing. Something snapped between her fingers and the old woman behind her moaned, gasping as she crumpled to her knees. Thanie clutched at her stomach as if she'd been kicked, and Ran let another orb of magic form in his hand.

He didn't know what was happening, but it wasn't good.

Around them people screamed and ran, some drawing weapons while others herded children to safety. He vaguely heard Erlon bellowing orders, but there was an unnatural wind swirling in the courtyard now, circling him and Sellan as another shot of blue lightning arced, this time between each of Sellan's hands.

'You just couldn't leave it alone, could you?' she growled. 'Pick, pick, pick; like a child with a scab.'

'All I wanted was the truth!'

'You don't want truth! You want *death*! That's all you Orthian's ever want from those of us with power. Just blood and death for something we had no say in.'

'You murdered innocent people!' Ran shot back, buffered by the wind Sellan called out of nowhere. He fought to keep his feet on the ground and his eyes open against the onslaught of dirt and debris until he couldn't take it anymore and plunged his magic into the earth, grounding himself with power that might have resembled tree roots if it could be seen above ground.

'Innocent?' Sellan screamed at him. 'Those "innocent" people would have killed us as soon as looked at us! You know it's true, Orthian. Did they accept you? Did they let you stay in your home, tucked up with your family once they knew what you were? Or did they run you out and hunt you like a stray dog?'

Her words cut deep, but he held, something in him roaring defiance.

'No,' he replied, almost too quietly to be heard over the howl of Sellan's wind and the crackle of her magic. She was a powerful elemental, at the very least, and somewhere behind her, someone screamed her name, hoarse and harsh, but the pleas went unheard. 'They hunted me. But that didn't mean any of them deserved to die.'

Whispers from long ago slipped unbidden into his mind and he gave them voice, drawing strength from them when he knew his was failing.

'People fear what they don't understand, and hate what they cannot control,' he told Sellan, repeating Sasha's words from the barn at the Parry farm. They meant more to him now than they ever had, facing the woman who had turned on the world because of their hatred of what she was. 'People are animals, just like any other. Base fears will take them over, but that doesn't mean they deserve to die for their misgivings.'

'Ha!' Sellan's laugh was hard and callous. 'You're a fool if you think they'll ever change their minds about people like you, people like *us*.'

Ran fired his magic and she swatted the shot away like a fly. A sizzling bolt tore through the air toward him and he twisted aside, the screams behind Sellan growing louder, pitched and keening, until they were one with the lightning crack of her magic.

A furious barrage of shots snapped back and forth, Ran fighting to keep his feet against the onslaught as the woman threw bolt after bolt at him. Surely, she'd weaken soon. Surely, she didn't have more in her reserves than he did? He would have sensed it. He would have seen...

Realisation slapped him in the face as Sellan staggered away from his last shot, revealing the woman doubled over on the ground behind her. Thanie lay curled on the dirt, her hand stretched toward the younger woman, pleas lost to agonised screams as thaumalux poured out of her. It pooled across the ground, visible only to Ran, a silver stream flowing from one woman to the other, then disappearing into the soles of Sellan's feet. Blood dripped from Thanie's nose and eyes, crimson tears coursing down her cheeks.

Her voice reached them as the wind died, no longer under Sellan's control, and Ran wondered if she'd reached her limit. She couldn't have much left. But then, she didn't need to. Somehow, she was drawing from Thanie without touching her, pulling away whatever power she wanted, and the older woman had no choice but to submit, or perish in the attempt to stop her.

'Please... Sellan, please...' Thanie's hoarse, broken words whispered into the lull left by the fading wind.

Sellan turned, her gaze falling on Thanie as she staggered away from Ran. Exhaustion rippled over her features and Ran knew she was spent. She'd fought hard, and likely for the first time in a long time. He was surprised she'd lasted as long as she had.

'Don't do this…' Thanie begged.

'I have no choice. Don't you *see*?' Sellan's pitch rose, verging on hysterical, maddened and desperate. Something glistened on her cheeks and Ran realised they were the tracks of tears. 'No one ever gave *me* a choice.'

'Mam!' Lidan screamed from behind him. He whirled around, saw her held back by her father, saw the pain in the bruised lines of her face. 'What are you doing? Stop! Please!'

'Oh, Liddy.' Sellan shook her head sadly. 'If only you'd seen that this was all for you.'

'Ma, no!'

Ran spun back, staggering, as Sellan stepped toward Thanie.

'Sellan, please…' Thanie pleaded.

'I've got no choice. They've left me no choice.'

No… Iridia breathed.

Sellan reached for Thanie, clamping her hand around the back of the woman's neck.

Ran! Iridia screamed.

Resignation settled on Thanie's face as Sellan dragged her up to her knees and stepped behind her, mere seconds passing before Ran realised what she was doing.

Too many seconds.

A dark, jagged smile broke across Sellan's face and her hand flexed around Thanie's neck. Ran lurched into a run as power coursed out of the older woman into the dana and an ear-splitting crack broke the air.

Chapter Fifty-two

Tingalla, Tolak range, the South Lands

Ran sprawled on the ground, his face buried in the dirt. His ears rang and his body thumped with the beat of his pulse, his arms shaking as he lifted himself up. There were no more screams, or at least, none that he could hear. People seemed to have stopped running and shouting. Those he could see just stood and stared.

There was a body on the ground, a crumpled heap that might once have been a living, breathing person, but it no longer moved as though it was. There was dust, settling slowly from the air, sweat stinging his eyes as he shielded them from the sun.

Sellan was gone.

The air where she had been had spilt, the smell of residual magic burning in the atmosphere. There was nothing left, not even a scrap of fabric, and a heaviness settled in his gut.

A pair of large hands wrapped around his arm and pulled him upright, gently but firmly, and they did not let go when he found his feet.

'Where is she?' Erlon's voice reached through the buzzing in his ears.

Ran shook his head. 'I don't... I don't know...'

'Is she dead? Or is she gone?' Erlon pressed, his grip tightening on Ran as though he could squeeze the truth out if he just pushed hard enough.

'I don't think she's dead, unless something went wrong. She's gone... somewhere...' He glanced around through the clearing dust. 'Zarad might be able to...'

Lidan appeared at the edge of his sight, moving at a slow limp, as if caught in a stream and fighting against the current. Her eyes were ringed with red, puffy and glistening. She'd likely shed every tear her body held, and she trembled, her good hand quivering at her side as she stepped toward the motionless figure on the ground. Ran broke the daari's weakening hold and followed, cautious of Lidan at first, not wanting to startle her.

'Lidan?' he whispered.

If she heard him, she ignored him, instead kneeling beside the body and staring as though it might burst into flame at any moment. Her hand reached for the figure's shoulder, its garments unmoved by the frame underneath, and Ran watched.

Lidan pulled at the shoulder gently, and the body rolled onto its back. It was Thanie, by her clothes at least, but something was happening to the features of her face. In the light of the morning sun, deep creases of age faded, lightened and smoothed. Most of the grey in her hair darkened, leaving only a little at the edges of her face and a thick band of it that began behind her ear. Aged lips became a little fuller and a little darker, until they let out a single, shallow breath.

'Fuck me...' Ran muttered.

'What is this?' Lidan turned her teary eyes on him, expecting answers like her father, when he had none.

'A disguise?' Ran ventured, unsure even as he said the words if it was possible. 'She must have been using magic to disguise herself?'

'As a decrepit old hag?' Lidan spat, venom souring her words.

'She... They must have known they'd be pursued, so when they fled, they disguised themselves...'

'What?' she pressed. 'How is that even possible—'

'I have no idea! I've never seen this before! I have no fucking clue what's going on here!' He stabbed a finger at Thanie. 'The only person who can answer these questions, is her. But as she's dead, she's no fucking use to us at all.'

Lidan staggered to her feet and glared at him. 'She's not dead, you fucking idiot. She's unconscious.'

Ran blinked and something stirred behind him that might have been Iridia. 'She's what?'

'Alive, albeit barely. And who the fuck knows for how long. So, if you'll excuse me, I need to save her life.'

At the northern edge of Tingalla's walls, a tower stood overlooking the river far below, and the vast, expanding vista stretching out to the north and east, mottled and shadowed by approaching storm clouds and dark grey columns of rain. Lidan wished she had the time or energy to appreciate the beauty of such a sight, but for now, her admiration would have to wait.

She followed Vee, limping along the top of the wall and through a door in the stone and timber tower, spiralling down a staircase to the base of the structure, where the stairs changed from timber to cut stone and plunged into the cliff below. There were no windows in the tower, no way to access it from the ground. There was only one way in and that was the heavily guarded door on the palisade, which had been closed and secured behind them.

The stairs continued to spiral until they levelled out into a tunnel, and Lidan drew a deep breath into her chest. It was cool here, much cooler than the air above, where humidity rose like steam from roasted meat, calling down the rain and the storms, singing them closer to the village to wash it clean. A deluge might come, she supposed, but it would never wash away what she had seen and heard.

Her mother…

Her mother was a magic-user.

Ran had called her a witch, the same word the strange woman had used in the white place. She knew now what it meant, what it *truly* meant, even if she still had no idea who that woman was or what she'd been doing there with Ran. She still didn't understand why they had met in the white place at all, but she quietly suspected it had something to do with the Crone and her magics.

Of course, her mother being a magic-user wasn't the worst of it. Not by half. Her mother, the dana of the clan and first wife of the daari, had apparently *created* the scourge of foul beasts that had been tearing through the South Lands for the past five years. Ran had his own tales of the monsters, and they left her with the stinging knowledge that it was *her* mother who had begun it all. It sickened her to her core.

Her boot caught on a stone and she staggered, sucking air through her teeth as pain lanced up her leg into her chest. Her wounds would heal eventually, if she gave them time, but she had none to spare right now.

She'd just have to push through this pain, like she would all her wounds, until she emerged on the other side.

'Witness?' Vee asked.

Lidan nodded and stepped forward.

'This way. Master Jarrah said it's this way.'

'Is Siman down here?' Lidan asked, following the tine-woman along the tunnel, their voices and footsteps echoing off the slick rock walls.

'I believe so, Witness. He'll remove the locks and stay by the door.'

'All right... Good...' She hadn't expected to fear this moment, but when Ran had sent Vee with a message that Thanie had woken from her stupor, her stomach had clenched and she'd immediately questioned if she hadn't gone completely mad.

She'd watched the woman change from a bent, haggard old crone, to someone at least a decade younger. Even her teeth had revealed themselves, no longer obscured by magic, while her hair had almost entirely changed colour, and her hunch had vanished completely. She now appeared no more than a handful of years older than Sellan, nothing close to the wizened elder named the Crone, and Lidan was voluntarily entering a room with her. Someone, who by Ran's estimation, had far more power than he, Zarad and Eian combined.

They rounded a corner in the tunnel and she saw him standing there, arms folded, his face turned toward a door set in the wall to Lidan's right. At her approach, he nodded at Siman, and the two of them stopped Vee and Lidan in the corridor, blocking the way.

'You're sure about this, Liddy?' Siman asked, light from nearby torches dancing across his face.

She nodded. 'I am.'

'It can wait a few days, surely?' Ran suggested. 'Give yourself some time to rest. She's not going anywhere.'

'I wouldn't be so sure of that,' Lidan countered, and Siman and Ran frowned at her. 'I've seen you use your magic, Ran. I've seen how it wears you out, but I've also seen how quickly it comes back.' She pointed an accusing finger at the door. 'I just watched my mother disappear into thin air, and if *she* regains her power, what's to say she couldn't do the same?'

Ran cleared his throat and looked awkwardly at Vee and Siman. 'It's not in my nature to talk about these things *publicly*. Think of it as self-preservation.'

'Keeping secrets more like,' Vee snapped.

Lidan stared at the woman, then turned a sly smile back on Ran. 'I rather tend to agree with Vee, actually.'

'Fine. Fuck it, whatever.' Ran turned to the side and pointed back at the door. 'The sheer volume of magic it took for your mother to transit to wherever she went was far more than one person can hold in reserve. Just like when Zarad...'

He hesitated and Lidan tried not to let the pain of the memory show on her face. She bit the back of her lip instead, and let him finish.

'When Zarad broke the cliff in the gorge, he needed a loan from Eian. Eian had to let the magic go voluntarily, or the force of it would have broken his spine and killed him. That's exactly what your mother did.'

'Don't call her that.'

'Call her what?'

'My mother,' she muttered. 'Use her name, or call her whatever you want, just not that.'

'All right, fine, but my point stands. Even at full force, I would eat my fucking boots if Thanie could manage to transit anywhere that was more than a few hundred feet distant, or do it more than once in a short period of time *without* the aid of a loan.' The look Ran gave her wasn't entirely sympathetic, but he seemed to understand.

'And when her magic returns? What then? What's to stop her blowing the door off this place and escaping?' Lidan looked at them, as Vee steadied her from swaying a little. 'I need answers before that happens.'

'We've got rangers all over the place, Liddy; she's unlikely to make it far,' Siman told her, though Ran seemed less convinced.

'I don't know what steel and stone could do to stop her if she wanted to get free, but the energy she lost, and the fatigue of the fight, and of keeping that disguise in place all this time, will have drained her so completely that I would be surprised if her magic ever returns at all.' Ran shrugged. 'It really depends how deep those wounds go and how terrible the scars are.'

'But it might?' Lidan pressed. 'You don't know that it won't.'

'You're right. It might. I don't know.'

'And you don't know how long it might take to come back?'

Ran shook his head slowly. 'No.'

'Then I'm going in there.'

Vee shrugged and Siman rolled his eyes, as the man was wont to do when Lidan got an idea that she refused to let go. She pushed past the men and stopped at the door. There was a small wooden flap set in the thick panel, and she lifted it to peer inside. A lumpy shadow lay against the right-hand wall, and Lidan motioned for Siman to pull a cord. In a jerking motion, a window opened in the far wall, no more than a slit to let fresh air and light into the dank cell, but it was enough to illuminate the body curled on the floor.

Siman tied off the cord and set to work on a series of latches and bolts that held the door closed, then swung it inward. With a sigh, Lidan turned to Ran.

'Coming?' she asked.

He blinked, seemingly surprised by the invitation. 'If you'd like me to?'

'She's your prisoner as much as mine. And there isn't anything she has to say to me that I wouldn't want you to hear.'

'You're sure?' he asked again.

She couldn't tell him she would have preferred to do this with Loge beside her. She couldn't admit that she needed someone to stand with her who had experienced even half the things she had been through, and until she drew her last breath that person would be Loge. But at least Ran had faced the ngaru, and he knew the history of these women better than any of them. He was a poor substitute for the man she missed so desperately it knocked the air from her lungs, but he would do in a pinch.

She nodded, and they stepped inside the cell.

CHAPTER FIFTY-THREE

Tingalla, Tolak range, the South Lands

Fresh air swirled in through the open window, taking away the musty, damp scent of the cell. Thanie hadn't been down here long enough for there to be more powerful odours, and for that Lidan was thankful. There was a small stool in one corner, and Ran collected it, depositing it on the floor in the centre of the room and nodding at Lidan that she should sit. Her body protested as she folded herself onto the seat, but the chance to rest her aching legs and back was sweet relief as Ran moved to lean against the wall behind her shoulder.

They waited.

For a while, nothing happened. The youthful face Lidan saw tucked into the crook of an arm was uncanny. She was most certainly the woman Lidan had known all her life, at once utterly different and eerily the same. It was like looking back through time, to a past she had never lived, at someone she vaguely remembered.

Lidan cleared her throat.

Nothing.

She glanced over her shoulder. 'You said she was awake?'

'She was,' Ran whispered for no reason, stepping forward. 'Let me try…'

The burning sting at the edge of her awareness told her his magic was moving, and Thanie jerked up, gasping, her eyes casting around for a threat. Her gaze settled on Lidan, and she recoiled, thumping back against the wall.

'Good afternoon, Thanie,' said Lidan in her best attempt at a casual, flat tone. Except she wasn't cool or calm, and this wasn't a casual conversation between friends. Her heart hammered harder than a horse running at a gallop, and she shook with nausea.

'Dead Sisters, save me—you scared the breath out of me!' Thanie gulped and panted, drawing her knees up to her chest with a pained wince. 'How long...'

'Only a few hours. It's well past midday,' Lidan told her.

'Sellan?' Wide, cloud grey eyes searched Lidan's face.

Lidan sighed. 'She's gone.'

Thanie looked away, staring at something Lidan couldn't see, and took a deep breath. 'Well then...'

Her accent was thicker than Sellan's and slightly different to Ran's, and her voice less ragged and strangled than it had been in all the years Lidan had known her. She hadn't ever realised how different her mother and the Crone sounded to the rest of the clan; it was just how things were.

'I expect you'll be executing me, then?' Her question echoed off the walls and Lidan swallowed an unexpected tightness from her throat. She glanced back at Ran.

'Your crimes were committed in the north, so you'll return there to face the Duke's Justice,' Ran said quietly. 'But first you have questions to answer.'

'And your treatment and conditions will depend entirely on your coop-eration,' Lidan put in.

Thanie nodded and ran her tongue across dry lips. 'I shall do my best. But first, who is that?'

'Excuse me?' Lidan asked.

Thanie pointed at the empty corner of the cell behind Lidan's ruined left shoulder. 'That presence over there. The one who's trying to watch me while hiding at the same time.'

Ran's boots scuffed the stone floor and he cleared his throat awkwardly. 'She's someone from your past. I doubt you'd remember her, given how many of them you killed.'

'Ah,' Thanie nodded sadly. 'She's attached to you then? From Lackmah?'

The whispering began an instant later and Lidan spun on her stool, staring at the corner of the room and expecting to find someone there, yet seeing nothing at all. Someone was talking, quickly and with a fury, but the words were lost to Lidan. She felt them though, their anger and their pain, stoking a fire in her for the injustice of so many lives cut short.

'Iridia was among those you murdered,' Ran said, turning back to Thanie with a sneer on his lips. 'She helped me find you.'

Again, Thanie nodded. 'She had best decide which side she's staying on.'

'What?' Ran snapped.

The woman whisked her hand in the air. 'If her story is true, she's been wandering this plane for a long time, when she should have moved on. The Rider will only abide that for so long. She can hear me, I'm sure, so I'll say it straight.' Thanie gave Ran and the empty corner a pointed look. 'Girlie, you need to make up your mind—you're either staying here or going where the dead belong. Make a decision and get it done, or all manner of ill will come down on both of you.'

Ran stood rigid by the wall, gaping at Thanie, and while Lidan didn't understand the meaning of what the woman said, it was as clear as day that Ran comprehended every last word.

'Now that's been said, best get on with it then.'

Not knowing what else to do, Lidan shifted on the hard timber of the stool, ignoring the protest of her broken body. 'Why?' she asked simply.

'Why what?' Thanie frowned at her.

'Why did you do all this? Why go to these lengths, why disguise your-self, why insert yourselves into our clan and stay?' Exasperation drove the pitch of her voice ever higher. 'Why did you make those *things*? Why did you kill all those people and sew weapons to their bodies?'

'I didn't do the sewing. Or the killing.' Thanie watched her carefully. 'Did you see that in a dream?'

Lidan stared, her mouth agape. 'How did you know that?'

'I sent you those dreams…' she said with a shrug.

'What?' Lidan's face contorted, and every muscle down the left side screamed. 'Why?'

'You needed to know. I was trying to show you who she was, *what* she was… trying to explain… I couldn't say the words, but perhaps I could show you…'

'You were there, though? You saw it happen?' Ran asked, his voice betraying the rage he held inside, shaking as he spoke.

Thanie nodded.

'Why didn't you stop her?' Lidan's whisper fell from her barely moving lips.

Thanie shook her head. 'I wanted it too… I was angry, as angry as she was, possibly more so. I loved her, Liddy. I loved her like a sister. She was all I had, and I was furious they'd tried to send her away. She would have gone to her death, and all because she had too much power and anger for one small body to hold. All she needed was time and love and they gave her neither. They just decided she was too much.'

She began picking at a thread in her skirt, as if pulling at it would unravel the lies she and Sellan had woven for the world. Lidan watched the memories crawl up from Thanie's soul for the first time in twenty years, their grip so hard it brought tears to her eyes. For the first time in her life, Lidan saw the woman behind the facade, and realised Thanie was as broken as the rest of them.

'Who did those things to her?' she asked.

'The Empire and their precious Academy… I gave her everything I had, Liddy; just to keep her safe. I held all her power in me, keeping her together, giving her time and somewhere to fall when it got too hard. You saw what it did to me.' She held up a hand, her fingers trembling in the air between them. 'What it's still doing to me…'

There was a past here Lidan still didn't understand, but a memory of a dream played before her eyes—two young girls running, hand in hand, escaping. Fire and death all around them, and a pair of eyes she had recognised then that refused to look at her now. Thanie, and a much younger Sellan, fleeing from something she couldn't see. Had it been the Empire they were running from? Was it the Academy engulfed in flame?

'But *why*?' Ran pressed, cutting into Lidan's recollections. 'Why murder all those people? What was the point?'

'To show them.' Thanie looked up at him, still tugging at the red thread with her trembling fingers. 'We had to show them what she could do, prove her value so they would let us come home. But we were discovered, and we fled again. We found a trading caravan just north of the Pass and followed it here. The rest is history—or rather, *your* history, Lidan—but that's how it went. We were forced to abandon our work before it was finished, unleashing those things on the world before they were fully ready.'

'They… they weren't finished?' whispered Lidan, her throat contracting and her stomach roiling. She was going to be sick.

'No… they couldn't be controlled. There were further steps, more things to be done. Had we the time, we would have owned every single one. Instead, they were left to roam, and we ran.' Thanie sat forward, her trembling hands open toward Lidan in a desperate plea. 'It would have been the work of moments to finish the task, and if she's allowed, she'll do it all again.'

'What?' Lidan and Ran asked in unison, and a chill shivered through Lidan as the words hit her.

'I fear that's her plan.'

Lidan stared at her. 'So where did she go?'

'I have no idea—'

'You've been controlling her magic for at least eighteen years!' Lidan's shout cracked against the walls and Thanie flinched. 'Don't tell me you can't sense where she's gone!'

The woman looked away, tears welling at the edges of her eyes, her lips pressed into a hard, angry line. 'She's going home.'

'Home?' Ran asked, his brow furrowing as he stepped forward and looked Thanie over with an expression of furious contempt.

'The Empire. Wodurin. She's going home.'

'But they banished her. She was a derramentis!' Again, Ran's words made little to no sense to Lidan, but she absorbed them, tucking them away in her memory. This was important. Somewhere in all this was the key to understanding her mother and the reason she had done all these things.

'She was cast out, yes.' Thanie turned her cold grey eyes on them. 'But those creatures had a purpose, a reason for being. They were not some experiment, or a frivolous joke. They were an army.'

Silence pooled in the cell. Ran glanced at Lidan, and Lidan set her jaw.

'An army for what?'

'To march into the capital and show them just how wrong they were. To show them just how powerful a derramentis mage can be.' Thanie leaned forward. 'And if she is allowed, she will start her work again, and this time, she will finish it.'

'She's going to march an army of dradur to Wodurin?' Ran's voice rose with disbelief. 'That's insane! She'd never defeat—'

'Oh my dear, sweet boy,' Thanie said with a dead smile. 'She doesn't want to *defeat* the Woaden. She wants to give them a weapon. She's going to give them the dead walkers, and she's going to turn them on the Empire's enemies.'

'Fuck,' Ran breathed. He started to pace, and Lidan watched, worry coiling in her gut. She'd always feared her mother, feared her brutal hands and her whip-like tongue, but the fear she saw in Ran went deeper than that. He raked his fingers back through the waves of his hair. 'I have to get home... I have to warn people. Fuck!'

'Indeed,' Thanie nodded and looked back at Lidan. 'She never forgave the Empire for casting her out, or Orthia for pursuing us across Coraidin until the only safety to be found was in the bed of a powerful man, behind the shield of her new title. She always intended to go back and show them what she could do, how valuable she was, how much they need her to win their wars and take new lands.'

'So she's going to be their general?' Lidan asked in a hoarse whisper.

Thanie shook her head slightly. 'No, child. She means to be their empress.'

To be continued...

ACKNOWLEDGEMENTS

It's incredibly easy to lose track of those who help you along the way to bringing a story to life. It's impossible to recall the name of every reader who sent you a message, or mention all the friends who shared their joy at what you have accomplished. And while I'm driven to try, I'll have to be content with thanking you together, with one collective hug, for everything you have done and said. This was the most difficult book I've ever written, not simply thanks to its subject matter, but because of the whirlwind that my life has become in the past few years. I wouldn't be here without each and every one of you. You've buoyed my heart, dried my tears, laughed with me, held me together while I broke apart and stood guard as I put myself back together. I hope you know who you are, because I'll never forget a single one of you. There are of course, a few very special people who I must thank explicitly:

Anne & Ian—for your endless support, putting a roof over my head and carpet bombing Central Queensland with promotional material for Blood of Heirs. Easily the best sales team in the history of publishing.

Hadrian—the dragons are yours, from your boundless imagination. It's always a privilege to bear witness to your creations. I could not be prouder of you and the glorious person you are. Never change.

Graham—for everything, always.

AJ Spedding and Matthew Summers—you work wonders with words, magic with punctuation, and your grammatical witchcraft is awe inspiring.

Pen Astridge—for another stunning cover to bind these pages and for bringing Ran to life.

Clare Davidson—for formatting this monster and wrangling it into something that resembles a book.

The Cabal, which of course does not exist. Everything you've heard is lies, and everything you haven't is true.

About the Author

Living in Central Queensland, Australia, surrounded by coal mines, snakes, marsupials and a wide blue sky, Alicia is a writer, a mum and a cat-herder. There are rumours she may in fact be a quokka in disguise, but these are not to be believed.

She began writing in her teens and never grew out of the phase, working in her spare time until the birth of her son allowed her to focus on writing full time. She has also dabbled in editing and blogging while completing a Bachelor of Education and studying a Post Graduate Certificate in Ancient History.